END GAME

NEW YORK STARS: ONE

G. A. MAZURKE

Photograph: Rafa Catala

Illustration: Chelsea Chira

Editing: Anne-Geneviève Ducharme-Audran

Proofreading: Norma's Nook

To D & H
You should always have been each other's end game, but you're not, so here's one I could fix.

PLEASE READ: FOREWORD & TRIGGER WARNINGS

HEY LOVELIES!

Welcome to the first-ever novel in the New York Stars' series.

This is a complete standalone and requires no other reading to enjoy this book.

This is a cherry popper for me, guys, but, I've been blessed with a hockey-obsessed Canadian who also happens to be an ex-sports reporter for an editor. Yeah, you read that right. Like any pusher, :P, Anne-Geneviève has made me addicted. To hockey players. She took me to my first game in Denver in March and I've been OBSESSED ever since.

What she doesn't know about hockey hasn't been written, and I consider myself freakin' lucky that she worked on this book with me to bring you a hockey romance that she isn't ashamed to tell her ex-hockey-player buddies about LOL.

Just FYI, this whole story came about because of something called a billet family. If you don't know what that is, it's where a kid from Québec, for example, can play for a team in Winnipeg because a billet family brings him into the fold and raises him like he's one of theirs. They're trusted families and members of the hockey community and these boys can grow up in safe environments while fulfilling their goals.

I also reference something called PALs - that's an abbreviation for 'partners and lovers' which Joe Arden coined, so thank you to him for that inclusive title!

Writing this book brought out my Canadian pride. *And I'm British!* But these characters **are** from Canada, so you will find dates and, perhaps, cultural references that seem foreign to you because they are... They are Canadian! For example, July 1st is Canada Day and their tax deadline is April 30th. Regardless, I hope you will follow me down this path, with maple leaves shining in your eyes and maple syrup running through your veins!

Triggers:

On the page:

References to kidnapping, as well as a character with an eating disorder, another with a terminal illness, and another who overdoses.

Off the page:

References to torture, drug overdose, and child neglect.

You should also know that none of the NHL team names match the ones in my league.

Don't forget when **END GAME** reaches 500 reviews, head to my reader group for a bonus scene! www.facebook.com/groups/SerenaAkeroydsDivas

Much love and happy reading,

G. A. Mazurke

xo

THE NEW YORK STARS

FORWARDS

35 Liam Donaghat C (C)
11 Max Fortin LW
26 Zeke McIsaac LW
22 Henri Boucher RW
28 Kyle Lewis RW
4 Jasper Campbell RW

DEFENSEMEN

13 Jude Gagné LD (A)
23 Jean-François Deschamps LD
50 Lars Raimond RD
5 Ruben Kerrigan RD

GOALTENDER

50 Ryan Greco

Governor
Conor O'Donnelly

General Manager
Justin Delaney

Head Coach
Allan Bradley

Assistant Coach
Tony Bratt

NEW YORK
STARS

GLOSSARY

CURSE WORDS

FRENCH CANADIANS USE Catholic words as swear words.

Cibole - (colloquialism) fuck = derivative of ciboire which is the chalice used during Eucharist.

Tabarnak - (colloquialism) fuck = derivative of the tabernacle which is the ornamented box in which Communion hosts and wine are kept.

Ostie - (colloquialism) goddammit = the host/sacramental bread for Eucharist.

En ostie - for fuck's sake

Mon Dieu - my God

Mon cul - my ass

ENDEARMENTS

Ma belle - beautiful

Ma chérie - my dear

Minou - kitten

Mon petit chou - my darling (literal translation = my little cabbage)
Another variation in this book: Mon p'tit cabbage

Bébé - baby

GENERAL WORDS

Maman - mom

Tu ne comprends pas? - you don't understand?

Cabane à Sucre - sugar shack = where maple syrup is made and many commercial sugar shacks have restaurants where they serve dishes with maple syrup as a component. The dishes are traditional Québec fare.

Oreilles de Christ - a type of pork snack

Mon frère - my brother

Oui / Ouais - Yes / Yeah

Pour toujours - forever

LIAM

The Donnghals

father — **Padraig aka Paddy**

sister — **Jennifer**

nieces — **Luciu**, **Saverina**, **Bella**

BIL

THE O'DONNELLYS

aunt — **Lena**

cousins — **Star & Conor, Katina**, **Aela & Declan, Shay &**, **Cameron**, **Camille & Brennan**, **Savannah & Aidan**, **Inessa & Eoghan**, **Aoife & Finn**, **Victoria**

Gracie

Oliver aka Ollie

family

The Bukowskis

parents — **Hanna & Fryd**

brothers — **Trent**, **Cezary aka Kow**, **Noah**

billet boys — **Cole**, **Gray**, **Matt**, **Oren**

PLAYLIST

If you'd like to hear a curated soundtrack, with songs that are featured in the book, as well as songs that inspired it, then here's the link:

https://open.spotify.com/playlist/1fFSpfoM6xQyKcEeRfnWhy?si=213a2e3a64e348bc&pt=96bb924854658a66a6150b76d2044420

NEW YORK
STARS

END GAME

USA TODAY BESTSELLING AUTHOR SERENA AKEROYD WRITING AS

G.A. MAZURKE

GRACIE

Teenage Dirtbag - Wheatus

"PE-TER PAN! PE-TER PAN! PE-TER PAN!"

From the friends and family box, I sit with my eyes locked on the tunnel.

Waiting.

Seething.

Ire building.

Patience draining.

The fans are chanting for "Peter Pan," aka Liam Donnghal, a guy who billeted with us from sixteen until he left to play for the Montréal Mounties when he was drafted into the NHL.

Next, they start singing for my brother, Kow, because they're a power duo that's had the talking heads beaking up a storm this season.

Neither of them has left the locker room yet, but they'll be on the ice soon.

I can't goddamn wait to see them.

Beside me, Mom, Dad, Trent, Noah, Cole, Gray, and Matt are waiting in the wings. The whole family, billet boys and all, have never made it to a game before, but this is the first time that if Liam and Kow win, they'll be in the Stanley Cup final.

Trent and Gray, eighteen months older than Liam and Kow, are still in the minors, making this the first big-deal NHL game the Bukowskis have ever played in. Hell, even Liam's absentee dad, Padraig, traveled from Québec City with his mom to watch!

It's an important occasion.

Huge.

A lifetime of familial support got them here. The fans aren't calling out the moms' and dads' names, though. They're the ones who scrimped and saved for endless stick purchases and paid hundreds of bucks a week to fill those bottomless pits they have for stomachs.

For almost two decades, life has centered around the ice like it was our church…

The god of the NHL has finally heeded the Bukowskis' call.

My teeth grit as I wait with the rest of the stadium, which practically glows red for the home team, until finally, the lights stop dancing like we're in a nightclub and blare on for the players to start stretching.

"I can't believe it. We've waited so long for this moment," Mom cries, her hands clapping together like a seal.

Dad grabs one of them, presses her knuckles to his lips, and, in his thick Polish accent, declares, "Boys good. They win. We take Stanley Cup to print shop."

Because Dad said it, I don't roll my eyes, just duck in my seat.

"Furball, you get any lower, you'll slither onto the floor," Gray rumbles, scuffing a hand over my tuque, tugging at my hair, and prompting me to glower at him as I right it on my head. His gaze sharpens when he takes in my expression—he's the first one to realize something's wrong with me. "You okay, sis?"

There's an irony to that—he calls me 'sis' and treats me better than my biological brothers do.

Along with Liam, Gray, Matt, and Cole have billeted with us for years—they're found family. Trent, Noah, and Kow were mistakes the stork brought along to make me suffer.

"I'm fine," is my wooden response.

His focus turns concerned. "You look like you've been crying. Has Kow said something to piss you off again? Someone had to tell him,

Gracie," he assures me. "He needs to cut out the drinking and he only ever listens to you."

Oh, yeah, he *really* listened.

"I don't cry over that loser."

"Gracie! Don't call your brother names. What's gotten into you?" Mom chides, her voice high enough that the people in front of us twist back to stare.

What's gotten into me?

Ha, more like what has my brother gotten *into*.

My best friend, Charlotte, that's who.

Or, should I say, 'so-called' best friend who's only ever hung around with me because of Kow. Go figure.

If it didn't hurt so much, I'd laugh it off because it's creepy as shit.

But it *does* hurt.

I thought we were like sisters.

Honest-to-God BFFs.

Yet, I learned she was stringing me along to hop into bed with my skank ho of a hockey-boi brother who only fucked her to get back at me.

How dare I tell him that he was partying too hard and that it was affecting his performance...

How dare I care when our whole family has waited years for this opportunity that he's pissing down the drain...

What an asshole.

Matt gets into my face. "What did he do?"

"Nothing."

"Little bit, you forget that we know when you're lying," Cole says, sticking his nose in.

I glare at him and repeat, "Nothing."

They glance at one another.

"What did *you* do?" Gray asks slowly, like he's approaching a ticking time bomb.

This time, I smile.

Cole grunts. "Fuck."

"Fryd!" Mom cries. "What on earth—"

Her gasp snatches my attention. Quickly, I study the ice, but I don't have to hunt for long.

There, amid the bright red jerseys, are two teens with green grapes for heads.

A choked chuckle escapes Matt. "You didn't!"

"You dyed them green? How—" Cole sputters before he almost rolls off his seat he's laughing so hard.

"Fuck, Gracie. *FUCK*. That's just cruel." Gray cackles. "My God, they look like the Philly Fanatic's twin brothers—"

With vengeance served, I get to my feet.

"Where do you think you're going, young lady?" Mom barks, but then she sees my glee. Her eyes widen in horror. "Gracie, you didn't—"

Dad demands, "What they do?"

God, I love him.

So. Much.

He's always on my side.

Always.

"GRACIE AGNIESKA BUKOWSKI! What did you do?!" Mom shrieks as my green-as-grass brothers, Liam and Kow, start skating around the ice.

Payback, *that's* what I did.

Which is when Kow makes my decade by kicking off a fight with one of the Lumberjacks, who are obviously giving him shit for doing a four-leaf clover impression.

Before my delighted eyes, he gets tossed from the game.

Satisfaction slides through me, warmer than hot cocoa in the winter and more delicious than iced tea on a summer's day.

Though Liam isn't to blame, he kind of is for being my brother's best friend.

For choosing *him* over me.

But then, why am I surprised?

Everyone chooses my brothers over me—even girls I've known since I was little.

If he'd have loved her, I'd have understood and accepted them getting together. But Kow is incapable of that; he only loves himself.

Mom tries to snag a hold of my hand to stop me from leaving but I snatch it away and head for the tunnel. There, I shake off the day's misery and grief and betrayal as I rush toward the outer hall.

I can hear Gray and Cole as well as my dad shouting my name, but the stadium's buzzing. People who were taking the last-minute opportunity to grab snacks before the game starts are rushing for their seats when the news that Kow got tossed spreads around like a game of telephone.

Taking advantage of the chaos, I slip among the crowd to elude them.

A few minutes of keeping my head low and I'm through security.

Gaze locked on my phone, I snap off a text in the family chat, telling them I'll loop them in when I get where I'm going—Vancouver —so they can call off the search.

"Ms. Bukowski?" Erick from security calls before I leave. "You okay? You look like real upset."

For the past year, I've been the resident ghost, shadowing my brother and Liam, so the stadium staff knows me.

As I swipe at my cheeks—I didn't even realize I was crying—I shoot him a weak smile. "I'm fine, Erick."

"You sure?" he pesters.

As I head outside, I turn back to nod at him. "You won't see me again, Erick."

His brows lift. "Do you need me to call someone—"

I hold out a hand. "I'm moving to Vancouver so I can go to college in the fall."

"You are?"

"I am." I suck in a breath. "It's time I started living for me and not hockey."

He looks more confused than ever, but that's the funny thing—my mind is clear. Like crystal.

At that moment, I don't realize I'll make history for what will become known as the 'green dye affair.'

Nor do I know that Liam will, from here on out, cease being known as 'Peter Pan' and will be called the 'Leprechaun' for scoring his first hat trick.

Nor do I realize it'll be almost eleven years before I set foot in a stadium again.

All that matters is… I'm out of here.

1ST PERIOD

SEVEN YEARS LATER

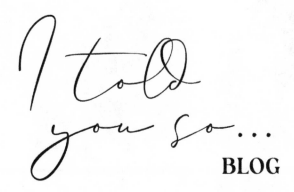

BLOG

RUMORS abound over Liam Donnghal's absence at the latest Mounties vs. Bolts game.

The captain and last season's Stanley Cup winner has an impeccable attendance record, and no injuries have been reported by Montréal.

I can't help but wonder where he is, and the moment I know, you will too…

CHAPTER 1
LIAM

35

Goodbye My Lover - James Blunt

I NEVER THOUGHT I'd die before I hit the big three-oh.

I really didn't.

I'm rich, I'm successful, and I'm healthy.

Moreover, I'm a hockey player.

A good one.

Hell, some might even say a *great* one.

I didn't think I'd die in a godawful basement that stinks of piss and shit.

I didn't think I'd die of sepsis.

I didn't think—

God, that's just it.

I didn't think.

If I had, I wouldn't be here because I was snatched from some nightclub. I would have gone to a skate park and done some tricks before I got taken—fuck my contract. In fact, no. Screw skate-boarding. *I'd just have called Gracie.*

The kid next to me, a fellow hostage, whimpers in his sleep.

Who can blame him?

These assholes not only took a child, but we've been here for too long.

We haven't seen our kidnappers' faces, so the situation isn't that dire yet, but the fact we're still here has my anxiety spiking.

Something has to be wrong.

My absence *must* have hit the news.

I mean, I've already missed a couple games by this point. Though the Mounties are a solid team without me, there's no way the press hasn't realized that the captain has gone missing.

I live in Montréal—we jack off to hockey there.

My fellow Quebeckers somehow worked out I visit my favorite coffee shop on Tuesdays, but they don't recognize my absence on the ice?

I don't buy it.

Digging my fingers into my eyes, I try to understand why my ransom hasn't been paid.

Even if the Mounties couldn't shell out because of years of misman-agement, my personal accounts would—

"Shit," I whisper.

Now that Mom's gone, no one aside from me has access to my money.

I went a little crazy and built up my own trust fund so that my father couldn't get his hands on my assets. The markets haven't been as stable either, so whatever they're asking, I might not even be able to cover—

I scrape a hand over my head, ignoring the blunt, throbbing pain from my injuries.

"Why did you have to buy that new house?" I ask myself.

And why didn't I just mortgage it like everyone advised?

Paranoid... that's me. Especially when it comes to my father.

Padraig has a habit of sniffing around when he's run out of cash, which is always.

It's like water to him, and it easily slips through his fingers.

How ironic that being tight-fisted with him will bite me in the ass in the *short* run because I don't have the funds to cover my ransom.

The Bukowskis and my billet brothers might be able to pitch in, but that I'm still in Lucifer's idea of a vacation hotspot doesn't give me much hope.

"I'm going to die here," I rasp, closing my eyes to quell the stinging from pointless tears.

Maybe that belief is why I see *her*.

Not my whole billet family who took me in and made me one of their own. Who sheltered me from the age of sixteen and who, after Mom died, drew me deeper into the fold.

No, I just see Gracie.

She's the only girl in the Bukowski family.

She's a nag.

She's got a loud mouth.

She's... *magnificent.*

Smart and unafraid, strong and ebullient.

Fuck, when was the last time I even saw her?

She moved to New York, what, two years ago?

She hasn't come to Thanksgiving for a while, and though I tried to pay for her flight back for the holidays, as have the rest of her brothers, she always claims that she needs the overtime...

She's been saying that for years.

We used to be close.

What went wrong?

Did the fame get to my head? Did she think I was an asshole hockey fuckboi like Kow and stopped wanting to hang out with me?

I know the game's changed me. How could it not? Sex and money on tap—aside from when I need to pay off a ransom *apparently*—and I'm supposed to be living my dream.

God, if I make it out of this then I need to be a better person. Someone who Gracie actually likes.

The kid screams something in Mandarin as a nightmare awakens him. The abrupt shout jerks me from my thoughts as he scrabbles into the corner where his camping bed nestles against the wall.

"Hey, it's okay," I try to soothe, but it doesn't stop his sobbing.

He's too petrified for comfort from me to do anything other than scare him further.

I rub the side of my head where my ear used to be—they cut it off to send with the ransom demand. Ever since then, he's looked at me like I'm a monster, and I'm starting to feel as if I am one.

Blood has dried down the side of my cheek where it escaped the bandage they placed there after I passed out. The itch has started. Infection's set in and the pain is bad. Really bad. I have a high tolerance after years on the ice, but it's starting to be something I can't shove aside, a solid fifteen on a scale of one to five.

"How do you get yourself into these situations?"

I can almost hear Gracie chiding me while she simultaneously gifts me her patented finger wag.

I wish I told her that my feelings for her were never *brotherly*.

I wish she knew she meant more to me than just my best friend's sister.

I wish I'd gotten to kiss her.

Fuck, I wish for so many things that'll never happen now.

God, I miss her.

And, I guess, I always will.

CHAPTER 2
GRACIE
SIX MONTHS LATER

Fuck Her Gently - Tenacious D

"SING, SING, SING!"

My younger brothers, Kow and Noah, practically frog-march me to the stage where Liam is watching us as they chant the words in stereo.

"I hate you for this," I snipe at Noah, who just grins dopily at me. "You're lucky you're massive or we'd have a problem."

It's my unfortunate fate to get my mom's height and my dad's weight and for it to be about two feet less than my massive brothers, who got all the inches, whereas I got all the pounds.

It means that when he scrubs my hair, I can literally only punch him in the stomach.

His grin widens because he knows that hurt me more than it hurt him—jerkface. "You love karaoke."

"Not in front of snooty people."

"Look at Liam," Kow whispers in my ear as I shake my wrist.

I do. And, hell. He's smiling for what seems like the first time in months.

I only agreed to attend this wedding because A, my cousin decided to hold it in her groom's hometown in New Hampshire, which is too close to NYC for me to lie about being unable to make it. And B, because I wanted to check in with Liam.

Ever since he came home from the kidnapping, he's been acting a little off. Noah and I aren't the closest, but he's gotten used to me calling him simply because, until his recent trade, he was also a Mountie which meant I could check up on Liam via him.

His move made attending this vainglorious wedding all the more important—I haven't had a recent update in weeks.

Seeing Liam in the flesh hasn't granted me much relief.

He was wicked thin when he got out of the hospital after he was returned to us. He's yet to bounce back much even though Noah told me he was focusing hard on his fitness levels and their coach had him working with a nutritionist.

The problem is, of course, his agent will be working on convincing him to keep his weight low to improve his speeds. The laws of physics agree, but dropping thirty pounds because you were starved under a hostage situation is different than shedding weight for your sport.

At least, morally, it should be.

These goddamn hockey agents don't give a fuck about morals.

Did I mention that I hate people? Especially bottom-feeders.

"Jesus Christ, Gracie. Cheer up, would you?" Kow argues, but that's because he's had one too many beers and is feeling brave. "It's only a song."

"She'll get you back for that," Noah says, his tone a singsong that's bizarre on a man who bench-presses double my weight for funsies.

"You know it," I promise, watching Kow raise his hands and quickly dart off the stage, hauling Noah with him, leaving me on there with Liam while the whole six-hundred-strong wedding party peers at us like we're bacteria on a petri dish.

It's enough to make me want to die because the bright lilac brides-maid dress Amelia *forced* me to wear and the many chocolate-covered strawberries I ate for dessert mean my shapewear is *not* as effective as it was this morning.

Shooting Kow a glower to cover my agitation, I turn to Liam and warn, "If this is your idea, I'll make you pay as well."

His smirk is so normal, so pre-kidnapping Liam, that the sight of it floods me with delight. "I'm a victim too."

"Yeah, yeah, I'm sure you are. This has your pranking signature all over it."

I still want to trace his smile with my fingers though.

Which would be bad.

Very bad.

Because this is Liam.

A fact I'm having to remind myself of more and more often.

Like 'every time I talk to him on the phone' often.

Like 'whenever he texts me' often.

This is a problem I can't solve.

He's Kow's BFF. Family.

Except, you don't want to kiss family.

You don't look at family and think about running your fingers through their messy chestnut-brown hair or want to stare soulfully into their blue eyes...

Before the kidnapping, Liam always had scruffy stubble on his cheeks. You don't see that so much anymore. You don't look at family and think about how wonderful it'd be to test how smooth their silken jaw is, right?

"This isn't a prank," he assures me, which is the opposite of reassuring.

"Which song?" I ask uncomfortably, voice tight with the longing I'm trying and failing to repress, aware that people are starting to talk.

It makes me super self-conscious in my really tight, too tight, wedgie tight, (I hate you, Amelia) dress.

That's when the opening chords sound behind us and I have to hide a snicker as recognition hits.

"You didn't," I whisper, my agitation fading in the face of his wickedness.

He winks at me, making the gauntness in his cheeks more apparent. "I did."

"How did you convince the DJ to play it?"

"I can make magic happen," he says smugly.

"Thought you weren't involved."

"Adjacently."

I snort.

As Tenacious D starts to play and Jack Black's lyrics evolve into social discourse about the appropriate way to fuck a lady in front of Amelia's new family who is hella conservative, I beam up at him.

Not only is this song a mutual favorite of ours, but the sense of justice is too delicious.

Amelia is a grade-A kiss-ass who's marrying up and who my mom wishes were her daughter instead of me.

When the chords drift to an end and Liam's croon does too, I don't give a shit if both of us were flat. I'm just enjoying his grin and the buzz of adrenaline that's flooding my system in a way that has nothing to do with chocolate and everything to do with Liam's vibe.

Man, I missed that.

The urge to kiss him is back.

With a vengeance.

But nope, can't do that.

No, sirree!

As the song dies to nothing, the silence spreads and the crowd gawks at us for singing about smooches and sexy times in front of Amelia's new father-in-law, who's the town mayor. Liam proceeds to hook his arm around my shoulder and leads me toward the stage steps when, finally, there's a reaction.

My brothers as well as Uncle Jak and Aunt Ginnie, who dislike their new son-in-law, start cheering.

In my ear, Liam whispers, "That's for Amelia making you wear lilac. *And* a dress."

I bite my lip to hide my smile. It's worth Mom grabbing my hand and hissing, "What were you thinking?" when we return to our table as if it were my fault that Liam picked the song he did.

It's worth the disappointed headshake from my dad and Amelia storming out of the room like a drama queen.

Kow, of course, loves the chaos.

He sits back like the king he thinks he is, bumping his fist with Noah's as he declares, "There's another player in town, sis. Liam's got his wicked streak back."

That means they really were in on it together—okay, so my siblings don't always suck.

Just sometimes.

Not that Liam is a sibling.

He's not.

He's a friend *of my brother.*

A fact I'll scream after I dig out my vibrator tonight as the lopsided smile he shoots me when he's sneaking away from the hall for a breather will become a feature in my spank bank.

Only, in my fantasies, that smile wouldn't be from across a room... It'd come from directly above me and I'd get to taste it.

Maybe that's why I get up after yet another scolding from Mom, and maybe that's why I decide to follow him.

And why, after I slip out of something a lot uncomfortable in the bathroom, I pick up a bowl of lime slices and a salt shaker to go with the bottle of tequila I saw him slink outside with...

CHAPTER 3
LIAM
LATER THAT NIGHT

35

One Day / Reckoning Song - Asaf Avidan, The Mojos

GRACIE GURGLES around a laugh as she sinks back a shot of tequila and almost chokes on a slice of lime she stole from the party.

Dopily, I grab her chin, pop my fingers into her mouth with an ease I wouldn't be feeling if I were sober, and pluck it out. "Dangerous, Gracie. Dangerous." I wag the mauled slice at her as I relinquish ownership of the bottle too. "You just gotta drink the tequila, not the lime. I'm cutting off your supply."

Her nose crinkles but she hands over the dish of deadly citrus fruits to me.

Like the sprite she is, she twirls on her bare toes, skirt whipping around her legs as she raises her arms to the sky, both dancing and beckoning me closer.

Her almond-shaped eyes angle upward at the corners, lending a mischievousness to her expression that fits considering her family. Her cheeks slope inward toward pouting, naturally dusky pink lips that lead to a chin with an indentation made for my thumb to sit in.

All that beauty is set beneath a dainty button nose like Tinkerbell, except she's a brunette. Her face is round, and her mop of hair with bright red tips dances and bobs around her jawline like Rachel's from *Friends* did.

Fuck, my crush on her is more gargantuan an issue than the one I had on Jennifer Aniston when I was growing up.

"Isn't it beautiful, Liam?" she crows.

My focus doesn't shift to the night sky or the lake.

It stays locked on her.

"Yeah, yeah, it is."

I know I'm drunk. Hell, I went so far past drunk an hour ago that it's only my metabolism that's stopped me from needing to head to an ER to get my stomach pumped. But looking at her twirling in the moonlight, fireflies bobbing around her—she's like a dream.

My fantasy.

My dick gets hard when she runs onto the lakeshore, water splashing high as it makes the dress cling to her even more than it already did.

I tormented Amelia with the karaoke thing because she made Gracie wear a dress. See, I learned my lesson—always have Gracie's back—when she transmogrified me into a four-leaf clover, but I don't get why she hates 'em.

She's hot in a dress.

H. O. T.

I've seen chicks at Chez Parée look less fire than she does right now.

Why she hates herself in dresses is so incomprehensible to me that the mental power it requires has me staggering backward.

I plunk my ass onto the pebble-strewn shore before I fall and watch her with a weather eye. She's too drunk to go into the water, but I'll keep her safe.

She twists around again, letting loose a holler that's drowned out by the music from the other side of the lake where the reception's at.

We snuck away from there two hours ago—me because I needed a breather (and alcohol) after being at the center of everyone's attention, Gracie because Hanna was still scolding her after our stunt.

The tequila I snagged from the open bar encouraged her to stick around longer than I know she intended, so that's what we've been doing—drinking too much. Honestly, this is the happiest I've been in months. I wish the night'd never end.

"Come in the lake, Liam," she croons.

Man, if mermaids look like her, no wonder men have always been lured into the water by them.

"Why? So you can dunk me?" I scoff. "Did you dye this lake green too?"

Her croon turns into a wicked cackle. "Tell me you didn't deserve it."

Technically, all I did was back my bud up when she said he was partying too hard, but—

"I can't."

I blame myself for not seeing the warning signs.

Kow can be an asshole when crossed, but fucking with Gracie's best friend just to hurt her? Prompting her to leave us behind for Vancouver when she could have gone to university in Montréal? I didn't speak to him for six months afterward.

She beckons me with her fingers again as I take another gulp of tequila. "No dye. Just me."

So, what she's saying is the water is even *more* perilous then?

Propping the bottle between some pebbles, I flop onto my back and cup my head with my arm. Tilting forward, I study her and the darkness of the night sky. It's warm out, comfortable, and I'm with my favorite person in the whole world.

"I'll just stay here." *And enjoy the show.*

"You're no fun!" she grumbles. "Come and swim with me."

Tequila.

That's the only reason, the *only* reason, why I yell, "If I come in that water, Gracie, we won't be swimming."

The sounds of splashing stop. Then, I hear the crashing of her feet on the shore. One second, I'm just lying there watching her, the next she's straddling me and plunking her ass on my stomach.

Half dazed, I slur, "Jesus Christ, Gracie!"

"What did you mean by that?" she demands, pushing her hair out of her face and almost punching me with her elbow in the process.

When I don't answer because I'm busy trying not to focus on the heat of her butt against my abs, she leans over me.

Droplets of water sprinkle on my face, cooling me down some as she insists, "Well?!"

Feeling like I actually fell asleep and this is a hazy dream, I cup her chin. "You're so beautiful."

Her stare is owlish. "Why won't you come swim with me?"

"Because you're too beautiful."

"I'm so not," she argues, brow furrowing. "Stop messin' 'round. S'posed to be in veeeeeeno vertiras—berrytus, veraturas?"

"Think you got that wrong," I retort, smirking a little because that's a reminder this is real, not a dream. Reality has never been kinder to me than it is right now. "And you are. You're so fucking beautiful, Gracie. I can't even look at you without it hurting."

She squints at me. "I'm beautiful like this?"

I nod.

She sticks out her tongue. "How about now?"

"You stick that out any farther and I'll do something with it."

Rocking back, Gracie gasps. "Liam!"

"What?"

Her eyes blink. Once. Twice. "Do you have...," she whispers, only it's loud enough to be a shout. "...a boner?"

I grin at her. "Sure do. Ain't ashamed of it either. I can see your tits."

She peers at them. "Huh. You can."

"That dress wasn't made for water, but it was made for me," I sing as I settle my hands on her hips. "You gonna fall asleep on me, Gracie? I'd like that. Maybe it'd make the nightmares stop."

In an explosion of wet hair and drenched silk, she surges on top of me, her elbows settling on either side of my head, pinning me in place, surrounding me with the scent of lime, tequila, perfume, and *her*.

Flowers.

She always smells like flowers.

Fuck, I love flowers.

"Liam?"

"Hmm?"

"What if..." She sucks in a breath. "...I don't want to sleep?"

"What ya wanna do, Gracie?"

She wriggles slightly and suddenly, her core is no longer on my abs but lower. Right there. Where I need her.

"You're drunk."

"You're drunk too." She pouts. "You got whiskey dick?"

I sniff. "Would I have a hard-on if I did?"

Gracie winks as she wriggles some more and her hand is there. On top of me. Shaping me.

"Fuck. Stop it, Gracie. No fair."

"I'm not a cocktease, Liam," she chides before, sitting up fast enough to give me whiplash, she grabs the bottle of tequila at my side and pours some into her mouth.

Then, she stuns me. She doesn't swallow.

She looms over me again.

Her lips press against mine.

Like the fool I am, I part my own, and a slow trickle of unholy water streams into my mouth.

Swallowing quickly, I watch in a daze as she starts rocking her hips, grinding into my dick while her breath tickles my jaw until, finally, she joins us together.

When she thrusts her tongue into my mouth, I groan. Hands tightening around her hips, I encourage her to ride me that little bit harder, loving the friction and craving more.

I tangle with her some, adoring her taste, half-stunned that this is happening while half-bewildered that Kow hasn't popped up out of nowhere to drag us apart.

That jackass always has *the* worst timing.

Moving one hand to cup her nape, I tilt her head to find a better, deeper angle.

For the first time since the kidnapping, I feel like I can breathe.

As if my head is clear.

As if the shadows aren't as dark.

As if the stars themselves are illuminating my path.

Cupping her chin, smoothing my thumb over her jawline, I rumble, "I want to touch you, Gracie."

A soft moan escapes her but she nods.

I encourage her to sit up again and allow my hands to stroke her calves and along her thighs. Eyes locked on her, I wait for her to tell me to back off, but she doesn't. She just watches me as I find—

"You're not wearing panties?" I croak.

"I got sick of being strangled by my shapewear and you could see my VPL through the dress," she whispers.

I'm not sure what a VPL is, but I *am* sure that it means she's naked beneath her skirt.

I have never loved VPLs more in my life than I do right now.

"Fuck, fuck, fuck. I didn't need to know that."

She lets loose a laugh, one that's wicked and wild and so much freer than I'm used to hearing from her. "Why? Would you have been trying to look up my skirt, Mr. Donnghal?"

Grunting, I let my fingertips trail over the line of her hip. "I still can."

As her brows lift, I cup her ass and haul her higher. She shrieks but starts cackling like a lunatic when, snagging the hem of her dress, I duck beneath it.

"Oh, *my*, God!" she cries around another burst of laughter before turning into Scarlett O'Hara on me. "Why, Mr. Donnghal, I do declare you're a pervert!"

Fuck, she smells like heaven. She's even flowery down here.

Motherfucking addicting flowers.

Ignoring her chortles, I settle her so that her knees are on either side of my head and I urge her to take a seat exactly where I want her.

The second I've got her positioned, she yelps, finally realizing that I'm not messing around.

A shaky breath drifts from her before she holds it for the longest time, her tension ratcheting ever higher with every missed inhalation until she releases the deepest, longest groan that sets off an intonation in my veins.

I purse my lips and blow a stream of air along her slit, aware that my cock has never been harder. I'm in agony, but what a way to go.

"Oh, fuck," she whimpers as my tongue finds her pussy.

No way this is a dream. Not when I'm tasting silk.

Not when her scent is all around me.

Not when I'm breathing her in because she's the only oxygen I ever want in my lungs.

In a flurry of movement, she crumples a touch, spreading her legs wider, angling her hips, rocking forward and back, suddenly unafraid to take what she needs.

How did I know she'd be like this?

How did I fucking know she'd be perfect?!

I groan against her as I suck on her clit. She cries out, deeper than before as I start to press wet kisses around the nub then trail my tongue down her channel.

"Liam," she moans, and my name has never sounded so sweet as it does on her lips. "How am I... You're Liam. You're not supposed to... This is too..."

She jerks up, but I follow, continuing to suck on her clit like I've got nothing better to do with my night—spoiler alert, I don't.

"Liam, you can't... I'm going to..." She releases a guttural grunt. "No. I mean, this is... too... Stop!"

I do.

Her frantic breathing sounds overly loud as she scrambles away from me.

Away.

From.

Me.

As my heart starts to shatter, that's when she twists around. I figure she's about to run off but she doesn't.

She turns.

Repositions herself above me.

Her hands—

"Fuck," I bite out before she chokes off my air by settling that delicious pussy where it should always be while her fingers are fussing with my fly.

As she delves between the zipper, drawing my dick out into the open, I hide a grin when she whimpers, "Jesus, Liam, what is this? An ana-freakin'-conda?"

Preferring to stay silent and to get back to work devouring her cunt, I savor her moans and bitten-off cries and her curse words that tell me what I'm doing to her is driving her wild.

Me.

Only me.

When she sucks the tip of my shaft between her lips, I have no idea how the fuck I don't come. Little brain down below seems to recognize that while he's currently in heaven, there's nothing better than this pocket of paradise between her thighs.

Nibbling the edge of her clit with my teeth, I wait for her squeal then suckle it. Wet and noisy and hungry, I feast on her, getting her juices all over my face, wanting to drown in her, craving her orgasm more than I do my own.

When she gasps around my dick, I know why.

The keening sob that vibrates around it has me almost seeing stars, but I hold off. I hold and I hold and I fucking hold. As I lick and flick and torment her pussy, I go through plays in my head, fighting the urge to explode in her mouth.

Cibole, *I wonder if she swallows?*

When she sags on top of me, I go slow, teasing her until she's twitching in overload.

Cupping her butt, I shuffle away so I can mumble, "Gracie, you trying to torture me?"

A soft, hiccuping breath is my only answer, but she doesn't argue when I maneuver her around.

I grin. "You gonna let me do all the work, huh, *ma belle*?"

She mutters nonsense that sounds like, "Dying. Phone later, caller."

Snorting, I get her where I need her then I twist us over. It's a pebble shore but we're in a semi-sandy patch so I don't feel like a jerk for letting her lie there.

When I kneel between her thighs, carefully shoving her skirt high on her hips, I rest my dick against her pussy as I reach for the condom that's only in my wallet out of old habits dying hard—thank fuck for them.

"You with me, Gracie?" I ask as I cover my cock.

She flops her hand on her forehead. "You deserve a reward for good behavior," she agrees, but the words fade at the pressure of my dick sinking into her.

My tip stretches her slit to the point where her eyes pop open and she blinks blindly at me. Carefully, I start to rub her clit with my thumb as I rock my hips, needing to keep her slick so that she can take me.

Aware of my size because it's been a problem in the past, I push deeper, taking this slow, loving her hiccuping breaths, the sharp sighs, how her hips rock up and back to help me slide home.

When, finally, I'm there, we're both panting like crazy and I'm pretty sure I've got an aneurysm in my future because the blood vessels in my brain want to pop at how good she feels.

I push my forehead into hers. "Your pussy is so fucking tight, Gracie."

Her moan is half-laughter and half-sigh, but she shrieks when I flip us over so that she's back on top.

Her gaze is wide-eyed and wild as she presses her hands to my chest.

"I want you to strangle my dick. I want you to come so goddamn hard that you cut off my blood supply. That's an order, do you hear me?"

She tears at the buttons on my Oxford and her fingers brush over my skin. I feel the dig of her nails as she starts to ride me, slow at first, but gradually getting faster as she finds her rhythm.

In the moonlight, she glows.

All around her, the silvery atmosphere makes her appear ethereal.

This is starting to seem like a dream again, but I know this one won't end with me screaming in terror as I wake up.

Needing to get lost in her, I find her clit, rubbing it so that she feels it with every downthrust. When she grinds into me, when her hips start to wriggle, I know she's close—I can sense it.

She clutches at me like a vise and whispers, "Liam, I-I think I'm going to come again."

"Give it to me, Gracie. I want it. I need you to come or I can't. My cock is so hard for you, *bébé*. You and only you. I want to come in you, fill you full. Want you to explode around me and—"

"Liam!" she gasps, her body shimmering with tension as she shudders above me.

That's when I let go.

That's when I groan as her cunt teases my cum out of me, blowing my mind and tearing the walls of my heart wide open.

"Gracie," I moan as I come and I come and I come.

As the earth shudders beneath me.

As my whole world detonates in on itself, imploding before exploding because this is where I'm supposed to be.

As my heart stops racing, as my body comes back to reality, I can feel her soft weight above me.

Her breathing is low and steady and the gentle puffs of air at my throat key me into the fact she's either passed out or sleeping.

Carefully, I pull free of her, taking note that she doesn't wake up. I lower her skirt, close my fly, try to tug my shirt into some semblance of decency, and haul her against my chest as I carry her back to the lodge where I'm staying.

I know she intended on driving home, but that's not going to happen.

There's only one problem with my plan.

Kow.

Not because he thinks I just fucked his sister, but because he's always the problem child. It's one of the reasons I had to befriend him —the fucker has no limits. Since I've known him, he's had *thirteen* near-death experiences.

I'm not sure if I'm his unlucky charm or not, but I swear I'm the one who's kept him alive this long.

Still, his timing is better than it usually is.

At least he drove his dumb ass into some bushes *after* Gracie and I got it on and not before.

With her still in my arms, I stride over to the parking lot where Kow's snoring away against the steering wheel, somehow ignoring the seatbelt alarm that's bleating and the stench of burned-out tires from the foot he's pushing the accelerator with.

The dipshit is drunk as a skunk—what the fuck was he thinking getting behind the wheel in this state?

Mouth tight with annoyance, I snatch the keys from the dash before carefully shifting Gracie in my hold. Her face falls into the curve of my neck and the whisper of her breath there has me wishing I could keep her in that spot for the rest of my life.

As that wonderful thought hits me and I let loose a dopey grin, that's when Kow lets loose too.

In my direction.

I stagger back to avoid the impressively projectile vomit he sprays my way but it gets on my shoes—*asshole*.

Eyes narrowed, I stride off, his keys in my pocket, as I take Gracie to my room, knowing that I can't do much to help him while she's in my arms.

After I settle her on the bed, I stroke a hand over her hair. "I'll be back soon, okay?"

Her lips purse but she sighs in her sleep and rolls onto her side with a discontented mewl before her features flatten out in a deep, true rest.

God, she's beautiful.

Like an angel.

Which is such false advertising that it makes me snicker.

The last thing I want to do is go, but I can't leave Kow out there. He'll probably fall in the lake or be barreled into by a lawnmower that's inexplicably running at midnight or somehow manage to choke on a cupcake—weirder shit happens to him on the regular.

I find him, thankfully, where I left him.

This time, however, I'm prepared.

I toss the bucket of iced water I stopped off to collect from the wedding reception at him, enjoying his shriek as he wakes up with a bang.

Snarling, I grab him by the ear. "Drunk driving, Kow, really?"

I haul his ass out of the car and snag one of his arms in my grasp. Then, I toss him over my shoulders and carry him like a scarf.

A part of me even hopes someone takes a snapshot of us—just so I can prove that losing thirty pounds has done nothing to fuck with how much I can bench press.

I carry him to his room like that, dumping him in front of the door so I can pat him down for his keycard. Once I find it, I open up and drag him over to the bathroom where I drop his groggy ass again.

Knowing he's a kinky, sex-obsessed moron, I find what I'm looking for in his nightstand.

"What are you doing?" he slurs, head flopping back and forth as I make my return, swinging the furry leopard-print cuffs between my fingers.

Ignoring him, I fix one around the bathtub handle and with the other, I fight for control of his left hand.

Because he's a lot drunker and slower than me, I manage to tie him in place without too much difficulty. "That's for being an idiot. You have a room here, you dick. Why did you try to get into your car?"

His head lolls forward, chin butting his chest. "Seemed like a—"

He starts puking again.

"That's why I cuffed you to the bathtub," I tell him unapologetically as he practically crawls over the side of the tub and lets it free flow.

By the time he's done and I'm sure he's not going to choke on his own vomit, I leave him cuffed in the bathroom and make a return to my bedroom.

Gracie's still asleep so I quickly shower because I stink, and that's when I edge my way into bed.

Of course, that's also when I realize the Bukowskis exist simply to turn me prematurely gray.

Because Gracie's watery eyes pop open.

Wait, she's crying?

She squints at me.

Then, she breathes, "Liam?"

FOLLOWING MORNING

Gracie: Still can't believe you did that.

Liam: What do you mean? What did I do?

Gracie: Put me in your bed! Ugh. You could have dropped me into the shower before you left this morning. I feel like hell.

Liam: You do?

Gracie: Yeah. My head's banging and I'm pretty sure I died and was reborn with a migraine. Anyway, where are you? Sorry I stole your room.

Liam: I'm heading out of town. :-)

Gracie: What?! Already?! I thought we could hang out before I had to leave!

Liam: Tried to wake you up but you weren't having it.

Liam: I had an emergency.

Gracie: What kind of emergency?

Liam: A Kow-shaped one.

Gracie: Say no more. Everything okay?

Liam: Yup.

Gracie: We had fun last night, didn't we?

Liam: I mean, I did. I hope you did too.

Gracie: Sure. No one better to hang out with than you. I forgot that.

Liam: You liked... hanging out with me?

Gracie: I did!

Liam: Good?

Gracie: Why the question mark, lol?

Liam: NVM.

Gracie: I need to figure out a way to thank you.

Liam: For what?

Gracie: The karaoke, duh.

Liam: Oh.

Liam: Well, Amelia shouldn't have made you wear a dress or purple.

Gracie: What were you talking about?

Gracie: I feel like this conversation is at cross-purposes lol. I'm too hungover for this.

Liam: Nothing. Doesn't matter :-)

Gracie: Sure it does! Did something happen?

Liam: Nah. GTG. Speak later.

YOUR DAILY DOSE OF SPORTS NEWS

THE 'LEPRECHAUN' WINS HART MEMORIAL TROPHY FOR THIRD TIME AFTER SHOCKING KIDNAPPING SCARE

BY MACK FINNEGAN

Montréal Mounties' forward, Liam Donnghal, was selected by the Professional Hockey Writers' Association as the Hart Memorial Trophy recipient this season, marking Donnghal's third nod in as many years, already having won the Conn Smythe Trophy for playoff MVP as well as the Stanley Cup this season.

Donnghal was recently seen attending a family wedding in New Hampshire, where he seemed in good spirits following the tragedy that befell the center.

Details of his kidnapping have never been released to the media, but those close to the 'Leprechaun' state that he was taken for ransom and was held hostage with the child of a New York businessman whose name remains unknown.

After his release, Donnghal came back onto the ice with a vengeance, breaking Gretzky's record of most goals in a season with a total of 95, making him the obvious choice for the Hart Memorial.

Mounties' fans are anxiously awaiting his first game of the new season to see what magic the Leprechaun can sow for Montréal.

THREE MONTHS LATER

Gracie: Saw this and thought of you.

Gracie sends picture

Liam: Why would a dick pic with a tattoo of a mountie on it remind you of me?

Gracie: Because you're a Mountie. And I figured it'd make you smile. ;)

Liam: I don't want to know what goes down in your brain. That's a literal mountie. Not the team logo.

Gracie: :P

Liam: And, for future reference, a picture of tits with the tattoo of a mountie on them is more likely to make me smile than a dick.

Gracie: You ruin everything. *pouts*

Liam: It's a gift.

Liam: What kind of jerk-off is sending you a dick pic?

Gracie: A guy who doesn't realize that's not the way to get into my pants lol. Great game last night, btw.

Liam: Thanks. :-) Surprised you watched it. Thought you'd gone cold turkey on hockey.

Gracie: Bad date. :P Your shoulder acting up?

Liam: Nah. It's fine.

Gracie: You sure? You looked like you were favoring your right one.

Liam: Got into a fight in the tunnel. Doesn't matter.

Liam: Today was the first day of your last year of law school, right?

Gracie: It's cute that you know that. And yes, I'll allow you to change the subject.

Gracie: But...

Gracie: Let me guess, the guy you fought with...

Gracie: Greco.

Liam: Know-it-all.

Gracie: :P

Gracie: Who won?

Liam: I'm offended you have to ask. He punches like you.

Gracie: You're lucky you're six-hundred clicks away.

Liam: ;-)

Gracie: My punch makes grown men weep. Or it will the next time I see you.

Liam: Love it when you threaten me with a good time, Gracie.

Liam: How did it go today?

Gracie: It went. I'll get there.

Gracie: How are the nightmares? Are you sleeping?

Liam: Things are better, yeah.

Gracie: You sure? Always here to talk.

Liam: Thanks. :-) Your brother convinced me to switch therapists btw.

Gracie: Which brother and why? You liked that one, didn't you?

Liam: Kow said she was a fan girl.

Gracie: Ah, Jesus. What did she do?

Liam: Offered to suck my cock to make me feel better.

Gracie: And you needed talking out of switching therapists, huh?

Liam: I liked her. I mean, the offer was nice but not what I need right now.

Gracie: Ya think? Well, I hope the new one is better.

Liam: I haven't found a replacement shrink yet.

Gracie: What?!

Gracie: Ah, shit.

Gracie: GTG, something's just come up. Take care of that shoulder, huh? And TTYL.

TWO DAYS LATER:

Gracie: Here. He's posted on his Facebook page that sports are how the government controls the masses.

Gracie: He's straight with three kids and I don't think he's in the closet. Not from the memes he shares.

Gracie: He's a commie supporter with Marxist leanings and Nihilist tendencies, but he's confident in his sexuality and won't be offering to suck you off midsession.

Liam: You stalked his Facebook profile?!

Gracie: Of course. Anyway, sign up with him. TODAY. You hear me? Don't make me make the call, Liam.

Liam: Okay, okay. Chill. I'll do it now.

Gracie: Good. Got a class. Talk later.

An hour later
Liam: Session with him next week. TY

Gracie: <3

VOICE NOTE

"Merry Christmas, Liam! I hope you have a wonderful day. I
   hereby donate all the riced potatoes that I'd have eaten to
   you and your plate. The carbs are gift enough, but knowing
   you, you're still trying to live clean—bleugh—even on
   Christmas Day, you heathen. So, because you won't accept
   them without a fight, here's my real gift to you.
"Now, don't laugh. I know it might seem crazy, but as long as
   you have this, you'll always be able to find your way home.
   Take care of yourself for me, Liam.
"Yours,
"Gracie."

VOICE NOTE

"I love the compass, Gracie. Thank you. Merry Christmas. I just... I just wish you were here."

Gracie: Got the bling yet?

Liam sends picture
Liam: Does look good on my finger.

Gracie: Stop preening. :P

Gracie: I'm sure the Stanley Cup rings get gaudier every year lol. Kow wears his to bed. Did you know that?

Liam: More like he wears it EVERYWHERE. He almost got mugged in a bathroom last year in Kansas LMAO.

Gracie: He did? Fucker. I didn't know that. My brothers are going to be the death of me. Why was he wearing it in the first place?

Liam: He's a show-off? Anyway, well done! I don't really understand it but you got a scholarship or something?

Gracie: I did. It eases things substantially. When next semester starts, I'll be able to relax on the financial front.

Liam: I'm glad to hear that. Always here if you need me, Gracie.

Gracie: I know and I've already said it, but thank you for those tickets.

Liam: Next time The Arctic Monkeys play in the city, we'll go together.

Gracie: I'd like that :)

Liam: Hell, the next time I'M in NYC, never mind the band, WE need to meet up. I mean it this time lol. No more ghosting me.

Gracie: That'd be cool. BTW, your gift is in the mail.

Liam: Is that a hint?

Gracie: Yes.

Liam: I'm not Kow lol. I never forget your birthday.

Gracie: Good.

LIAM'S JOURNAL

Hi, Gracie,

I know this is strange but my therapist suggested that writing you a note might help me make sense of things.

Not that you'll see this. It's in a journal. Yes, a journal. You'd be proud of me if you knew, you little stationery whore.

It's blue leather and from Mont Blanc because when I told Kow what I have to do, his bougie ass sent this to me. You know he's worried if he actually went out and bought something for me.

He's more like you than you realize.

Well, aside from that weird ability he has to almost die once a year... Thank God you don't have that, too, or I wouldn't just be going gray, I'd be losing my fucking hair.

Still, I'm not sure where I'd have been without you guys the last couple years. Unfortunately, since Noah got traded, I'm alone in Montréal.

And...

Christ, Gracie, I'm scared.

No, I'm petrified.

All the goddamn time.

I don't feel safe anywhere because nowhere is safe.

I wish I could talk to you about this, and I know that you'd be mad at me if you realized I was holding back, but some stuff, I just can't say out loud.

My house isn't safe. The rink isn't safe. Nowhere is fucking safe. All the places where I found peace away from the spotlight were used to target me.

It's not like I can even carry here.

You know I hate guns, but it's starting to feel like having one nearby is the only way I'll be able to sleep at night.

I guess it's weird that my therapist wants me to talk to you. Well, it'd be weird for you. Not for me. It's starting to make sense.

You're my safe space.

I didn't realize it until everything... happened, but you are.

It'd be easier if Kow were my safe space, I guess, but he isn't. He's not you. Maybe if I could tuck you into bed next to me, I wouldn't need a gun...

I cannot wait until you're 35.

I'm not known for my patience but fuck, for you, I'll wait.

So, this is my first 'letter' to you. Mike suggested it because I'm struggling to journal my feelings, but he says if it feels like it's an open dialogue, it might seem more natural to me.

I figure he's right because this is the first time I've written more than three words.

Mike intends on reading it. I'm sure you were right about him having communist leanings—he's definitely a tin-pot Lenin. But he doesn't offer to suck me off every time I break down during a session like you promised, so yay?

I miss you.

I can't tell you that either.

Not IRL.

Here I can.

I can't help but feel like you've been pulling away. I wish I knew if it was something I've done. I know your mom gave you shit for that stunt at Amelia's wedding. You've been distant since then. It's not like you even remember what we promised each other afterward, never mind what happened, so I don't understand what made you back off.

Some days, that makes me sadder than memories of 'that time.'

Couldn't believe it when you didn't make it home for Christmas—the level of devastation I experienced was a new low.

I'll write you tomorrow and, just so you know, the compass you bought me keeps pointing south because that's where you are and where I'm not.

Liam

THREE MONTHS LATER

Liam: Hey, I'm in New York.

Gracie: I saw on PSN TV lol.

Liam: Wanna meet up?

Gracie: I've got a crazy schedule right now. :/

Liam: You're the only woman who'll blow me off. You're good for my ego.

Gracie: Pfft. I'm sure, in your head, you don't have me down under the label of 'woman.'

Gracie: More like 'Kow's sister.'

Liam: *rolls eyes*

Gracie: You're here tonight and tomorrow?

Liam: I have a business meeting tomorrow, but yeah.

Gracie: Ah, shit, I've got to work tonight and I have a meeting with one of my professors. I'm so sorry. Is everything okay?

Liam: Yeah, it's fine. No worries. I'll message you in advance next time. ;-)

Gracie: Best way lol. Have a good game tonight.

Liam: I'll try. :-p

VOICE NOTE

"Love that you keep living up to the name, Liam. Though
Leprechaun gold is supposed to be fake…
"My Canadian heart salutes you for winning the gold medal,
though.
"Remind me to make you some pierogi the next time I see you."

Gracie: YOU FUCKING DIDN'T.

Liam: :-p

Liam: You liked it?

Gracie: LIKED IT? FUCK YOU, LIAM DONNGHAL.

Liam: I mean I wouldn't say no lol. ;)

Gracie: Pfft.

Gracie: You cannot get me a Cameo from Papa Roach and ask me if I 'liked' it.

Liam: LOL. You're welcome?

Gracie: *sobs*

Gracie: Jacoby Dakota Shaddix asked me, ME, MEEEEEE, if school was going okay.

Gracie: I can't. I'm going to expire.

Liam: No expiring.

Liam: Happy birthday, mon p'tit chou.

Gracie: FUCK YOU calling me a cabbage again! I love you so much. I hate you. AGGGHHHH. Now I have to go to work and I look crazy.

Liam: Hey

Gracie: WHAT

Liam: Love you too ;-)

LIAM'S JOURNAL

Hey, Gracie

I'm getting traded to New York.

I'll be making the move as soon as my house is packed up.

I don't want to play for the New York Stars, and I'm definitely being pushed toward it by my agent and Paddy, but the only reason I went ahead with the deal is because you're there.

Maybe I won't need this journal anymore.

Maybe I'll be able to talk to the real deal.

Maybe I can fast-forward our schedule by a few years.

I've always been an overachiever...

See you soon, .

Liam

CHAPTER 4
GRACIE

PRESENT DAY

Breezeblocks - alt-J

"WHAT ARE *YOU* DOING HERE?"

Liam might be the best thing since sliced bread in the world of ice hockey, but to me, at this moment, he's a pain in the ass for coming into my place of work with that face of his all out in the open.

That very recognizable face.

That very recognizable, very gorgeous, very droolworthy, very *kissable* face.

It's all out there.

For everyone to see.

Honestly, it should be illegal.

What *is* illegal?

My crush.

On. Him.

I'm screwed.

"Such a welcome, Gracie," he drawls, tugging on his baseball cap.

Ha. As if *that* disguises his identity.

"If you wanted a welcome, you should have gone to a different bar," I grumble as I set down the menu in front of him. In a low voice, I mutter, "Thank you for the Cameo, by the way."

His smirk is annoyingly hot. "Liked it?"

I huff. "Blink-182 asking me if an MBA stands for Mothers Breaking Ass? Um. Yeah. Anyway, what do you want to drink?"

"Water."

"Water?" I repeat. Though I know his penchant for lean proteins, I needle, "Chuck's is famous for hot wings and beer, Liam. You can't come here and have water."

"I didn't realize there were rules. You know I can't eat hot wings."

"Because you're a pussy. Nothing to do with being a pro hoc—" I stop myself before I can finish my sentence.

The last thing I need is for the nosy fuckers around here to eavesdrop on our interaction.

He doesn't comment on me stuttering to a halt, just rumbles, "That sounds like trash talk."

I smile. Slowly. "You know it. What are you doing here? You didn't answer my question."

"It's a bar. Why do people come to bars?"

"Not to drink water," I retort, and because my boss isn't an asshole and I'm practically management, I plunk my butt opposite Liam in the booth. "What's up?"

"Nothing," he says quickly.

Too quickly.

Having grown up around hockey players my whole life, I know their various quirks and the BS they spew.

This is grade-A, toxic BS.

Mostly because Liam's been in the crapper for a while now.

Not hockey-wise. Nah, on the ice, he's practically a god to fans. The idolatry people have for him is only getting worse.

See, Liam's one of those unusual players—the more depressed he is, the better he plays because he puts his whole focus into hockey.

It's when he's happy that his game suffers and Liam hasn't been happy for a while.

He'd played like Hermes on ice during the playoffs. No wonder the Mounties won the Stanley Cup *again*, despite him not being in top shape mentally.

That's why his excuse of 'nothing' doesn't ring true.

"Tell Aunty Gracie your problems, Liam," I state, moving my fingers in a 'gimme' motion.

"I don't have any problems."

"Your life's perfect, huh?" I mock, knowing that's a lie.

It's not like I'm unhappy to see him. In fact, I'm very happy, just not here and without any notice.

"Well, no, but nobody's life is perfect," he remarks, flicking a look at the table then back to me. "Don't you have to work?"

"You didn't come here for water. You didn't come here for hot wings. You came here to talk to me."

"I thought you were studying for your MBA. Why are you working in a bar?"

"And what does that have to do with you?"

"I'm... family." He scowls. "Saying that no one in the family knows either." His scowl darkens even more. "Kow seemed to think you were working on a sex hotline."

Barking out a laugh, I shake my head. "Only Kow."

"You don't do that... right?"

I bat my lashes. "I've got the voice for it."

His gaze dips to my mouth and quickly flashes away. He clears his throat. "You have a great voice, yeah. If your mom and dad knew you were doing sex work—"

I snort. "Puritans."

"No lie." He clears his throat again. "So, I mean, are you?"

"Would you tell them if I were?" I purr.

He immediately tenses—smart guy. The softer my voice, the deadlier the threat. "Of course not. I was just thinking out loud. They give you shit for living in the US when Canada is the best country on earth—"

"—best country on earth—"

We say that at the same time.

"—so I don't think you working a sex hotline would go down well."

Sitting back in the booth, the red vinyl creaking, I murmur, "They can sleep peacefully in their beds because I don't." *Anymore.* I'd done it for three months two years ago though. Had a whale of a freakin' time until I'd gotten laryngitis that wouldn't quit. How Kow knows any of that is a mystery. "But to answer your question, I'm waiting tables because I have rent to pay and I enjoy it. I'm pretty much management here and it's a nice change of pace from my studies."

Though his scowl lessens, he still seems confused by my life choices when we both know my brothers would pay my way through school.

To be fair, most of the men in my life have worn that look around me at some point—I'm used to it. But this is *my* show. Not theirs.

"How did you even know I worked here?"

"Got my own ways of doing things," is all he says, making me roll my eyes because he probably got it out of my landlord for twenty bucks before he remarks, "I don't think it's possible for you to be my aunt. You're barely six months older than me."

For a second, I'm in the dark, then I realize he's pivoted back to my earlier 'Aunty Gracie' comment.

He didn't like that... Huh.

Not giving a damn whether he likes it or not, I get to my feet because something's going on with him and I need to get to the bottom of it.

The second I start to walk away, however, he snags my hand. "Don't go."

That has my brow furrowing with concern. Not just the request, but his tone.

Liam's cocky, but without being a jerk. Of the best friends my three brothers have, as much as I love them, he's the only one I can stand for more than two hours without wanting to whack him between the legs with a hockey stick.

And while my brothers got all the talent, I inherited the swing too.

"I'm not going anywhere," I inform him, aware that my voice is pitched softer. "I have to tell Chuck, my boss, that I need to cut my shift short."

"You don't have—"

I huff. "Make up your mind, Liam. Do you want me to go or not?"

He squirms in his seat, and that right there is worth losing an hour's pay.

There's nothing like making a hockey god *squirm*.

Millions of women around the world drool over the IG stories he shares of him diving into a pool in designer swimwear for dough, men knock beer bottles over the chicks he's reportedly banging while wishing they were him, and here I am, little Gracie Bukowski, making the Leprechaun squirm in his seat.

Honestly, nothing beats that.

"Yes. But I'll make up the pay," he offers quickly.

With a grin, I duck to kiss his cheek. It's not where I want to kiss but beggars can't be choosers. "I'm not too proud to take it," I declare.

As I rush to the bar, Mia Charles, bartender, my work wife, and the owner's niece, mutters, "Who's the hottie?"

Chuck's plays nothing but baseball on its fourteen TVs, so that's why she doesn't recognize Liam. Mia and I are birds of a feather—we freakin' loathe sports.

Everything sports.

Except with two differences.

One, she's a figure skater so she doesn't hate that.

Two, she never tried to use sports as a bridge to connect with the rest of her family how I did.

My desire to stop feeling like an outsider in my own home means that I can tell you who won the soccer World Cup in 1962 (Brazil), the male 1989 US Open winner (Boris Becker), and the PGA Championship Winner in 2017 (Justin Thomas with the US), even as I loathe every single sport I've ever come across.

Though, it *is* a great party trick for trivia night.

"He's best friends with my brothers."

That's about as deep into it as I can get without having to explain what a billet family is to someone who doesn't give a damn about hockey.

She whistles under her breath.

I snort. "Shut up."

"What? I didn't say anything. Anyway, you've got eyes. I've got eyes. Hell, honey, every woman in Chuck's has eyes too."

"It's just Liam."

"'Just' Liam, my ass," she retorts.

Glancing across the bar, I see 'Just Liam' is watching me and I wave at him.

"He's been checking you out since he sat down."

"Shut up."

Mia raises an eyebrow. "Baby, I'm telling you, he's been watching you."

"Probably because he wanted to talk to me. Speaking of," I demur. "I need to duck out early."

"It's quiet tonight, so you should be all set."

"Where's your uncle?"

"Playing pinball. Where else?"

With a nod, I nudge my hip into hers. "He wants some water. Could you get me a bottle while I go talk to Chuck?"

Her expression's puzzled. "Water?"

I shrug. "Water."

"Does he know we've got a gazillion different types of beer on tap?"

"He does. He wants water."

I leave her shaking her head over the oddities of mankind and stroll toward the vintage arcade games in the back corner.

I can't blame her for finding his order strange. It's not often that a single guy comes in on a Thursday at 9pm with water on his mind. Liam couldn't do incognito if he tried.

"How's my favorite warrior princess?" my boss exclaims.

Snickering, I knock elbows with Chuck, amused as always by how his focus can be on pinball but he somehow knows everything that's going on around him.

Chuck really does have eyes in the back of his head.

"How many times, boss? It's Gracie, not Xena."

"Well, Princess Gracie, how ya faring?"

Though I pull a face, I know that he was super proud of me yesterday. I'm pretty sure he's got the news reports of what went down outside the bar recorded from a few shows.

Chuck's an indeterminate age of somewhere between fifty-four and seventy-four. I've seen pictures of him at thirty-two and he looked like he was in his fifties back then.

His grizzled features, bulbous nose from a history of an alcohol problem, and full head of silvery white hair set him apart. Last year, when he redid the logo on this place and was going to go all fancy, Mia drew him and he's now the symbol of Chuck's.

The funny thing is, Mia told him it was a portrait, but it's his caricature.

That's just Chuck, though—he's got a face only a cartoon animator would love.

"I'm fine, boss. How are you?"

"Back's aching—"

"That's because you're hunched over these games all the time," I immediately retort with zero pity.

He harrumphs. "You ain't got no sympathy for an old man."

"I'm still not sure if you *are* old," I reply with a grin.

"Trust me, my arthritis says otherwise."

My nose wrinkles. "It's quiet out there, Chuck. You mind if I take off early? I'll make it up tomorrow. I'm on a half-shift."

He waves a hand. "Sure thing, kiddo. Everything okay?"

"Yeah, an old family friend popped in and he's looking..." How did Liam look? I mean, Mia's not wrong about him being a hottie. He never looks *bad* per se. But whatever's wrong with him, it has me offering to take off work early, so I noticed *something*. "...odd."

Chuck tuts. "Odd? Is he painted blue like that kid last week?"

When he says 'painted blue,' he means in his entirety.

The idiot had covered every inch of his body with paint and he'd ended up riding to the hospital in an ambulance.

That was an expensive game night. One that made me reminisce about the time I turned Liam and Kow green.

"Nah. He's just..." I purse my lips. "...sad."

Yeah, sad. That fit.

"Huh. Go for it, sweetheart. I'll see you tomorrow."

I knew he wouldn't mind, and not just because he's a great boss, but I'm usually the first to volunteer whenever he needs an extra hand.

Seeing as I live on the same block, he knows he can always rely on me; it's how I became 'management' without the job title but with a pay raise.

Plus, I'm not a jackass and don't take advantage of his kind nature.

We both know that I could pick up and leave at any moment and get a better job, but I meant what I said to Liam—I'm happy here.

I tap him on the shoulder. "Thanks, Chuck. You need me to get you some ibuprofen for your back?"

"You're a good girl, but nah. It's fine." He stretches. "You're right. I've been playing this too long. I should probably sit down and do some bookkeeping anyway."

"Yeah, you should," I retort, aware that Chuck's filing system is a walking hard-on for an IRS auditor with a quota to fill.

"You go cheer your boy up," he shoos.

My boy... *I wish.*

"Night, Chuck."

Having made my retreat, I dump my order pad on the counter when I'm back at the bar and toss my apron on top of it. Next, I grab the tray Mia has loaded up with Liam's bottle of water as well as my regular order of cream soda.

Ice clatters in his glass as I ask, "Mia, babe, do you mind putting my apron in the hamper?"

As she snags the bright orange fabric, she informs me, "He's still watching you."

With a sniff, I wiggle the cream soda at her. "Thanks."

"You look like you need it."

"Yeah, it's been a long day."

"Maybe you'll get lucky and it'll be a long night too."

"Shuddup," I retort, flinging my order pad at her.

Catching it, she just winks and walks off when someone calls out for a refill.

If it *is* a long night, it won't have anything to do with what she's imagining. Hell, what I've been imagining for far too long—one of my fave fantasies involves us, a lakeshore, moonlight, and the number 69.

Bad Gracie!

I tried the old-fashioned way to cure my crush—distance—and that hasn't worked.

The nuns in school were liars when they preached that suffering leads to rewards.

Though, I guess the rewards they were talking about are of the heavenly variety, not earthly, which means I'm plain screwed all 'round because this crush isn't going anywhere.

Years after his kidnapping, it's still an uncomfortable ache I can't fight.

And him being *here*, all up in my space *and* one of my booths, with that gorgeousness of his spotlighted from on high, while a choir of angels sings, isn't helping.

Why do men never do what you want them to do?

Still, if he needs me, that changes things.

Retreating to his table, I drop a napkin and place his water on it then drink directly from my bottle of cream soda as I plunk my butt opposite him. He frowns at the soda so I tip it forward.

"Go on, preach about clean living to me, Liam. I just dare you."

He pours water into his glass and takes a sip. "I don't preach."

"No? You looked preachy to me."

"Kow's the preacher. The whiner too."

I don't bother to hide my smirk. "Yeah, he is. 'Gotta live life to the fullest, sis.'" I mimic my brother's baritone voice. "God, I'm glad I don't have to share a bathroom with him anymore. If I never have to hear him puking again, I'll die a happy woman."

His jaw works. "It sucked when you left for Vancouver. I missed you."

That has me blinking.

What's with him tonight?

"*You* missed *me*?"

"That so hard to believe?"

Short answer, yes.

Long answer, yes.

I pick at the sticker on the perspiring bottle in my hand. "I guess that's nice."

"Nice?" He squints at me. "*Nice?*"

"Oh, Liam," I mock, my voice high and breathy, "I'm so grateful that you missed me. What a compliment coming from *the* Liam Donnghal."

"Don't," he grumbles, tossing the napkin at me.

It's my turn to smirk. "With an arm like that, it's a wonder you were scouted at all, never mind drafted."

He rolls his eyes as he takes another sip. "It's good to see you, Gracie."

"Good to see you too. Didn't realize you were in New York. You never messaged. The Mounties have you down here for publicity or something?"

He shakes his head. "Got traded."

Well, that's news to me.

Brows high, I ask, "Does Kow know?"

"Everyone does now. You're losing your touch if you weren't clued in."

My lips purse. "When was it announced?"

"Today. You clearly didn't check the family group chat," he mumbles.

Ha. I haven't checked that in a week. I don't seek out stress—do I look insane? "Where?"

"The Stars."

I gape at him. "*The Stars?*"

"Yeah, the Stars," he growls, his fingers fussing with the bottle in front of him.

"Wait, what?" I mutter, rubbing my forehead. "Did you not just win the Stanley Cup? Or am I dreaming? I must be. What the fuck are *you* doing playing for the Stars?"

They were bottom-of-the-division losers for a reason.

"It doesn't matter."

"Um, yeah, it does. I'm so confused and you know I hate being confused."

"That's because you're too clever for your own good," he grouses, his gaze flickering around the bar rather than at me.

Shaking my head, I ask, "So, did you fall or were you pushed?"

"Pushed."

"By?"

"The new owners of the Stars."

"Who are they?" My mind races as I try to assimilate what the hell's going on. A snippet from a PSN clip on Tiktok comes to mind. "Acuig Corp? Didn't I read that that fancy real estate firm was diversifying into sports teams or something?"

"Yeah. But that was midseason last year. Their overhaul is all the news has to talk about right now."

"You might be into stocks and shares with your fancy investment portfolio, but I have enough to do without reading that section of the paper when school's out for the summer and I'm working sixty-hour weeks."

But this is... *huge.*

It's like Tom Terrific playing for the Buffalo Bills in the '71 season when they went 1-13.

It just doesn't compute.

Taking a deep sip of my cream soda, I muse, "I think you need to start at the beginning."

CHAPTER 5
LIAM

35

Come A Little Closer - Cage The Elephant

YOU KNOW that one person in your life who'll tell you the truth, no matter what? Who'll call you an asshole while everyone else blows smoke up there?

That uncomfortable person who you love but who you don't open up to because if you do, it'll sting?

That's Gracie Bukowski for me.

Just sitting with her in this shithole of a bar is already making me feel a thousand times better, too.

Once upon a time, we'd been close friends.

Sometimes, I wonder what would have happened if Kow hadn't almost died that day twelve years ago.

If he hadn't fallen through the ice in the Bukowskis' backyard pond, my allegiance wouldn't have shifted.

Everything would have been different.

That was our beginning.

But I know she isn't talking about when I dumped her for her brother, switching friendships like I'd switched underwear.

God, I'd been an asshole.

"Do you want some wings?" I ask, desperately trying to shift my thoughts away from shitty memories of a time when I had nothing to be proud of and everything to be ashamed of.

Confusion's cute on her as she states, "They have saturated fat in them."

I shrug.

"A million calories."

Over my glass of water, I pin her with a look as I take a sip.

"And I hate to besmirch Chuck's rep, but I doubt the chickens are free-range or organic."

That has me wincing.

She chuckles. "I know you too well. Don't think you can distract me with promises of food. Especially when you wouldn't be the one clearing the plate."

I grimace.

Kow had made her weight a running joke at one point during our teens, but she'd always told him to shove it. The last thing I wanted was for her to think that I was calling her out—

"Come on, we can go back to your place. I'll cook."

I gape at her. "Jesus, do I look suicidal?"

She kicks me under the table. "Don't even joke about that."

"I won't, I won't." Mostly because both of us know how close it's come these past couple years. "Sorry. That was in poor taste."

"It was, but don't be sorry. Just shut the fuck up about being suicidal. And screw you," she says lightly. "I can cook. It's been years since I burned those noodles. Despite all those hits to the head, you guys never freakin' forget, do you?"

"Memories of elephants when it comes to fuckups."

She hums, but I can see the concern in her eyes. I'm getting tired of seeing that, of facing people's worry over my state of mind, but with Gracie, it doesn't feel like a burden.

She never makes me feel that way.

"I heard from Kow and Mom that you've been pulling away...," she mutters, bringing me back to the subject at hand. "They never said anything about *this*, though. I mean, fuck, the Stars? You're a Hall of Famer—" Her mouth gapes wider. "Wait a minute, you've had a no-trade clause for years! Why would you agree to go to the Stars? What was your agent thinking in letting you accept the trade?!"

He was thinking that the payoff was phenomenal because, even with the salary cap, the money was great and the sponsors based in New York that he had lining up for me meant a couple more million in the 'just in case I'm kidnapped again' fund.

He was thinking that I'd likely be captain again.

He was thinking I could be pivotal in bringing the 'new look' Stars to the Stanley Cup.

As for myself, I was thinking that *Gracie* was in New York.

She, without knowing it, without anyone else knowing it either, is the real reason I'd signed on the dotted line.

"You probably need to fire Andrews." My agent. "Immediately."

I shake my head. "He's earned his commission."

"Liam, how has he? This is a terrible deal! It's like you've started playing for Russia in the Olympics. You and the Stars? It doesn't make sense."

I stare at her, wanting to open up, wanting to share, but it's hard. Really hard. Impossible, even.

When I'm in therapy, the same thing happens—it's like my tongue freezes.

Hell, it's as if *I* freeze.

Mike, my therapist, says it, and a whole host of other shit, is a form of PTSD. PTSD or not, I'm hoping Gracie will defrost me.

She achieved it by sitting on my face, so why wouldn't she come through this time with a dose of common sense and real talk? Okay, the stakes are different, but she doesn't remember when she sat on my face, does she?

Fuck. My. Life.

"You want ice cream?" I ask her, needing to change the subject.

Gracie frowns. "The day just gets weirder and weirder. Sure, I'll take ice cream. We can stop at a store because there's no way you have any in your freezer."

I nod as I get to my feet.

Tugging on my cap, I drag the visor farther down to cover my face.

If Gracie worked in a regular sports bar, I'd be fucked. Instead, this place appears to value baseball and chicken wings above all else so I should be okay.

When she approaches the counter, Gracie snatches a lightweight hoodie that someone from behind the bar tosses to her, then we walk outside.

I let her go first.

Not because I'm a gentleman, which I kind of am, but mostly because Gracie looks good going.

Coming too.

Kow would break my jaw for thinking it, but I've got eyes.

So do Chuck's patrons.

Fuck if it doesn't grind my gears to watch *them* watch *her* leave. They wave at her as she weaves through the tables, patting some on the shoulder and jeering at others, talking smack about their team in a way that's purely Gracie because I don't know anyone with as much random sports trivia in their head as her.

That's what happens when you grow up in a household with three brothers and a variety of billet kids over the years, I guess.

When a guy taps her on the ass, before I can do dick—hell, I don't even have time to get angry—she grabs his hand with a smile and shoves it behind his back, giving me zero opportunity to wade into the fray and smash the fucker's face in. Shame.

"Now, Jason, what did we say about getting handsy with the servers?" To the woman behind the bar, she yells, "Mia, cut Jason off, would you?"

Mia shakes her head and tuts. "Jason, this is getting to be a regular thing. You know what that means, don't you?"

Jason pouts. "It was only a little tap."

Gracie wags her finger in his face. "Is one little tap on my ass worth being beaten with that Jung-ho Kang signed baseball bat Chuck just bought?"

His eyes widen to a comical degree. He clearly knows that she can put her money where her mouth is as he sputters, "N-No."

"Good answer." She claps him on the shoulder, hard enough for him to cough and almost face-plant into the table. "Right, I'll see you guys tomorrow. Don't get into trouble unless I'm here. Twinkle Toes behind the bar can't bat for shit."

"Fuck you, Gracie!"

She winks. "You know you love me, Mia."

Mia boos and hisses, but Gracie just smirks at her as she sashays out the door.

"You handled that well," I say once we're standing on the sidewalk, my tone uneasy. "You have to deal with that on the regular?"

It's an unseasonably chilly night for mid-June, but it means that she loops her arm through mine as she huddles into me for heat.

I don't want to think about why that feels so fucking good.

"Sometimes, but Chuck isn't afraid to toss out patrons so it's mostly okay. Jason's different. He's… loopy." Her nose crinkles. "He used to play college ball and was on his way to the NFL, but he took too many hits to the head. His boundaries are still back in 1999 when you could do shit like that without it being called sexual assault."

That's a lot of information to process. "It's not your job to police him."

She shrugs. "He never takes it too far."

"*Yet,*" I point out.

"What are we supposed to do? The boys in blue do dick if a woman gets hit, never mind tapped on the ass in a bar, Liam."

If that was supposed to make me feel better, she failed.

"Anyway, he's a good guy, just stuck in a different era. It's sad, really. The game fucked him up." Gracie drags her hood over her head, whacking me in the arm when I try to tug it down at the back. "I worry about you idiots turning into him, to be honest. One too many pucks to the face and you'll have cognitive issues as well."

I snort. "Kow says it was worth it to get new teeth."

She shakes her head. "He would. I'm surprised he bothered."

"He's too vain not to."

When she laughs, I dislodge my arm from hers and curve it over her shoulder, tugging her deeper into my side.

God, that feels good.

"You guys are always so warm. I need that superpower," she grouses.

Another woman would be giggling and flirting as she said that, but not Gracie.

Charlotte, that so-called friend of hers, told Gracie her only worth was her brothers, that she was destined to be surrounded by hot hockey players who'd want to screw puck bunnies but never her.

I heard all about it secondhand from a snickering Kow whose nose I proceeded to break.

I don't know why Gracie listened to that bitch, I just know that she did.

That was the year she stopped following Kow and me from city to city after she turned us green.

That was the year I started to miss her. Our talks. Her smack. That damn tuque she practically lived in. The way she braided her hair as she recapped a game with us.

Sometimes, the moves she lauded were better than what our coach at the time developed. What she knew about the sport was unreal back then, and her capacity for strategy was seriously impressive.

That was the first phase of her fading from my life. Moving to New York had pretty much been the final period. I'm hoping this is my shot in OT.

I don't say any of that. I just tell her, "You can thank oatmeal for why we're always warm. Central heating for the bones."

"I hate that shit. Don't even talk to me about overnight oats. Mom's trying to get me onto those and I told her that anything that can soak overnight, be mush, and still go viral on social media is the work of the devil."

My lips quirk into a grin and a slither of something I haven't felt in a long while rushes through me—happiness.

"Thanks, Gracie."

"For what? Hating oatmeal?" She drags me to a halt. "There's a Duane Reade on that corner. We can pick up some Ben & Jerry's. Swedish Fish too. It's been a day."

Grimacing, I say, "Sorry. You don't need my crap on top of it."

"Don't be a doofus."

"I'm not. I can't just wade into your life and expect you to drop everything—"

"If you'd expected me to drop everything, I wouldn't have dropped dick. You came in to talk, we got to talking, and now we need to talk because I can tell something's going on with you if you can downgrade to the Stars." Her scorn is impressive. "Kow's got about as much sensitivity as a drunken donkey, as do the rest of the boys, so you need to chat with someone who actually has sense." She pats my abs in what I assume is supposed to be a comforting gesture, then she pauses. "Man, you've been working out."

Automatically, I tense the muscles in my abdomen.

Automatically, she pulls back and punches me in the gut.

She waggles her fingers, teasing, "Man of Steel."

"You Bukowskis fucking suck," I complain, even as I guide her across the street.

"You knew it was going to happen."

"Yeah, because I've been around you heathens for too long."

Still, it's good to be back with at least one of the 'heathens' again. Kow moved home to Winnipeg last year after a stint in Denver, and Trent got traded and will play for San Jose this upcoming season. As for Noah, he's in Dallas, Cole's in Newark, and Matt's heading to Boston. Gray's still in Tucson.

We're spread out, far-flung, and though we're technically living our best lives, at the top of our game, I've missed them.

At my lowest point, through no fault of their own, my adoptive family has been far away. They've tried to reach out, but Christ, there've been times I've felt unreachable.

If I can thank the collusion of my agent and father for one thing, it's for getting me traded to the same place where Gracie is.

Not that Padraig has admitted to being a part of this, but he can deny it as many times as he wants—his sticky fingers are all over this deal.

He's got connections now.

"Did you keep ahold of that tuque you used to wear?" It's a random question. Not even I'm sure why I asked it.

She pauses in the doorway to the convenience store. "Which tuque?"

So, some things *do* change.

"Never mind," I dismiss.

When we walk into the convenience store, I grab the Phish Food container before she does because I know that's one of her favorites, then I realize she got a basket, so I dump in another carton of Butter Pecan, as well as Swedish Fish, some of those crazy hot Takis because I know she loves them, and then a bunch of other snacks she likes.

"You getting anything for yourself?" she asks, peering at me though she knows the answer.

"Nah. I'm good."

She rolls her eyes as we stroll over to the cashier. While the guy checks out our stuff, he keeps glancing at me in that way I've come to recognize. Gracie elbows me in the side, telling me she knows I've been spotted too.

Neither of us says anything, but as he scans our purchases, I know he's going to.

"You were on the news yesterday, weren't you?" he blurts out.

"No," I answer. Today, sure. Not yesterday. It's Gracie who surprises me, though.

"Yeah." Her cheeks turn pink. "Just a small segment."

Bewildered, I demand, "What happened?!"

Sighing, she shoots me a look before starting to tuck her stuff into a reusable grocery bag she liberates from one of her pockets. "This asshole grabbed a kid off the sidewalk and threw him into the street for shits and giggles. This city, man, it's becoming a gong show."

"A gong what?" the cashier mutters.

"What did you do?!"

"Managed to snatch him before the boy could get hurt."

"And beat the shit outta the guy. Don't forget that part." The cashier makes a few 'pow-pow' noises as he copies what I assume were Gracie's moves in the altercation. "You got him real good, lady."

She waves a hand. "I have a lot of brothers. Practice makes perfect."

The guy chuckles. "I noticed on the TV that you were tiny, but seeing you in real life, that douche is gonna get his ass kicked for being beat on by a little girl."

That has Gracie's embarrassment turning into annoyance. "I'm not a little girl."

Before the cashier can get a taste of her knuckle sandwich, I quickly pay him and tug her out of the store. With one hand on the bag, the other I use to dig inside for a glucose hit.

Tossing her the pack of Swedish Fish, I mutter, "Here, start eating!"

It's always wise to appease the beast.

She harrumphs but does as I asked. "Want one?"

It's on the tip of my tongue to say no, but I waggle my fingers at her instead. She tosses a couple onto my palm, obviously too annoyed to comment on me eating junk food, and starts chomping on the candy like she's eating rocks.

"So, you're a hero then?"

She squints at me. "I just did what anyone would do."

I hide a smile to dispel my panic. "I mean, save the kid, yeah. Get into a fight with a lunatic, no."

God, that could have gone wrong in so many different ways.

"Asshole deserved it." Her harrumph is louder this time. "I couldn't believe my eyes. He thought it was funny. The kid was screaming and a truck was incoming and..." A gust of breath escapes her. "It was a nightmare."

"You were brave—"

"I did what anyone should have done."

That has me curving an arm around her shoulder again. "Yeah, but no one did, did they? Just you." I press a kiss to her forehead. "You shouldn't have gotten into a fight. You could have been hurt."

She chuckles. "That guy had a fist made of glass. Talked the big talk but had nothing behind it."

The idea of her punching above her weight makes the Swedish Fish in my gut start swimming.

"I know we said we'd head to yours," she asks, voice kind as she changes the subject. "But this is my place. Want to hang out here?"

I study the street, the area, the building itself and pull a face.

If Kow and the rest of her brothers knew where she was living, they'd hit the roof.

"Yeah, let's. There's barely any furniture at my apartment," is all I say. "I have to set it up this week. That was supposed to be on today's to-do list." My nose crinkles because I got dick done.

As she unlocks her door, she offers, "I can help if you want."

"I mean, I'd appreciate it, but I don't want you to think that's why I came to the bar."

"Oh, it's not as much of an offer as you think," she teases. "You haven't seen my place yet. It's a dive."

"Do your brothers know?"

"Know what? That I have shitty taste? I think they figured it out when I wallpapered Benji Madden everywhere."

I grin at the memory. "Remember when you snuck into Noah's room and covered up all his titty models with Justin Bieber's face?"

Cackling, she nods. "Good times."

Her amusement fades like a lightbulb just went out. Switched on and immediately switched off.

"You okay?" I ask her as we start to walk up the rickety stairs to her apartment.

"Yeah, I'm fine," is her breezy retort.

Why don't I believe her?

When we reach her door, she opens it and walks in after she toes off her shoes. Knowing that's her mom's house rule, I obey the silent prompt and take the opportunity to look around.

While she was exaggerating about having bad taste, that she runs so much toward neutrals comes as a shock seeing as Gracie is the opposite of neutral.

Her apartment is a two-room space with a tiny bath. My fancy mud room is bigger than her kitchen/dining area/living room combo and her bedroom barely fits a double bed.

"Compact and bijou," she jokes, sensing then disregarding my disapproval, while she walks over to the freezer and shoves in the cartons of ice cream. "I made pierogi yesterday. Want some?"

"Your mom's recipe?"

"Of course."

"Polish potstickers?" I ask hopefully.

"Yeah, yeah. We can have some."

"Cheese?"

"Stop with the puppy-dog eyes," she grumbles. "They're cheese."

Beaming, I rub my hands together. "The best." Watching as she draws out a pan from the stove, I grimace. "You've been working all day. I should—"

"Yeah, you should." She wafts a hand. "Get cooking." Then, she wriggles her shoulders. "Give me five. I'll get showered and changed."

She's already walking out the door or she'd probably have noticed my reaction to those words.

A stupid reaction.

Out of place, unnecessary, making me no better than that jerk from the bar Jason.

'Showered and changed.'

I lived with her for three years. She's showered and changed plenty under her parents' roof, never mind mine and Kow's place in Montréal.

This is no different.

"So why is it different?" I ask myself as I dig around in her refrigerator and find the dumplings in question.

Hanna made sure all her boys could cook. It's probably why each of us handles our own food even though we started making enough our first year of playing to hire private chefs.

Despite her ability to burn water, some recipes were purely for the only girl of the family, with pierogi being one such mythical food item.

I'm not about to look a gift horse in the mouth.

Drawing the large Tupperware dish from the refrigerator, I pop the lid and groan with delight when I find thirty tiny carb bombs that are worth the destruction of a day's macros.

Mouth already watering, I stick the pan on the stove, drop in some butter, let it get nice and hot, then I position the dumplings in the fat so I can get as many in as possible in one go.

Over the sizzle, I hear the water come on in the bathroom next door.

It's more difficult than it should be to shift focus away from what's happening in there.

"Stop making this weird," I mutter to myself, giving the pierogi more attention than they need, seeing as you have to leave them to crisp up on the bottom and that's pretty much it.

After I've flipped them over, that's when Gracie walks into the kitchen.

Except, it's not the Gracie I'm used to seeing.

The kid who lived in hoodies and jeans... even at home. Even at *night*. I didn't see her in PJs because she'd switch out a day hoodie for a night one and would throw on some jean shorts.

Gracie, the adult, is wearing a bathrobe, with her hair tucked into one of those towel turban things. Her face is pink and clean. Her scent is gardenias—I know because I always buy them for her mom on her birthday since Gracie told me they are her favorite.

They aren't.

They're Gracie's favorite, not Hanna's.

Gracie had pranked me and I just always kept it up.

As I try not to stare, I'm still left dealing with the aftermath of my dick reacting to the only stimuli it's been interested in for the last couple years.

Quickly glancing away from places my eyes have no right landing yet, I tell her, "I hope you don't want any of these."

"I made thirty," she complains.

"Yeah, and I'm a growing boy."

She scoffs, but there's a smile on her face as she drags out the bottle of milk from the refrigerator and glasses from the cupboard. If she leans into me to reach above the sink in her tiny ass kitchen, well, I know she doesn't realize how close that shoves us together.

Nor does she realize how goddamn addictive her scent is.

Or that I can see down the robe.

Fuck.

When she pours herself some milk and then wiggles the bottle at me, I nod as I dish out Poland's version of potstickers between two plates.

"It's weird they don't have milk in a bag here."

"You get used to it. All Americans are faintly weird," she advises me. "You get used to that too."

Ketchup soon finds its way onto the table because I'm an animal and she remembers and forgives me for it, and both of us take a seat so we can dig in.

At the first bite, I groan. "Jesus, these are almost better than your mom's."

She smirks. "I have a secret ingredient she doesn't."

"Tell me more."

"Wouldn't be secret if I told you, would it?" She pours me some milk, too, then snags her glass and takes a sip. "You owe me big time for sharing these. They're a pain in the ass to make but I was feeling nostalgic yesterday."

"I'll love you forever."

"Ha! That won't sustain me."

I place my hand over my heart. "That's just rude."

"Who said I was polite?" There's a gleam in her eyes as she studies me while I chow down on Polish potstickers. "Must have known you were coming to eat them all."

"Fate has a way of working out in my favor."

"Never thought I'd be sharing my pierogi with *the* Liam Donnghal tonight," she breathes mockingly.

"Shut up."

"Don't pretend you don't love it."

"Maybe before."

She grimaces.

I point my fork at her. "No pity."

"I don't pity you. I can wish it didn't happen though."

"Fair. Did I ever thank you for coming to the hospital the day I was rescued?"

She hitches a shoulder, and maybe she doesn't know it or maybe she does, but the deep V of the bathrobe gapes at her neckline. Her words are unfortunate as she says dismissively, "We're family."

"Yeah," I say gruffly, aware that, not for the first time since I moved in with her kin, I wish we weren't. "We are."

CHAPTER 6
GRACIE

Sign Of The Times - Harry Styles

I'M NOT sure what I expected when Liam came to my place, but a night watching old movies wasn't it.

After dinner, he seemed to clamp down more than at the bar so I suggested we just hang out and I enjoyed it.

Too much.

I always got along great with him, even consider myself his 'first friend' in the family, but I was pushed aside when Kow decided he wanted Liam to be his BFF.

Not that Kow called him BFF, but, given time, I could have. And, after, I'd always been jealous and kinda hurt.

Just one more way I didn't measure up in the Bukowski household.

So, it's nice to drift into wakefulness the next morning with memories of last night putting a smile on my lips.

We watched three Groucho Marx movies and while it definitely wasn't the first time we'd seen them, we'd sure as hell laughed like it was.

Good times.

I take a deep breath and gently pry open my eyes.

That's when I realize he's behind me.

On the sofa.

My really small sofa.

His arms are around my waist.

His face is burrowed into my neck.

And all his hard bits are pressed into my soft bits.

Including his morning wood.

A long time ago, if I even dreamed of waking up like this, I'd have died and gone to heaven. Now, it's awkward. Hella awkward.

I want to melt into him.

I know I can't.

How do I escape the only place I want to be without waking him up?

For a minute, I just stare at the TV screen. The news channel is on like always and I groan at the headlines.

"God, talk about a slow news week," I mutter, more embarrassed about that than waking up with Liam's morning hard-on burrowing between my butt cheeks.

That's probably why dubious fortune is on my side.

If I'd *tried* to maneuver off the couch without disturbing him, I'd never have managed it.

But when I surge upright because I see Chuck on the big screen, he doesn't even stir behind me.

Grabbing the remote, I tap the unmute button, realizing Liam must have turned off the volume at some point during the night.

"Gracie's always been one of my best servers. Great kid. Can't help that she loves hockey over baseball, you know? But the facts that girl has in her head." Chuck whistles. *"Honestly, I always tell her she belongs on* Jeopardy."

My eyes narrow.

'Love' hockey? Ha. Hockey ruined my freakin' life.

"How long has Ms. Bukowski worked for you, Mr. Charles?"

"Oh, three years now. She's Canadian, eh," he says, laughing like he cracked an original joke. *"Call me Chuck. My bar is named after me. Anyways, she came over here for her studies.*

"I reckon the reason she's so brave is because she grew up with so many boys. She always talks about her brothers and —"

I close my eyes.

That is why this is on *TVGM's Morning Show.*

Them.

Always them.

This is why I hate hockey because everyone will always value it over me.

Case in point...

"—Liam Donnghal. *Didn't realize until last night who he was when he came in to visit. Just clicked when you guys called.*"

"*Yes, Ms. Bukowski is related to Noah, Trent, and Kow, isn't she?*"

Chuck beams at the news reporter. "*She sure is. I bet they taught her all their moves.*"

"Shall we break his heart and tell him that you taught them all yours first?"

Liam's voice is gravelly and low. Deep and rumbly. I mean, it's first thing in the morning, so that makes sense. What doesn't make sense? My reaction to it which supersedes my annoyance at the systematic destruction of my privacy that's going down on the TV set.

Agitated, I whip around and find that he's watching the TV *and* that he's covered his dick with a strategically-placed throw cushion.

That I notice the tactic, period, when I'm as furious as I am tells me something I'm not ready to think about.

"Did you plan this?"

Liam gapes at my seething retort. "No, of course not. How could I? In fact, fuck that—*why* would I?"

I close my eyes and release a hissed breath. "Yeah, you're right. Sorry. Wishful thinking."

"I'm offended," he grouses.

I rub my forehead. "This must be Chuck." Which hurts. Sold out by my boss. A boss I liked. *Great.* "Fucking asshole. Sell me out for some free publicity, why don't you, Chuck."

It's not as if I can help noticing that the storefront windows, which I complained about being overdue for a cleaning two weeks ago, sparkle like diamonds in the low morning light.

A soft buzz vibrates between us. It's followed by a couple more until Liam retrieves his phone.

He clears his throat but silences his cell. "They know."

My mouth tightens.

'They' being the whole Bukowski clan.

"It's on PSN."

"How the hell is this on PSN when it's not even sports related?"

Liam grimaces as I surge to my feet and start pacing in front of my TV. Which, in my tiny apartment, doesn't give me a whole lot of distance to goddamn cover.

"Well, you know what the networks are like when it comes to anything Bukowski," he tries to appease, but he fails. "It's no wonder it's gone national."

"Do you know how hard I worked to stay under the radar here?" I demand. "No one knows me as anything other than Gracie. They don't think hockey's in my blood. They don't see me as someone to use to get to my brothers. They just think I'm a regular person."

"Nothing regular about you, Gracie," Liam quips.

I freeze. "Is that supposed to reassure me?"

With a stretch that has his entire body moving—no, I did not notice—he yawns. "Not reassure you but it's the truth."

"Not in my family."

He squints at that. "What are you talking about?"

"Nothing."

"No, not nothing." He angles his head to the side. "Your brothers love you like crazy." He waggles the phone. "When I say crazy, I mean it. They saw you take on that kid. Not sure if they're impressed, terrified, or both."

My mouth pinches. "It wasn't about them. It was about some asshole stoned out of his mind on crack who thought it was funny to throw a toddler into the street. I just saw red."

"And that's why you're not regular, Gracie. Anyone else would scream and try to call the cops. Not you."

I don't bother to skewer him with a glower, not when Chuck introduces Mia, my so-called work wife, to the nation.

Bitch.

Before my very eyes, lies about Mia hanging out at the bar with me and my brothers when they're in town between games start falling from the cow's lips.

"I can't believe this is happening. I do something nice, something decent, and even then, it's about them," I rasp, both bewildered and unsurprised because when isn't everything about my brothers?

And no, I don't mean to seem petty, but I'm just tired of this. Of *their* fame affecting *my* life because this is just the start.

The baseball bar will turn into a hockey one overnight as fans crowd in to see if my brothers will visit their poor, unfortunate server sister.

I'll get hounded. My anonymous life here will change forever if I don't cauterize this wound before the infection can spread.

Tears of fury prick my eyes as I contemplate what Chuck has unleashed.

Hockey fans are crazy for my brothers. *CrAZy*. Then, he had to make them feral by dropping Liam's name. This won't end—

I jolt when Liam places a hand on my shoulder. "It's not about them."

Gaping at his naivety, I gesture at the TV. "I beg to differ." I release a second hissed breath. "I'm going to have to get another job."

"No—"

"Yeah, I am. Of course I am." I motion to where Chuck's standing—strategically so that you can see the bar in all its cleaned-up but still grody glory. "This is a walking ad for Chuck's. People will visit because they think you or my brothers just drop by for a beer every now and then. Throw in your recent trade and it'll be like a circus in the bar.

"I liked it there. I liked them." My mouth trembles. "How could they do that? How could they sell me out? I've been there years, Liam. *Years.*"

Before I know what hit me, I'm crying and he's hauling me into his chest.

He smells like laundry detergent and aftershave that costs more than my rent, but I slide my arms around his waist and let him hug me because damn if I don't deserve a Liam hug.

I love my brothers, I do. I love my family. I just get sick of everything being related to goddamn hockey. Of it controlling *my* life when I have no horse in that race.

"I'm sorry. I didn't mean to make this happen," he rumbles as he places his chin on my head. "The guy on TV mentioned my name. I-I didn't think when I... I just wanted to see you. It'd been too long, you know?"

I can hear his guilt but don't know how to assuage it. Right now, I'm having to replan my life because I can't *not* work.

If I ask my parents for help, Mom will tell me again that my MBA is a waste of time because all my problems would be solved if I'd just come home and work for the family printing company.

That will make me want to smash her over the head with one of the many hockey sticks that litter our basement.

I don't need a murder one charge to add to my woes.

And I won't ask my brothers.

Sure, they'd cover my costs but I'd never hear the end of it.

A hand smoothes over my still-damp-from-last-night hair, and I jerk back to the moment.

I should pull away, but the comfort feels good, nice, even if it's from Liam and he's a no-fly zone.

Still, I squeeze him harder, trying to fight how right this feels, how much his embrace helps calm me down.

"You did something good, Gracie. You don't deserve to have it used against you."

My bottom lip trembles at his validation of my feelings, and I know it's dumb to cry, but I do. I can't stop the tears from falling.

Pathetic it may be, but I'm used to being pimped out by people to get access to my family. That Mia and Chuck betrayed me on *TVGM's Morning Show*...

Clearly, they don't get what they've done.

They tried to grab five minutes of fame for themselves and the bar, but they just wrecked my life and I doubt they'll care.

Everyone wants a piece of the spotlight nowadays. Me, I want to stay in the shadows and do my own shit.

Turning my face to the side so I can see the segment that, of course, has moved onto my brothers' stats and where they're currently playing, I bite my lip as old photos flash onto the screen.

Me at games with them, cheering them on. Me hanging out with them afterward, lingering at their sides after they played at the World Junior Championships and, of course, won the gold.

A strong hand smoothes up and down my back.

I grit my teeth at how good that feels then gently dislodge myself from him, explaining, "I need to email over my resignation. Effective immediately." If that came out sounding like a growl then so be it.

No more wasting my tears on people who don't give a shit about me.

"Won't you forfeit two weeks' pay?"

"Look at you, knowing the little man's labor laws," I mock.

He squints at me. "Ouch."

"Don't make it seem like you've worked a regular job in your life."

"Hey, I—"

When he stops, I arch a brow at him. "Yeah, thought as much."

Shoving his hands into his pockets, he huffs. "You don't have to work."

"Don't start."

"I know for a fact Noah said he'd pay for your student loans."

"And what about how I lead my life makes you think I need one of my brothers to pay my way?"

He purses his lips. "Nothing."

"Exactly." I jab him in the chest. "Nothing." Swiping my hand through my hair to gather it into a bun, I grab a tie from the coffee table and fix it into place. "Do you want some breakfast?"

"Please."

I stride over to the kitchen. "Bacon? Eggs? Toast?"

Watching me retrieve my laptop from a side table, he clears his throat. "Back bacon?"

Despite the situation, I hide a smile. "What do you take me for? An American?"

He grins a little. "Then, sure. But I can make it."

"I know you will," I agree, staring at him from over the device as I take a seat at the table. I shoot him a sweet smile. "Get cooking, Liam. You owe me for the pierogi. Three pieces of bacon and one egg, sunny side up, please."

He chuckles as he walks toward the refrigerator and retrieves the fixings for breakfast.

Absently, I watch him bend over now and again, trying not to focus on the fact that he takes up a lot of freakin' space as I type out an email to Chuck.

Another person might think I'm overreacting by resigning without having another job lined up, but I made it a rule that if anyone in my life tries to use the ties to my family for their own gain *again*, I cut off the dead weight.

Immediately.

I owe it to myself to not be used.

When I hit send, even though everything is still up in the air, I feel better about it.

That's when I realize Liam is watching me. "You okay?"

"Yeah, I'm fine."

"This happens a lot, doesn't it?"

I could be facetious and point out that this is definitely the first time I ever got into an argument with some dopey kid on the street while saving a toddler from a head-on collision with a Mack truck, but instead, I just nod.

"I'm sorry."

The sincerity in his voice hits me on the raw. Hell, it does more than that—it chokes me up.

Bowing my head, I shrug. "It's life."

"Doesn't make it right."

"It's *my* life then," I snipe. "I should be used to it, but I'm not. Mom says I let it get to me too much."

A frown flashes over his face. "Hanna says that?"

I sniff my disdain. "Yeah, she does. Then she wonders why the last time I went home for Thanksgiving was two years ago." And only then because Liam had still been fragile after the kidnapping.

"We miss you. At Thanksgiving, I mean," he says uneasily. "And Christmas."

I want to believe him, but I'm not entirely sure that I do.

It's not that my family doesn't love me; I'm just not sure if I'm relevant.

I have no idea why I'm prodding this particular wound, but... "Is the best son competition still ongoing?"

His grin is wry. "Of course it is."

Slowly, I nod. "Thought as much."

"Why do you ask?"

I tap my nails on the table. "Not very inclusive, is it?"

"No." He winces. "I guess not."

"But then, they never expect me to actually do anything worth *winning*, do they?" I heave a sigh. "It doesn't matter. It stopped mattering a long time ago. Some days, it just pisses me off more than most." I point to the stove. "The bacon'll burn if you don't turn it."

He shifts focus to the food while I bring up some open positions at local places that are looking for staff.

When he serves us breakfast, I close my laptop and vow to have the situation under control by this time tomorrow.

In a sense, I'm fortunate that I'm a year into getting my MBA. I'll be able to work in my field sooner rather than later. *Plus*, it's summer break. I have time to get my feet back under me before the semester starts.

Thanks for nothing, Chuck.

Getting up, I collect the cutlery and some glasses that we'll need, then the OJ from the refrigerator.

After, I dive into my food. With my thoughts definitely elsewhere, it's all quiet in here. Liam, obviously aware he's on thin ice already, doesn't push his luck and stays silent. It might be awkward, but I've had thousand-plus breakfasts with him over the years. If anything, I appreciate the company.

When I'm almost finished, Liam rasps, "At the risk of you jumping down my throat for thinking this is about charity… I need some help."

"I'm not too proud for charity," I drawl. "Independence comes with a requirement of common sense. What help do you need?"

"PA."

"Pennsylvania?"

"No," he says with a chuckle. "A PA. An assistant."

My lips twitch. "You couldn't handle me as an assistant."

His chuckle dies and a slow grin makes an appearance, one that has me questioning all kinds of things when my body responds to it like it wasn't Liam frickin' Donnghal who just smiled at me.

Good God, he's pretty.

He's got a scar on his eyebrow from a run-in with Trent's skate when he was seventeen, and a couple more nicks and bumps from hockey, but he's the epitome of male beauty to me.

His eyes change color depending on his mood—shifting from green to gray to blue thanks to a play of the light. His jaw has these dimples on either side where my thumbs were made to slot into. His lips are wide and soft but when he gets mad, they firm up into an almost-pout.

As for his hair—seriously, I want to rake my nails through it and use it as a steering wheel.

Short and wavy, chestnut brown—everything about him is catnip to me.

"Why? Would you ride me hard?"

My nails dig into my palms.

To play dirty or not to play dirty—*that* is the question.

For a few seconds, I fight myself.

Then, I live up to the rep of having three massive hockey players for brothers and four *other* hockey stars who'd billeted with us when I was growing up.

"Hard and wet, Liam," I retort, brow arched. *If only.* Then, I mock, "It's okay if you want to rescind the offer."

He doesn't take the bait and I'm not sure why I'm disappointed. Of course, he didn't.

I'm just Kow's sister to him. He was messing around. That's it.

Simmer down, Gracie.

"I don't know anyone in the city," he admits, "and those I do know, I don't want to ask."

My brow puckers. "That's an oxymoron."

"What is?"

"How can you not know anyone but know enough people not to ask them for their input?"

He purses his lips. "My father's moved to New York."

Everything's illuminated.

Still, that has me gaping at him. "Padraig moved to the States?"

"After the kidnapping."

I cover his hand with mine. It's a reflex because Liam and his father have never gotten along great. After his mom died and the kidnapping, shit just got worse.

Biting my lip, I tell him, "If you don't mind the fact that I won't cut you any slack, I'll take the job."

"Gracie, I never imagined you'd give me any so we're all good."

A thought occurs to me. "Is that why you came to the bar last night?"

"Partly. I was going to offer you the job anyway but mostly, I just wanted to see you."

I don't want to admit, even to myself, that that makes me feel better.

"Why?" I ask softly.

"Because when you're with me, I'm reminded of what I like about the world." His hand turns so that he can clasp my fingers in his. "I've missed that. Missed you. But I'm sorry for... *everything.*"

When his thumb smoothes over my knuckles, I catch his glance with my own, and my heart falters in my chest.

It has no business stuttering, but it does.

Twice.

Dad: What you thinking?! Putting yourself in danger like that!

Gracie: I thought you'd be proud, Dad.

Gracie: I took him down.

Kow: Mowed him down more like lol

Mom: Don't encourage her.

Gracie: I'm not a vigilante.

Gracie: It's not as if I'm going to go around looking for trouble!

Gracie: It was a one-off.

Kow: That we had to hear about on the news...

Liam: Shut up, Kow. Leave her alone.

Kow: Where'd the fun be in that, Leprechaun?

Kow: Maybe it's a good thing you're going to be in New York from now on. You can keep an eye on our sis. Keep her safe. She's clearly incapable of staying out of danger.

Liam: You're one to talk.

Kow: I'm being serious. You gotta take care of her.

Trent: Still can't believe you're going to be playing for the Stars!

Noah: You were the Mounties' franchise player. They should have made sure they kept you this season.

Liam: Well, they didn't.

Dad: Stars made good offer. Liam boy smart. Think with brains not balls.

Liam: Um, thanks, Fryd lol. I try.

Mom: They'd BETTER have made you a good offer. You won the Stanley Cup last season!

Liam: I don't think now's the time to talk about this.

Liam: Gracie did a good thing.

Noah: And got exploited by her boss on live TV. Great going, Gracie.

Gracie: You're an asshole. A massive asshole.

Noah: It takes effort.

Trent: Not much.

Gracie: Thanks, Trent.

Trent: I'm not on your side. I think it was crazy of you. I saw the footage. He was double your size.

Gracie: Oh, and I should have just let that kid die?

Mom: You should have called the cops.

Gracie: Before or after the Mack truck killed that innocent little boy? People were too busy filming what was happening to get involved. That kid is alive because of me.

Gracie: Screw this. I have stuff to do. TTYL

Mom: She's always got such an attitude.

Mom: Liam, maybe you can fix her up with someone. She needs to settle down. By the time I was her age, I'd had four children.

Liam: That's not my place, Hanna.

Liam: Anyway, I doubt she'd want to date a hockey player. They're pretty much the only guys I know.

Kow: As if a hockey player would date her.

Dad: Son! That mean.

Kow: What? It's true. She's a bulldog.

Mom: I think that might be why she's still single, Fryd. Even you can't deny your golden girl has always been prickly.

Liam: I GTG. But you should know that Gracie was being Gracie and deserves to be treated better by so-called friends.

Mom: I'll call you later, Liam. I want to know where you're living.

Liam: :-) Okay, Hanna. Talk to you soon.

Liam: And you, asshole, @Kow. You should apologize to your sister.

Kow: *snorts* Like that's gonna happen.

LIAM'S JOURNAL

Gracie,

You've no idea how fucking happy I am that you agreed to become my assistant.

I'm pretty certain I'll drive you insane, but I figure you'll forgive me like you always do.

You're a blessing in my life—I don't think you know that and you should.

Maybe I can prove that to you over the next couple months. Maybe I can show you how you make me feel because, fuck knows, telling you is impossible.

Why is it hard to be open with you? You're so fucking blunt and easy as hell to talk to, but when it comes to this shit, I just can't get the words out.

I know for a fact you don't remember what happened at Amelia's wedding. I'm not sure if I'm sad about that or annoyed.

Still, the deadline hasn't hit yet. There's no need to push things, and if I have my way, we won't need to wait until we're 35.

Liam

2ND PERIOD

CHAPTER 7
LIAM

35

She Moves In Her Own Way - The Kooks

MUCH AS I expected when I made the offer, Gracie *does* rattle some cages once she's instated as my PA.

I don't know if it's the Pole in her, the fact that she's been raised with more testosterone than can be healthy for an impressionable girl, or that she had to deal with Kow for eighteen years solid—regardless, she gets shit done.

My bare apartment suddenly has furniture in it—within the week.

She gets me a bed and a TV, some sofas and armchairs, as well as a dining table and stools within a day of starting to work with me so I can leave my hotel room and set myself up in my new home.

By Sunday, she's put rugs down, has flowers in vases, and there's a housekeeper who comes in four times a week with the proviso that she'll bring food and will prepare something to eat on the days she works.

Gracie's to-do lists—always legendary—take up notepads.

Plural.

Just to get my apartment to her satisfaction.

Within two weeks, it's painted in the rooms that we discussed I wanted some color, there's carpet everywhere, the living spaces have drapes, the cinema is good to go, and I've got my man cave set up too. I even have an office arranged how I like it—all without an interior decorator muscling into my home with her opinions.

More than that, *she* is everywhere.

In my apartment, my car, my rooms, my gym, my kitchen.

To me, she's the white noise a city slicker needs to get to sleep after he heads to the country—I haven't felt this relaxed in months despite the fact she's about as restful as an overdose of Adderall...

"Ready for tomorrow?"

As I spin my office chair a full 180 degrees to face the woman who's unaware she just killed my buzz with talk of hockey, I mutter, "As I'll ever be. I'm not looking forward to being Captain again."

When she leans against the doorjamb, folding her arms across her chest, what she does to her tits is criminal.

Ostie, qu'elle est belle.

Those pouty lips—

"Why not? You coped with the Mounties."

"I didn't. Remember Poirier?"

"Yup. The goalie."

"He managed things behind the scenes. I just wore the patch."

She straightens. "Seriously?"

I scoff. "You really think I was in my right mind to deal with a bunch of egos when I could barely sleep two hours a night?"

"True." Concern creeps into her expression. "How are you gonna cope here, then?"

"Million dollar question... probably gonna be a dumpster fire."

Her lips purse. "You never did tell me why you came to the Stars."

"I'm still not sure if you'll believe me," I mumble, tone sullen, "and if you *do* believe me, then you'll give me shit over it."

I don't ask for trouble. Not where Gracie's concerned anyway.

She's quiet for a moment, then she moves closer to my chair and snags a hold of it to keep me in place.

I've had PAs in the past—they either simper or swoon or are afraid of my temper.

Gracie's none of those things.

I'm not sure why I haven't hired her before. My life has never been this organized, and it's nice not having to tiptoe around her.

Not one of my previous PAs would have dared stop my chair.

Yesterday, she told me I stank after my workout and she made me get into the shower before she agreed to eat breakfast with me. Last week, she canceled a blind date Noah had set me up on before I had the chance to because there was no time for 'me to get boned' when we had so much to do prior to my first practice with the Stars.

Gracie's balls, I swear, are bigger than her brothers' combined, and fuck if it isn't a breath of fresh air.

A twister of it, in fact.

I need that in my life.

"Why are you playing with the number 35 when you've always been 14 before?"

"What is this? Twenty questions?"

"Just lubing you up for this conversation," is her pleasant retort.

Pleasant?

Walk carefully, Liam, the path ahead is treacherous.

And sexy.

Rubbing my thumb along my bottom lip to hide my smile, I murmur, "14's been retired with the Stars."

"How can it be retired when they didn't exist until recently?" she scoffs. "That's moronic that they wouldn't let you play under your number."

"I'm fine with it." Put in the request myself.

Her eyes narrow with suspicion. "You're being weird."

"I am weird. Perks of being a pro athlete," I inform her, knowing that will annoy her.

"Don't get Mr. Bighead Bigshot with me," she immediately snarks, huffing like Puff, the Magic Dragon.

"You're the one who just said the Stars should unretire a number for me!"

"Yeah, well, I'm allowed to say that. You're not."

I snort. "Your logic... I swear."

"It makes sense."

"If you say so."

She taps my sneaker with her Converse. "Anyway, spill."

I squint at her—not to be difficult but to try to remember what she's talking about.

Then it hits me.

The *why* of my relocation to New York when I'd helped win the Stanley Cup for Montréal six out of the ten seasons I'd been playing for them.

"It's not important," I dismiss.

"Sure it is. I have to confer with that crazy bitch you introduced to me yesterday—"

My lips twitch.

Kara Kingsley *is* a little crazy, damn good at her job, though—she's my new publicist.

"—and if you expect me to keep you ahead of the gossip, then I need to know what the potential for gossip *is*."

"Why didn't you go into PR?"

"Does that matter?"

"I'm interested."

"No, you're procrastinating."

I study her. "Those new jeans?"

"Yes. You pay better than Chuck's," she drawls, slamming her hands on her hips.

Sure, I'm trying to stay off-topic, but those jeans look too good on her. Hell, all of her is looking too good right now. The jeans are black, high-waisted, and she's wearing a kind of navy-blue sweater that is doing phenomenal things to the tits I can't stop wanting to drool over. Her Converse sneakers—All-Star Lifts—match the sweater. It's not PA attire, but I find I don't care.

I prefer her to be comfortable.

If she's comfortable, she won't leave me.

"Concentrate, Liam. Jeez."

I grin at her when she pinches the bridge of her nose. "This drama queen thing you've got going down is new."

"You bring out the best in me," she retorts. "Okay, it has to be bad if you're avoiding answering as much as you are." She plunks her ass on the edge of my glass desk. "Hit me with it. I'm not moving from this spot until you tell me what's going on."

"I could move instead," I point out.

Right between those legs of yours, Gracie.

"Yeah, but you won't," she grouses.

She thinks of you like a brother, Liam. Stop being a fucking pervert.

"You've been wanting to talk about this since you first walked into Chuck's." As always, she's unaware of the direction of my thoughts. "Now's your time before you have to report for training camp tomorrow."

I hate that she's not wrong. I also hate that I'm no longer thinking about what's between her legs and we're onto this shitty topic of conversation.

"Padraig isn't who we thought he was."

I have no idea why that's the first thing I think of to say, but think of it I do.

"Who is he? I'm not sure I thought much about him other than the fact that he was a crappy dad."

"You got that right," I mumble.

She nudges my leg with her toe. "Stay on track."

"He's the son of a mobster. The brother and the uncle of one, well, several, too." I'm not surprised when she starts to chuckle. "I wish I were lying, Gracie."

Her laughter fades, but she sits up straighter. "Is he the reason you were kidnapped?"

"No."

"You sure?" she demands.

"Yeah. That was just for money. The usual." My jaw works. *The usual.* Like it's normal to be kidnapped.

"You promise?"

"I've no reason to lie. It wasn't mob-related. But he *is* why I got traded."

"The mafia owns the New York Stars?" she sputters. "Wait, that's not possible—"

I shrug. "Padraig's an O'Donnelly. Of The Five Points' Mob O'Donnellys."

Though her eyes widen, she shakes her head. "No, he's a Donnghal."

"He bastardized the name. Anyway, he was a better uncle than he was a dad because he pulled some 'favors' recently and their front,

Acuig, bought the Stars because he wanted me to move nearer to him.

"He said that being alone in Montréal wasn't, 'What I needed to heal,'" I mock, though my agent had been the one to say the words, not Paddy.

My father's smart enough to know that I don't respond well to requests from him.

Of course, I would never have gone ahead with any of this if she didn't live here.

I'd been happy to wait for her, content to let her lead her life, to watch her attain her goals and fulfill her dreams while I bided my time in Québec.

The parameters have shifted now that we're in the same city.

I'll still be patient, but I'll make my move the second I can.

She blinks then her grin slowly forms again. "You're joking, aren't you? Good one, Liam. You almost had me with that prank."

Rocking back in my chair, I heave an impatient sigh. "Why do you think I've put off telling you this, Gracie? I knew you'd think I was either crazy or joking. I wish I were but I'm neither. I found all this out when the contract was dropped in front of me."

Her expression turns serious. "This is…"

"A lot? Trust me, I know."

"Do they expect you to fix matches?"

"If they do, they're in for a goddamn disappointment. My wins are fairly fucking earned. Apart from the first Stanley Cup with the Mounties," I concede. "You dosed me with some magic when you turned Kow and me green. How did you do that, anyway?"

She snorts. "Like you said—magic. But I think that win has more to do with finally convincing you to—"

"We don't talk about that!" I blurt out.

Gracie's grin is wicked. "I signed an NDA."

"Only because you suggested it and insisted upon it." As if she'd *ever* betray me.

"Yeah, so that I could talk smack about you to your face! What's the point of knowing all this crap about you if I can't bring it up? And the fact that you guys started—"

"Don't say it."

She chuckles. "I saw the barre in the gym."

"Shut up."

"No. It was *my* suggestion. It worked, too, didn't it? As well as the yin yoga and pregame hot tub soaks. Your jackass Neanderthal coach insisted I was trying to turn you all gay—" That triggers an eye roll. "—but instead, I perfected your skating and improved your healing times."

Not a single word of that was a lie.

Nor was it smug.

Just amused as hell.

She deserved to be smug, though. We'd given her shit for her suggestions until we realized how beneficial ballet, yoga, and the soaks could be.

"No one knows about the ballet."

"Like it matters. This isn't 1988, Liam," she retorts.

"I have sponsorship deals with Mega XY," I counter. "Their demographic would prefer to think I pump up with steroids than with pliés."

"That's because they're idiots. Those energy drinks are liquid sugar. And that's me saying that, the lover of cream freakin' soda."

"Capitalism pays the bills."

And I'll be retiring in a couple years.

My choice of sponsorships hasn't been as discerning as it was back in the early days of my stardom, I'll admit.

My agent loves me though—his commission is going through the roof.

"Capitalism can suck my dick," she snipes.

"You grew one?"

"It's bigger than yours."

"Didn't know you'd looked, Gracie."

She freezes at that. Then swallows. Ever so faintly, her throat bobs, and she licks her lips.

All the while, I'm left wondering what the hell I was thinking saying *that*.

All the while, I'm waiting, hoping, fucking dying to know if she'll glance at my cock.

She doesn't.

Just stares at me in bewilderment.

Inwardly sighing, I tug on a strand of her hair. "This is different."

She blinks.

"The tips—weren't they red?"

"They were," she croaks.

They're definitely not anymore.

"Navy..." I smirk at her. Then, a thought hits. "The Mounties play in red."

She sniffs.

Ha!

I fucking knew it.

"You represented my team, huh?"

Her scowl tells me I'm playing with fire. "I can be supportive from afar."

Afar?

I'd prefer her to support me, oh, from nine inches away with six inches of that tucked inside her.

"You look good in my colors," I rasp.

She swallows.

"How come you didn't represent your brothers?" I inquire, trying to sound innocent.

"Because I like you and I don't like them," she grumbles with a sniff, flicking my hand away.

Am I surprised when she walks out of the room?

No.

Still, when she goes, it's not her back I'm studying.

Just her ass.

That's probably why I don't catch her peeping a look at me.

Maybe if I had, shit would be different...

CHAPTER 8
GRACIE

A MONTH LATER

Light Me Up - Ingrid Michaelson

WHEN I CAN'T GET a hold of him, I try not to freak out.

In my defense, as normal as working for him has been despite his status as an NHL demigod, cue eye roll, staying at his apartment last night has amped up my concern.

I mean, logically, I knew the nightmares were happening. Mom has mentioned it and his PTSD a few times over the past year, and I know he's still seeing that shrink I found him.

But knowing and *hearing* them are two different matters entirely.

So, when he goes AWOL, my heart definitely can't handle it.

I pull some homeland security stalker moves I perfected when I was shadowing them during their first NHL season, because Kow has some magic juju powers that always puts him in danger, and learn that my negotiating skills haven't lessened any from lack of practice.

I find him in West Orange, New Jersey, of all places.

When my taxi stops outside the rink, a flurry of bikes pass by. Impatiently, I wait for them to fuck off before I can get out.

Through the flapping of Satan's Sinners' MC leather jackets, I see Hudson, Liam's driver, waiting in the parking lot. He raises a hand in greeting, and I nod at him in thanks—he's how I found my asshole boss.

An asshole only because I now owe Hudson three dozen pierogi in payment for the intel.

Then again, pierogi as blackmail fodder is cheap in the grand scheme of things. Especially when I know getting an in with Liam's driver is smart if he's going to pull stunts like this in the future.

When the dozen or so bikers finally get out of my way, I pay the fare and jump onto the sidewalk. It's a warm day, but knowing this was where I was heading, I dressed up for the occasion, hence my matching mittens and tuque with 'Make Emo Great Again' embroidered on them.

Just *thinking* of the slogan makes me smirk to myself.

It's a public rink we're at but it's dead. Liam must have handled this on his own because I never arranged for some private ice time, and when his bodyguards let me in, I threaten the one I know is the leader:

"You should have told me where he was when I rang you."

The jerk just shrugs. "You're not my boss, Ms. Bukowski."

I sneer at him but swipe past, aware that Liam must have given them the order to let me through *if* I found him.

When I make it to the board, I yell, "You jerkface!"

In a spray of snow, Liam stops sprinting across the ice. Red-faced from exertion, he skates over to me. That's when I take in the 35 Esposito jersey and the backward Stars' baseball cap, his own.

Just sucker punch me right in the ovaries, why don't you, God?

"Hey," he greets.

Because I'm turned on as well as annoyed, my scowl is meaner than before. "'Hey?!' Why didn't you tell me where you were? I've been looking for you for hours."

His gaze turns inward. Distant. I don't know why but it makes my throat grow tight. "Just needed some peace."

"One minute I was in my office, dealing with a deluge of manga comics that showed up from out of nowhere—thirty, Liam, really?—and the next, you were gone."

"Thirty-five, actually, and they're for you."

Thirty-five? "What are?"

"The comics."

I blink. "For me?"

"Yes."

"Thirty-five different ones?"

He shrugs. "Gotta be some perks to working weird hours."

"Thirty-five?" I squeak.

For the first time, he seems amused. "Excessive spending is a form of therapy."

"Since when?" I scoff, but I'm still trying to get my head around him buying thirty-five monthly subscriptions for *me*. "Do we need to stage an intervention?"

"No. But we can get you some skates."

"I don't skate."

"You do."

"I don't," I retort.

"You *can*."

"Yeah, but not with you. I'll make an ass of myself."

"I'll fall over if you get on the ice."

I squint at him. "You won't fall over."

"On command." He presses his hand to his heart. "One push of your pinkie finger and I'll flop onto the ice. How's that for a deal?"

With a huff, I nod and start to make my retreat to the counter for rentals. That's when he calls out, "Where are you going?"

"To rent some skates, dingbat."

"Got some over by the bench for you."

I twist around to gape at him. "You did not." I snort. "Let me guess, *thirty-five* pairs?"

His smile is slow.

He doesn't mean for it to be sexy, but oh, dear Lord, it is.

Whipping away from him so he can't see my reaction to that smile, I call out, "How did you know my size?" *And why did you plan for me to show up without telling me where you are?*

The man is such a weirdo.

"I looked at your shoes?" he repeats back at me like it's a question.

Fuck.

I pull a face at the three-hundred-dollar pair of skates.

Why does he have to keep doing this stuff?

What, with the Cameos and the show tickets, now the comics and then this?!

You cannot kiss him, Gracie.

STOP.

Huffing and grunting and snarling under my breath like a rabid dog, I put on my skates, hating that they feel like a second skin.

As I tie up my laces, I watch him make a couple practice shots as he flies across the ice like Peter Pan.

I want to ask him if he's okay, but I already know that he's not.

His concentration is locked in a way that tells me this practice isn't about working out or the sport itself—it's about him. About escaping. About finding peace in the muscle memory of the stick in his hand as it winds up when he shoots the puck, of his blades on the ice, of the chill in the air biting at his cheeks.

I could watch him for days.

I guess it helps that it's the first time he and I have been alone at a rink in years.

I know that he'll remember I'm here soon enough, so I grab my compact from my purse and quickly check out my face—swiftly, I rearrange my features so they're blank.

My earlier desire to maul him is no longer evident in my expression, nor is the faint hurt I felt from hearing him being terrorized in his dreams.

That's when he wings across the ice, so fast it looks as if he's going to crash into the boards, but instead, he swings into a one-foot spin that has me choking on a laugh.

And the desire to attack him is back.

Every part of him.

Every.

Inch.

There were rumors back in the day that he's massive too.

Fuck.

My pussy clenches.

NO.

Do. Not. Go. There.

I smile at him as I carefully clamber onto the ice.

The smile has his brows lifting. "You like them?"

"Yeah, I do. Thank you."

He shrugs. "Figured I'd get you here sooner rather than later."

Jerkface.

Perfect, perfect, perfect jerkface.

With kissable lips.

And that baseball cap.

CUTE.

I'm so screwed.

He skates over to me like he's flying and his hands grab mine. That's as rough as he gets. The next five minutes he spends coaching me on how not to fall on my ass.

When I can finally stand up straight, I can't say that it's like riding a bike, but the motions are definitely coming back to me.

I eye him up. "You ready?"

Because he's perfect, he knows exactly what I'm talking about.

His lips twitch. "Yeah, I'm ready."

I swipe my pointer finger against his chest and like magic, he takes a dive with all the theatrics of an overenthusiastic *Glee* kid who's also a star of the hockey team.

When he stares up at me, not looking at all winded despite wearing no padding, he grins. "There, your ego's been stroked. You okay now?"

I skate over to him.

Hold out my hand.

Wish like hell I could straddle him.

Then, the asshole tugs me down so I'm on the ice too.

In a flustered array of limbs that is the least graceful fall in the history of ice skating.

"You dick!" I cuss, embarrassed and mortified and everything in between.

He smirks and drawls, "You didn't forget how to land."

I squint at him, flustered and suddenly really freakin' hot.

My hands are on either side of his shoulders, so I slide them out and plunk on him, giving him all my weight. My nose brushes his and I snarl, "That's what you take from this?"

His breath whispers over my mouth.

That's the first warning sign.

Oh, fuck.

Why was this a good idea?

Why didn't I—

My knees scramble over the ice but instead of helping me up, they work against me—one slides close to his crotch.

So close.

Fuck.

I gulp when I see his pupils have—

No, that's wrong. They're not dilating. Are they?

It's just all the light in here—it's too goddamn bright.

He smells like Juicy Fruit.

I want to taste that.

I could—

Jesus Christ.

I could kiss him now.

CHAPTER 9
LIAM

35

DOES she know how easy it would be to tip my head forward and let our mouths collide?

The thought is the opposite of helpful.

I can already feel my dick starting to respond after years of being left out in the cold.

She smells like pansies.

She feels like heaven.

God, I want her.

I want her so fucking bad.

I raise my head, angling forward so that I can—

She rolls off me, tumbling onto the ice in a flurry of movements that are the opposite of graceful.

Fuck.

Why does my front feel colder than my back now?

God, I miss her.

And she's never been so close yet so fucking far away from me either.

CHAPTER 10
GRACIE

My Favourite Faded Fantasy - Damien Rice

THE MOMENT I GET HOME, I slam the door behind me.

Four hours of torment later and I'm about to explode.

My fingers are shaking as I mess with the hundred thousand locks I need to keep NYC out as per Dad's orders.

With that done, I race through my sardine-can apartment to my bedroom and start to dig through my nightstand drawer.

"Come on, come on, come on," I mutter, retrieving the smorgasbord of vibrators I have stored in there, hoping, *praying* that one will have enough charge to get me through.

But the pink rabbit, the purple wand, and the bright green Hulk dildo with the bullet vibe are all dead.

As dead as my sex drive was before Liam came to the city.

"Fuck!" I groan, pulling out the drawer in its entirety, on the hunt for anything that will take the edge off.

When I find a small bullet vibe that's shaped like a lipstick, I hit the 'on' button and almost weep with frustration—no dice.

"Okay, low-fi it is."

My tuque and gloves go flying, as does my sweater when I strip off. My jeans, on the other hand, are clearly a part of Satan's clothing line because I end up plunking my ass on the bed with them around my knees, my panties tucked into them.

Sucking in air, I think back to the rink.

His breath on my lips.

His eyes locked on mine.

His dick brushing my knee.

Then, the memory shifts. Morphs into my favorite fantasy where Liam and I are on a lakeshore of all places and I'm on top of him and he's beneath me.

I know what that feels like now for real.

"God," I groan, feverish with need as I think of my knees burrowing into a sandy shore as I cling to his hips, digging my thighs into his sides as I grind on top of him.

He'd only take so much teasing, though. I know him too well. He'd spin us over so that I was beneath him. While I never wear dresses, I do in this fantasy for some weird reason, so he's got the easiest access ever.

In no time at all, his fingers would be plucking my panties away and they'd be sliding through my core. Gathering my juices, getting me wetter, preparing me for his dick.

Groaning, I whimper as I rub my clit, circling it with the flat of my hand how I like. It doesn't have the same punch, but just thinking about him filling me, stretching me, thrusting into me, taking me…

"Oh, fuck," I whine, curling onto my side when my orgasm hits.

In the grand scheme of things, it's a sneeze.

But fuck if I didn't need that sneeze.

Panting, I rock my hips to eke out every last bit of pleasure, then I push my forehead into the pillow as I get my breath back.

The need for him is overwhelming.

It isn't new, but it's starting to hurt.

Working with him was the worst idea in the world, but like any addict after falling off the bandwagon, the need for my fix reigns supreme.

Eyes fluttering with fatigue, I almost fall asleep.

But then I remember my current state of affairs and, drowsily, I clamber out of bed and waddle over to the toy I tossed on the floor as I simultaneously try to shuck off my jeans.

Mid-shuck, my cell buzzes in my pocket.

Liam: Hey

Liam: Today was a good day, non?

Eyes wide, I shake my head. "Ended better than you think, Liam."

I think of the thirty-five mangas in his apartment and smile to myself.

Me: It was great. Thank you

For the orgasm inspiration.

That's when I grab every single goddamn wire for each vibrator I own and I set them up and get them charging.

"Be prepared," I mumble to myself. "Girl Scouts will come in handy for something."

CHAPTER 11
GRACIE

Still Waiting - Sum 41

FOR A WOMAN who claims to hate hockey, how my eyes track Liam on the ice makes a mockery out of me.

I forgot.

That's my only defense.

I just forgot.

But after I joined Liam at the rink last week, he managed to wrangle the promise out of me that I'd come to a practice—in my defense, I'm a sucker for his puppy-dog eyes.

Now that I'm here... God, it's like coming home.

The *swoosh* of the blades, the *tuk* of the stick hitting the puck, the *thud* when it collides with the net...

I can see why Liam finds comfort in those sounds because I do too.

I've got a childhood mixed in with those noises. A lifetime of hockey games that I shoved to the side to get away from the massive egos in my family. But it's a language I speak fluently and it draws me in like a warm hug.

Cones are dropped and as the forwards on the ice transition from shooting to skating drills, Liam's father takes a seat beside me. I can't say that I didn't see him coming, more like I hoped he'd just continue on his way.

Taking my eyes off the sheer poetry in motion that is the Leprechaun on the ice, I greet, "Padraig."

"Gracie." Unlike me, he's not interested in the game. Paddy never enjoyed hockey, one of the many disconnects between father and son. "Didn't expect to see you here."

"Disappointed? The last time we met, hadn't I turned your son green?"

His grin makes a lightning-swift appearance—man, that reminds me of Liam. "Nah. I'm not disappointed. You're good for him. Always have been. Just came as a surprise. Thought you were still in Canada, to be honest."

Something about that doesn't ring true, but Coach Bradley barks, "How are you in the goddamn NHL, Kerrigan? TURN. LEFT. It's the opposite of *right*," and distracts me.

Watching the right winger's shoulders hunch mid-drill, I say, "Haven't been back in a long while. Moved here years ago. I'm working toward my MBA. School starts up again tomorrow actually."

He scratches his chin. "Thought you were close to your family?"

"You really want to hear the answer to that?" I mock, eyes tracking Liam as he clocks up some impressive speeds.

Knowing him as well as I do, that concerns me.

The better he plays, the crazier his mind is.

And last night, he had another nightmare.

"Sure. You've always mattered to Liam so that means you matter to me."

That has me frowning.

"What?" he demands.

"You weren't exactly a helicopter parent, Padraig. Let's face it, my dad did most of the heavy paternal lifting when he was a teenager."

"A man can change," he retorts, "when his son's gone through what Liam has."

"If you say so."

"I do," he states, tone firm.

"Do you know it's been years since I've been to a hockey rink?"

"Really? You were obsessed the last time we met—"

"I just stopped letting hockey be the center of my world. It's strange coming back here," I muse. "I missed it more than I realized."

His grimace says he and I aren't on the same wavelength—no shit.

"Are you sick?"

Confusion lacing the words, Padraig mutters, "No. Why would you think I am?"

I wave a hand at the rink where Bradley's put them back on shooting drills. Liam's having a real good time trying to hit Greco, the goalie, in the face with the puck. When he catches five in a row, I want to groan because he winks at Liam.

Freakin' winks.

Liam's shoulders jerk like he's been struck by a lightning bolt and I know that's game on now.

Men and their egos—sheesh.

"Seems like a big gesture to make," I mumble, watching as Liam works extra hard to score. Every time he does, his smirk gets wider and wider. "Forcing Liam here."

"Forcing?" He scoffs. "The Stars will be the best team in the NHL by the end of next season."

"You get an inside scoop?" I rasp, pinning him with a glare, the Greco and Liam byplay forgotten for the moment.

"You could say that."

"Liam was assured there'd be no funny business—"

"He told you that?"

His surprise is evident, enough that it leaves me feeling smug. "He told me that the Stars' new owners are the Irish Mob."

"Jesus Christ, Gracie! Keep your mouth shut." He looks left and right to make sure no one can hear him. "If there's even a hint of corruption, we'll—"

"What? Get the SEC in? The feds?" I snort. "Like the mafia hasn't been fixing games for decades."

Padraig scowls at me. "I don't remember you being this ballsy."

"Turning Liam and Kow green didn't give the game away?"

He flushes. "Liam told me what happened."

"That I stopped being a pick-me girl and got out from under my family's thumb?"

"A pick-you what?"

"Never mind," I say with a sigh, watching as Liam skates rings around Greco's net. The goalie seems to be whispering to his goalposts in the wind up to Liam taking his shot. "He won't stay if the games are fixed. You should know your son well enough to know that."

"There ain't no funny business in the Stars."

"If you say—"

Coach blows his whistle when two of the players start fighting but both men ignore him.

Greco drops to his knees, spreads 'em butterfly style, but no amount of sweet talk to his posts stops the puck from ricocheting off the left and settling in the back of the net.

I clap at the goal but shake my head when Liam weaves past and flips Greco the bird.

Padraig chuckles, making me grumble, "Don't encourage him. Greco started a fight with Liam two seasons ago and bad blood has been flowing between them ever since."

"What was the fight about?"

"Greco said Liam had fucked his girl." I roll my eyes when Padraig preens.

Men.

"Did he?"

"I can't say." Doubtful—he's been like a monk since the kidnapping according to Noah. "You'd have to have a conversation with your son's penis to know for sure."

When Padraig chokes on the coffee he's sipping, I don't slap him on the back. "You've learned to stop pulling your punches."

"You can survive or thrive."

"Heard you're his new PA," he rumbles as Liam starts bouncing around the ice like the Energizer Bunny.

"I am."

"You're probably why his energy is up."

"You said that before but I don't get it. I'm not going to shepherd him out of nightclubs he shouldn't be in or get him out of trouble—"

"Chance'd be a fine thing. Maybe *you* can get him out of his damn apartment for more than just work. The trouble we're talking about has nothing to do with shotgun weddings, Gracie."

"This isn't 1962."

"Might not be, but he almost lost his fucking head—" Padraig sucks in a breath. "Apologies for swearing."

"Heard worse with my brothers," I dismiss.

He adjusts his tie. "Yeah, well, the lady in my life don't like me swearing around her and I'm trying to break the habit."

"What trouble?"

"Did you sign an NDA?"

"Now you ask?" I sniff. "But yeah, I did."

Reassured, he nods. "He tell you he's been having nightmares?"

"Heard him have them. Surprised you know about them."

"After the kidnapping, I spent the summer with him."

My brows lift. "You? And Liam? I didn't know that." He never said, just that Padraig moved to New York after that summer.

Padraig hitches a shoulder. "Wasn't about to leave him alone."

So, he stepped up when it counted.

For the first time since Liam came into my life, I can feel whispers of respect begin blossoming into being for his father. He's never acted like a dad before. At least, not in my opinion, which left mine to do the aforementioned heavy lifting.

When you come from a big family, I think it's safe to say that every kid feels like they flow under their parents' radar. Too many kids, not enough time or energy to balance every plate.

In this case, me.

Especially when my brothers started playing bantam hockey.

The minute the oldest, Trent, reached that level, we began billeting kids from around Canada.

Four ultimately became eight.

Less time, less energy, more hockey, more travel to hockey games, more hockey-related bills, more, more, *more*…

Did I resent that growing up? When there was no money for piano classes but there was for skates? Yeah.

Do I still? In a sense because I don't like how hockey makes me feel forgotten and isolated.

I guess it's a sign of how much I've matured that I'm just glad Liam had Paddy as well as my family to fall back on after the kidnapping. That spiteful pick-me bitch of before would probably have been jealous.

"You're living with him?"

I'm jerked back to the conversation, but before I can answer, my cell buzzes.

CHAPTER 12
GRACIE

> Unknown: Gracie?
>
> Unknown: Please talk to me.
>
> Unknown: We didn't mean to hurt you.
>
> Unknown: If you'd let me explain, Chuck really needed the exposure.

MIA.

Oh, hell, no.

I blocked hers and Chuck's numbers the day they appeared on TVGM, so she must be using a different phone but fuck this.

BLOCK. BLOCK. BLOCK.

I've got *zero* time for users.

Speaking of users, Paddy gives me the side-eye. "Everything okay?"

"It is now."

He clears his throat. "Sure?" My glower has him lifting his hands in surrender. "Like I was saying before... You're living with him?" he asks while we watch the first string attack Greco. When he holds off a goal, only one of them bumps fists with him in celebration. "That how you know about the nightmares?"

"No."

He frowns. "Okay."

"I'm not," I grumble, annoyed by his disbelieving tone. "I just stay at his place from time to time. It's easier to sleep in his spare room than go across Midtown at 2am." Before he can comment, I huff. "What do you want, Paddy? I don't have all day to talk about this and I'm trying to watch Liam."

"Why?"

"Why not?"

"You're his PA," he points out. "Not his coach."

"You don't say."

"Aren't you supposed to be polite to me?" Paddy complains.

"Nowhere in my contract does it say that," I disagree. "I don't even have to be polite to Liam. Now, *that* is in my contract."

"You two have a strange relationship," he grouses after harrumphing. "I'd say that you're like his sister but if my kid was looking at his sister how he looks at you, I'd have a problem on my hands."

I frown at him. "He doesn't look at me any type of way."

I wish.

But Paddy knows Liam as well as I know egg white omelets—i.e., not at all.

Yolks FTW.

He snorts. "If you say so. Anyway, this is the first I've seen you here."

Squinting at him, certain he's trying to throw me off, I mutter, "Liam asked me to come. Watching him and the rest of my brothers play is an old habit. I pick up on stuff that the coaches don't."

"Like what? These are pros, Gracie."

"And I've got more family who are heading for the Hall of Fame, Padraig, than these so-called pros. I've also attended more hockey games in my time than you've had hot dinners." I arch a brow at him. "Liam's a leftie so why's he favoring his right side?"

"Huh?"

I shrug. "Just something I noticed. You should tell Bradley."

"Why's it matter?"

"Could be overcompensating for an injury. Might be nothing."

"I don't have any sway with the coach."

"That's a lie. Liam's only here and not in Montréal because of you. If you can move that mountain, you can make sure his coach uses his eyes to check in with the players."

"If he was still in Montréal, Gracie, then he'd be losing his mind up there." He turns to me, letting the soft scent of Cool Water, something that always reminds me of my Uncle Jak, drift toward me. "Still, maybe this hyperawareness will come in useful. If you could keep an eye on him, I'd appreciate it. Liam could have gotten into big trouble last year, Gracie. He bought himself a gun—"

"What?!" I shriek, gaping at him, aware that my shriek was loud enough to draw attention from the players on the ice. Ignoring them, I lean into Paddy's side and demand, "You better be kidding me."

"I'm not. Got himself a ghost gun of all things."

"A *what* gun?"

"No numbers on it, ya know? Untraceable."

I don't think it's possible for my mouth to be any wider but hey, never say never. "What the hell did he get one of those for? And where did he even buy one?!"

We're Canadian, for chrissakes!

"Illegally," is his wry answer, but I can see his worry in the pucker of his brow and the way he gnaws on his cheek.

"Where? How did he even know to get a gun?"

"An MC."

I blink. "My Liam approached an MC and bought a big gun?"

Padraig's lips twist. "*Your* Liam?"

"That's the part that stuck out to you?"

"Like a sore thumb. But yeah, he did, and into shit he found himself. Only my connections got him out of trouble. They were going to blackmail him into throwing games, Gracie."

I rub my forehead where a headache is suddenly gathering, and this is when it hits me—that 'thing' Liam hasn't been telling me? That big secret that has him freezing up every time we approach it?

It's gotta be this.

And somehow, it's so much worse than I thought it could be.

I figured he had a cash flow problem—his investment portfolio might be solid, but hey, no one's safe when a financial crisis hits. Or perhaps some weird aftereffect with his health after those bastard kidnappers cut off his ear.

I never suspected anything like this.

Turning back to stare at the guys on the ice, I find Liam skating around the rink again. His eyes are on me, though. Beneath his visor, he's chewing on his mouthguard.

I wave at him, and he nods before refocusing on what's happening around him now that I've checked in.

Bradley starts an off-the-cuff scrimmage which is downright cruel after two hours of nonstop power, shooting, and skating drills and, in the chaos of that, my mind's able to wander.

Because I'm not the most linear of thinkers, as the game gets underway, I mumble, "Kerrigan's hogging the puck rather than looking for an open teammate. It's a team sport. These assholes forget that sometimes."

Liam intercepts a pass from the dark team's right defender, shoving the other guy into the boards in the process before passing the puck to Lewis despite the fact he isn't wide open. Unlike Kerrigan, who is.

Lewis scores and he and Liam bump fists while Lewis does his crazy version of a celly.

Here's one guy who isn't ashamed of his ballet classes.

"The gun... It was to protect himself, right?"

"He didn't buy a gun to break into a bank, Gracie," Padraig retorts.

"I've noticed he's spent a fortune on personal security. Almost twice what my brothers spend."

Padraig sighs. "He's had it rough the last couple years."

"I still can't get over what happened. It's so hard to believe. Like something from a book."

His father hesitates. "I didn't have the cash for the ransom, Gracie, but I did everything I could to get him back, I swear.

"I know we're not close, but he's my boy. This isn't about making up for the past, just trying to improve things for the future.

"There's family here for him, family that he can claim or not. He was pretty much alone up in Montréal. He needs people right now. He needs to know he's safe. I figured that's why he offered you a job."

"I'm safe?"

I'm not sure if that's a compliment or an insult.

Padraig scrapes a hand over his head. "Sometimes, in life, you meet people who bring out the best in you. That's you for him."

Before I can tell him he's wrong, that Liam and I haven't hung out in years until recently, that there's no way the absentee dad can even judge *that*, Padraig pats me on the shoulder.

"I'll let Bradley know about your suggestion regarding Kerrigan."

"And that Liam's favoring his right side," I call out as he walks toward the aisle.

Then, he leaves me to my thoughts.

Which got a whole lot darker all of a sudden.

CHAPTER 13
LIAM

35

AFTER A TORTUROUS PRACTICE that saw Lars Raimond, on defense, and Kyle Lewis, a forward, coming to blows yet again and with my asshole dad sniffing around Gracie in the stands, I head to the showers and slam the water to boiling hot to ease the tension in my neck.

Once I'm done, I head into the dressing room where Greco's talking about this chick he banged on the dance floor of some club—Russu.

Man, I've told stories like that in my time, but Jesus Christ if it doesn't bore me shitless now. We're the same age as well. Isn't it time for him to grow the hell up?

Scrubbing the towel over my head, I walk to my locker and start to drag out the things I'll need to get changed.

As I pull on some boxer briefs, Raimond, living up to his asshole rep, shouts, "Is it true you can't hear no more?"

"I heard that," I growl, twisting to glower at him. "And shut the fuck up about shit like that. You don't hear me talking about your microdick, do you?"

I'm too used to the chatter to try to cover up where my ear once was and it even puts me on a go-slow to reapply my prosthesis.

Raimond turns bright red, but he grabs his crotch and sneers, "Didn't know you were interested."

"I wasn't." The lie trips easily off my tongue: "But the bunny I fucked last night was whispering sweet nothings in my ear about how I'm the biggest she's ever had and how you're the smallest."

Lewis hoots. "Sweet nothings for you, bitter nothings for Raimond. Exactly how I like it."

Raimond grits his teeth. "You need to shut your trap, Lewis."

"Or what?" His top lip curls. "Yeah, I'm condemned to abide by that goddamn NDA, but you and me are fucking done, assface."

Leaving everyone in the dark about what the NDA is covering up, he dismisses him and starts dragging on a tee shirt.

Raimond, being the moron that he is, comes after him—with Lewis's back turned.

Before any hit he pulls can collide, I grab his fist in mine and clamp down on it. There's an advantage to being six-five—big fucking hands and big fucking feet.

I squeeze on the moneymakers. "You wanna watch yourself, Raimond. Hitting a man when his back's turned?" I tsk. "Doesn't seem very sportsmanlike to me."

"What? And breaking my nose is?" He snarls as I squeeze harder before I let go. "Fuck you, Donnghal. Fuck you and your one ear."

I tug on the one that didn't get cut off by my kidnappers. "You just hurt its feelings," I mock. "You should—"

"Okay, everyone. Got some news." Bradley's declaration breaks things up before we can get started. "I know we've been keeping this under wraps for longer than usual but we wanted to be sure our picks were right."

Turning to face the guy who coached Canada to a gold medal at the Olympics two years ago, an asshole whom I've never liked, even if one of my medals at home is in part thanks to him, I give Bradley my focus.

Assistant Coach Brall starts tossing out jerseys. One plunks on my chest and I see the 'C' on it before I shove it into my cubby.

Though I knew this was coming, a part of me doesn't want it.

I've never wanted the responsibility. It's why I let Poirier take on the role of Captain in the dressing room back in Montréal. But now, I genuinely don't know if I'm equipped to handle it.

"Waiting was wise of us seeing as Lewis was in line for alternate captain, as, in fact, was Raimond," Bradley snaps, "but seeing as you two morons can't even keep it in your pants for a scrimmage and repeatedly fighting, you lost the privilege. Gagné, we'll have your jersey ready for tomorrow."

"Fucking disgrace that Raimond was anywhere close to the role of alternate captain," Lewis mutters as Bradley fades into talking about what the next couple weeks of practice will look like once the season kicks off for us tomorrow.

It's not unusual for a team to almost start up from scratch with all-new players, but *everything* is new for the Stars. Not just the roster, but the goddamn coaches and the support staff, as well as the management and the sponsors—even the uniform. Gone are the red, white, and blue of the Liberties, in with the navy and white.

Acuig came in and wiped every inch of the old away.

Only time will tell if their investment'll pay dividends, and I can't help but hope that it doesn't, even if my trophy room could use some more Stanley Cup silver.

"NDA aside, you gonna spill why Raimond's a disgrace?" I ask Lewis.

"Wish I could, man. Just know that I wouldn't hate his guts if the cunt didn't deserve it."

I can feel the makings of a grin start to form but then I study the jersey in my cubby. That 'C' patch meant so much to me once upon a time...

"You going to be able to play with him? I need to know, Kyle."

"I can try."

"Gonna need more than that, man. You know how this rolls."

His gaze drifts over to Raimond, who's literally standing in front of the mirror and preening.

"Think it talks to him like how Greco wishes his posts could answer him back?" I mock-whisper.

Lewis knocks shoulders with me. "His reflection is the only person who'll put up with him."

Gagné approaches his cubby beside mine, rubbing a towel over the back of his head. "Heard he won't fuck without a mirror there anyway."

"How do you know that, *priest*?" Lewis mocks.

"You younger fools think fucking puck bunnies is the only way to get it," Gagné intones, but there's no heat to the words. "You'll learn that there's a difference between Wagyu and Spam."

My nose crinkles. "What the fuck, man?"

Lewis gags. "What kind of pussy did you tap that was like Spam?"

"It's called an analogy." He throws his towel at Lewis. "Read a book. And I heard about his love of mirrors from Ella."

Brows lifting, I ask, "Your wife?"

He nods. "She's friends with some of the bunnies."

"That's weird."

Gagné smirks. "I like her weird."

"So, she told you Raimond needs a mirror to get it up?" Lewis inserts. "And you don't think she's messing around with him?"

"With his pencil dick?" Gagné snorts. "No."

I frown at Lewis. "Hey, you shouldn't have gone there, man. Everyone knows they've been married for a thousand years."

Tying his shoelaces, Lewis sniffs. "You can't trust women."

Gagné and I share a look before we both settle down and start getting ready to leave...

Guess we just got confirmation of *why* Lewis broke up with his long-term girlfriend.

TEXT CHAT

Liam: Fuck.

Gray: Hello to you too, Liam.

Cole: How was your day, honey bun?

Matt: Honey bun?! Jesus Christ, Cole lol.

Liam: They made me Captain.

Cole: Dude, you're the second coming of Gretzky.

Gray: Yeah. DUH.

Liam: I can't deal with this shit.

Matt: Can't you do what you did in Montréal? Get the goalie to manage the dressing room?

Liam: GRECO is the goalie, Matt. GRECO.

Matt: Ohhh, yeah. You and him never got along, did you?

Liam: He's an asshole.

Matt: So, you're stuck with the C.

Gray: Excuse me while I play my miniature violin for you.

Liam: You know I hate this shit. So, Kyle Lewis?

Cole: What about him?

Matt: The kid whose cellys are like a trip to the ballet?

Liam: Yeah, him.

Liam: Well, Raimond did something while they were both with Chicago. Something that had the team forcing the other players to sign an NDA...

Liam: They only came to blows on the fucking ice today.

Liam: I swear, I don't have the patience to baby these fuckers.

Matt: Then tell your coach you don't want the responsibility.

Liam: Don't know who else would handle it. They were going to make Raimond and Lewis alternate captains, FFS. Management clearly has no idea what they're doing.

Cole: Gagné's a decent guy. I know he got traded to the Stars.

Liam: He got the A instead of Raimond and Lewis. Coach demoted them for fighting.

Gray: Pull some of the heavy lifting on the ice and let him handle the dressing room, then?

Liam: Maybe. :-/

Liam: How's it going for you guys?

Cole: My coach has Stalin's mustache and I think he might be his love child.

Gray: My PA quit.

Matt: My shoulder's acting up again.

Liam: Cole, Stalin died decades ago and mustaches aren't hereditary.

Liam: Gray, Trent played in Tucson a couple years back. Could you hire his PA?

Liam: Matt, get your ass to the physio.

Gray: Awwwwwwwww, and you say you're not ready for the C.

Liam: Fuck off.

CHAPTER 14
LIAM

"WHAT DID HE WANT?"

It's not the politest way to greet someone, but after I jump into my ride once I've nodded at my bodyguards to make sure they're there and find Gracie in the backseat of my SUV, it's the only thing I can think to say.

Her attention doesn't deviate from the textbook she's reading on econometrics—with the start of school on the horizon, she's been lugging textbooks around and skimming them in between work. "Hudson likes emo rock."

I cut the driver a glance in the rearview mirror. Hudson is one of many perks the Stars have given me—Acuig went above and beyond to bring together an all-star team. He hides his smirk by looking away.

"Yeah, he does," I lie.

"Do you get him Cameos too?" she drawls. "Is this an employee perk that everyone receives?"

Ignoring her, I demand, "What did my dad want?"

"He said that I bring out the best in you."

My mouth rounds because whatever I thought my father would whisper in her ear during practice, it wasn't *that*. "He did?"

"He did."

I have no idea how to respond to that.

Gracie snorts. "Cat got your tongue, Donnghal?"

I grimace. "I thought he was coming onto you."

A hoot escapes her, one that's loud enough to make Hudson jump. "Your father's like seventy years older than me."

"More like forty," I correct.

"I might be into older guys, but grandads aren't for me."

"Reassuring."

She likes older guys.

Fuck.

I can make a lot of shit happen, but being born *after* she was isn't one of them.

Ridiculously disappointed, I almost miss her saying, "Anyway, he's taken."

"No, he's not," I scoff.

My father is a perennial flirt. A fuck 'em and leave 'em kind of guy. Exactly how he was with my *maman*. The asshole.

"According to him, he is." She pins me with a look. "When was the last time you talked to him?"

"A while ago." When she hums, I grimace. "What?"

"Nothing."

"Not nothing. What?"

"He said you spent the summer together after the kidnapping."

"We did. So?"

"You never mentioned him at the time…"

Because it had been hell. "Almost killed each other."

"Fun times," she mocks.

I grunt.

True, yet there's no denying he got me through those weeks when I could only practice and didn't have games to escape in.

The memory has me rubbing my temples.

"He says he's got a lady friend who doesn't like him cursing in front of her."

"A lady friend?" I sputter. "He used those words?"

"Well, he called her a lady."

"I didn't know that he knew any."

"I'm offended on your mom's behalf."

"She showed bad taste the night she met him," I dismiss, methodically cracking each of my knuckles then flexing my fingers as Hudson guides us through the crazy traffic toward my building.

"I don't think she did."

That has me frowning at her. "Don't think who did what?"

"Your mom." She rolls her eyes at my blank stare. "Don't think she had bad taste. You exist, after all."

My lips quirk into a dopey grin. "Was that a compliment?"

"I'm capable of them," she drawls, then her brow furrows. "How big of a problem is Greco going to be for you?" When I just shrug, she sighs. "Come on, Liam. How am I supposed to fix things if I don't know what's going on?"

"Nothing is going on."

"There is. *Did* you fuck around with his girlfriend?"

Deep inside, tension crawls up my spine as I grind out, "You're not my PR rep. You don't need to know that. And even if you did, you shouldn't have to ask—"

She tuts. "I didn't think you had, but I needed to check."

My nostrils flare with irritation. "I guess."

When Hudson drives over a pothole, it shoves us closer together, but she doesn't seem to notice, just carries on as if nothing happened.

"So? What's the beef with him, then?"

I, on the other hand, *do* notice our new proximity.

Does she know that she smells of lilies today?

We also have a change from regular jeans and a hoodie or sweat-shirt to an actual pantsuit.

In the semi-formalwear, I've been more aware of her than usual.

How can someone so short have such long legs? It's a crime.

Against nature.

"Liam?" A nudge to my side has me blinking at her. "Did you get hit in the head or something when I wasn't looking?"

I huff. "No."

From this position, I can see straight down her—

"What's the beef with Greco?"

"The beef could be pork for all that matters. Greco's making shit up. He somehow passes his drug tests but I swear he's on LSD or something. Trippy motherfucker."

"Not possible."

Sniffing, I retort, "Anything's possible with enough money."

"True. Did you know that cocaine only lasts two days in urine? It's why the NHL finds it so hard to clamp down on its usage. Party on a Friday but it'll be out of your system by Monday."

I arch a brow. "Is that a random fact or something you want me to know? Am I being accused of taking coke now as well as being an asshole who fucks my teammate's girl behind his back?"

Though her eyes widen, she angles her head to the side in a way that, I swear, would make her a perfect grade school teacher. "I think you need to check yourself, Liam," she says calmly. So calmly that it makes my right eye twitch. "What about my questions felt like an attack?"

"You mean this wasn't a character assassination?"

"No. You're being paranoid."

"Maybe that's because of all the coke I take. Jesus Christ, Gracie. I don't even eat refined sugar. I'm approaching thirty. If I want more years on the ice, I have to take care of my body. Coke or whatever isn't on anyone's list of superfoods."

"I never thought you were taking cocaine, dammit! I was thinking out loud, that's all. Why does Greco believe you were with his girl?"

Turning my head to the side as I watch Midtown fade into Hell's Kitchen, I mutter, "Because his ego is the size of the US and he couldn't handle thinking she didn't want him anymore."

"If it's going to affect your game, then maybe you need to tell Greco you didn't mess with her. Explain things."

"I don't owe him dick."

She growls beneath her breath. "My God, you're infuriating."

"And you're not?" I snap. "Do you know how I've spent the last three years, Gracie? Not fucking anything with a pussy, that's how. I've been on the ice, on the road, or in my home. A home that I didn't feel safe in. A home that, even though the kidnappers didn't get to me there, they might as well have.

"I went to bed with a knife beneath my pillow, a gun in my night-stand, not some chick's pussy sitting on my face—"

A hand settles on my shoulder. At first, I think she's trying to shove me, but she isn't. She does this pinching thing that's too soft to be corporal punishment.

"I genuinely never meant for you to take this how you did, Liam. I wasn't accusing you of anything, just trying to understand so I can maybe make the situation better for you." She looks up at me, her eyes big and wide and so fucking beautiful that I grit my teeth. "I can't do that if I don't know what's going on."

Though I purse my lips, mostly I'm just wondering how I can stop thinking about her legs being wrapped around my head, her butt in my hands, and those big wide eyes staring at me as I plow into her with my tongue...

"Right." It's easier than arguing, especially when I know I *did* just jump down her throat.

Which, of course, makes me think of stuff I'd prefer to go down there...

Focus, Donnghal. Get your head out of your ass. Or *thoughts of your little head in her mouth.*

"Paddy told me about the gun." She coughs. "Before you did."

I think back to what I just blurted out. "I didn't mean to tell you period."

"Thought my very Canadian self would be ashamed of you? If so, you'd have been right." But then, she nuzzles into my side. "I'll protect you, Liam. I'm better than a gun."

My laughter is sheepish. "Shut up, furball."

Her nose crinkles. "That's Gray's nickname for me."

"And? Possession is nine-tenths of the law."

"I think I prefer it when you call me a cabbage."

I snort.

"You think you're funny, don't you?" she grumbles.

"I know that I am."

Gracie sniffs.

"Why did you let Gray call you furball but you whacked Kow in the shin with his stick when he called you a rink rat?" Which, to be fair, was a pretty standard term in Canada for someone who loves ice hockey.

Her eyes narrow. "I'll take any opportunity to whack Kow with his stick. Plus, Gray means it in a nice way. Kow didn't." Before I can pick that apart, she slides in for the kill: "So, why does Greco think *you* were with his girl? It's not like you've played on the same team before."

"Whenever the Mounties were eliminated from the playoffs, he was the goalie."

"So it's a *you* thing, not a Greco thing?" she mocks.

That has me folding my arms across my chest. "He's been an asshole since we came up together in juniors."

Her eyes get even narrower. "If I find out you're lying to me about this…"

"What?" I jeer.

"I know where you sleep and I know where your food is."

I frown. "Poison's illegal. Whether it's laxative or cyanide. You know that, right?"

Her smile is evil enough to make me huff. "Yeah, it's illegal," she agrees. "But maple syrup isn't."

"You wouldn't!"

"Oh, yeah, I would." She smirks. "Watch it, Donnghal. No kidnappers will get through me before I get to you."

"Man, is that supposed to reassure me?"

I mean, if she were built like Noah, maybe. But she's pocket-sized on a good day.

"It's my job to reassure you," she purrs, her rosy pink lips puckered as she croons the words.

I inch back in my seat.

Suddenly, I understand why a male black widow willingly succumbs to its fate.

LIAM'S JOURNAL

Gracie,

Now that the season is underway, it got me thinking.

Having you around, watching in the stands, following stats, listening to you recap a match, the random shit you pick up on, it all brought it home.

Do you remember when you traveled around the circuit with Kow and me?

There was a point where you were the only person I listened to. Not my teammates, not management, not even Coach, and certainly not Kow.

You.

What you don't know about hockey is something that I can write on a postage stamp, but it's more than that. Your insight has always been impressive. How you view the world has fascinated me since forever.

Now that that's back in my life, I truly feel blessed.

I didn't realize what I lost until you were gone.

Do you know what sucked the most?

You walked away from Kow but you left me behind too.

I didn't talk to him for months after you moved out.

I should have seen the writing on the wall when you started giving him hell for drinking too much and partying too hard... He can be a vindictive piece of shit when he wants.

I'd have helped set that whole 'green dye affair' up, Gracie. I'd have willingly gone green so you could get your payback. I know I told you to back off him, but listening to you two argue requires the patience of a saint. We both know I'm no saint, Gracie. Because of that, you put me on his team instead of believing I'd automatically be on yours. If you'd known I'm always on your side, maybe you wouldn't have gone to university in fucking Vancouver.

Four-and-a-half-thousand clicks, Gracie. Could you have moved farther away from me?

I still think back to those days with fondness, you know? Before New York, I missed them so much. I never imagined that these past couple of months with you would be a thousand times better. Without Kow to mess shit up, without him to rile you into a bad mood, this, us, it's too good.

Too perfect.

The only thing that'd improve perfection?

If, whenever you bite that lip of yours, I had the right to kiss you out of your funk.

If, whenever you snarl at me, I had the right to drag you into my arms.

If, whenever you laugh, I had the right to taste your happiness.

One day...

Until then, I'm going to spoil you. I'm going to insert myself into your life until you don't remember a time without me.

Round one, two, and three are already underway, but round four is just about to begin...
   Liam

YOUR DAILY DOSE OF SPORTS NEWS

NEW YORK STARS LAUNCHES THIS SEASON WITH A BANG!

BY MACK FINNEGAN

The Stars have won their first 3 games of the regular season to take the lead in the Eastern Conference.

On opening night in Montréal, marking Liam Donnghal's return to the stadium that he called home for over a decade, the Stars beat the Mounties 4-2. Donnghal led the offense with 2 goals, while Lewis and Kerrigan completed the score for NY.

The following day, they visited Ottawa and shut them out 3 to nothing. The Otters' fans witnessed the birth of what has all the markings of being the new power duo in the NHL when Lewis and Donnghal's line scored all 3 of the New York goals.

Two days later, it was Washington's turn to feel the heat. Lewis and Donnghal again with a goal each, Danny Fisher being the only one to score for DC. Greco was barely under threat, his defense keeping the Diplomats out of their zone.

Where the Liberties failed, the Stars appear to have found the right combination early on. But the hockey season is a long one. Let's see if they can keep this streak going!

CHAPTER 15
GRACIE

Gray: Dumb question

Gracie: There are no dumb questions, only dumb people

Gray: Umm, okay. Lol.

Gracie: Hit me with it. I'm tired and I'm in class.

Gray: Is Liam not sleeping?

Gracie: No.

Gray: Short and sweet as always, G.

Gracie: Sorry. I'm not sleeping either, because he's not sleeping.

Gray: Whoa

Gracie: Not what you think.

Gracie: Unfortunately.

Gracie: Oh, shit. I didn't mean to say that!

Gray: Wait.

Gray: Nothing's going on between you and him but you WISH there was?!

Gray: Furball, what the fuck?

Gracie: YOU CANNOT SAY ANYTHING.

Gray: It's between me and you, but seriously, this is huge.

Gracie: Not really. It's just a crush.

Gracie: I have to go. Professor Donaldson might not give a shit because he's got tenure and everything but I don't want to push my luck.

Gray: WAIT.

Gray: It's okay.

Gray: If you have feelings for Liam, you can tell me.

Gracie: How can I tell you that?

Gray: You already did, furball.

Gracie: Yeah, but you can erase that or we can excuse it with you getting hit on the head with that puck last night.

Gracie: BTW, don't think I'm not taking count. That's two concussions in the past two seasons. You need to protect that pretty head of yours, dude.

Gray: It's nice to know you care, G.

Gracie: *snorts*

Gray: So, Liam, huh?

Gracie: He's not sleeping.

Gray: (I see what you did there.) Nightmares again?

Gracie: He mentioned them?

Gray: Couple times.

Gracie: They're terrible, Gray. I mean, we know what happened to him in a sense, but I didn't KNOW until I heard him. And I feel like shit because there's nothing I can do to fix this.

Gray: Not on you to do that.

Gracie: No, but I can't help but wonder if I should sneak down the hall and, I dunno, wake him up?

Gray: Blowjob's always a nice way to wake any dude up.

Gracie: GRAY!

Gray: Too soon? Gotcha.

Gracie: FML. If you tell him or any of the brothers about this, I will make sure Mom thinks you're allergic to gluten.

Gray: You wouldn't.

Gracie: I would. No. More. pierogi. For. YOU.

Gray: :O

Gracie: Exactly. We understand one another?

Gray: Totally.

Gray: So, you're staying at his place?

Gracie: He made an office/bedroom up for me.

Gray: That's unusual. I never did that for any of my PAs but you're you so, I guess that makes sense.

Gracie: We work late sometimes.

Gray: How late? Lol.

Gracie: Too late to cross Midtown at 2am, late.

Gracie: Plus, when he gets in after being on the road, we have shit to catch up on.

Gray: If you say so.

Gracie: It's not affecting him on the ice. He's playing better than ever. What made you ask if he wasn't sleeping?

Gray: Saw a close-up shot of him. He just looked exhausted.

Gracie: Guess having to relive being tortured every night is tiring.

Gray: When you put it like that...

Gracie: Hey, would you do me a favor?

Gray: Aside from not being allowed to tell anyone you've got a crush on Liam?

Gracie: Yes, aside from that.

Gray: What?

Gracie: Liam's been collecting these mugs from Starbucks for me.

Gray: Why?

Gracie: Guess he knows I like collecting stuff.

Gracie: Anyway, the schedule is really tight for when you face off in Tucson. Would you get them for him to save him some time?

Gray: Sure. But you can never threaten me with a gluten allergy again.

Gracie: Deal.

Liam: You going to be okay without me?

Gracie: Lol, I think I'll manage. I have plenty to keep me occupied while you're gone.

Gracie: Kara's been messaging me... She wants you to attend some events for that new brand of boxer briefs who wants to sponsor you. Andrews is insisting that you go to at least one.

Liam: I'm already in a bad mood because we've got three away games in six days, Gracie.

Liam: Can't even hang out with Gray.

Liam: You trying to make things worse?

Gracie: Stop being a baby.

Liam: o.O

Liam: I'll handle Andrews.

Gracie: I told you to fire him lol.

Liam: Meh. He's a good agent. I can't fire him for doing what I pay him to do.

Gracie: Even though you never want to deal with any of the bullshit he heaps your way?

Liam: Even though.

Liam: Anyway, are you going to get that essay on econometrics finished while I'm on the road?

Liam: Please say yes so I don't have to hear you whine about it anymore...

Gracie: I'm flipping you the bird.

Liam: Shame I'm not there to see it.

Liam: I know where you can put it.

Gracie: LIAM!

Liam: What?

Liam: 😊

Gracie: You're about as angelic as Lucifer.

Liam: Lucifer's sexy, so that's a compliment.

Liam: At least he's active in the community.

Gracie: You've been watching Family Guy again.

Liam: Gotta do something on the nights I'm stuck in a hotel room.

Gracie: Better than watching porn, I guess lol.

Liam: Oh, trust me, porn is watched.

Gracie: Didn't need to know that.

Liam: You didn't?

Liam: Not as if you don't watch it too...

Gracie: You been checking my browser history?

Liam: Didn't have to. Everyone watches porn.

Gracie: Even Father Gutierrez from St. Mary's?

Liam: Hahahaha. OMG, you know it.

Gracie: :P Take that back. He's eighty. Porn would probably give him a heart attack.

Liam: Tbh, I have a good imagination.

Gracie: What's that supposed to mean? You imagine Father Gutierrez watching porn?

Liam: Oh, yeah, Gracie. That's what gets me going. *eye roll*

Liam: You wanna know what I think of?

Gracie: Liam, what are you doing?

Liam: You like it when I open up to you, don't you?

Gracie: Yeah, but this is weird.

Liam: Nothing's weird between me and you, Gracie. Plus, I talk about this shit with your brothers all the time. It's just talk.

Liam: So, I got a thing for squirting.

Gracie: You do??

Liam: Yup. Only fair if you share with the class too...

Gracie: Jesus Christ.

Gracie: Umm, I guess overstimulation.

Liam: Huh. Like too many orgasms overload?

Gracie: Yup.

Liam: Well, I know what I'm watching tonight lol.

Gracie: ....

Liam: ;-) See you in a week, Gracie. While I'm gone, get that goddamn essay done!

Gracie: Yes, boss.

Liam: Please, tell me you saluted. Sharing is caring.

Gracie: I wasn't before...

Gracie: ...but I am now.

Gracie: And don't forget my mugs!!

CHAPTER 16
LIAM

"WHERE THE FUCK HAVE YOU BEEN?"

I scowl at Kow. "Like you can talk, asshole."

For a month solid, I've been trying to call the jerk since our face-off in Winnipeg.

"What's that supposed to mean?"

"You think I haven't seen you in all the tabloids? Or are you still sore because we whupped your ass four-oh."

Kow sniffs at me. "Since when do you read that trash?"

"Since your sister became my assistant," I drawl.

Yawning, he scratches his nose. "I still think you're crazy to have done that. Who invites Gracie into their life to organize them?"

"Me?"

"Apparently, but I'm not sure if something is going on with your brain. Some kind of malfunction. That last punch from Juarez maybe?"

"Fuck off. He didn't hit me that hard."

"You can lie to my mom but not to me," he says piously. "It's the bro code."

I sniff.

His smirk fades. "Seriously though. You okay?"

Because it's not often that Kow is solemn, I shrug. "Been better since your sister started taking over everything."

"She's good at that," he grouches. "Don't you ruin him, Gracie!"

His sudden bark startles me, prompting me to twist around where I find Gracie making faces at her brother.

When the hell did she come in? She has a key but I didn't hear anything.

I hate that my heart is pounding extra hard.

Cibole, I'm a pro athlete. My heart rate and endurance are tested by universities, and here I am, feeling like I've been playing on the ice for a whole game with no break.

"You're the one who ruined him, Kow. What the hell is this shower-in-a-bottle bullshit he said you taught him?"

I can't even groan that it was *one* time before they're back to facing off. Still, they don't notice how the interaction affects me.

Thank God.

I already feel like a freak for not being able to get over this shit without Gracie making things worse if she recognizes what's happening. If she does, then she'll encourage me to talk to Mike, my shrink, more, and once a week is enough.

Therapy is like having a putrefying wound and scraping off the gunk on the surface then pouring vodka on top of it.

Sure, it heals a bit better but it's still goddamn sore.

Leaning my elbow on the counter as my heart rate starts to slow, I perch my chin on my fist and watch their bickering continue.

"Do you even know how bad you guys stink?"

"Marigold loves it. Says I smell like victory."

"Marigold? Well, there's your problem. Fucking women with names like that."

"Fuck you."

"Fuck you right back." She crows, "Victory stinks like wet socks and fish feet, does it? I don't even have to—"

And on it continues. I've never understood where they get their energy from.

"*This* is why I haven't called you in ages, you jackass—"

When Gracie said she stayed disconnected from her family, she meant it.

"Why would I want to talk to you anyway?"

"If you'd just—"

"Listen—"

"...fuck off. I'm telling you, you're skating weird."

"Weird? WEIRD?" Kow bellows. "My speed is up."

"Yeah, and it's fucking with your knees. When you need knee surgery, don't say that I didn't warn you."

Kow, though pissed, stares down at the joints as if they'll tell him the truth.

My lips twitch. "She told me my skates were too small if that helps."

"And weren't they?" she snipes.

I nod.

Kow huffs. "You're a pain in my ass, Gracie Agnieska Bukowski."

Man, I went two decades without knowing that name. This is the second time I've heard it in three years—since Amelia's wedding to be precise.

"You brought out the full name?" I whistle, watching as Gracie literally turns hot pink.

Honestly, the only place she wears pink is on her cheeks when she gets mad at her brothers.

"I won't dignify that with a response," she growls. "But when you need surgery, you owe me a thousand dollars. Deal?"

Kow nods, but I mutinously insert, "Are you two seriously betting over knee surgery?!"

Grunting, Kow retorts, "Make it five thousand."

"I'll start researching the best orthopedic surgeons in Winnipeg," she says smugly.

I shake my head. "You two are crazy."

Both Bukowskis ignore me, too busy staring each other down to care about my opinion.

Before either of them can argue, I grab my cell and cut the video call.

Gracie blinks at me. "What did you do that for?"

"I'm not in the mood to hear both of you bicker for an hour." *Or more.*

Getting to my feet, I round the kitchen counter and move to the fridge to pick out some hummus and celery sticks. Right next to them are the 'healthy' bagels Gracie eats for lunch, and fuck if I don't want to snag the bag and dump them in the toaster.

Like always when she's in the kitchen, she withdraws two items from her satchel—a massive bag of seeds and nuts that she grazes on all day and a carrying case with a tablet, keyboard, and her massive agenda.

As she sets herself up, I watch her from the corner of my eye when she starts nibbling on a Brazil nut.

Then, she wiggles in her seat.

God.

I gnaw extra hard on a celery stick.

Talking to Kow should have been a boner killer, but it's not.

If only it were.

Every goddamn day, it's getting harder to ignore her, because this is *Gracie*—the straight-talking, caring, sincere, loyal hottie that's had me ensnared for years.

"You're staring."

I don't bother denying it.

She peers at me over her tablet which she's leaning against a textbook on business analytics. "What's wrong?"

"Nothing." I tip my chin at the textbook. "Need me to quiz you?"

"No. Thank you. But you better stop with the judging. I can feel it from over there."

My brows lift. "I'm not judging you."

Does my 'I need to get rid of this boner' face look like I'm judging her? The fuck?

"I deal with my brothers on my own terms."

Ah.

"You think I haven't figured that out yet?"

She sniffs. "You were surprised by how distant I am with them. I just thought you were slow on the uptake."

"I was *surprised* that you hadn't talked since you started working for me." I shrug. "But ten minutes of listening to you bicker was a reminder of how you roll."

"How *he* rolls. I never bicker with anyone else."

"Since when?" I hoot.

"I don't!" she insists. "I argue with people who deserve to be taken down a peg or two. With my brothers, I bicker. They deserve the low-level sniping for being big-headed pains in the ass."

"What about with me?"

"You usually listen to me so, no, I don't need to argue with you," is her simple reply. "I tell you about the skates, for example, you go up a size. Ergo, no need for sniping.

"Kow will have knee surgery in two years because he'd prefer that than to listen to me."

Because I have a feeling she's right, uneasily, I mutter, "You normally talk sense. I'm not sure why he fights you so much."

"Because to him, I'm a nobody and he's a somebody."

I shake my head. "You're the only one who can talk him into anything."

"Respectfully, I disagree. With you, I always have a voice. I have meaning outside of being my brothers' sister. That matters more than you know."

Hearing her sincerity, I don't play it off, but she's left me speechless.

I know she has identity issues, and to be honest, I don't blame her. Having witnessed with my own eyes how she disappears into the woodwork in people's minds whenever her brothers are involved, it's small wonder she fled to the States to make a name for herself.

Back home in Winnipeg, she'd never be able to forge a path that wasn't 'Bukowski brothers' tainted.

Their family uses it for publicity—their printing company has over twenty stores in the Peg because one of the guys always stars in their ads.

I don't blame Fryd, not after the sacrifices he and Hanna made to get the brothers where they are, but Gracie isn't like that.

She wants to make her own way, and that's something I respect.

"You have a meeting today," she drawls, her tone making it clear that she's changing the subject.

The irony is that this wasn't something I intended to discuss anyway. Though it *has* killed my boner so, win-win?

"With whom?"

"Bradley."

I grimace. "I forgot about that."

"Nah, it's your jam. I spoke with his secretary to learn what he wanted and it's about the outreach program the Stars are starting."

"Outreach program?" I question, not remembering anything about that. "This is the first time I'm hearing of it, right?"

"Technically, the meeting would be that," she corrects. "He wants the Stars to start working with inner-city kids."

I shrug. "Sounds cool to me."

"Didn't think it wouldn't but wanted to warn you that he expects you to deal with convincing the rest of the team to get on board. It's in the players' contracts but that won't stop the whining. He doesn't want to hear it."

That has me groaning. "Fuck, it sucks being one of the older players. They mistake me for being the responsible adult."

"That's why you wear the C," she says, unimpressed.

I wince because she's right. Of course.

She knows it too.

Her smirk is cocky. "I can take some of that off your shoulders."

"How? And if so, I owe you."

"I know. Your team, your team's endeavor, your teammates... Yeah, you owe me. B.I.G."

Cibole.

I want to fuck her when she's smiling that smug smile at me.

And my dick is back in business.

"Whatever you want—" *'Bébé'* is so close to tripping off my tongue.

Instead of saying what I want, I snag a hold of her hand. The slide of her fingers against mine, the silk over the calluses, has her mouth trembling before she tightens her grasp around my fingers, clearly understanding my game.

"I'll take a day trip to Coney Island as a down payment. But that's not the end of it," she warns huskily.

I shake her hand.

But I don't let go.

I rumble, "That can be done. Easily. How are you going to reap miracles?"

She blinks when I keep a hold of her fingers.

"I'll twist the girlfriends' arms to get their men involved. Greco and Raimond will be a problem though."

"Seeing as they have a revolving door on their bedrooms?" I ask as

I allow my fingertips to slide around to the inside of her wrist. "They're the worst."

"Leave it with me."

I wink at her. "Gladly. And when you decide on your price... I'm all in."

Her pulse stutters beneath my fingers.

"Your heart's racing, Gracie. Is everything okay?" I ask blandly.

"Y-Yeah, it's fine. I'm fine." She's not. Her voice is high and squeaky. Totally un-Gracie-like. She pulls on the hold I have on her, but I maintain my grip and gently turn her arm inward.

Thirty-five—that was the deal.

But fuck if rules weren't made to be broken.

I bow my head and hear her sharp inhalation as I press my lips to that point that's proof I'm having some kind of effect on her—her heart is pounding like crazy. I can see the soft leap in her veins as she reacts to my proximity.

"You sure about that?" I ask, uttering the words against her skin.

Today, her scent is fresh—freesias. Another flower I only know exists because of her.

"Y-Yeah, it's the energy drink I had on the ride over here. Caffeine's bad for you," she chokes out, tugging on my hold again.

Amused at how she always has a damn answer for everything, this time, I peer at her, making sure I have her whole attention as I place another kiss on her pulse, which is pounding harder than ever.

With our eyes locked, I let my tongue flutter out.

Just the once.

At her shocked gasp, I finally let go of her.

Immediately, she swallows and scuttles backward, nearly toppling off the damn stool in her haste.

I grab her and drag her forward to save her from falling, and when her hands collide with my chest, she stares at me, wide-eyed and bewildered.

Keeping it light, I tap her nose with my pointer finger. "You have to be more careful, Gracie. Or did you catch whatever curse Kow's got?"

She swallows. "I'll be more careful."

I dip down, invading her space by pressing my lips to just above her ear, letting my breath wash over the tender flesh there. I can hear her sharp inhalation even before I whisper, "Good. You're precious cargo, Gracie Bukowski. If you think I won't wrap you up in cotton, you're mistaken."

Her pupils are shot when I pull back. "G-Good to know," she croaks as she leaps from the stool and, before I can say a word, darts off.

I watch her go.

Try not to chuckle when she glances back at me.

Try not to groan when she almost walks into the door.

Then, she's gone.

And she leaves me alone.

In the sudden silence, that's when I start to wonder if that was too much, too fast.

Convincing her I don't see her as Kow's sister isn't something that can happen overnight.

"If you fucked that up, Donnghal," I mutter to myself as I scrape a hand over my jaw when the bathroom door slams shut. "I'll fuck *you* up."

But her pulse... that gives me hope.

Gracie: Your first goal tonight was chef's kiss good. You worked well with Kerrigan too. Though, I agree, he's a total goal suck.

Liam: You keep giving me compliments. I'm getting a complex.

Gracie: Fuck off. You did great.

Liam: ;-)

Gracie: Still on track to be back in the city at midnight?

Liam: Yup. You gonna be at my apartment?

Gracie: Yeah. Thought I'd sleep here tonight. You can debrief me in the morning about how things went with Noah. He was pouting like a baby even before the OT.

Liam: That's offensive to babies.

Gracie: Still a sore loser, I take it lol

Liam: The worst.

Gracie: Did I tell you I got Greco on board for the outreach program?

Liam: That you accomplished that makes you more terrifying than homeland security.

Gracie: Now who's giving compliments?

Gracie: Don't you want to know what I did?

Liam: It's either sex-related blackmail or some other BS that's compromising and it'll kill my buzz.

Gracie: You'd be right.

Liam: As long as it's not illegal, I don't give a crap.

Gracie: They're hosting weekly parties where they bring in a bunch of hookers and take this new drug that's doing the rounds.

Liam: FUCK.

Liam: Have you reported them?

Liam: Dumb question. Of course, you haven't. I just played a goddamn game with them.

Liam: You should have told Bradley.

Gracie: And fuck up the roster? Nah. I'm not about to ruin that when this drug, RED, isn't gonna show up on any blood tests.

Liam: You don't know that.

Gracie: I do... It's not that kind of performance-enhancing drug.

Liam: What?

Gracie: Oh, Liam. Stop killing MY buzz. ERECTIONS, dude. It's to maintain erections for longer.

Liam: Viagra?

Gracie: Nope. RED.

Liam: What did you do, Gracie?

Gracie: Got one of your bodyguards to follow them and to take photos of the deal going down.

Gracie: Unfortunately, I didn't kill two birds with one stone. Only Greco was there... That's why he's not gonna bitch about the outreach program. I'm working on Raimond.

Liam: Jesus Christ, Gracie!

Gracie: I stayed out of it!

Liam: You. Should. Have. Told. Bradley. For no other reason than it would have kicked that asshole off MY team.

Gracie: He's one of the best goalies around. Don't kid yourself and think he isn't.

Liam: GTG. Sleep. Don't bother waiting up. We'll talk about this tomorrow.

Gracie: Fine, fine. See you in the morning then.

Gracie: Killjoy.

CHAPTER 17
LIAM

Unforgettable - French Montana, Swae Lee

SLIDING the puck across the ice, I watch Lewis snatch a hold of it like his stick is magnetized. I swear we're on a roll this season—something that's backed up when two Seattle defensemen almost collide with me to stop the pass from happening.

Lewis, practically on his own now, slips the puck into the goal. As the stadium roars in triumph, he skates over to me and bumps my fist before turning into his signature goal celly—a pirouette.

"Fucking cocksucker," the defenseman, a jerk by the name of Condon, mutters under his breath.

Just loud enough for me to hear.

And that's it.

Off the gloves come, off with the helmet too.

One second, Condon is skating away, and the next, my fingers are on his jersey as I drag him back and he's flat on his ass on the ice as I punch him.

The crowd goes wild. Roars from the Stars and boos from the Killer Whales accompany each of my hits like an aria, but I don't give a fuck.

A linesman scurries over and grabs my fist before I can lay into Condon again.

In the background, I hear Lewis calling, "Come on, dude, he's down. He's down."

I point my fingers at my eyes and jerk them in Condon's dazed direction. "You back the fuck off with that homophobic shit. You hear me?"

"I'm not gay," Lewis drawls, amused.

"Don't give a shit where you stick your dick," I disregard. "It's the principle."

He peers at me. "I get it all the time."

"I know. But not on my watch."

His lips quirk into a smirk as he bumps fists with me again. "Appreciate the backup, man."

I tip my chin at him then accept being tossed from the game with grace as I skate over to the bench, snagging the puck on the way.

Condon, struggling to get off the ice, is helped up by two of his teammates. I took him by surprise, which wasn't exactly an example of sportsmanship, but I'm sick of this BS.

It's a goddamn pirouette—not an orgy in the neutral zone.

The shit Lewis gets for his celly is ridiculous and bullshit macho nonsense taken to the extreme. To be frank, it's happening too frequently for my liking.

When Condon is guided not just off the ice but to the locker room, I figure I went a little too *Mad Max* on his ass.

Oh, well, shouldn't have been a fucking douche bag.

As I storm down the tunnel, stopping only to toss the puck at one of the kids in the stands, behind me, the crowd goes wild. I'm not sure who scored but it ends up being a Stars' 4-1 win.

In the locker room, after Bradley's debrief which consists of him throwing shade my way, the journalists wade in.

Ordinarily, I'd do my time and head for the showers, but in this instance, I'm the first to face the fray.

"Chase Winnows with NYCT Sport. Liam, any clue as to why things turned aggressive between you and Condon?" one of the reporters asks.

Bradley glowers at me in the background, warning me with his glare to keep my trap shut, but I don't.

I can't.

"One of the ways to talk smack to other men is to diminish their masculinity. And, you know what, that's life. That's how things go. It's just talk. But I can't help but notice how what we say verges on hate speech." I shrug. "When a player calls someone a derogatory term in front of me, as captain, I think I'm within my rights to defend my teammate.

"Especially when that derogatory term spews hate toward a subsection of the population who are already underrepresented in this sport."

One inserts, "Mack Finnegan with PSN. Condon was being homophobic?"

"I have no desire to get into fights with anyone. Violence is not a language I want to be fluent in. But when adrenaline is high and tempers are surging, things get out of hand. I regret what I did and know that it was wrong, but so was what he said, which is between Lewis, Condon, and me.

"The toxic masculinity in hockey goes much deeper than this and everyone here knows it."

Feeling like I accomplished something, even if it's only small in the long run, I head for the showers, ignoring the barrage of questions that follow me.

But even there, I'm not granted any peace and quiet when Raimond hollers, "You need to cut that shit out on the ice, Lewis. We can't have our captain getting into brawls to defend your honor."

He meant it as an insult, but I chuckle. "Fuck you, Raimond. I'll defend your right to be an asshole out there too. Isn't that what teammates are supposed to do, or didn't you get the memo?"

Raimond's scowl follows him out of the showers.

The heat of the water feels good on my bones as I let it pound away some of my annoyance.

The growing pains of a new team have faded, but there's no getting away from the fact that some guys will grind your gears more than others.

When I'm through, I head out and see Raimond hovering by my locker.

"What do you want? I already spoke to you more than once today. That's my quota done."

He swipes a towel over his head. "You don't need to get into shit for that kid."

"Says who?"

"Says anyone with sense. It isn't a good look."

"A good look?" My frown shifts into a scowl. "And who the fuck are you to decide what is or isn't a good look for me? Lewis is carrying this team right now. He's the golden boy.

"You're managing to hold things up in defense, but that's more by luck because the last couple games, you've all been slow as molasses. I think those parties you're having are messing with your game."

Raimond's eyes narrow. "What do you know about my 'parties?'"

Aware that I owe Gracie big time, I smirk at his finger quotes but zoom in for the kill. "A) it's my job to know what you're up to as your captain. I'm watching out for you, dipshit. B) You've been bringing hookers in and messing around with that new 'performance-enhancing' drug that's doing the rounds."

"I'm not taking—"

"Not steroids," I immediately counter. "RED. You need to watch yourself. Eventually, they'll start testing for it."

"When I need your advice, I'll come and ask for it."

That has me barking out a laugh. "Like I asked *you* for advice. Whatever problem you have with Lewis is between you and him. So long as it doesn't mess with the team, I don't give a shit, but you stick to your end of the locker room and we'll stick to ours, okay?"

He grunts but starts to slouch off like the jackass he is.

That's when I remember the outreach program.

Fuck.

"Raimond," I call, watching as he glances at me. "Coach will be hitting you up for a couple of hours a week to deal with the outreach program."

"What outreach program?"

"The one the Stars is organizing to help inner-city kids. You know, the one that everyone is talking about? Who's the guy with one ear here?"

He scowls. "Why the fuck would I want to help out with that?"

I didn't need confirmation he was a jerk, but I got it anyway.

"We're all contractually obliged to donate at least three hours a week."

"I never agreed to that—"

"Yeah, you did. Get your lawyer on it if you're that much of a selfish jerk, but when Coach hits you up, you make time, got me?"

"My agent will hear about this," he growls.

"Good. Cry to him," I call to his back. "Maybe it'll take your mind off your dick and hookers!"

He flips me the bird over the top of his head.

Lewis, making his way out of the showers, sees him go. Because his cubby is next to mine, he quietly asks, "What did RaiBoy want?"

I snort at the name the press have given Raimond, a moniker they only use when he's fucked up. "To tell me to stop defending you."

His brows lift, but he shrugs. "He's not wrong. I can defend myself."

"You didn't hear him talk smack about you. I did." I eye him. "I practice ballet too. I'm just not as... effusive as you are and I don't think it's right that I feel I have to hide it as if it's a crime."

Lewis elbows me. "You practice ballet?"

My grin is sheepish. "Have a barre in my apartment and an instructor comes by once a week."

"I just go to a studio," he admits. "Mom wanted me to be a primo ballerino so I'm comfortable there."

"She did?" I laugh. "Man, she must have been disappointed with the multimillion-dollar contracts for hockey teams, then. What a letdown."

He rolls his eyes. "I never hear the end of it. Anyway, thank you. I appreciate you having my back."

"Told you before that I would."

"Yeah, but you keep on proving it." His brow furrows. "I don't get it, to be honest. I appreciate it but why do you care?"

"We're teammates," is my simple answer.

I'm saved from saying that I like him and that I think RaiBoy is an ass when the door to the locker room blasts open.

Silence throbs through the space at the explosive sound, and trust me, that we noticed in this chaos says a lot...

CHAPTER 18
LIAM

"MS. BUKOWSKI!" Coach yells.

"Bradley, if you think these jerk-offs have something I've never seen before, you're mistaken."

Facing the door, I watch as she storms toward me. I know I'm in for the Gracie Bukowski special—the finger wag—but I don't have it in me to care when I notice *her* notice I'm naked.

Apart from a towel.

Is it my imagination or does she not even *glance* at any of the other guys who are all in middling states of undress?

Maybe that's just wishful thinking.

She's been acting like a cat on a hot tin roof ever since that day in my kitchen when I kissed her pulse, so it's nice to see her back to normal.

Even if 'normal' involves her snarling at me: "Liam Donnghal." Her finger is out and wagging in my face. It'd be inappropriate to snag it in my hold and suck on it, right? "What the hell were you thinking?!" she demands, prompting me to tune back into the conversation.

Some guys wouldn't appreciate this going down in front of the team, but they're clearly not comfortable with their masculinity. I, on the other hand, just grin at her. "Gracie, what was I supposed to do when Condon was throwing out slurs?"

"He *what*?" she screeches, focus shifting.

"You heard me."

"I'm not gay," Lewis grumbles, but he's watching Gracie like the unexploded hand grenade she is.

Most of the guys are.

Which means her rep from the early days, a rep that's *ten* years old, is still making the rounds.

What, with the 'green dye' incident and how she knocked Kow out that one time, it's no wonder she's famous behind the scenes.

"Would it matter if you were gay? Just you wait until I tell that piece of shit what I think of him. I know his sister Lorie. As if he can judge anyone with a name like that. I'll show that Condo*m*—"

"Ms. Bukowski," Bradley snaps. "You will leave this to the appropriate channels—"

"Why would I do that when you never get anything done? One word to his sister and it'll pass back to his mom. *His mom*," she repeats. "Have you met Jessica Condon?"

Bradley squints at her. "I've had the pleasure, yes."

"Then you'll know that she's more terrifying than the NHL Player Safety Committee," she retorts with a sniff. To me, she snipes, "I'll see you outside. Leave this with me."

That's when Lewis slips in, "Hey, I'm Kyle—"

The fact he *tried* to talk to her in this state tells me where his mind is at—his dick.

Jealousy whips through my veins, making my fists ball at my sides and my nostrils flare with agitation. I can't help the visceral reaction, not when my teammate wants to get it on with *my* Gracie.

But of course, she never disappoints.

And as much as my blood pressure surged, she works on it better than a beta blocker by scowling at him like he's plankton when he tries to snag a hold of her hand—the dude's got a death wish.

"I know who you are."

In fact, no, her stare tells the locker room that, to her, he's *worse* than plankton. He's the mold on a grilled cheese sandwich that's been forgotten on the countertop, which just so happens to be the only kind of cheese she'll never eat...

Unaffected, Lewis slides in with a grin he probably thinks is charming. "That's good you know who I am. I'm—"

"—getting in my way?" she grates out.

Lewis blinks. "I just wanted to—"

"—get in my way?"

I cough to hide my laugh. Instantly, that draws her attention. As she pins me with a glower, I raise my hands in surrender.

That's how she'd look if I accidentally made her gag on my dick.

I just fucking know it.

Outraged but hot as hell.

She sniffs at me and waves a hand at Lewis, who needs to get better at reading the room.

"Kyle, get out of her way, dude," I insert quickly.

Gracie dips her chin. "Thank you."

"You're welcome." I grin at her. "Didn't want to presume that you couldn't defend yourself, Gracie."

"We both know I can and we also know that I can't afford the lawsuit if I knee Lewis in the balls for touching me without my permission." Instantly, he rears back, grabbing his junk. That has her shooting him a pleasant smile. "That's right. Just consider me a contagion. No touching!"

The *Arrested Development* reference has me snickering as, feathers well and truly ruffled, she storms off.

With a final glance at my chest.

That was *not* a figment of my imagination.

"You need to make sure that doesn't happen again, Donnghal," Bradley snaps.

Shifting my attention from her ass to his beet-red face, I arch a brow at him. "You try and stop her, Coach. No one gets in the way of the Bukowskis. They make Jessica Condon seem cool, calm, and collected."

He grimaces but doesn't reply—he knows I'm right. He's dealt with the family many times as coach of Canada's Olympic team. Though, admittedly, it's Fryd who's the nightmare parent on their side.

Lewis whistles. "Your assistant is terrifying."

"What the fuck was that about?" I demand, slapping him upside the head because I can *hear* him drooling over her.

"She's hot."

"You don't fuck with a teammate's PA, *bruh*."

"I like a woman with a fiery temper."

"Yeah, well, that fiery temper is *mine*. Got it?"

"You put a ring on it?" Gagné surprises me by asking.

"What's that got to do with anything?"

"Just curious," he says blandly. "Gracie *is* as terrifying as ever, by the way."

"Nah, not really."

"Didn't you notice? No one hooted or catcalled while she was in here," Lewis points out, his tone practically dreamy.

"They wouldn't dare." Fuck if that isn't hot.

The irony is that she's a sweetheart. I've never known anyone more genuine or with a bigger heart than her.

"Exactly," Lewis enthuses. "Is it true she stormed into the locker room at the World Junior Championships?"

My mind trickles back to that day. She always managed to get in where she wasn't supposed to and though Kow and I didn't have the clout we do now, it didn't stop her.

Nor did it stop her from making herself heard.

"Yeah, she did. She doesn't understand 'No Entry' signs," I answer as I pull on a pair of boxer briefs that Kara's trying to get me to be the spokesperson for.

They're comfortable but tight in the glutes.

"What made her storm the barricades?"

"She said Kow was skating like he was high. The funny thing is, they argued loud enough for the Russians to hear in their locker room, but he started skating better afterward. She's a good influence on him."

He just doesn't want to admit it and, in two years, he'll be five grand lighter and Gracie will be giving him advice on the best orthopedic surgeon in his area.

Lewis hums under his breath as he draws on a tee shirt. "Wanna go for a drink?"

The offer comes out of the blue, in the middle of a conversation about Gracie… Is he going to ask me to set him up with her?

Getting ahead of that bullshit, I growl, "I'm not setting you up with her."

Lewis's grin is sheepish. "I never hooked up with an older woman before."

Gagné muses, "Which part of 'mine,' *tu ne comprends pas*?"

With my eyes narrowed upon him, Lewis shrugs. "If she's off limits because she's a Bukowski, how about we hit up a club together? There are puck bunnies just waiting to meet—"

"It has nothing to do with her last name," I interrupt, dragging on my chinos. "Public spaces aren't for me. Thanks for the offer, though."

Lewis blinks, and I can tell he doesn't understand my refusal. Our rapport is great. We should be closer than we are, but I'm so shut off outside of the rink that we only meet here.

It takes him a few minutes, probably with help from Gagné who, from my peripheral, looks like he's having some kind of episode with how hard his brows are wriggling, before he nods his understanding.

"No problem." He clears his throat. "If you change your, er, mind, you know where I am."

"I do." My smile is tight. "Leave Gracie alone, you hear me?"

Nodding, he coughs. "Anyway, I heard about something called the 'green dye affair.' Is that true?"

"Where the hell have you been, Lewis? Everyone heard about that. She turned 'em into four-leaf clovers," Gagné jokes. "Saw them myself."

"Fuck off."

"We had no chance of winning that game with him on the ice. Why do you think his name went from Peter Pan to Leprechaun?"

Even *I* chuckle at that.

When Lewis's cell rings, he strides off to take it elsewhere.

"You dating her?"

Gagné's question has me growing tense. "Why?"

"Like that, huh?"

"Like what?" I retort, trying and probably failing to sound nonchalant.

Gagné claps me on the shoulder. "If it's any consolation, the only ass she was studying was yours."

Because he's been married since high school, I don't get pissed at him for looking at her.

I scrape a hand over my jaw. "Really?"

"Really. I get you, bro. We both like 'em crazy."

We share a grin and bump fists.

Fuck if that doesn't improve my mood for the rest of the day.

TEXT CHAT

Liam: Talk me down.

Gray: From what?

Liam: Wanting to kill Lewis.

Gray: Should I feel special that you singled me out for this pep talk, lol?

Liam: You're the rational one.

Gray: I went from feeling special to feeling insulted. Thanks.

Liam: You're welcome.

Gray: Why do you want to kill Lewis?

Liam: He was trying to flirt with Gracie.

Gray: Oh. Asshole.

Liam: Right?

Liam: She's clearly too good for him.

Gray: She's too good for anyone with a penis.

Liam: Exactly.

Liam: He's getting over his ex as well. Like, what would Gracie even be? A rebound?

Liam: Ha. No way. Not on my watch.

Gray: I'm sure if he was flirting she could turn him down if she wanted to.

Gray: You're taking the protective 'brotherly' role a bit seriously, Liam, lol.

Liam: Maybe I don't feel like her brother.

Gray: You had a falling out?

Liam: What? With Gracie? Of course not.

Gray: Then

Gray: OH.

Gray: What?!

Liam: You can't say anything.

Gray: What's there to say?

Gray: Fuck, this is huge, Liam.

Liam: I know.

Liam: Trust me, I know.

YOUR DAILY DOSE OF SPORTS NEWS

DONNGHAL FORCES THE LEAGUE TO TAKE A STAND ON HOMOPHOBIA!

BY MACK FINNEGAN

The hockey world is left reeling from Liam Donnghal's accusations of toxic homophobia in the NHL.

The Leprechaun didn't hold back any punches in the dressing room last night after he was tossed from the game for instigating a fight against Condon (6 weeks ACL) who had allegedly uttered homophobic slurs

John Newton from Idaho, 46, says, "Why is he bringing politics into this? It's a game! Donnghal was out of order for dropping the gloves. Especially with Condon out for weeks."

Mario Chester from Illinois, 23, says, "Representation is important. What these guys do on the ice matters. I can't condone violence, but at least someone is taking a stand where it matters. These things are important. It saves lives."

What's your take?

Mom: Gracie, are you done with that class of yours? Your father could use some help with the printing shops.

Gracie: No, Mom. The semester hasn't finished yet. And, it isn't a class. It's a postgraduate degree.

Liam: Gracie got an A on her recent paper, though, Hanna. Isn't that awesome? I'm sure she aced her mid-terms too.

Dad: Well done, girlie.

Mom: Dad's barely home at all. It's so busy right now with everyone wanting something printed for the holidays.

Kow: It'd be neat if you could help out, Gracie.

Dad: Leave girlie alone. I fine.

Mom: You're not, Fryd. Working all these hours isn't good for you. You should be retiring soon.

Dad: I retire when dead.

Mom: Don't even joke about that!

Noah: Can't you make it home early, Gracie? If Dad needs help then...

Gracie: If things are so busy, then Dad needs to expand his workforce. :)

Kow: Took that fancy business thing you're studying to work that one out, did it?

Gracie: I'm surprised you can even spell business, Kow. Didn't you go bankrupt last year?

Kow: ALMOST.

Gray: *snorts*

Cole: That you think that's a defense is embarrassing.

Gracie: Apparently, there are positions in Dad's shops if you need some extra cash...

Mom: Gracie, that was mean.

Gracie: The truth stings. Anyway, I have to go study for my business thing so I can give advice that no one listens to.

Kow: You telling me to save for my tax payment wasn't advice.

Cole: Did you save for it?

Kow: No.

Matt: And isn't that why you almost went bankrupt, lol? Sounds like advice to me.

Kow: ALMOST is the keyword.

Liam: I think I remember you hitting me up for a loan around April 30th last year...

Kow: Are you taking Gracie's side?

Liam: Yeah, dumbass. You still owe me BTW.

Mom: Boys! Stop arguing. Look at what you've done now, Gracie.

Noah: I don't see why she can't help out. Winter break has to start soon, doesn't it?

Liam: She's working for me full-time on top of school. Her schedule is crazy.

Mom: I just don't understand why she's doing all this. The firm could be hers. It's not good enough for her. That's her problem. She always did have her head in the clouds.

Liam: Hanna, that's not fair! Everyone should dream big. You taught us that we could aim for whatever we set our hearts on.

Dad: We did, Hanna. I told you you hard on Gracie girlie. Leave her be.

Dad: I no want retire.

Mom: Oh, Fryd. Hush.

YOUR DAILY DOSE OF SPORTS NEWS

NEW YORK STARS' PERFORMANCE REMAINS STRONG

BY MACK FINNEGAN

As the ultimate holiday gift to fans, this year the New York Stars beat Philadelphia 5-4 in a close-won game that saw Ruben Kerrigan get tossed for unsportsmanlike conduct toward referee John Arcey.

Still, with twenty-five wins and nine losses, the Stars will be heading into the post-Christmas games against New Jersey, Arizona, and Colorado in better standing than the 'Liberties' saw in the previous eight seasons.

CHAPTER 19
GRACIE

I'd Do Anything - Simple Plan

WHEN LIAM TURNS up at my apartment at 7am on Christmas Day, red-faced and dressed for a run, I blink away the sleep in my crusty eyes and don't question why he's here, just trudge back to bed and climb under the covers.

I hear him chuckle but to be honest, it's 7am.

On Christmas goddamn Day.

It takes me a while to remember that but when I do, I shriek, "Liam?"

No answer.

Wait—did I dream all that?

I mean, he's been the star of a few recently. What, with how touchy-feely he's become, my subconscious has gone into overdrive.

Since I saw him in the locker room, half-naked, it's been getting worse.

Watching him suck his self-imposed allotment of maple syrup off the spoon twice a day has also started featuring heavily in my fantasies.

It's only fair that he pays well because good vibrators aren't cheap and I'm burning them out with how weird he's been acting lately.

As I contemplate whether I should go back to sleep or make myself a coffee, that's when I hear the sound of water coming on.

"So he *is* here," I mutter, rubbing my sleepy eyes.

Then, it hits me.

He's naked.

I flop back onto my bed.

"This is torture," I whisper, trying not to think about what he's seeing right this second.

Since I started working for him, his pecs are bigger.

His shoulders wider.

His abs more defined.

He might be finding clean living a strain, but my God, it's doing him a world of good.

In the middle of an all-out swoon, I finally realize the shower turned off.

The door doesn't open but I can hear footsteps.

"Did he just shower with the bathroom door open?!" I can't cope with that knowledge, knowledge that proves I'm a peeping Thomasina because I would *so* have looked if I'd have known, I shriek, "LIAM!"

"Yeah?" I can tell he's nearer because he doesn't shout as he asks, "You decent?"

"Never," I mumble. "What the fuck are you doing here? I booked your flight. You were scheduled to leave last night."

Last night when I came home, ate too much ice cream because I was missing him already, and dove face-first into the case study I have to hand in on January 3rd.

"Didn't feel like going." When he pops his head around the door, his cheeks are loaded with shaving foam and one of my razors is in his hand. "Figured I'd come and keep you company after I went for my morning run."

That, right there, is why when my dad tried to make me a hockey player, it never worked out. Not only is my coordination shit and I'm short as fuck, but I can't cope with this whole torture thing they do on the daily. Even if I can appreciate the end result.

"You ran here?"

He knows what I'm asking. "It was rough but I did it. I sent Jonathan home too... so what are we going to do?"

"I sleep on Christmas Day. And you should as well. Who runs on Christmas morning?! Before 7am?" I mock-retch, trying not to swoon when he leans against the doorframe and I see he's wearing gray sweatpants.

Gray. Motherfucking. Sweatpants.

Santa really did visit good girls last night...

"You sleep?" he demands, ignoring my criticism. "The *whole* day?"

"I do. It's tradition." One I made for myself after I left Canada.

No arguing, no brothers, no hockey. *No sports.*

Heaven.

"A tradition," he repeats.

"If you're going to parrot everything I say, you can fuck off into the kitchen and make me some coffee."

"Latte with two shots of espresso?"

Ugh. He knows me too well.

Squinting at him, I whine, "You're a monster. Who wakes someone up on Christmas Day at 7am who's over the age of five?"

His snicker is all the answer I get.

I hear him return to the kitchen, next comes the hisses and spitting from my coffee machine, and then he's back with liquid gold in his hands, *sans* the shaving foam and with a jaw made of silk housing a grin I'd want to smack if he weren't so pretty.

When he settles it on my nightstand, I yawn around a mumble: "You didn't use a Liam cup."

Dropping to one knee beside the bed, he studies me with a perplexed frown. "A Liam cup?"

Sleepily, I nod. "My 'You are here' cups. I have fifteen now and you go pick an old mug?"

He clears his throat. "I'll know for next time."

"Good. Coffee tastes better in them." Because *he* bought them for me.

His dopey grin makes my heart flutter. "Really?"

"Really."

"I'm glad. Just, you know, wanted you to remember I was thinking of you when I'm on the road."

He's so sweet that he's going to make me diabetic.

Curling onto my side to hide my face in the comforter, I mutter, "You're supposed to be at Mom and Dad's now."

"Didn't feel like going."

"Since when do you not feel like going home for Christmas?"

He hitches a shoulder. "Since I didn't feel like going."

What with that and the run, concerned, I flip around and lean on my elbow so I can touch his forehead. "You're not coming down with something, are you?"

Backing off, he snorts. "I'm not sick. I just didn't want to travel. It's been a hectic month."

I continue studying him. "I'm not going to entertain you."

"You entertain me without trying, Gracie," he says glibly, but I can see the hint of amusement in his eyes that backs up his words. "Like when you cornered Condon on his way to the Killer Whales' bus? Priceless."

"His sister wasn't answering her phone," I dismiss. "I wasn't about to let him get away with…"

My words fade as he crawls onto the bed beside me.

And he says, "Scoot over. I didn't get to sleep until late."

My mouth rounds and any cerebral short-circuiting at Liam's presence in my bed fades as I screech, "You could have slept in in your own damn bed and not have woken me up!"

"And you could have flown with me to Winnipeg," he snipes. "Decisions have consequences. This is one. You're right, though—I shouldn't have gone out so early. Now, I want to nap too."

Appeased because he admitted I was right, I shift aside, letting him have more space. Even so, his feet stick over the edge.

Sucks to be him.

That's when he stuns me by snagging me in his hold and sliding his arms around my waist. Eyes wide, I don't shift a muscle as he tucks me into him so that his head is resting on my shoulder, my back is pressed up against his chest, and my butt is in the curve of his thighs.

"Now sleep," he retorts.

I'm about to start hyperventilating here! How the hell can I sleep?

Oh, God, he feels so good.

And he smells even better.

And he's this *wall* at my back.

Fuck.

He's so warm.

This is—

"You made me coffee," I croak. "I should drink it."

He doesn't let go of me when I stick out a hand to grab my cup.

"You can drink it when it's cold. I'll even put ice cubes in for you and transfer it to one of your Liam water bottles and that's when we'll exchange gifts."

"You ran here with it?"

"Sure did."

Before I can respond, a round of bullets sounds on the TV that has us both jolting in surprise.

"I'm making an executive decision," he declares, twisting around while somehow maintaining that firm grip on me. I try not to think about other places he could be gripping right now. Goddammit, he's so close. I could reach back and— "No news on Christmas Day."

Without waiting on an answer from me, he reaches over my head and snags the remote. In the background, I can hear—

I groan. "Not *It's a Wonderful Life*."

"Only *you'd* have a problem with a classic."

"It's sad."

"It's a *classic!*"

"Classics *are* sad. Put something else on."

"Do you know you're difficult?"

I don't know why I do it.

I really don't.

I wriggle my hips.

Then, I still when I realize what I just did.

Both of us are frozen on the mattress.

Both of us remain locked in place as, in the background, all of George's prayers are answered with a basketful of cash.

Then, I release a breath.

He does too—I can feel it whistle past my cheek.

I could turn around.

I could kiss him.

I could—

"Do you want to order Chinese food?" I choke out. "If I have to watch this, then you can break with the health freak stuff for the rest of the day."

He turns his head. My heart feels like it's going to start stuttering in my chest. His nose rubs gently against my cheek. "General Tso's cauliflower sound good to you?"

I snort, and the tension between us breaks. "No. Not if you're going to make me watch suicide films on Christmas Day."

"It's a classic!"

"If you're just going to keep on saying that, I'll put the news back on."

"It was nominated for five Oscars."

"Nominated. Not won. Even the judges agreed with me."

"*National Lampoon's Christmas Vacation?*"

"Deal." I rock my head back to study him and that's when I do something stupid…

But he's so mussed, and clean, and gorgeous, and he smells better —honestly, it'd be a crime *not* to—

I press my lips to his.

And it's like the world itself stops turning.

The kiss is chaste.

Nothing fiery. Not passionate. No tongues, even.

It's still the best kiss I've ever had.

He pushes his forehead onto mine and for endless moments, we just breathe each other's breaths.

"Merry Christmas, Liam," I whisper, aware that my tone is deep and warm and sugar-cookie sweet, needing him to know that he just made my morning.

Fuck, my *year*.

He swallows. "Merry Christmas, Gracie."

I stare at him.

He stares at me.

Something flickers to life in his gaze that has me jerking back and rasping, "Is it too early for takeout?"

He chuckles, which shatters the lingering tension between us.

But… that was relief in his eyes, wasn't it?

My heart sinks.

What did I expect?

For him to tip me back onto the sheets and ravish me?

The agoraphobe ran through Manhattan before 7am on Christmas Day to avoid crowds and people with his *bodyguard* yet here I am, mauling him—

"Yeah. Nap. We can order after."

When he curls me into him again, it comes as a surprise.

I don't know what I was doing, and I don't know what he's doing either, but when I settle against him, I feel *him*.

My eyes are wide as I look at the wall opposite my bed in my sardine-can bedroom and I try not to be aware that a simple, chaste peck on the lips gave Liam Donnghal a boner.

So, why didn't he—

I'm confused.

He wants me. I can feel it. It's not as if he's ashamed of it, but he doesn't act on it, just holds me close.

Adrenaline is winging around my veins, so there's no way I can sleep, but it's good. *Nice.* It's Liam. And me. We're here. Together. It's Christmas Day.

Which is when I realize a solid truth.

There's no one else I'd rather spend it with than... *him.*

Which is also when I realize we're on the same page. Because his presence in my apartment tells me he feels it too.

We want to kiss each other.

We want more but more puts this, *us,* in danger, doesn't it?

It could put pressure on a relationship that is starting to feel like solid ground for me. For him too, maybe. I know he's been brighter since I came in and organized his life.

Messing with the status quo, doing something that could potentially destroy this?

I can't.

I... just can't.

And that's why he didn't deepen that kiss.

Because he can't lose me either.

That right there is the moment I start to cry.

Silently, so he doesn't know that my heart feels like it's breaking.

CHAPTER 20
LIAM

WHEN OREN, one of the more recent Bukowski billet brothers, stops a third scoring chance from the Stars, I start to get pissed.

I mean, it's his job to stop us from scoring, but when did he get to be so fucking good at it?!

It's a relief to be on the ice, though. A relief to be focusing on the game.

Things have been weird with Gracie for a while, but they've worsened since Christmas. Just when I think we've stepped things in the right direction, she does a full one-eighty. It's driving me insane. The irony of that, of course, is the more I fuck up my life, the stronger my game is.

Go figure.

Pittsburgh's playing aggressively, so it's a good thing I'm on top of my shit tonight. They're not giving an inch on the boards.

When Lewis sends the puck sailing toward me, I dig it out of the corner and circle the net. When I shoot, Oren blocks it. Again.

Fucker!

Lewis grabs the rebound and passes it to Kerrigan, who takes his shot.

It fucking goes wide.

Not just that time either.

Why Coach keeps playing him on the first 2 strings is beyond me.

With three minutes left on the clock, they're up 2-1.

It's more luck than skill that Lewis and I manage to eke a draw out of Oren, who's blocked at least ten scoring chances in the last fifteen minutes.

Kerrigan misses a perfect shot in OT, but we finish the night with a 3-2 win only because Lewis and I gun for the victory so hard that we'll probably be pissing blood tomorrow.

Absolutely exhausted by the end of the game, the only thing I want to do is go home and get Gracie to drink a maple syrup chaser on my behalf.

Which she does.

Except, as she pours the combination of creamer and ambrosia into her mouth, a few drops ooze from the corner of her lips.

For the rest of the night, as she tries to talk about tomorrow's schedule, that's all I can see.

There'd been amber striations to the mixture, but the droplets had looked like cum.

Fuck.

After the day I've had, that's what I need too.

To escape through her. To find release in her. To *join* with her.

When she eventually leaves, citing that, 'My grumpy ass had better cheer up before tomorrow,' the first thing I do is head to the guest bathroom because the need is too urgent to waste time heading to my connecting bath.

As I wait for the shower to heat up, I strip to nothing and duck under the spray once it's tepid.

My cock is an aching, throbbing mess—pre-cum is every-fucking-where and I'm so close to release I feel like a goddamn teenager again.

All it wants is to sink home into her, but that's not an option right now.

I think about those droplets that had seeped from the corners of her mouth, imagine that *was* my cum, picture her swallowing every drop and, in the aftermath, that she'd even go as far as to stick out her tongue so I could see the mess I'd left behind.

Gritting my teeth at the imagery that's better than porn to me, I start to stroke my hand along the length of my dick.

As the water pounds my nape, I think of her sitting on her knees as I lean over and taste myself on her tongue.

With a growl, my fist starts to move faster.

She'd whimper as I kiss her. "Liam, I need you." She'd moan, her hand slipping between her thighs so she could touch her clit.

Together, we'd—

"Liam? Where are you?"

My eyes flash open as I realize the Gracie mewling in my imagination isn't the Gracie shouting my name.

Fuck if that doesn't have my screwed-up brain reacting, though.

Knowing she's here, that she's outside the bathroom in the hall has me biting off a snarl as cum slaloms out of me, spattering the shower wall and the cubicle door, sliding into the water before it sinks down the drain.

"One minute," I yell hoarsely as I pump my hips, eyes closed, brow furrowed as I take every ounce of pleasure I can get.

Breathing heavily, the release of tension a welcome relief, I stare at the tiled floor as the evidence disappears.

Then, I turn off the faucet, grab a towel, and head out to find her.

I catch a glimpse of her in her bedroom, her ass right in my fucking face as she waggles it while she bends over beside the wall.

Wondering what she's doing, I tilt my head.

That's when I see it—the vibrator.

Charging.

Fuck. My. Life.

Scrubbing my hand over my jaw as I try to contain my reaction to that temptation, I clear my throat. "You forget something?"

She yelps, drags out the wire from the socket, tosses the vibrator on the floor then, on her way up, manages to knock her head on the stand before she whips around to glower at me.

Her eyes immediately widen as she takes me in.

Her tongue peeks out.

She licks her lips as she gawks at my seminudity.

"Um," she croaks, "I forgot m-my—"

Despite the torment she gives me on the daily, I have to hide a smile at how blatant her reaction is to me.

Hope flickers inside me with the force of a fireworks display on July 1st.

After the past couple of hope*less* weeks, it puts a spring in my step as I stride into the room, prompting, "You forgot your...?"

It should be impossible, but her eyes grow even wider. Those dove-gray irises turn stormy as Gracie, who never squeaks, *squeaks*, "Nothing! Never mind."

When she knees the nightstand this time in her haste, my amusement dies as she starts to hop on one foot.

"What the hell did you do now, Gracie?" I grumble as I reach her.

"Fuck if I know," she whines, cupping her knee as she continues bobbing up and down.

It's my turn to stare when I see the blood dotting the denim of her jeans. "You're bleeding!" I rasp, urgency firing through me at the sight.

My gaze darts to the nightstand where I see one of those Stanley knives she uses to cut open my PR boxes and parcels peeping out from the mess she has exploding from the drawers. Her jeans have rips in the knees which is where she was cut.

"Gracie, you have got to be more careful. Why wasn't the blade retracted, dammit?"

Before she can answer, I sweep her up in my arms, ignoring her shriek as I carry her to the guest bathroom.

It's still humid from my shower as I sit her on the toilet, which is when she mumbles, "It's just a cut, Liam."

I ignore her and reach into the vanity to find the first-aid kit. With that in hand, I kneel in front of her.

She hisses when my fingers carefully move around the cut and I pull at both sides of the rip in her jeans and make the space bigger. "Liam!"

"What? Would you prefer I drag your jeans off, Gracie?" I croon, knowing that'll stop her whining.

Her lips form an 'O.'

An 'O' that just starred in my fantasies.

"This is totally unnecessary," she whispers when I force myself to glance away. "It doesn't even hurt."

"Good. But there's no harm in me cleaning it up and sticking a Band-Aid on it, is there?"

She stops arguing then, letting me set out the things I need to doctor the cut.

The steam from the shower makes her skin dampen and when I stare up at her, I can see tiny whorls of hair have stuck to her forehead. But that's also the moment I realize she's not looking at me anymore.

No, she's studying the shower.

With a frown, I follow her line of sight and my eyes flare at what I see.

Cum—streaks of it on the glass cubicle door.

It could be shower gel or shampoo, but the way she licks her lips tells me she's reached her own conclusion.

Unashamed, I study her and rasp, "Are you ready for the hydrogen peroxide?"

When her head whips around at the sound of my voice, I see that her pupils are pinpricks.

Fuck.

"I-I'm ready."

With our focus on one another, I carefully press the cotton ball soaked in the peroxide to the small wound. As it fizzes, I ask, "Do you want to spend the night?"

Her mouth works.

Words form on her lips.

I can practically see them and my heart pounds, just waiting for her to—

Her phone rings.

Both of us jump at the sharp noise.

She's flustered as she reaches into her pocket for her cell, almost dropping it in her haste once she draws it out, then she groans. "It's Mom."

What goes without saying is that Hanna won't stop calling until she answers.

I have no idea what just happened between us, but I can't help but feel that we made major progress. Progress that Hanna wrecks as she crows about Kow's win tonight.

With every gloated, bloated, praise-loaded word Hanna utters, I can practically see Gracie retreating from me even though she hasn't moved a damn inch as she's reminded of exactly what I am to her —family.

That cockblocking, motherfucker Kow—his timing, I swear, will be the death of me.

3RD PERIOD

STARS' PLAYER DOMINATES ALL-STAR GAME

BY MACK FINNEGAN

Liam Donnghal took part in this weekend's All Star festivities for the 3rd year in a row and his 9th in career, skipping only the game that took place under somber circumstances when he had been kidnapped.

He led the Metropolitan division to its 3rd tournament victory in the 6 years since the new format has been adopted.

CHAPTER 21
GRACIE

FEBRUARY

Dandelions - Ruth B.

WHEN I ARRANGE our schedule for the week, I play with the Christmas gift Liam got me, a diamond-studded '35' pendant, and release a contented hum—I *live* for this bullet journaling shit.

My double-page spread is split into seven days, and after Liam took me stationery shopping, I have color-coordinated stamps and Washi tape that helps me identify with a glance what Liam's doing and when as well as—

"You're cute."

His interruption has me glaring at him while he makes us both a protein shake.

"I am not cute."

As the blender does its thing, I wait for him to finish up, reading the morning's headlines on the TV in the kitchen until he's done when I warn him, "Take it back."

"Or what?"

My eyes narrow as he slides a 'Dallas' water bottle over to me. "Or else."

His lips twitch. "You're not cute, Gracie."

"Thank you," I exclaim before I take a sip of my breakfast. *Yum.* "For how much this shake costs," I say happily, "it's only right that it tastes like peanut butter."

"What kind of peanut butter do *you* eat?" There's a morose tinge to his expression as he glowers at the drink. "This tastes of what it is: chemicals."

Shrugging, I lick my lips. "I like it."

"That's because I put two tablespoons of maple syrup in there for you."

"That explains it then," I admit, tone guilty now because I know he only allots himself two *teaspoons* a day.

Not wanting to waste a drop when I feel a pearl of maple ambrosia beading at the corner of my mouth, I catch it with my tongue.

He studies the movement.

That's something he's doing more now since the night after that showdown with Pittsburgh. On Christmas Day, I felt like we were on the same page, but he's changed. I can sense it.

He's never blatant but he's always watching me, and I can feel the momentum building.

It's like when you're a kid at the top of a hill with a snowball. Gradually, as gravity does its thing, it's going to turn into a Grinch-sized ball that'll make a great snowman's body.

Except this snowman will be bigger than the Stay-Puft marshmallow giant from *Ghostbusters* by the time it comes to a stop.

Is it too late to yank on the brakes before we ruin one of the closest friendships I've ever had?

And if it is, do I even want to?

That's the real question here.

In December, I did.

Then I saw his cum on the shower cubicle door...

It was a catalyst.

I'm starting to feel like if I don't kiss him soon, *properly,* I'm going to explode.

Or implode.

I'll take either at this point.

Peering over my bottle, aware that my cheeks are flushed at the thoughts of the many ways a man as strong as Liam could make me shatter into a thousand pieces, I recognize a distraction is required and work is exactly what I need.

"Stop bugging me. I have to sort out my organizer."

Closing this conversation, I reach for my agenda and start to check off the shit I've done today.

Honestly, my planner has never been this full.

Or pretty.

Liam gave me too much money to spend in this Japanese stationery store over by Bryant Park. That means this bullet journal is loaded with colors and designs and all kinds of shit that I refused to buy in the past but it's on his dime, so hell to the yeah.

I got midliners in different shades of sakura—cue sobs—a Sarasa Nano pen that makes me write like those peeps who design typography on social media videos. Washi tapes, special rulers that let me convert any standard diary into a bullet journal, rubber and wax stamps, bento-shaped erasers, and a massive case to haul around this shit with.

Honestly, I'm in stationery heaven because I didn't just buy *one* of everything—oh, no—I bought a rainbow's worth of colors *on top of* ten different kinds of styles because, hello, there was a zodiac and an astronomy pattern and a—

"Hey."

Disturbed from my paradise, I glower at him. "What?"

When he picks up one of my erasers and starts tossing it in his hand, I quirk a brow at him and watch his eyes roll before he puts it down.

I wonder if the calluses on his palm would feel good rubbing along my inner thighs.

"I was thinking about your graduation ceremony."

My brows lift. "Why were you thinking about that?"

He clears his throat. "I'd get there."

I frown. "Get where?"

"To the ceremony."

Oh.

Ohhh.

This is about the other day.

"Look, Liam, I don't want to hurt your feelings but—"

"Thought you specialized in being a ball buster."

"Proud of it," is my cocky retort. "I'd prefer that after my name—Gracie Bukowski, ball buster—than MBA."

He snorts. "Yesterday, you lived up to the title."

Though I sniff, I'm also smiling. "Got to look after you. Especially when Bradley is frighteningly disconnected from reality."

Like hell, I wasn't going to read him the letter of NHL law after Liam's head collided with the boards during drills and that old-school moron wanted him to jump straight into a scrimmage.

Little tap to the head, my ass.

"Yeah, but I didn't think you'd tell him that to his face. I thought he was going to have a heart attack when he ordered me to make my assistant *stand down*." He barks the words like Bradley did.

"As if anyone could make me stand down. Joel Quenneville couldn't get me to close my mouth if I think something's shady."

"You and your obsession with Quenneville." He harrumphs. "The stats are indisputable—Scotty Bowman has the record for the most games coached, the most wins, and the most Stanley Cups! How can you argue with that?"

"I can argue with myself in a locked room, dude." I wag my finger at him. "That'll be to your benefit when Kara and Andrews arrive."

"Oh, Christ, I forgot that they're coming." He scrapes a hand over his head. "I'm going to reschedule. I can't deal with their bullshit today."

I frown. "That's not like you."

He heaves a sigh. "I'm talking to Mike later." His therapist.

"You normally speak on Thursdays," I point out.

How his jaw locks tells me more than words can.

I haven't been staying over lately, trying to avoid temptation, so I have to assume he's been sleeping like shit.

His answer is continued silence.

It makes sense, to be honest. We didn't use the concert tickets that were his Christmas gift from me, and I know it's gotten to him.

"I'd make it to your ceremony," he grates out.

Sheepishly, I admit, "I wasn't going to invite you anyway."

His eyes bug out. "What?!"

"You'd want to come?" Embarrassed, I bow my head. "Look, this isn't important. Finals aren't even in my near future yet, and I could fail them all. *Massively.*"

"Failure is an alien concept to you," he dismisses. "And of course, I want to attend. *Cibole!* I mean, I knew I'd need an invitation but never thought I'd have to ask you for one. You seriously didn't think I was coming?"

Graduation ceremonies are in May and if the Stars continue in the same trajectory, they'll likely be in the playoffs.

Which, if they take it all the way, would probably have the semis lining up with the ceremony.

In that situation, I know what would suddenly stop being important...

Do I set myself up for heartache or tell him he can't come?

"You really want to attend?" I ask hesitantly.

"Of course." His head tips to the side. "I'll sit with your parents and—"

"I wasn't planning on inviting them either."

"Why not?"

"Because I'm protecting future Gracie from being sad when they don't show up on the day." I heave a sigh. "I don't want to talk about this."

His confusion *hurts*, but I know the score—Mom wouldn't come because she doesn't approve and Dad will have to work.

It startles me that he lets the topic drop long enough for me to get back to my task, but he makes my heart clutch in my chest when, tone ardent, he vows, "Even if we have a game scheduled that day, I'll find a way to be there. I'll just have to wear a hat."

I'll find a way to be there.

Why does that make me want to cry?

Still, the sappier he makes me, the brisker my tone is as I snipe, "Because that worked in Chuck's."

"I can grow a beard?"

I purse my lips. "That *might* work. A big bushy one? You've never gone that long before, have you? That would make you more incognito."

"How bushy are we talking here?" he asks warily.

"Hohenheim long."

"Ah, fuck. You and anime."

I shoot him a smirk. "Never let it be said you don't know what to buy me for my birthday."

"True. You *are* easy."

"You, on the other hand, are not. What do you get the man who has everything?"

His brow furrows. "I've never needed any gifts from you. Even for Christmas. The best part of opening your presents are your voice notes. I always keep them."

I have no idea why, but that makes my cheeks tinge pink. "No way."

"Of course." He grins at my embarrassment then straightens up and leans over the counter to snatch his phone from the other side. As he does, his shirt ripples and tightens, snagging on his hip, revealing very touchable areas that are a 'no-go' zone.

His abs are thick with muscle, gleam like silk, and there's a faint smattering of hair too.

As my nails curl into my palms, palms that instinctively know how good he'll feel, he messes around with his cell.

A couple minutes later, he plays a voice recording I recognize from this past year, though we'd ended up spending it together.

"Okay, dingbat. Aside from the show which needs no explanation and I won't sing to you because I don't want your ears to start bleeding, this is a book. You read it from left to right. It's full of information that will prove my love of Joel Quenneville. You'd better read it. There will be questions. Merry Christmas, ya filthy animal."

He grins at me. "I finished it."

"I thought you would have googled the CliffsNotes," I say sheepishly.

"Nah. It was a great book, but you're still wrong."

I blow him a raspberry then, with a small smile, ask, "You want to come even though you have to grow a beard?"

Scratching his short, blunt nails—also sexy—over his bare jaw— sexier—he says, "Luckily for me, I don't have to do much for it to grow. Doesn't need watering but even if it did, I'd be there. Guaranteed."

He doesn't look at me, finishes off his shake instead, but if he did, he'd see how much that means to me.

My feelings for Liam have been messed up for years, but the urge to smack him and hug him is tipping evermore toward the hug side, and the craving to touch him is growing as well. Never mind the fact that he does and says shit that squeezes my heart with the ferocity of his cold-press machine.

He's just...

'Thirty-five hundred bucks on Japanese stationery' sweet.

'A bedroom in his swank apartment in colors of my choice in case we work late' sweet.

'I'll attend your graduation ceremony when getting out of the door is hard' sweet.

Actions speak louder than words and his confirm that we're reaching a turning point.

This is honestly the first time in my life that I've lost sleep over dating a guy.

But Liam isn't *just* a guy.

He's... everything.

And if I fuck this up by being me, how am I supposed to live in a world where the one person who makes me feel seen hates me?

LIAM'S JOURNAL

Gracie,

Watching you in that stationery store last week gave me a chubby.

Honestly, seeing your joy, feeding your addiction... it's the most innocent way I've ever gotten a hard-on in public.

Most women want jewels, clothes, shoes—not you, Gracie. You've always been unique.

I love that about you.

When I see you hauling that massive case around or trying to decide which color pen to use, it makes me smile.

Never change, Gracie. Never stop surprising me with how you view the world because it's a brighter place than the shit-hole I inhabit.

And I'm sorry about the other night.

I wanted to go.

You've no idea how grateful I was for the tickets to the Damien Rice show, but I just... couldn't.

You didn't have to stay home with me, so thank you. Even if you made me watch that Akira movie. AGAIN.

*Still, for you, I'll watch it a thousand times. :-) But...
please don't hold me to that.*
     Liam

CHAPTER 22
LIAM

I Wanna Be Yours - Joel Sunny, Arctic Monkeys

"'*STILL, for you, I'll watch it a thousand times. :-) But... please, don't hold me to that.*

Liam.'"

Mike tilts back in his lounger and pulls the tab on a can of pop as he finishes listening to me read the last entry in my journal, one that I wrote after Gracie left earlier. "You want to talk about the concert?"

"No."

I eye the Coke.

God, I'd kill for one right now.

Mike is my therapist.

Despite my move to the US when I requested we work outside of his office hours, he agreed to stick with me so long as he could talk to me in his La-Z-Boy at home.

I wasn't about to argue, not when opening up to him was impossible. I don't want to have to go through that again with someone new.

"How are you?"

Scraping a hand over my face as I contemplate the answer to his question, I eventually say, "I feel bad."

"Why?"

"For Gracie."

Mike scratches his jaw—I can hear his stubble rasping against his nails. The noise is worse than if he scratched them down a chalkboard. "You write about her a lot."

"The diary entries are addressed to her," I defend.

"Yeah, but you could write about anything and you don't. You always write about her. Plus, you consistently talk about her. Did you know that?"

"She's an active part of my life."

Mike hums. "I'm *your* shrink, not hers."

"I know that," I mumble.

"Why do you feel bad for her?"

"She's studying for her MBA."

"On top of being your full-time assistant?" His brows lift. "That's a lot of work. She must be very proud of herself."

"Yeah. I'm proud of her too. Her family isn't though."

Mike takes a sip of coke. "From what you've told me about your billet family, they're very kind, warm people."

"I think that's why I feel bad," I mutter instead of answering his question. "I guess I didn't realize how things were for her."

"In what way?"

"I know how close the Bukowskis are, but it's like Gracie's an outsider. I was talking to her about her graduation ceremony this morning—"

"That's not until May. Doesn't she have two sets of exams to pass first?"

"Yeah, but this is Gracie. I mean, she'll ace them."

"Your faith in her is cute."

"Fuck off, Mike."

He slurps his Coke. Noisily.

Jerk.

I narrow my eyes at him. "I probably paid for that Coke."

"You probably did," he agrees with a shit-eating smirk as he smacks his lips. "And it's so good.

"You want to talk about why you're struggling with your diet at the moment?"

I huff. "No."

He heaves a sigh. "So, why were you talking about Gracie and her graduation ceremony?"

"It just came up in conversation."

"You need to be taught how to flirt with a woman," he says with a snicker, "because you've clearly been relying on your status to reel the chicks in for too long."

I don't want to talk about the show and how pathetic I felt for not being able to attend and how terrible it was to waste her gift when Gracie saves every cent she has.

"*Anyway,* she was saying that she won't be inviting her parents which means she won't even tell them it's happening! Can you imagine?"

"Why won't she tell them?"

"She thinks they won't be interested."

"Would they be?"

"I—" Pinching the bridge of my nose, I admit, "I don't know for sure and that makes me think they wouldn't."

"So, what's the problem then? She's correctly assessed her situation and is making smart decisions that will protect her state of mind."

While I know he's right, the whole situation doesn't sit well with me.

I rub my bottom lip with my thumb. "I just assumed I'd be going to the ceremony but then I realized that wasn't a given."

"Your fame tends to overshadow everything else in the vicinity," Mike muses. "Maybe she—"

"No, she didn't think I'd make the time for her."

He's silent a moment, then he admits, "That *is* sad."

I clear my throat. "I offered to grow my beard to try to hide my identity."

Mike, who's heard crazier stories about the stunts I've pulled to stay under the public's radar, inquires, "Are you sure you're going to be able to cope with that?"

I wish that were a dumb question. "It's a beard."

"Yes, and the last time you had a beard was because you weren't allowed to shave, weren't allowed to wash, and were kept in unsanitary conditions... Does she know what you're going to be doing for her? Does she understand the sacrifice you're willing to make? Because, buddy, if she did, you'd have her hook, line, and sinker."

"I'm not going to tell her that I can't have a beard because it's a trigger, Mike. *Cibole*." I roll my eyes at the prospect.

Mike frowns. "I don't understand."

"What, my *Québécois*?" I mock. Then, when his frown deepens, I mumble, "What's to understand?"

"She's one of your oldest friends. You've trusted her to organize your whole life. From what I can tell, the only thing she doesn't have access to is your internet browser history. So, why can't she know *this*?"

I'm not sure why his question has me tapping my fingers against the kitchen counter where I set my laptop up earlier.

"I need a beer."

"You don't."

"I do." I release a breath. "Or white bread."

Mike snorts. "Get an apple."

God, I'd kill for a smoked meat sandwich from Schwartz in Montréal.

My jaw aches with how badly I grit my teeth.

"Hmm, this is new. I was aware of your struggles with food, but comfort eating? Have you gained any weight?"

"No. If anything, I've lost some. And stop humming," I grate out, rubbing a hand over my hair.

Mike arches a brow. "Why are you agitated?"

I can already feel the tension in my throat spreading wider, locking out the ability to answer him and making my temper surge.

"Liam, it's okay to be annoyed about the limitations you're experiencing in the aftermath of the kidnapping."

"It was three years ago," I snap. "I should be over this by now."

"You were tortured, Liam. For cash. Because of your fame. Because of your money. Because of your skills. And you still use these skills, and money, and fame to get by. Your lifestyle hasn't changed—that's why you're scared about your security. Hence the issues with that motorcycle club last year."

I can sense his disapproval at that. To be fair, I was lucky he didn't report me to the cops or something, if shrinks can even do that.

My fingers dig into my eyes as I mutter the one truth that I can get out, "I don't want her to think that I'm weak. I can't even go to a show. That ticket must have cost her a fortune and we had to stay in. What the hell can I offer her if I can't even leave the apartment unless it's for work?"

Maybe I'm the one with my head in the sand.

Maybe she doesn't want me.

Maybe she's been letting me down gently and I'm too bullheaded to see it.

"You're not weak. You're a survivor. If anything, what happened to you affirmed that." Mike falls silent for a moment, then he soothes, "Inhale through your nose. Hold one, two, three, and four. Then exhale. Long and steady. One, two, three, four. And again."

He breathes with me until I can sit up, until my jaw unclenches and I'm not digging my fingers into my eyes.

"I like her."

Mike cuts to the heart of the matter, "You're sexually attracted to her?"

Stiffly, I nod.

"Words."

"Yes," I bite off.

"That's the first time you've admitted that outside of a journal entry." He purses his lips. "You're wooing her. No man goes stationery shopping in his free time unless he's looking to get laid, never mind one who has your issues with public spaces, so what's the problem?"

"Kow would probably kill me," I murmur, my tone dispassionate.

"Kow would go to jail if he did."

"If Kow didn't, the others would."

"It's a legal requirement of all brothers to make that vow."

I snort. "In which province?"

"The world..." He studies me. "Not that you care. I can tell. You're—"

"'Wooing' her," I concur.

He smiles. "It's good that you're interested in her. You've been celibate since the abduction, haven't you?"

Looking away from him, I nod.

"That's what we call progress, Liam. Especially as she was important to you throughout the hostage situation, wasn't she?"

Again, I nod.

"She got you through it, no? And I'm going to need words, Liam. No more nods."

"Yes, she got me through it." I blow out another breath—a harsh one. "She's the only thing that—" I grunt, then I hear the door buzzer. "Wait a minute, Mike."

"It's not as if I charge by the hour," he shouts, but I ignore him as I head to the intercom. When I see her standing there, my brows lift. "Did you lose your key?"

Her jaw works.

Then...

Tabarnak.

She starts crying.

And I feel like my heart is going to explode.

I shift into panic mode. The only thing on my mind is getting to her, making sure she's safe, and bringing her back to me.

I hit the buzzer to let her in but I run out, barely remembering to take my keys with me, and head to the elevator before she can call it down.

On my way to her, my brain is more focused on the fact that she didn't appear hurt other than her tears, because if she *was* hurt...

Well, I'm related to the goddamn mafia.

I text my bodyguards.

> Me: Gracie was hurt. Do you know anything about it?

The doors open onto the lobby, and she's not surprised to see me standing in there because she immediately hurls herself at me.

That's when I notice a few things.

One: Her knee has a bad graze on it, one that's already bruising.

Two: She stole a hoodie from me at some point today because it's hanging to her knees. Even if it's torn and ripped now, she looks adorable.

Three: She doesn't have her purse. That purse is as big as a suitcase because of all the goddamn stationery she carries around. Everywhere. Which means the purse is gone. And the tears are...

Fuck.

The tears are for the stationery. I'd bet last season's championship ring that she's not crying about anything else, which means she's been mugged.

Some motherfucker dared target her.

"Who did this to you?" I demand, but I don't expect an answer as I hold her, cupping the back of her head to my chest. When she starts shivering in shock, I call out to the doorman, who's hovering in the lobby. "Call the cops, Quentin, please."

"They're already on their way, sir. I'll direct them to your apartment if you'd like to take Ms. Bukowski with you?" He wrings his hands. "Miss, please don't worry. I know someone in the NYPD and they'll get your stationery back for you."

Gracie, who didn't even cry when Bambi's mom died, sniffles and turns to him. "Do you think so, Quentin?"

"I do."

"T-T-Thank you for being s-s-so kind, Quentin."

"I appreciate it," I tell him before hustling her into the elevator. "I can buy you some more."

She peers at me then, her bottom lip wobbling. "We can't spend another thirty-five hundred on p-pens, Liam. That's f-fiscally i-irresponsible."

Fuck.

I'm going to have to do it.

I will.

I need to.

I'm only a goddamn man and no one can resist that much temptation.

Fuck waiting. Fuck patience.

She needs *me*.

I lower my mouth and press it to her trembling one.

The quiver stills.

A breath rushes out and drifts over mine.

Then gently, so fucking gently I'm not even sure it's happening, she kisses me back.

And the doors close.

Startled, she pulls away to stare at me.

My tone is low, throbbing with unrestrained and unfiltered need for her. "If you need thirty-five hundred dollars' worth of pens, you can have them. Okay?"

"Why is everything about thirty-five with you?" she mumbles, swiping the sleeve of my hoodie over her cheeks.

Ignoring her, I plead, "Don't cry, *mon p'tit chou*. Please."

Her eyelashes are little spikes from the tears gathering there. "Why not?"

"Because it kills something in me to see you cry. You were never made for tears, *minou*."

She swallows then wipes at her cheeks some more. The sleeve is gathered between her fingers, tucked to hold it in place. "This is embarrassing."

Whatever I expected her to say, it isn't that. "Why is it?"

"Because I was on the news for stopping some jackass with my fists, then I get mugged and fall apart?! God, Kow will never let me live this down."

"He doesn't have to know."

"You won't tell him?" she whispers.

As I hit the button for my floor, I assure her, "I won't."

If he ribbed her, I'd have to kill him and he *is* my best friend.

But he wouldn't. He'd be more likely to read her the riot act.

Still, her words are just further confirmation of the communication issues she has with her family.

At my promise, she bites her lip. "Thank you. F-For that, for the pens, for being nice."

As the doors open, I guide her into the apartment and toward the kitchen, ignoring her last words to ask, "What happened?"

Nice.

I'm not nice.

Dippin' Dots at the stadium are *nice*.

Unaware of my train of thought, she grumbles, "I can't believe he got away with my purse."

Though I'm irritated by her choice of adjective, that she's sounding more like her regular ornery self comes as a relief.

"There's more to life than a purse."

Like that kiss.

Which you haven't mentioned.

Fuck.

"That's because you're rich. I'm not. I had a lot of stuff in there," she snaps.

"Whatever you need replaced, I'll replace." I shrug. "Simple."

"For God's sake, Liam. Didn't anyone tell you never to diminish a woman's possessions? Sure, you can buy more, but each item in that bag probably holds a memory. That's impossible to replicate."

"Who the hell said that?" she demands, twisting around in the kitchen to see who's with us.

"Shit," I mutter, genuinely having forgotten that Mike was on a video call with me. "Gracie, meet Mike. Mike, this is Gracie."

Gracie peers at my computer. "You're the therapist."

"I have many other labels," Mike says serenely. "I don't just answer to the capitalist title that's been assigned to me, much as I was assigned a number at birth like I'm cattle instead of a human being."

"Mike, cut the spiel. Now isn't the time for it."

He harrumphs. "It's a pleasure to finally meet you, Gracie."

"It is?" she asks, her tone loaded with distrust as she glances at me, clearly surmising that she's been one of the topics of our conversations. "I hope you've only heard good things."

"Now *that* I can't say," is Mike's cheerful reply. "However, I can tell that you're distressed. What happened?"

"I was mugged. The bastard got away with my purse."

"I'm sorry to hear that. Are you all right?"

"Just a little shaken up."

The renewed cocktail of fear flooding my veins has me grabbing her and starting to check her over for cuts and bruises. "Aside from the knee, where are you hurting?"

"Knocked my elbow," she grouches but levers herself onto one of the stools at the breakfast bar. I say 'levers' because she's obviously hurt something else but isn't willing to say what.

And I don't just think it's her pride either.

"I'm going to get the first-aid kit. Mike, keep her company while I'm gone."

"It's your 1%er dime," he yells as I leave the kitchen and stride into the bathroom.

I listen to them talk but tune out the moment I lean into the vanity. My brain's a mess, and it has nothing to do with yesterday's hit to the head.

She was mugged.

And...

I kissed her. *She kissed me back.*

Yet... crickets.

Still, she was fucking mugged.

When I look into the mirror, deep in my eyes, I notice something that's been missing for too long though.

Life.

It might just be a spark now, but Gracie never does anything by halves. Soon, it'll be a forest fire if she doesn't put it out.

And she didn't earlier; *she kissed me back.*

If she really is ready for more...

I scrape a hand over my jaw as I come to a split-second decision— no more waiting, no more patience.

I need her.

In my life.

In my apartment.

In my bed.

I want her under me and over me.

I want to sleep with her.

I want to eat with her.

I want her in the stands. Not as my PA but as my girl.

I want her in my jersey. God, *Cibole*—naked.

Fuck, I just want *her.*

All of her.

Every short-assed, curvy inch of her.

So I need to win her. No more patience, no more long games. I'm good at winning and I need this victory. It's what I do for a goddamn living—

That's when my phone vibrates with an incoming message.

The bodyguard on duty today, Jonathan, has replied:

Jonathan: We have security footage of the incident. We'll forward it to the police in charge of the investigation.

Me: You need to put more bodyguards on her. How did your men miss this?!

Jonathan: We have bodyguards on her when you're together.

Me: WHAT?! Make that make sense.

Jonathan: You'll have to speak with the company about scheduling issues. You're our client, sir. Not Ms. Bukowski.

Me: Not anymore. Make it happen. She gets a 24-hr shadow from now on.

Jonathan: Fine, sir. The contract changes will be sent over tomorrow.

Me: Good.

I feel like throwing my cell at the wall. How the fuck did my security company misunderstand a direct email about her having a bodyguard?

That's when the buzzer sounds at the door.

What's with all the interruptions in today's life-changing moments?

Still, knowing her, she'll try to get it, so as I grab the first-aid kit, I call out, "Gracie, keep your ass on that stool if you don't want me to swat it later."

As her shocked gasp at my words echoes down the hall, a smile curves my lips despite my agitation.

Liam 1 - Gracie 0

CHAPTER 23
GRACIE

Boom Clap - Charli XCX

I GOT TAKEN down by a two-bit punk.

I cried like a girl.

I lost my pretty case with all the Japanese stationery in it.

I got kissed by Liam.

I was informed by said brave, brave, *brave* man that he'd spank me if I moved from the kitchen...

What else is the day going to bring?

Instead of the cops, is a glittery and bejeweled Sam Smith about to waltz in through the door?

Because hell if that wouldn't round things out nicely!

Unfortunately for me, I get a Sam, but it's a uniformed police officer—Samuel Brownhill—and not the singer.

As Officer Brownhill introduces himself and his partner, Adamson, to me, Liam works on cleaning the graze on my knee. It stings like a bitch, so I hiss a little when Brownhill, taking the lead, asks me to explain what happened.

After I manage to recall what went down in between more hisses,

Liam presses a kiss to the top of my bandage once he's done then stares up at me from his place on the floor.

He's kneeling.

At my feet.

For the second time this year.

I mean, I'm not a Dominatrix or anything, but my gawd. What, with the kiss and the threat of a spanking and now *this*? My amygdala can't handle any more. Seriously. It's going to fritz out soon if I'm not careful. It's supposed to be flight, fight, or freeze—not *melt* into a puddle of goo.

This is Liam goddamn Donnghal at my feet, kissing me and looking at me like I'm...

Fuck.

Like I'm everything.

That's when it hits—we *are* on the same page.

We're at the same chapter.

And we're in the same damn book.

Hallelujah.

When Adamson starts talking, his gnawing voice grates on me.

I need them gone.

Stat.

"I recognized my attacker." Not sure why, but now that I'm calmer and thinking about sex, my fight/flight/melt response has relaxed enough to remember details that were a blur before.

Brownhill frowns as he and his partner share a look. "Excuse me? I was asking about where the mugging took place?"

"Just at the end of the block."

"Where did you recognize the guy from?" Liam demands, his hand settling on my thigh.

Oh, fuck.

His fingers curl inward, right at the seam between my legs. He might as well have hockey gloves for hands they're that big, and he covers a lot of space on my not-so-long limb.

Focus, Gracie. Focus.

"He was with the jerk I got arrested—"

Brownhill, who's starting to look like he thinks this is out of his league, mutters, "Who did you get arrested?"

I waft a hand. "He deserved it."

"I mean, I assumed so. There's protocol—"

Liam ignores him, and he seems to be looming over me more than before. Hell, he's sucking up all the oxygen in here too. That glower, man, the intensity is thrilling. 'Ten seconds on the clock and a penalty just about to be called' thrilling.

That's when I realize he's speaking, "...there's CCTV footage of the day when that guy threw the kid into the street—"

"You're Kow Bukowski's sister? Oh my God! I knew I recognized your name but hell, Gracie Bukowski's not exactly unique." His interest in a routine mugging deepens.

Adamson joins in, "You beat the shit out of that guy when he tried to stop you from helping that kid. I recognized Kow's style. Did he teach you?"

Brownhill gasps. "And, wait. You're Donnghal. DONNGHAL. Oh, man. Just wait until we tell the guys at the precinct that we met the Leprechaun and Kow Bukowski's sister!"

As my lips purse in irritation, it's Liam who snaps, "She was just mugged, officers, so could you dial down the fangirling?"

Brownhill blushes. "Sorry, sir."

"Apologies," Adamson mumbles.

They're more professional after that, but only barely.

When the officers leave once Liam informs them his security will be in touch and he gives them the number he has for business calls, a cell he's said I can use from now on, that's the first time since the kiss that we're alone.

At least, that was what I thought.

"Does that happen a lot, Gracie?"

I jump at Mike's voice.

Twisting on the stool, I stare at the computer screen and find Mike's watching us with a massive bag of popcorn on his lap.

At least we're entertaining someone.

"All the time."

"That must be tiring."

I heave a sigh. "Very."

"Gracie had to leave her last job because they exploited her family's fame."

Mike's frown is reassuringly unimpressed by such behavior. "Some people will sell their souls for the media machine."

"True dat," I agree. "I worked there for a long time too. Thought they were my friends."

"It must have been hard coming face-to-face with them in the aftermath."

"I didn't. I resigned, effective immediately, and then Liam sent his driver to get my things."

"It's handy having a hockey player around, hmm?"

"Stop with the humming," Liam growls.

Absently, I pat his shoulder. "Think they'll catch him?"

"It's more than just a random mugging, isn't it?" Mike inserts. "You were targeted by what sounds to me like a gang."

Liam nods. "I agree. If they don't figure out what's happening, I will."

"Take a chill pill, Bruce Wayne. You're not a billionaire with a bat cave yet," I mutter, gingerly prodding my knee around the bandages he fastened there while Brownhill was hovering.

"I won't charge you for tonight's show, Liam. You're better than anything my wife would make me watch."

"Happy to be of service," Liam grumbles.

"If you need someone to talk to, Gracie, then Liam has my details."

"I'm the one who found you for him," I reply.

"So, you're to blame, hmm?"

My eyes widen and I glance at Liam, wanting to see how he feels about his shrink ribbing him, but he smiles at me too. "Mike's relaxed some since he agreed to speak with me outside of his office hours. I prefer this side of him for some reason."

"For a man whose life is regimented down to what you can and can't eat for breakfast, I think you enjoy the lack of structure in our sessions now." Mike's gaze is gentle as he directs at me: "Muggings can be traumatic events, Gracie. If you—"

"That bastard will be more traumatized than I am." I sniff. "When I said I whacked him with my purse—"

Liam snickers. "Oh, yeah, I forgot. You carry about eighteen pounds of crap in that thing."

"Exactly. I got him between the legs *and* managed to bite his ear. I think I did pretty well coming out of it with a graze or two."

"You Mike Tysoned him?" Liam sputters around a laugh. "Jesus, Gracie! Kow told me you used to get into trouble for biting in school but—"

Mike hums. A-goddamn-gain. "You were a biter?"

I frown at his tone. "I'm not paying for any armchair psychoanalysis, Mike, though I appreciate what you're doing with Liam."

"I'm sure I could add it to your benefits if you need it," is my hockey god's soft response.

I cast him a look, can see that he means every word, and have to hide a smile. "I'll think about it. You'll be the first to know if I have any issues after today," I assure him, leaving it to Liam to end the call.

Mostly, I'm pissed. About the mugging, about potentially being targeted by a gang, about losing my damn purse.

Today, however, could have gone down so much worse than it did.

My purse was snatched—my dignity alongside it.

The guy didn't have a knife and I wasn't dragged into some dark alley.

All in all, as muggings go, it wasn't that bad.

Tonight could have veered down so many different paths and none of those alternatives would end with Liam kissing me.

So, I'm going to take my blessings, count them tomorrow, and in the meantime...

"Did you mean to kiss me?"

CHAPTER 24
LIAM

35

I SHOULD HAVE KNOWN—IT'S Gracie. She's upfront. Ballsy. Strong. Even when she's literally been kicked down, she'll pop right back up again, fists in the air, dancing on her toes because that's how Fryd taught us to fight.

"Light on toes, kids, light on toes."

"Balls of your feet, Dad," Trent would correct, but Fryd would waft a hand and dismiss the correction.

My lips quirk at the memory even as I can see she's getting impatient by my lack of an answer.

"You think I make it a habit of accidentally kissing women? That's one way to get put into a database somewhere."

She sniffs. "You know what I mean."

I move, surging forward with a speed that makes her jolt when she sees how close I am to her.

The color on her cheeks is all mine. And that slight flare of her nostrils? *Green light.*

Slowly, I lower my head, giving her time to back away.

She doesn't.

Gracie stays right where she is, and I stay right where I am.

My mouth hovers over hers.

Her breath becomes mine and mine becomes hers.

"Liam?" she whispers.

"Gracie."

She swallows.

My finger traces the bob of her throat, and I enjoy the soft moan she releases at the tender touch.

"I-I... I want this but our friendship..."

Ah.

Now, I understand why she's been weird since Christmas.

Studying her, I take a moment to bask in her scent.

Roses today.

God, she drives me crazy without even trying.

There's a whole host of words I want to say, that I *need* to say, but my little brain is almost in total control...

Almost.

"This changes everything and nothing."

"What?"

"I mean, it changes everything because once I kiss you again, there's no going back. No hiding away. No embarrassment." I let the tip of my nose brush hers. "No wondering if I want this. If I'm going to use you for sex. No fear."

"O-Okay. Why nothing?" she whispers, clearly invested in my answer.

"Because no matter what—" *I'm never letting you go.* "—we'll still hang out, we'll always have spent a part of our childhoods growing up together, and we'll still be a team. No resigning, you got that?"

I don't know if she can see how imperative that is to me. I can't deal with *this*, any of this, the New York Stars' this, Greco this, my goddamn father this, PTSD *this*, without her.

And I won't.

My life is better with her in it and I won't stop until every part of her day is better too because I'm hers and she is fucking mine.

"Kissing you, having sex with you, being with you, will *not* change our trajectory," I rumble, watching her pupils flare in response.

"Trajectory?"

I'm not about to tell her that I've been driving us down this path for goddamn years. It's time I stop Gracie's mind from racing.

The good old-fashioned way.

Letting the tip of my tongue flutter to the corner of her lips, I trace a path to the other side.

The soft groan she utters will never leave my memory banks. It will remain there, locked away, until the day I die.

And then I get confirmation that Gracie's okay, that she's back to herself because her impatience gets the better of her. I also get confirmation that she wants this, *me*, as much as I want this, *her*, when her hands slide around my neck and she drags me into her, her chin arching up as she joins us together.

I can't be rough—after the day she's had, she needs gentle. But nothing about her kiss is gentle.

Before I even get to peck the corner of her mouth, hers is open and her tongue is ready to tangle with mine.

A groan of my own escapes me as her nails dig into the back of my neck, and that's when she slays me—her legs part on the stool and she drags me into her, crossing her calves over my ass.

Cupping her chin, I tip her head back so that I can lean forward, letting her feel more of me. Her nails start to rake down my spine, hands shifting and flowing over me in a way I've been waiting to experience again. That's a lifetime's fantasies and dreams all in one.

As she fights for control in true Gracie fashion, I smirk against her lips then retreat and bite the bottom one before I sink lower, lower, lower.

When I find her throat, she moans again and that moan lights me up inside. It's deeper than before. Needier.

She's needy—*for me*.

As I nip her there, suckling the skin to leave a mark behind, she whimpers, her claws dragging at my tee before she scrabbles it higher so they can dig into me.

The scraping sensation has me shuddering in response.

"Fuck, Gracie, fuck."

As I nip the join between shoulder and neck, she shivers and, on an exhalation, admits, "Liam, God, that feels so good."

My name on her lips is what feels good. Better than her hands on me or her nails clawing at me, and that's so much better than epic, it ties with lifting the Cup.

My hand settles on her knee and brushes the bandage I wrapped there.

It's an immediate red flag that has me retreating and dropping a peck on her mouth. "You with me, Gracie?"

Dazed, she blinks. "Huh?"

Gently, I smooth my finger along the outer edge of the bandage. "Are you okay with this?"

Her pupils are blown now but she whispers, "Orgasms are good for pain relief, right?"

That kills my erection.

I cup her cheeks. "Where does it hurt, *bébé*?"

Her nostrils flare and her arms slide around my waist, dragging me closer to her with surprising strength. Not that I *should* be surprised when she's a pocket rocket.

As her thighs clutch at my hips, drawing me nearer, she mumbles, "Just my hands. My head. But don't stop."

I nuzzle my nose down the side of her jaw, wanting to take this further, not wanting to lose the progress we've made today, but my hard-on disappeared the moment she mentioned she was in pain.

With a final kiss to her temple, I snatch ahold of her fingers and gently drop more kisses along the curve of her wrist, murmuring, "Shall we test that theory, hmm? That orgasms are better than ibuprofen?"

She gulps but nods. Her breathing comes hard and fast as my hand moves to her waist, clutching there for a second, giving her a gentle squeeze, before it slides over her front.

This is Gracie.

Mon Dieu.

I've wanted her for so long that I don't even know when it started. Sure, I realized what I was feeling when I was in that goddamn hellhole, but I've wanted her for longer than that. Maybe... always.

How I missed her when she moved to Vancouver...

How I looked for her at Thanksgiving dinner when she didn't attend...

How I tried to meet up with her whenever I was in New York...

Those are instances that have been happening since she dyed Kow and me green.

As I slide my fingers over the front of her pants, I rumble, "Are you wet for me, Gracie?"

"O-Oh, God." She hiccups, eyes fluttering to half-mast.

I nip her bottom lip. "Is that a yes?"

Her nod is shaky. "I-It is." She reaches between us. I can feel her working at the buttons on her fly.

Curious, I let her take control, and I'm glad I do because when she unfastens her pants, she grabs my hand and tucks it down the front.

When my fingertips meet the crotch of her panties, they encounter slickness.

I groan at the proof that she wants me, *me, ostie, moi*, then I stroke her softness, murmuring, "Is all this mine, Gracie?"

Her hips rock forward. "This is so wrong, Liam."

My chuckle is dark. "Could something that feels this good ever be wrong?"

"I've—" She breaks off, but her arms tighten around my waist.

"You've...?" I ask, kissing her a second before I pluck her panties aside and slide my fingers along her bare slit. As she judders, her thighs squeeze me harder.

"I-I've?" she answers with a question.

"Concentrate, Gracie," I chide, nipping her bottom lip again. "Don't you like this?" I rub her clit, enjoying the keening sound that escapes her.

God, that's music to my ears.

The way it hitches in the middle, breaks as if it's too much, as if she can't cope with it—I need more of this in my life.

Her nails are back to digging into my spine. "L-Liam," she mewls, spreading her legs but only so she can maneuver me with her heels, hauling me tighter into her.

"What, *bébé?*"

She shudders. "Fuck."

Suddenly, it clicks.

What's that shit all the girls like on BookTok?

Praise?

I've never done this before, but I've watched the videos, seen how hot it gets them, so I give it my best shot: "You're so wet for me, Gracie. Such a good fucking girl."

She jerks against me. "L-Liam?"

"So fucking good," I rasp, encouraged by her response. "Creaming those panties for me. Do you like this?" When I circle her slit, a sob soughs from her. "Give me the words, *minou*."

"T-That f-feels s-so n-nice."

There's that goddamn word again.

I tut. "*Nice*? Then I need to do better."

I thrust my finger into her tight channel, enjoying the way it clutches at me, then I retreat, enjoying her whimper even more, and I find her clit again. The broken mewl she releases has my cock leaking pre-cum.

Erection reinstated.

Tabarnak, the sounds she makes.

"Still nice, *ma belle*?"

"So good. Don't stop. Please," she begs. "I need your dick. How the fuck is it not in me yet?"

That's what I needed to hear.

Pulling back so I'm looking into her eyes, I rest my forehead atop hers and I stop messing around.

Needing to give her pleasure, I whisper, "When you ask so nicely, *ma chérie*, how could I refuse? But you need more than that tonight."

That's when I slide my fingers over her clit, rubbing fast and hard, moving in circles, trying to ascertain her preference while encouraging her to fall off the cliff I want to build for her.

When she starts to pant, the susurrations shimmy over my lips, but it's how she clutches at me and clings that's poetry in motion.

When she comes, the sob she releases is the most beautiful sound I've ever heard.

Her back arches as she cries, "L-Liam, don't stop. Fuck, you can't. Please. PLEASE."

So I don't.

I listen, giving her what she wants because, ultimately, that's exactly what *I* want.

Her.

How ever she'll let me have her.

Whenever she'll let me in her.

Whatever she'll let me do to her.

When one of her hands circles my wrist, the nails digging in, I watch as she wriggles, angling her hips back. Letting her maneuver me, I quickly pick up on what she wants.

I circle her slit with three fingers, getting them wet before I thrust one in, following it with the second and third after she relaxes.

"You take me so beautifully," I rumble. "So fucking beautifully. Even better than I expected."

Instantly, her cunt clamps around me.

"God, how have I gone so long without experiencing this? You fill me so perfectly, Liam. I need you. I need to come around you. I want you to fill me with your cum. Fuck, I need that so much," she cries.

My dick aches with how badly I want inside her, but this is about Gracie. Not me. And definitely not my dick.

Still, I get my confirmation that whatever dirty talk I throw her way, she's more than capable of hurling right back at me.

Game on, Gracie.

With my thumb, I rub her clit, enjoying her whimpers and mewls, soft sounds that I've never heard coming from my abrasively delicious Gracie before.

When she presses her mouth to mine, diving into a kiss that peters to a halt as she climaxes, I grin in satisfaction, pressing against her G-spot so that she can eke out every inch of pleasure.

"Liam, oh, God. Please, don't— I need. Too good. Fuck. Yes. YES. Liam—"

Her heels dig into my ass, hips rocking and thrusting with wild abandon until she starts to come down, her tongue toying with mine gently, no longer feasting as she rides the high *I* gave her.

For endless moments, there's silence between us, just the quietness of our kiss. A kiss that doesn't stop, that we feed and nurture, cultivating with the connection of our lips and tongue and teeth, and it's heaven. Pure fucking heaven.

Everything I wanted yet somehow so much more.

We part, but only to leave tender, nipping kisses on each other's mouths.

"'Better than you expected?'"

The mumbled question has me rocking my forehead against hers as I realize she picked up on something I said earlier. "Yeah."

Her gulp is audible. "You've been thinking about this?"

"For years."

There's no point in bullshitting her here. Now that I've had a taste of her again, that's it. I'm done and I won't stop until I'm the only one who ever hears those soft sounds of release from her.

They're mine.

They belong to me.

"Since the kidnapping?"

I'm not sure why that has her tensing but it does.

Easily, I hitch a shoulder. "Missed you since you left Kow and me behind."

"Behind," she mutters with a snort. "Yeah, because your star stopped soaring after I moved away."

"I didn't realize how you grounded me until it was too late."

"Is that a bad thing?" she rasps, squirming as I pull my fingers from her, letting them drift to my mouth.

Watching her watch me slurp her cum off the digits, I murmur, "Not a bad thing at all. You know that. *Fuck, you taste good.*" She jerks as I carry on, "The kidnapping made me realize how long it had been since I'd seen you. It's easy to take people for granted in this life, and it put my priorities straight."

She studies me, her gaze locked on my hand as I move her panties back into place. "You're hard."

The shift in subject has me smirking but I just agree, "Very."

Her lip is sucked between her teeth. "You don't want to do something about it?"

"Not when you've just been mugged. Did the orgasm work?"

"Work?" She blinks. "In what way?"

"You said orgasms were pain relief."

Her grin is dopey. "Yeah, I did say that, didn't I?"

"Well?"

"Better than ibuprofen, not as good as morphine."

"That'd be an interesting stay in the hospital if it *was* as good as morphine."

Her snicker makes my heart do some interesting shit in my chest. "Damn straight." Her hand settles on my tee, fingers pinching at the fabric and pulling it taut to my torso. "Liam?"

"Uh-huh."

"We—"

"—are both adults?"

"We are."

"*Consenting* adults."

A sigh whispers from her lips and I just have to kiss her.

"Yeah," she breathes, her hand sliding over my shoulder now so she can hook it around my neck.

I don't think I'm being 'forward' by moving into her. "So?"

She stares me straight in the eye. "They're going to go crazy."

Knowing how to lay this to rest, I muse, "Since when do you give a damn about what your brothers have to say?"

Her mouth rounds into the most perfect 'O' I've ever seen in my life, then she jerks back, all fire and brimstone, to snarl, "It's none of their business."

"Agreed."

"They can go fuck themselves and their opinions!" she bursts, tone irate as if Kow has already condemned us for hooking up.

"They sure can," I say lightly, letting my thumb trace the line of her jaw.

"And if they have a problem, then we can duke it out!"

I hide a grin. "That's not fair."

She nods. "It's good that you know my right hook is better than theirs."

Happiness settles in my chest like the most delicious of weights. "So, we're doing this?"

Gracie stares straight into my eyes. "If we are, there are rules."

Amused, I tug her into a deeper hug. "I'd expect no less."

"If any puck bunny comes onto you, then I'm within my rights to smack the shit out of them."

"So long as it doesn't end up with you getting arrested, sure. But if you haven't noticed by now, I stopped giving a damn about puck bunnies a long while ago."

"I noticed," she concurs. "Kow asked me when was the last time you got laid."

"He wanted to know? Fuck, he's an oversharer." I groan.

"When was it?" she mutters, her cheeks tinging pink.

"For educational purposes?"

"Just so I know if Kow asks me again," she reasons.

Because she was my last 'hook-up,' I white-lie my way out of this: "Before the kidnapping."

Her eyes go big and round. "You're kidding me."

"Nah. My priorities changed, remember?" I could play it cool but instead, I throw myself into this wholeheartedly: "I stopped wanting the chicks who don't matter and realized the only woman I want is the one I've known for over a decade."

Her throat bobs as she squeaks, "Me?"

"Yeah, you," I agree, laughing at her surprise.

A breath gusts from her. "Wow."

"I have rules too."

"Technically, I only told you one of mine," she grumbles.

"If this doesn't work out, I'm still holding you to our agreement."

"Which agreement?" she demands, confused.

"The agreement we struck on the night of Amelia's wedding."

"Huh?"

I tap her nose. "Not my problem that you don't remember what you agreed to. Best get to thinking."

"That was years ago!"

"Sounds like a 'you' problem."

Her eyes narrow at me. "I'm not going to announce it to the world but I won't keep you a secret."

"Good," I counter, knowing she's taking back control of the conversation by returning to her rules. "I don't want you to."

"If Kow asks, I'll tell him."

"He won't have to ask. *I'll* tell him."

"You will? Huh. I didn't think—"

"*I've* been thinking about this for years," I say calmly. "It'll take some time for you to catch up."

Though she gnaws on her lip again, her nod is slow in coming. "Me and you, huh?"

I smile. "You and me."

CHAPTER 25
GRACIE

I DECIDE to spend the night at Liam's.

In his spare room.

Staring at the ceiling.

Wondering what the hell is wrong with me.

"Why didn't you go into his bedroom?" I mutter.

When I'd mentioned that I was tired, he'd told me to go to bed while he did his final workout of the day, and muscle memory had me heading in here.

Not his.

In my defense, I was thinking about Amelia's wedding.

What did I agree to?

All I remember is getting drunk on tequila—ever since just the smell makes me gag.

Still, it's Amelia's fault that I came into this room and it's her damn fault that I heard him go for a shower ten minutes ago and I wasn't there to see it.

He's under the spray.

Naked.

Liam fucking Donnghal is naked and, unlike on Christmas Day, I'm allowed to touch him.

I could go in there now.

I could see those abs up close and personal.

And his thighs.

Hockey players have the biggest thighs. The type of thighs that need tailoring and that standard pants don't fit.

Can you imagine how beautiful those muscular thighs are?

And I could be looking at them.

But I'm not.

Because...

"Jesus Christ, you're a moron," I grouse, rolling onto my side as I gather the comforter into a ball so I can hug it seeing as I was stupid and can't hug *him*.

Which I want to.

Just being in this room is a reminder of how slow on the uptake I am when it comes to Liam.

Either that or it took being mugged and sitting in a stinky alley for a half hour until my knee stopped throbbing long enough to let me stagger back to his building to draw the wool away from my eyes...

I could have died tonight.

Been raped.

It might have been my end.

Instead, I'm at the beginning of something beautiful.

This bedroom is decorated in colors that *I* chose because he designated it as my space when I helped him move in.

That means I have a change of clothes here, a desk where I work, and a computer he bought me too.

I have a bunch of flowers on the nightstand that he has a florist replenish every couple days.

There's always ice cream in the freezer even though he can't eat it.

And every time he leaves the state, he brings me back a Starbucks mug.

Manga comics sit on the coffee table in the living room; new copies appear every month.

Never mind the thirty-five hundred on unnecessary Japanese stationery.

I have a feeling that he's been *courting* me for a while and I was too afraid to see it.

Talk about being a slowpoke.

Brothers don't do that kind of stuff for their sisters. I've got three of them and none of them even know that I'm addicted to stationery, never mind which textbook is driving me crazy. They sure as hell don't offer to make up a pop quiz for me.

Liam did, though.

Pressing my face into the comforter, I hide from my idiocy.

Idiocy that would have made things a lot simpler for us both had I clued in a while ago.

How long have I wanted him?

Too long, that's how fucking long. Longer than long. Since Amelia's wedding long. (Irony.) Maybe even longer than *that*.

How many times, when I've stayed here, did I wish I had the right to enter his bedroom when he has a nightmare?

Too many times, that's how fucking many.

How often have I watched him on the ice and admired his moves? Wishing I could leap on him when he got out of the stadium and fuck all that power in the back of his SUV?

Too often, that's how fucking often.

Then a thought occurs to me.

Thirty-five.

Thirty-five manga comics.

And *thirty-five* flowers when he buys me a bunch of them.

Thirty-five hundred (and twenty-six cents) on the stationery.

His number.

My pendant.

"What the fuck is with 35—"

A knock sounds at my bedroom door.

I jackknife in the bed. "Liam?"

"Who else would it be?"

Grinning, tension abating, I answer, "I'm not sure. With the luck I'm having today, a home invader."

He snorts. "Well, opportunity knocks because it's me."

"Bigheaded much," I call back, but I scamper off the mattress with an eagerness I'm not ashamed of, ignoring my knee which is a touch sore.

The sap in me lurrrrrved when he pressed a kiss to the bandage earlier, never mind my other *boo-boos*—that deserves a special shout-out.

Pulling the door open, I stare at him. Really stare. Because he's half-naked with a towel wrapped around his hips and I'm *allowed* to look this time.

Jesus on a cracker.

No, *Mary* on a cracker because she'd dig what I'm looking at more than Jesus would.

Unable to stop myself, I whistle.

He snickers. "Like what you see?"

"Uh, *yeah.*"

"If you're allowed to objectify me—"

"You can objectify me too," I concur immediately, waving a hand over my form. "Knock yourself out."

His laughter hits a part of me that's not as good as the G-spot but almost. He's been so different since the kidnapping that these moments aren't exactly few and far between but they're more precious.

The realization that his happiness means as much to me, if not more, than my own is earth-shattering.

Not that he knows. He just groans. "Did you buy those shorts to torture me?"

I blink at him. "These ones?" They're cutoffs. Ancient. "Nah. They're from high school. They're comfortable as hell. I only wear them to bed now." Seeing as they're threadbare in some places.

"I thought I recognized them. Fuck." He grabs my shoulders and forcibly turns me around. "*Mon Dieu.*"

The sound is guttural.

I love it.

I love that I made him make that noise.

I love that I brought out the *Québécois* in him.

Still, I have to complain, "Hey, I can't ogle you from this side."

"You can ogle me all you want in my bedroom." His hands tighten on my shoulders. "No funny business. You're still reeling from what happened today. Just to sleep."

"And to ogle," I remind him, smiling a little. Twisting to look at him, I drawl, "How didn't I know you were a gentleman? And how did that happen when you're best friends with Kow?"

"He didn't rub off on me."

"Thank God for that."

He groans at my smirk. "Ugh. I know too much about him to go anywhere near him without disinfectant."

Laughing, I duck out of his hold and turn around. "That invitation still open?"

"Sure is."

Nodding, I grab his hand and tug him out of the bedroom and lead him down the hall.

"I guess I thought you'd have gone into my room anyway," he mutters, tone sheepish.

"I kind of meant to."

"Kind of?"

"I somehow ended up walking into mine though I shouldn't have entered yours without your permission anyway."

"You have free rein over my apartment. You could have gone in there *before* this afternoon, but if you need the invitation, here it is. Go in my bedroom whenever you want."

"As easy as that?"

"Nothing about you is easy, Gracie," he teases.

Though I huff, I grin at nothing—he knows me too well.

We head into his room, which is three times the size of mine, more of a suite than anything else. I peruse the space that I helped decorate and murmur, "You sure about this?"

"Nervous, Gracie?"

I squint at him. "No."

"Then why ask?"

"I don't know." I sigh. "This is just... Your bed is big."

"I'm a big guy."

I stare at his feet. "Is it true what they say about big guys with big feet?"

"What? That we have big shoes?"

I shove him in his side. "I was talking about socks actually."

"'Course you were." He hooks his arm around my shoulder. "You can go back to your bedroom if you want."

'Your bedroom.' Not the spare room. Not your office.

I want to believe that an evolution in our relationship won't wreck our friendship, but as much as I know that's wishful thinking, those words, along with his earlier vow that nothing between us will change, proves that he *has* been courting me.

He's done a damn fine job of it too. I definitely consider myself thoroughly courted and nerves aside, I'm ready to yank off my big-girl panties and for phase two to commence.

Letting go of his hand and embracing *carpe diem*, I toss myself onto his bed and immediately regret it when the dull ache in my head and the worse one in my knee throb.

No way am I about to tell him that, though. Or about how my wrist is hurting. He'll be chivalrous and that's the last thing I need tonight.

As the comforter explodes around me in a puffy cloud of feathers, I change tack: "What happened at Amelia's wedding?"

"You drank too much tequila," he replies, but his voice is muffled.

"Can't touch the stuff anymore," I grumble, leaning back on my elbows and seeking him out.

Ultimately, I find him with his head in one of the closets which is when he lets the towel around his waist drop.

Fuck.

Liam's ass.

My God.

I've seen it in shorts.

Boxer briefs.

But naked?

I wolf-whistle.

It'd be a crime not to.

He pops his head out so that he can grin at me, but he keeps it mostly R-rated, not X, by keeping the goods aimed at the closet. When he retreats, I get another shot of his ass as he bends down to put a pair of boxer briefs on.

"You did that on purpose," I grumble, sitting higher on my hands as I go hunting for a glimpse of his dick that gossip says is *gargantuan*. It certainly felt big earlier. "You could have gotten dressed before you came to my room."

"And miss the opportunity to tease you?" he chides, turning back to face me now that he's decently covered. "It's not the first time you've seen me like this. That was after that shit with Condon..."

My cheeks blossom with heat. "I mean, you were naked."

"I had a towel around my waist."

"With nothing on underneath it."

"So did a bunch of other players."

I scoff and, because I'm not thinking straight, speak without caution. "Why would I be interested in what they're packing?"

Triumph flares in his eyes and that, combined with how dumb I feel for letting those words slip, has me tensing up.

Like he knows, he strides toward the bed, and I watch him watch me. Watch as he climbs onto the mattress. Watch as he crawls over to the other half then rolls onto his side so we can stare at each other.

Fuck, he's gorgeous.

"What are you thinking?" he asks, tucking a stray strand of hair behind my ear. "Nothing good if that shadow in your eyes is any indication."

"You make it sound like I have cataracts," I grouch.

"Gracie!"

"Maybe I should book an appointment with the optometrist..."

His hand slides behind my nape and he takes the weight of my skull so there's no hiding when he urges me to look at him. "Gracie, what's got you all nervous?"

Nothing until I blurted out something that could push him away— guys don't like needy girls.

But because I have faith in him, and because he's staring at me with those eyes I want to drown in, I tell him the truth: "I don't want to lose you."

I'm a solitary person who's yanked herself out of the familial fold because I'm self-aware enough to know that their toxicity isn't good for me. It's only since he moved to New York that I've realized I don't want to be alone anymore.

I want to be with him.

When he shakes his head, my heart stutters, then he answers, "You'll never lose me. Ever. That's not going to happen. Anyway, I'm not the one who's the problem here."

Even as relief from his assurance settles in my soul—*his cockiness comes in good for something*—that last statement has my brows lifting. "Huh?"

"I've wanted you for years, Gracie. Which part of that aren't you understanding? *You're* the one who could change their mind here."

I don't know why that has me shuffling closer but it does.

Not stopping until our fronts are melded together, I mutter, "You know at Amelia's wedding?"

He rolls his eyes. "You'll have to remember what happened on your own—"

"I *know*. I'm talking about something else."

Liam chuckles but it's better than usual because his minty breath whispers over my face. It's an intimacy I've never experienced with him before and I like it.

A lot.

"What are you talking about, then?"

"After karaoke, I wanted to kiss you," I admit in a rush.

"You should have. It'd have made what happened a helluva lot more interesting."

Scowling, I shove his shoulder. "Tell me!"

There's a twinkle in his eyes that I don't trust. "Nah. It'll be fun watching you try to figure out what you agreed to."

Mouth gaping, I repeat, "What *I* agreed to? Not you too?"

He smiles. Slowly. Smugly. *Jerk.* "Now, I have to get some sleep so please stop disturbing the talent."

Before I can even huff about damn athletes being pussy teases, he twists me onto my side and tucks me into him.

Sometimes, it sucks being short, but now is not one of those times.

As Liam uses me like I'm a teddy bear, I don't even mock him for calling himself the 'talent.'

Instead, I let him draw the comforter from his side of the bed and wrap us up in it like we're the stuffing in a burrito.

It's only by chance that I see the clear stand housing the brass compass I bought him for Christmas a couple years ago.

He has it tipped forward so you can see where the compass points while also exposing the interior that I'd paid to have engraved with a quote from Winston Churchill, of all people, that I thought might resonate with him:

"Success is not final; failure is not fatal: it is the courage to continue that counts."

In the aftermath of everything that went down, it had seemed particularly apt.

As I stare at the old gift that he's placed on his nightstand, that he keeps *close*, Liam presses a kiss to my temple.

It feels... nice.

Warm and tender and sweet—things I couldn't have expected but that I love nonetheless. That, in all honesty, I need more than I do an orgasm tonight.

Something the aches in my body agree with.

Hand smoothing over his forearm, I study the compass until my eyes start to close as I realize I'm a million times more comfortable than I've ever been in my life.

Still, sweet or not, I can't let him have the final word.

"You're the talent because you got me off today," I mumble sleepily. "Not because you're a hockey star."

He kisses my temple again. "Wouldn't have it any other way, Gracie."

With a hum, I nestle into him and, almost immediately, fall asleep.

When I dream, maybe it shouldn't come as a surprise that it's of a compass. One that always swings a certain way, to a certain man, who might very well have his own gravitational field.

CHAPTER 26
LIAM

35

MORNING WOOD HAS NEVER FELT SO good.

Knowing *she's* there, that it's Gracie, that her ass is the one cushioning my dick makes waking up a thousand times better.

Until I remember the nightmare.

"*Tabarnak*," I grumble.

"Good morning to you too."

"You're awake?"

"Yup." She yawns. "Have been for about forty minutes."

"Did you sleep okay? You weren't in any pain?"

"My knee's stiff but it's fine," she says as she wiggles it. "My headache's gone, too, and my wrist doesn't hurt either. That fucker's probably suffering more than I am."

Hoping that's true, I ask, "Your wrist? You never said—"

"It was just a little stiff from smacking that ass."

I snort. "Why didn't you try to get out of bed?"

"Because you're my boss so if you're still sleeping then I can get away with dozing."

She stretches and, *Cibole*, that feels good. When her butt wiggles against my morning wood, she doesn't comment on it, just settles into me again.

"You have classes today," I point out, which has her turning so she can see me better.

"And? You have a meeting with Kara Kingsley and Andrews. We both have burdens to bear," she mocks before her expression turns serious. "She doesn't come onto you, does she?"

"Kara? Nah. She's a nightmare though."

"Good publicists are," is her pious retort, but she relaxes at my words. "You tell me if she does?"

"You going to get into a catfight?"

"You'd like that, wouldn't you?"

I hitch a shoulder. "Anything to see that right hook of yours in action."

Though she snickers, her hand comes up to cup my chin. "Bad night, hmm?"

"Good night," I counter.

"Didn't sound like it." She shivers, and just when I'm about to be more embarrassed than I was, she mutters, "I'm glad I was here. I hate hearing the aftermath and not being able to do anything to help ease what you're going through."

"Did I hurt you?" I ask, concern oozing through the words as I try to avoid the abject humiliation of waking her up that way.

Having never actually shared a bed with someone when I've had a nightmare, though, that I might have hurt her is a legitimate concern.

"Nah. You almost squeezed me to death but I can deal with that. Comes with the territory of being pocket-sized." Her fingers trail over my jaw. "You want to talk about it?"

My lips twist. "I'd prefer to talk about Kow and chlamydia."

"Gross."

"Exactly."

Though she sighs, I can see acceptance in her gaze, but I *feel* it too, which is so much better, when she presses her lips to mine.

The kiss is soft. Gentle. Close-mouthed. But it's also the fourth-best kiss I've ever had, with Amelia's wedding coming in first, yesterday in the elevator coming in second, and Christmas in third.

Although, yesterday in the kitchen needs to fit into that ranking somewhere too…

Her tongue rubs over the seam of my lips and I immediately part them to let her in.

One hand drifts to her ass as I tuck her tighter into me, but she's a step ahead—she scissors her leg to the side so that I can slide mine between hers.

"Fuck," I groan as that brings her thigh into contact with my dick.

Her guttural moan sends jolts of pleasure down my nerve endings as she starts to rock her hips. The seam at her crotch scrapes my skin as she grinds into me. My hands dig into her ass, holding her firm, drawing her deeper into my embrace. I love how she isn't afraid to take what she wants and how perfectly she fits me.

"God, Liam," she mewls as she pushes her forehead onto mine. "You know when I-I came back that night—"

It's a long shot but…

"The night you cut your knee? After we beat Pittsburgh?" I mumble as I nuzzle into her throat, sucking on the sinew there, letting my tongue palpate the sensitive skin until she's shuddering in my arms.

"You were jacking off in the shower—"

"I never did find out what you'd forgotten. Your vibrator…?"

"I left it charging," she keens as I slide my hand beneath her shorts to cup her butt.

"The thought of you using a vibrator when you could have used my dick instead makes me want to spank you," I growl.

She mewls in response but asks, "You were, weren't you? Jacking off, I-I mean."

As my fingers dig into the soft flesh there, I rasp, "You'd drunk that maple chaser for me, and small drops of creamer gathered at the corner of your mouth." Because I can, I stroke my tongue exactly where they'd been. "It looked like cum. All I could think about after that was picturing you swallowing mine." I rub my nose against hers. "Are you a good girl, Gracie?"

A soft snort escapes her even as it turns into a moan when I slide my hand over her butt cheeks and find her slit from behind. At first, I press the seam of her cutoffs inward, then I burrow beneath it, needing to touch her slick.

"Y-Yes," she cries as I thrust the tip of one finger into her. "Oh, Liam, that feels so good. So much better than when I do it. Deeper, please. Deeper—"

Cibole, I love how vocal she is.

Before I can tell her that, though, she reaches between us and starts to shape me through my sweatpants.

It's been goddamn *years* since anyone—

"Oh, fuck, Liam. I need you in me," she cries as she fumbles with the waistband. It's hard going because we're pressed tightly together, but we make it work. "*Now.* I'm going to—" She releases a satisfying hiss when she draws me out. "—Jesus, Liam. Where the hell do you put this? How do you walk?"

My amusement fades the second my cock is in her fist, it's my turn to hiss.

And to think of Bradley and plays and how much I want to beat the fuck out of Greco—anything but being a two-pump chump in her hand.

Pre-cum leaks from the tip as she starts to jack me off while I tease her slit and she grinds into me, putting pressure on the top of her sex, where she needs it most.

"I'd have taken it one step further that night. I wanted you to stay," I admit before I thrust my tongue between her lips.

As I fuck her there, she groans as she cedes to my ferocity. I feast on her like the starving man that I am all while she jacks me off, hard and fast, stroking me how I need to be stroked, her thumb rubbing over the sensitive glans until I'm bucking in her hold.

I freeze as I start to come, seed pelting her stomach and thighs as I finally get off after years in the goddamn cold in the hand of the woman I've been waiting for.

"There. *There.* Oh, my God. Liam, you... *Yes.* Right. I'm going to— Yeah. Oh, fuck—"

When she lets loose a cry of her own, jerking against me in response, it feels too perfect as we slump together, tumbling into a deeper embrace as she presses her forehead into my shoulder and I prop my chin on the crown of her head.

For endless moments, we're silent as our hearts stop racing, as our lungs return to normal, as the pleasure abates, leaving shadowy trails behind that are a promise for more. For later. For the next occasion when we can do this.

"We wasted so much time."

I smile, knowing she can't see me because we're ahead of schedule...

Rubbing my hand over her back, I appease, "We have a lot to make up for."

"We really do," she mumbles around a yawn, which is when her alarm starts blaring.

I nearly get kneed in the balls as she shrieks and scrambles off the bed, leaving me watching her as she races around like a mad woman in her haste to get ready for class.

Still, I grin as I watch the chaos, loving that I get to see her like this while my cum dries on her skin.

Today, I have to deal with my publicist and agent, she has to go to school, some heads are going to roll with my security firm, and Gracie's about to find herself with a shadow—whether she likes it or not.

For all that, as I watch her wreak havoc on my bedroom, shit finally feels like it's working out.

Thank fuck.

Liam: Hey, we need to talk.

Kow: Busy ATM. Will call you later.

Liam: Fine. It's important so don't forget.

Kow: *thumbs up*

CHAPTER 27
GRACIE

ON AN EXHALE as I leave the elevator, I whisper to myself, "Don't be ridiculous."

No one is waiting for me outside.

No one is going to leap on me.

No one is targeting me.

Doesn't stop me from tucking my tote bag from Trader Joe's closer to my side. It's a sucky bookbag replacement that'll have to suffice until I have time to order one online. It contains a card wallet and phone, both borrowed from Liam, inside it.

"You got this, Gracie Bukowski."

"Talking to yourself is the first sign of madness."

The voice is unexpected because in all the times I've come and gone in this lobby, I've literally only ever seen the doormen.

My head whips around to find the owner of that voice and I discover a woman sitting on one of the swanky armchairs that are usually empty. She's dressed in Chanel, her makeup is pristine, and she's so perfectly perfect that it's nauseating. Well, aside from the fact she has a baby attached to her boob.

I'd never have imagined that a woman like this would breastfeed, especially not in public, which I know is so judgmental but, sue me, it's my mind and I keep my thoughts to myself.

"Do I know you?" I ask warily, mostly because she's looking straight at me and hasn't looked away since.

"My name's Jennifer Valentini."

A whisper of unease forms in my heart and starts to coalesce as the baby gurgles. That's when I see another snoozing happily in her stroller.

Two kids.

God, this is a *Jerry Springer* show in the making.

Gulping down my anxiety, recognizing how badly I want things with Liam to work out, I rasp, "If you have a paternity claim, you can serve the man yourself."

Okay, that's even bitchier.

If Liam *did* father two children, and if the bastard *did* lie to me about not having sex for three years when both kids are under four, I'll castrate him and help her sue him for every cent of alimony she's owed.

Jennifer Valentini lets loose a laugh. "Even in the South, that'd be illegal."

I frown. "Excuse me? Look, I don't have time for this. I need to get to class."

"Class?" She tilts her head to the side, that perfect face and the perfect makeup not even cracking with her confusion. "I thought you were Liam's PA."

"EA," I correct with a sniff, giving myself the promotion in name only without asking him. Girlfriend privileges (also a promotion) aren't nepotistic when faced with a potential ex. "And though it's none of your business, I'm studying for my MBA."

"Cool."

Her gaze drifts over me, and I can feel her analyzing my outfit, my makeup or lack thereof, and my hair. I've experienced the 'scan' too many times to mistake it, and it never fails to annoy the fuck out of me even if I did just grace her with the same treatment.

Man, I'm such a hypocrite this morning.

"I'm Liam's half-sister."

My brows lift. "Excuse me?"

I did not just hear… She did *not* say—

"Liam and I are related. Padraig Donnghal is our father."

Mouth rounding, no longer caring that I don't have time for this conversation, I shuffle toward the seating area she's using and plunk myself in the armchair opposite her.

"You're Liam's sister?"

"Half-sister, but, yes." She tips up her chin. "My husband reminded me that blood is thicker than water so that's why I'm here."

"Because blood is thicker than water," I repeat, my confusion at an all-time high.

"In his words, 'The blood of the covenant is thicker than the water of the womb.' Know-it-all." She huffs. "*And* I lost a bet."

Amusement filters through me. "You bet with your husband?"

"Only over important matters."

"Like family?"

She clears her throat. "Yes. Which Liam is. I learned about him years ago. It's time I did something about it because I think Saverina and Bella should know their uncle if he'd like to know them in return."

I whistle. "You're going to give Liam a heart attack."

"I am?"

"Uh-huh."

I peer at the kid still breastfeeding without a care in the world and the one sleeping in her stroller. I know kids and I know these were born close together. Still, if I were Mr. Valentini, I'd lock Jennifer in the kitchen, barefoot and pregnant, too.

Oh, Paddy. What fine genes you have…

"Liam's great with kids, though," I inform her, aware that I was staring so long it was getting strange. "They'll have him twisted around their fingers before you know it."

Her grin is sheepish. "That's good to know. I wasn't sure how else to get in touch, to be honest. I could have gone through the Stars, but I thought that was too formal."

Through the Stars? If the Chanel outfit didn't give the game away, that did.

Even as I'm wondering precisely *who* her husband is, I ask, "You just thought you'd camp out in the lobby of his building? How did you even get in?"

"My best friend lives here," is her droll retort. "I'm multitasking— we're going shopping today."

I study her for a second. *"Who* exactly were you waiting for?"

Jennifer doesn't pretend to misunderstand me. "You."

"Not Liam?" I pepper.

"No. You're a first step."

"You want me to smooth the path for you?"

"For us both." Her gaze drops to my throat. "I think that would be wise considering how close you are to him."

I know I've got a hickey, but I don't bother hiding it. I quite liked seeing it this morning and if I'm not going to use concealer on the zit at the side of my nose, then I'm not going to waste my time trying to conceal the unconcealable.

Though if I had her mad skillz with makeup, I might try...

Considering her a moment, I muse, "I make no promises."

She smiles. "I expect none. Just a... gentle introduction. I know what he went through with the kidnapping. I have no desire to cause him any distress."

"What do you know about the kidnapping?" I demand, immediately curious.

She studies the still-suckling baby. "More than I'd like. My husband helped Liam's—" She sighs, corrects, *"Our* family free him."

Intently, I lean forward. "I thought the cops freed him."

"Unlikely." She harrumphs. "But I shouldn't be talking about this. It's not my place."

My lips purse as I think about the nightmare Liam experienced last night. "He still wakes up screaming."

"I can understand why. They kept him like an animal. And what they did to him..." She shakes herself then repeats, "I shouldn't be talking about this."

"How about we come to an agreement? I'll soften him up for you if you tell me what you know."

Her brow furrows. "Is that fair?"

"I don't particularly care if it is or not." Since Paddy told me that he was related to the Irish Mob, I've had the feeling that Liam's kidnapping was mafia-adjacent, no matter that Liam said it wasn't. This woman has answers—answers that might unlock his nightmares and help him move on. "Do we have a deal?"

"What I know wasn't obtained by legal means. I won't endanger my family by sharing anything with you."

"Did you hurt Liam?"

"No!"

"Then you have nothing to fear from me. I want to help him, not make things worse."

Her jaw works. "I'll think about it."

My alarm starts bleating, breaking up our conversation. "Shit." I scrabble to switch it off. "I have to go. My class is in a half hour. Do you want to give me your number?"

Like she was waiting for the offer, she slips an expensive vellum business card out of nowhere and passes it to me. "I hope to hear from you, Ms. Bukowski."

At her use of my name, a thought occurs to me. "How do you know my name and where Liam lives?"

Her smile is quick. "It pays to know people in the right places."

Annoyed by the nonanswer, wondering if everyone in Liam's family isn't on the regular side of the law, I'm prevented from bitching at her when my second alarm goes off.

"The name's Gracie." With a huff, I get to my feet. "I'll be in touch."

"I'm Jennifer. And I'll look forward to it," Jennifer says warmly, cupping the back of the baby's head and nuzzling her nose against her daughter's cheek.

The image sticks with me as I rush out of the building and, horrifically late now, start to hail a cab as grabbing the subway is no longer an option.

Until a car swerves beside me.

Forcing myself not to panic, I realize it's one of Liam's bodyguards —Ludvig—who opens the passenger door from the driver's seat.

"What do you want?" I demand.

"I'll be driving you to NYU from now on, Ms. Bukowski," he says like the robot he is.

I don't have to wonder on whose orders...

A shaky breath escapes me but I can't deny, I'm relieved.

Without any argument, I jump into the passenger seat and Ludvig sets off into the busy Midtown traffic.

Snagging my phone, I text:

Me: You could have warned me.

Liam: About?

Me: That Ludvig was going to take me to school.

Liam: I didn't know it would be him.

Me: But you knew there'd be a bodyguard waiting for me?

Liam: Of course. You'll have one on you at all times.

Me: That's too much.

Liam: No. It isn't.

Me: It is! I don't need a twenty-four-hour babysitter. I'm not even famous lol. But a ride to school and from work would be nice, especially when Hudson's busy with you.

I feel like a teenager for sending immediately after:

Me: <3

Liam: We can talk about this later.

Me: NO. We won't. I don't need a bodyguard, Liam.

Liam: Last night says otherwise.

Me: It's too much. Far too much.

Liam: Not enough IMO.

Me: Liam. Please? I appreciate it. But not 24/7.

Liam: It'll make me feel better.

Me: And it'll make me feel worse. Listen to me.

Liam: :-/

Liam: 12 hours a day?

Me: 8.

Liam: 10. Final offer.

Me: Deal. Speak later.

Liam: Fine. I'll introduce you to the other guy—his name's Harvey. :-(<3

Me: Cool xo

With that settled and a stupid warmth filling me from the <3 he sent, I take a deep breath, feeling relieved but, also, *heard*.

Liam: Done.

Ludvig's cell pings and from my seat, I can see his security detail has changed from guarding me and reverted to shadowing Liam.

He listened, all while acting to protect me without me having to ask.

Is he... *perfect?*

"Stop jinxing this," I mutter to myself as I input Jennifer's information into my contacts.

"Excuse me, Ms. Bukowski, did you say something?"

I wave a hand at Ludvig, who returns his attention to the traffic.

On the otherwise silent ride to my class, I think about our text conversation as well as that meeting with Jennifer while I try to calculate the probability of her intentions being negative toward Liam... I also throw in the fact that she might have answers that Liam isn't willing to give me.

I've always been too curious for my own good, and a mystery sister who knows more about Liam's kidnapping is a puzzle I have to solve.

Whether Liam wants me to or not.

Of course, that's when I get my notification from Cameo.

Any and all thoughts blur when I realize Liam got me a private note from Simple fucking Plan.

This.

Man.

My God.

CHAPTER 28
LIAM

"IT ISN'T enough to just play hockey, Liam. I've already passed invitations to Gracie that you should have accepted. You can't be a hermit!"

"Why not? I don't want to attend any of those bullshit events. I do the promo shoots. Surely that's enough," I demand, relieved that Andrews, my agent, had to split early because I rescheduled the meeting.

One-on-one, I stand a chance. Two-on-one? Not so much.

"They're not 'bullshit events.' You yourself told me that you want as many sponsorship opportunities as possible while you're based in New York. Has your intention to retire early changed and you haven't told me?"

"It hasn't, but I checked out each event. Do I look like the kind of guy who'd want to attend the release of an animated movie?"

"You're a hockey player. Your demographic is wide—"

I'm grateful when, in the middle of Kara's diatribe, my cell buzzes.

"Mr. Donnghal, Officer Brownhill here."

Immediately, I hold out a hand to stall my PR rep. "Officer, great to hear from you. I hope you're calling with good news."

"With the footage your detail sent over, we located Ms. Bukowski's purse—it was tossed in a dumpster. While most of the contents are in disarray, some of her personal effects aren't damaged."

"Also, we have a suspect in custody. However, Ms. Bukowski isn't answering her phone—"

"She isn't?" I glance at the clock.

Gracie should be out of class at this time.

"No—"

"Wait a minute. Let me message her." Concerned, I put him on speaker then switch apps so I can text her.

> Me: Are you okay? Officer Brownhill is trying to call you.

> Gracie: Still in my lecture. It's running late. If you can't deal with it, tell him I'll call afterward, please.

> Me: Will do.

"She says that if I can't deal with things, she'll call you back after her class is finished," I parrot to the officer.

"That'll be fine, sir. I'd like to arrange a lineup. Tomorrow at ten?"

Quickly, I look at the agenda Gracie finished for me yesterday because there's no way in hell she's handling this on her own.

"I have practice at ten," I tell him. "Can we hold it earlier?"

"Sure." I hear the bubble of excitement in his voice that appears because I'll be attending with her. "Eight?"

"Sounds good to me." Seeing as he's making my life easier, I offer, "As a thank you, I can arrange for you to pick up some tickets to this Thursday's game if you'd like?"

"Officially, I can't accept—"

"Unofficially?"

"I can collect them from the box office if you're amenable," Brownhill says quickly.

"Great. I'll place them under Ms. Bukowski's name."

"I appreciate that. I'll return whatever of Ms. Bukowski's belongings aren't important for evidence to the doorman so she isn't inconvenienced."

Aware that he's stretching the rules on our behalf, my voice softens. "And I appreciate that. Thank you."

"See you tomorrow at eight, sir."

With a hum, I cut the call and stare at Kara, whose lips are puckered in disapproval. "Gracie was mugged?"

> Me: They found your purse. Brownhill will leave it with the doorman.

> Me: There's a lineup tomorrow.

> Gracie: <3

Stroking my thumb over that emoji, I tell Kara, "Yeah. Yesterday. They think they found her mugger though."

"Is she okay?"

Because Kara is all business, I'm surprised that she cares enough to ask. "She was shaken up, mostly pissed off that they got the drop on her." I study her. "You should probably know that we're dating."

A gleam appears in her eyes. "At least Gracie will be able to convince you to attend the events I spoon-feed you."

"Always a silver lining," I grouse.

Kow: Bro, why isn't Gracie's number working?

Liam: She has a new one.

Liam: Why? What do you want?

Kow: Why did she change her number?

Liam: What do you want?

Kow: Jesus. Sure, you're her boss, but dude, she can talk to me outside of office hours.

Liam: You forget how well I know you.

Kow: I want to ask her what she's getting for Mom's birthday.

Liam: Ha. More like you wanted her to buy a present for you too.

Kow: Fuck off.

Liam: Can't fuck off. I'm comfortable.

Kow: Watching Noah before your game starts?

Liam: Yup. I'm in the hot tub. Think they'll win? Portland is doing great this year.

Kow: Got a hundred K on the game so if he doesn't bring the goods, I'll kill him.

Liam: You do know that's illegal AND against league rules?

Liam: Who am I kidding? Of course you goddamn do. MORON.

Kow: It's just this once!

Liam: Delete your messages. It's evidence admissible in court.

Liam: DOUBLE MORON.

Liam: FML.

Liam: And now I'm a party to it.

Liam deletes messages
Liam: Fuck you.

Kow: Gotta pay you back for my tax bill.

Kow deletes messages

Liam: I can wait, dumbfuck. You could have just given me your wager to cover part of what you owe me.

Kow: Have faith in Noah.

Liam: Is it my imagination or is he getting really good?

Kow: Nah, he's always been this talented but shit teams keep picking him.

Liam: He played for the Mounties!

Kow: Yeah, but he got traded just before you won the cup. That's your fault. Without you, they sucked, thought they were gonna lose, then BOOM. In your little green Leprechaun ass bounced and you brought home the silver cup. Again.

Liam: Do you expect me to apologize for getting kidnapped?

Kow: To me? Nah. To Noah? Maybe.

Liam: Cibole.

Kow: Why'd she switch numbers?

Liam: She just did.

Kow: Gracie has had the same number since she moved to the States.

Kow: What's going on?

Liam: Does it matter?

Kow: That my pain-in-the-ass sister who never does anything for no reason would just change her long-term telephone number out of the blue?

Kow: Yeah, it matters.

Kow: What's

Kow: Going

Kow: On?

Liam: She's fine so there's no need to worry but...

Liam: She was mugged last night. She didn't want me to say anything but I can see you spinning stories in your head.

Kow: Shit!

Liam: Like I said, she's fine. Few scrapes but she claims she wasn't hurt. Well, that's a lie actually. Her pride was lol. Mostly, she's pissed that they got away with her stuff.

Kow: Typical Gracie.

Kow: Gimme her new number?

Liam: What? So you can bombard her with messages to get her to pick out a gift for you? Nah.

Liam: And though she IS all right, the last thing she needs is a shopping list from you of gifts you want her to buy on your behalf.

Kow: Tell her I'll help her work on her right hook. Repayment for the personal shopping.

Liam: You begging for a fist to the face? Because I'll team up with her...

Kow: Nah. But it'll get her to grab a gift for me. A shit present is better than no present.

Liam: Get your assistant to buy you one!

Kow: Gracie's shit presents are better than a stranger's bland one.

Liam: You're a piece of work.

Kow: :P

Liam: BTW, we need to talk.

Kow: Later, dude. Charlene just came over.

Liam: Call me.

Kow: Sure thing.

Liam: I'm going to delete our whole text chat. Just in case.

Kow: Chill.

Liam: Fuck off. You'll thank me when this bites you in the ass ten years down the line.

CHAPTER 29
GRACIE

BACK WHEN I was following Liam and Kow around the circuit, though I used to sit in the friends and family box at home games, I never integrated with the wives and girlfriends.

Most of them weren't interested in me because I was just a sister, but I did get friendly with a few of the moms who used to hang out there—that's where I met Jessica Condon and her daughter Lorie.

It's always been my standard MO to sit in the corner and listen to their chatter, which is how I pick up on most of the info I have about the team, and I see no reason to change things just because I'm working for Liam. The majority of the women leave me alone and I'm not bothered about getting friendly until it's time to manage egos on his behalf.

Still, that's a 'me' problem, not theirs.

They could be nice as hell and I'd still maintain distance from them.

Mia and Charlotte are just two women who've betrayed me along the way.

I've no desire to make it three for three.

So, when Lacey Kerrigan sits beside me at the Stars vs. Bulldogs game, I cast her a surprised look.

In her arms, she's got their daughter who, amazingly enough considering the racket, is sleeping against her shoulder. Maybe it's how pink and plump the little girl is that draws my attention to how *bad* Lacey appears.

I mean, she's beautiful but frail. Really frail.

I'd even go so far as to say... *ill.*

We smile at each other in greeting, but it's only when the third period hits and Matt, one of my billet brothers, stops yet another goal from the Stars and she growls, "You asshole," at the same time as I do that we start chuckling.

"It's Bradley's fault. You can always tell when he's feeling like his manhood's being questioned—"

"He has them playing defensively. Ruben goes crazy about that."

"I don't think any of the offensive lines like Bradley," I agree with a snort. "Come on, LIAM!" I shout as he races around the back of the net, swiping the puck away.

He shoots, fails to score, but snags possession back after Matt deflects his shot and takes it toward center.

When the baby gurgles at my holler, I mutter, "Oops, sorry."

"You're kidding, right? She could sleep through a hurricane," Lacey says wryly. "That's why I bring her here. Honestly, it's great for sleep training. My mom always said to me, 'Lacey, don't tiptoe around your babies when they sleep because you're just causing yourself a whole lot of work in the long run.'"

"Huh, that's pretty smart."

"Yeah. She knew her stuff," Lacey agrees with a chuckle. "She had four kids, just like your mom, and billeted a few players as well."

Unsurprised she knows that about my family because every hockey lover in North America knows about the kids who billeted with us, I ask, "That's how you and Ruben met?"

"No. We went to high school together. I hated his guts throughout and even into his first year of college."

I chuckle. "Wow, I didn't expect that."

"Yeah, turns out the jackass was mean to me because he liked me." She rolls her eyes. "True schoolyard stuff. Can you imagine?"

"Yes, because men are idiots."

"They so are." Lacey presses her lips to the baby's head. "So many wasted years...," she whispers, her tone somber before she clears her throat. "Anyway, I sat next to you for a reason."

"You did?" I ask, watching as a Boston right winger gets in Raimond's face when he takes possession.

With a fight imminent because everyone knows Raimond fucked that player's girl and got her pregnant, he slaps the puck toward Gagné, who clears it down to the other end.

"Yeah," she mutters absently, her gaze locked on the ice. When Lewis snatches it and finally scores, we both shriek with relief before she continues, "It's looking as if we're going to be in the playoffs—"

"Damn straight we are!"

"—and no one else dared approach you."

"Approach me?" I repeat, both unsurprised and surprised. "About what?"

"For, you know, the PALs playoffs jackets."

"I'm neither a P nor an L."

She arches her brow at me. "Yeah, okay."

I scowl at her. "We've been dating for a day."

Lacey hitches her shoulder. "If you know the signs..."

Absently, I rub my temple. "I forgot about the playoffs jackets."

"To be fair, the last time you were on the circuit, it wasn't a thing."

"No, it wasn't, and I wouldn't have worn one because I wasn't a wife or a girlfriend back then," I drawl.

Her nose crinkles. "Are you going to turn me green for bringing it up?"

I snort. "No. I did that once. It's not something you can make a habit out of. People start to look suspiciously at you whenever you're near a body of water."

A soft laugh escapes her but it balloons into a coughing fit that hacks through her small frame with such ferocity that when I offer, "Do you need me to hold the baby?" Lacey actually accepts, leaving me with the kid and her to—

Shit.

I try not to stare when I see her press a tissue to her mouth and it comes away pink.

As her coughing fit lessens, I swallow as I look down at the tiny body in my arms before I pass her back to Lacey.

"Sorry about that," she rasps, her voice hoarse.

"You don't have to be sorry."

We share a glance.

It's an odd one.

It's a language that I'm sure only women speak.

That would go over the head of any and every man in the vicinity.

One that we know intrinsically, that's in our very DNA.

"The doctors say I have a year left."

My eyes flare wide. "I'm..."

"Please don't say it. It's not like you gave me cancer."

"No, but... that *sucks*."

"Yeah." Her focus is on her baby who's still sleeping peacefully in her arms, not the chaos as Boston manages to get one past Greco with two minutes left to the period. "It does."

Both of us focus on the game until the buzzer sounds and OT starts.

Hesitantly, I offer, "If there's anything I can do—"

Lacey peers at me just as her man misses a shot. "Get Liam to stop giving Ruben such a hard time?"

I blink. "He's captain. He has to push them."

"Yeah, and I know Ruben's game is suffering, but we've got a lot going on..."

"You really do," I agree huskily, and even though Boston scores and the game ends 2-1 with a Stars' loss, I assure her, "I'll talk to him."

"Thank you." She sucks in a breath that ends in a choked cough, one that she manages to control. Barely. Around a hoarse exhalation, she rumbles, "Now, the PALs jackets. We were thinking..."

CHAPTER 30
LIAM

Such Great Heights - The Postal Service

I SHOULD HAVE EXPECTED Gracie to return to her apartment.

That's what she does when she has assignments.

I figured she'd come back to mine because it was game night and we're a thing now but, no.

Mostly, I'm annoyed I had to hear from her bodyguards that she'd taken a taxi home. Still, that tells me she knew I'd have convinced her to stay if she'd waited on me and Hudson to take her back to her place.

I'm not too pissed about that.

One night with her in my bed, however, and it was already shitty going to sleep without her beside me.

I'm tempted to spank her ass for heading out without saying bye to me first, without even goddamn texting me, but my brain tells me that's like tugging on a tiger's tail and expecting not to get mauled.

The question is... would it be worth getting mauled by Gracie?

"Could be hot," I muse to my reflection the following morning as I scratch my chin, hating the stubble growing there which is a reminder of how rough last night was.

Saying that it's one of the worst night's sleeps I've had in too long is under-embellishing how awful it was thanks to a nightmare that saw *her* with my kidnappers instead of me.

I've leveled up to night terrors because of her.

My hands grip the vanity to contain the rage that fills me at the memory.

And now she's negotiated for having a bodyguard only ten hours a day...

She has me so riled up that I don't really care we lost last night. What the fuck is a game in comparison to her safety?

Agitated, I quickly shave, getting rid of the scruff and gracing myself with a few nicks for my troubles, and shower.

When I'm drying off, I hear Gracie in the kitchen.

The bolt of contentedness that hits me isn't surprising, not when I've been feeling it since she came back into my life on a permanent basis. The instant boner makes me laugh to myself though.

If it weren't for the police lineup, I'd probably try to convince her to take another shower with me...

Instead, I race through getting dressed and retreat to the kitchen after I've texted my request to the security company.

She never said anything about how many bodyguards I could put on her...

Gracie has her phone pinned between her shoulder and her ear when I see her, but it's her discontented expression that keys me into the fact she's talking to her family.

"Who is it?" I mouth when she sees me, trying not to feel elated when her eyes light up at the sight of me.

"Mom, look, I don't have time for this," she grinds out, answering me in the process. "I certainly don't need a lecture on being better prepared for living in a big city!"

Grimacing, I start making us both a shake while I chow down on a pasta salad the housekeeper left for me, one that needs about a bottle more of dressing.

As I eat, her temper ratchets higher and higher the longer Hanna keeps her talking.

When she slams my business phone onto the counter a couple of minutes later, she's lucky the screen didn't crack.

"Let it out. You'll feel better if you do," I advise, prudently hitting the blender's 'on' button at the same time as she releases a scream.

I let it run extra long so she can get it out of her system, then, when I'm done, a breath gusts from her. "Thank you."

"I'm surprised you told her."

Her top lip curls into a sneer. "I didn't."

Guilt hits me at the same time as understanding does. "Kow did."

"*You* told him. You said you wouldn't!"

God, I had. Fuck. Fuck. *Fuck!*

"He texted me before the game. Shit. I'm sorry, Gracie. He wanted your new number and I knew he wouldn't drop it." I scrape a hand over my face, feeling like shit for letting her down. "I should have warned you. I guess I just didn't think. I'm so sorry."

She bites her lip. "It doesn't matter."

That means it does.

My guilt triples down.

"I'm sorry, Gracie," I repeat for the third time. "I didn't mean to cause you any trouble."

"I know," she grouches, offering me a tight smile as she heads to the fridge where she snags the bottle of maple syrup that's always stocked there.

Before my eyes, she sets up a maple chaser.

"And, to be fair, if I had a normal family, it wouldn't have caused me any problems. It's just... Mom. You know?"

"I do," I tell her, watching as she sinks it back.

"What happened before I started working with you doesn't help," she mumbles.

I hum my understanding.

I'll never understand why Hanna gives her so much grief. She's a good girl. Hard-working. She forged her own path, sure, but that's not a crime.

Kow is constantly in the press for fucking the latest 'Page 6' darling, Noah gets into fights that end up being broadcasted on PSN, and Trent's so close-mouthed about his private life that he could be a spy on the side.

Out of all of them, Gracie's the best behaved, but you'd never know with the way Hanna jumps at her.

The thing is, I didn't realize any of that until she came back into my life.

Feeling doubly guilty and as if my lack of insight failed her too, I round the kitchen counter and tug her into a hug. She fights me at first, then it's like she remembers the last couple of days and she allows herself to slip into me. To lean on me.

The way we slot together is better than a jigsaw puzzle. My arms settle around her shoulders at the perfect height, and her face rests in the space that sits just below my heart.

As she returns the embrace, I feel her mumble as she whispers the words against my chest, "It'd have been nice for her to ask me how I was doing, you know?"

Anger rushes through me. "She didn't ask?"

"No. She was mad at me for letting my guard down. I mean, it wasn't my fault, Liam. He came out of nowhere. It's not like I wasn't paying attenti—"

Needing to stop her, I growl, "Gracie."

She pauses then blinks up at me. "What?"

"It was not your fault that you were targeted by a mugger. No matter what your mom would have you believe, you did nothing wrong. You were a victim. Don't let her twist things around, do you hear me?"

I think about how Gracie has been pulling away from the family since moving to New York, and I also think about how disappointed Hanna is when there's a space at the dinner table come Thanksgiving or Christmas.

Mon Dieu, I've seen her hiding her tears in the kitchen!

You don't cry about a missing kid at the table if you're glad to see the back of them.

It doesn't make any sense to me. None of this does.

I want to tell her that they care, that it's just not the kind of care she'd like to receive, but how can I even get those words out? They wouldn't be any comfort to her.

So, instead of trying to make things better when that's not on me, but on Hanna, I press a kiss to the crown of her head and state the one solid truth she can rely on, "I got your back, Gracie."

She stills. "You do?"

"Always."

Silence looms between us, then she murmurs, "You know I've got yours too, right?"

"Known you've had it from the moment I moved into your house when we were kids. I'm the one who let *you* down. Both times with Kow."

"Hardly," she says with a snort.

"What with dropping the ball yesterday..." I rub my forehead. "I know back when we were teens, I switched allegiances."

"You and Kow were peers. It makes sense that you'd hang out together."

From her expression, I know I hit the nail on the head—I hurt her.

Fuck.

I hate Old Liam. Sure, New Liam has nightmares, but give me that over the reckless hurt I laid on this woman, the only one who fucking matters to me.

"I regret it. I'm sorry."

"Things turned out how they were always supposed to." She places a hand on my chest. "We need to talk."

"Thought we were."

"About Kerrigan."

I groan. "What about him?"

"His baby momma's got cancer."

"What?"

"You need to cut him some slack."

"Cancer?" I repeat. "How do you know? He hasn't told anyone on the team."

"She knows he's playing like crap and she looped me in because she wanted you to stop giving him a hard time."

"Their kid's practically newborn," I rasp.

She nods, and the sorrow in her eyes tells me that whatever Kerrigan's woman's going through, it's not going to end well.

"I'll try." It's all I can promise.

What Kerrigan's dealing with is something no one should have to, but we've got responsibilities...

Man, I feel like a douche for even thinking that.

As if she knows, Gracie pats my arm. "The 'C' patch means you have to approach this with dual intentions, but if anyone can do it, it's you."

Though her confidence in me feels unwarranted, especially after I just failed her, I merely nod. That's when she changes the subject. Again.

But that's Gracie—four different conversations at once is the norm.

"By the way, I got my things back from Keith."

"Who's Keith? The doorman?"

Nodding, she bites her lip. "All my stationery is busted."

Tabarnak. "We can go to the store after practice."

"No, it's dumb to waste so much money on pens."

"You're going to need to stop being so practical around me."

"That's like telling me to stop being mean to assholes."

I grin. "No pouting. We'll head there after practice."

She doesn't argue. At first, I think that's because I did the impossible—convinced her—but no.

"I'm not looking forward to this," she mumbles.

"To the lineup?" I frown. "I'd have thought that would be satisfying. They've got the fucker."

"Why do they even need me if they found my stuff? Isn't being caught red-handed enough?"

"Brownhill said the purse was dumped." I study her. "What's going on?"

She sighs. "Nothing."

I don't believe her but I'm not going to push her. Today's already going to be stressful enough without me being a prick and mansplaining the situation to her.

"I'll put our shakes in tumblers. Give me five minutes?"

Her smile feels wry when I taste it. "You can have ten. I'm feeling generous."

Because we're going out, I transfer our smoothies into travel-safe tumblers that, as per my contract with them, are branded with Mega XY logos all over them and ask, "How's your knee?"

"Okay. It was only a small graze." She taps her nails against the counter. "I still can't believe that Mega XY is one of your sponsors. Didn't they put human nails in their protein shakes?"

My nose crinkles. "That was Mega X. Why do you think I switched?"

"What a difference a Y makes."

"Right. And we're good to go." I hold out my hand, watching as she studies it like I offered her a dead rat instead of my fingers. Gingerly, she slips her palm against mine. Squeezing it, I murmur, "Come on. Let's get this over with."

She's quiet as we ride down to the basement garage where Hudson is waiting to fight the morning traffic on our behalf. The rest of the journey is spent with her staring out the window, obviously thinking about whatever it is she doesn't want to discuss, while I check the invitations to various shitshows Kara sent me overnight.

Deciding to decline most of them, I accept the invitation to one, mostly because I know Gracie will enjoy the museum showing— Suffragettes and their contribution to society.

By the time we make it to the precinct, Gracie's pallor is unhealthily white. There isn't much I can do apart from wrap my arm around her shoulders and hold her close.

Brownhill's there, obsequious to the last. A couple of his buddies show up to get my autograph, and it's in such bad taste that I almost refuse, but it's never good to piss off the cops. Especially in a city like New York.

"Later, guys," I gently rumble. "After business is over."

They're not happy about it, but I don't care. I'll sign their damn shirts and programs but Jesus Christ if it isn't inappropriate timing.

Gracie doesn't say anything, maybe she's even too freaked out to notice, but inside, I'm cringing like fuck—*I* notice.

When we're guided into a small backroom, Gracie settles in front of the window but shrugs off my hold on her. Not wanting her to think she's in this alone, I stick fast to her side.

The lights blare on and a bunch of teenagers stride into the room. I can feel her eyes lock on them, her laser focus cataloging each of their features as they line up.

It's when she scans number five that I know he's the mugger. Even without the black eye, I'd know.

Christ, he's young. Maybe the youngest here despite being the tallest. Though he's a beanstalk, he can't be any older than thirteen.

She studies them all again, even after Brownhill asks the boys, because that's what they are, to turn to the side.

This, I realize, is why she was quiet.

It doesn't come as much of a surprise when she says, "It's none of them."

Brownhill frowns. "Are you sure, ma'am? These assailants were found very close to where your purse was dumped."

She swallows. "I don't recognize him and I got a good look at his face."

"He runs with the same crew as Kruger, the kid whose arrest you facilitated." Brownhill taps the window, pointing, unobtrusively, to number five.

Gracie sniffs. "I remember his name and I remember the face of the jerk who mugged me. I'm telling you that he's not here."

Brownhill grumbles but lets us go. He's annoyed enough that he forgets to pester me for an autograph. His other cockroach friends have scurried away too.

When we make it outside, she sucks in a deep breath and I can't blame her. That place was oddly airless. Desperation, shame, and remorselessness are not a pretty perfume.

Which is when I realize I didn't feel the walls closing in on me back there.

Progress? Or was I just hyper-focused on her?

I shove the thought aside for next week's session with Mike.

There are around twenty steps to the sidewalk, and it's only when we're standing on *terra firma* that I state, "The fifth kid was your mugger."

"I know it was," is her absent response as she turns to face the stairs. "It's even more embarrassing that I let an embryo get away with my stuff."

I hide a smile. "Hudson's waiting."

"Just give me twenty minutes."

I check my watch. "Practice is in an hour and it'll take a good half hour to get to the stadium."

"I know your schedule and the route we'll take better than you do, Liam," she grumbles. "Bear with me, okay?"

"Okay."

I shrug my hands into my pockets, uncertain what's going on here but knowing that it's important so I don't rush her.

Gracie is nothing but rational.

If she wants to wait here, then there's a reason for it. If she wants to lie about the kid who mugged her, then there's a reason for that too.

Fifteen minutes later, the *children* from the lineup sidle from the precinct. Some run down the steps, carefree and relieved to be out of there. A few slouch to the side and light up a cigarette, the doppelgängers clustering together in a fog of smoke.

Kid number five hunches his shoulders as he ambles toward the sidewalk but he keeps to himself.

The closer he gets, the easier it is to see the tear tracks on his cheeks.

Rubbing the back of my neck, I murmur, "What's your game plan, Gracie?"

She locks her gaze on the kid. "I don't know."

"Unlike you."

"Acting on instinct."

"More like *re*acting."

Pursing her lips, she mutters, "Remember when Noah got into trouble for joyriding?"

"I remember."

"Some kids just need direction."

"Noah didn't have much choice about his direction."

Her lips twitch. "No, he didn't."

Noah was the only Bukowski whose arm had practically been twisted into playing hockey.

Fryd had forced him to join a hockey team as punishment for his first offense.

In the Bukowski household, hockey was always the cure.

That's when it clicks.

"The outreach program."

She peers at me. "Tell me I'm wrong?"

"He's hanging around with a bad crowd," I point out.

"And Noah wasn't?" Her fingers find mine. "He just needs someone to take an interest. Someone to care. Look at him, Liam." Her voice breaks. "He's scared."

Unable to argue, I nod. "I'll sponsor him for the team."

"Thank you," she whispers, and just in time because kid number five makes it to the bottom step.

If I hadn't known he was her attacker, I'd have seen it in how his eyes flare wide—she got him good.

There's a faint graze on his ear as if she drew blood when she Mike Tysoned him, and the way his hands drop to his crotch before he fights the urge to cup himself is clue enough that she got him in the balls like she said.

With every step forward she takes, he cringes backward until she drawls, "You and I both know you stole my purse, you little shit," and he freezes.

I can almost see the smokescreen between kid and criminal quiver in place.

The criminal sniffs his disdain, but the kid's voice is a croak. "The pigs just released me."

"Sure they did," Gracie agrees. "Because I told them you didn't do it. But your freedom comes with a price."

If his eyes were wide before, now they're bugging. "You one of them perverts, lady?" he demands as he backs up, only to forget that he's on the precinct steps.

When he falls flat on his ass, Gracie approaches him with her hand held out. "You heard of the New York Stars?"

The kid blinks. "Sure. They were the Liberties and they sucked ass." When I snort at that, his gaze flickers toward me, and maybe it's the context that helps him out, but his mouth gapes before he squeaks, "Are you the Leprechaun?" If his voice breaks over two octaves, that's between him and his vocal cords.

I hitch a shoulder. "What's it got to do with you?"

I can support Gracie's plan without liking it—the little bastard scared her, made her goddamn cry. I don't have to cut him any slack here.

"He's a Star," Gracie confirms, snagging the boy's hand in her own and dragging him onto his feet. "The team has this outreach program for troubled kids. I think you fit the bill, don't you?"

"I don't play hockey."

"No? You're about to learn." She snaps her fingers. "I can tell the cops I was wrong in a heartbeat. I can say that I was confused, that my mind blanked for a minute. Next thing you know, you can be in juvie, kid.

"*Or* you can cooperate and you can find a better path than hanging out on street corners with jackasses who think it's funny to throw babies into the path of oncoming traffic."

The kid's so young that he doesn't have an Adam's apple. His throat bobs as he whispers, "Arnie didn't mean to do that."

"It sure as hell looked as if he did when he was busting a nut laughing over his antics," she growls, vibrating with her rage. Smartly, the boy takes another step back, making a near miss with the stairs again. "What I don't understand is why you mugged me. Retaliation?"

When he shuffles his feet, I ask, "What's your name?"

He swallows. "Oliver Nolan."

"Well, Oliver?" she persists. "What was your intention? To scare me?"

Oliver scrubs at his cheeks. "The others said we had to make you pay for sending Arnie up. One of 'em saw you heading into the Acuig building. I-I was watching you when you came out.

"They were really mad at you, lady." His bottom lip trembles, making him appear even younger than he did initially. "I figured if I mugged you and took your shit, they'd think that was it. You know, revenge? It worked."

Though relief the grudge match might be over fills me, I draw her under my arm, asking, "You sure about this?"

She nods. "Oliver, do *you* want revenge against me?"

"No. Arnie shouldn't have done w-what he did. I-I think he was trying to be funny, but he went too far." Another sniffle. For the first time, I see the tears in his eyes, not just the ones that have dried on his cheeks. More than that, I see the fear. "I-I don't want to get into trouble. This is the first time the cops have hauled me in."

"Where's your mom?"

He shrugs. "I dunno."

"You must have had a social worker with you?"

"He had to leave. He's busy."

Squeezing her arm, I pick up the slack. "You can stick to the path you're on, Oliver, or you can do something different."

"What if I suck at hockey?"

"Then you suck. You can still try. And if you hate it, we'll figure something out."

The hope in his eyes is brutal to behold. "Like what?"

"I have contacts," I answer in Gracie's stead. "I can find you a sport you *do* enjoy."

"What if I hate sports?"

Brat.

"Do you?"

He hitches a shoulder. "Maybe."

"The only choice you have is *which* sport you can practice, Oliver," Gracie practically spits. "That's it. Or I go back in there and I change the shape of your future forever."

"You're lucky she didn't do that already," I insert. "She could have. I would."

He bites the inside of his cheek. "I'm sorry, lady."

She sticks out her hand. "The name's Gracie."

Oliver tentatively slips his grubby fingers into hers and they shake on it.

CHAPTER 31
GRACIE

Head On Collision - New Found Glory

WE LEAVE Liam at the rink while Hudson drops both Oliver and me off at his tenement building.

If I were questioning my sanity, what I see makes me realize I'm doing the right thing.

His *home* is a desperate place.

A drug deal goes down on one corner, right out in the open, and I see cash exchange hands for what can only be a deal between a hooker and a john.

Aside from those heart-warming welcome homes, the entire neighborhood looks as if it were due for demolition ten years ago.

As I stare at it, Oliver fidgets on the back seat. "Lady."

I turn so he can see my arched brow.

God, he's young.

I didn't realize my attacker was practically a fetus until I saw him in the lineup. I mean, I knew he was young, but *this* young?

With a huff, he corrects, "Gracie."

"Oliver, what is it?"

"I don't want you to come up."

"Do you not want your mom to know what happened?"

He snorts. "Like she'll give a damn anyway. Nah, it's not safe for you 'round here. Arnie's family lives on my block."

Nodding my understanding, I mentally file what could be a future problem. "Will there be an issue getting away for practice?"

Oliver sucks in his bottom lip. "No."

"Convincing."

He wriggles his shoulders. "I can only try, right?"

"Not good enough. I think we should establish a baseline. If you can't make it to a scheduled practice, you text me. But if you do that more than three times in a row, I'll go to the cops. If you skip four practices in a month, I'll go to the cops. You understand me?"

He glowers at me. "How am I supposed to get away from my friends?"

"Maybe you tell them that you're one of the lucky few who gets to take part in this program."

"They won't think I'm lucky. They'll just be jealous."

"Then they're not really your friends."

His shoulders hunch, but he doesn't have an answer for me.

Facing him on the back seat, I murmur, "Hudson can pick you up if you have trouble getting to the stadium."

My words have him staring at me like I'm an alien. "I don't get it, Gracie. Why are you going to this much effort for me? Even I know what I am—a punk in the making."

"Who told you that?"

"No one," he mumbles.

"Liar. Nobody calls themselves that."

"Mrs. Hyatt next door. She says I'm good for nothing."

I scowl at him. "Don't you want to prove that she's wrong?"

"I don't know if I can." With ancient eyes, eyes too old for such a young boy, he studies his building. "People like me... we don't leave this neighborhood."

"This is your chance to. Maybe something will come of it, maybe nothing. You might suck at hockey, but you might meet a good friend in the program. Either way, it'll keep you off the streets and out of trouble... *and* it'll stop me from going to the cops."

"You don't gotta keep saying that," he grumbles.

"Sure I do," I say lightly. "I have to ram it home so you'll listen. I have three brothers. I remember what they were like as teens. Memories like sieves for anything that wasn't sex or sports-related."

I don't want to blackmail a preteen but if it keeps his nose clean, I will.

Though he blushes at the 'S' word, proof alone that the kid hasn't totally been corrupted by life in this tenement, he mumbles, "You'll send this fancy car to pick me up?"

"If you need me to."

"Mrs. Hyatt'd tell you that I ain't worth your time."

"I think we should prove Mrs. Hyatt wrong."

His grin is sheepish. "I'd like that. She's a real bitch."

"Not sure that's the way to prove her wrong, Ollie," I remark wryly.

"Oliver."

"Ollie," I insist. "You have my number?"

As he clambers out of the car, he nods. "I do."

"What's your social worker's name? I might need it for the paperwork."

"Jeremy DiPascale."

"I'll be in touch once everything's arranged."

He bites his lip. "You think Mr. Liam'll make it happen?"

"If he doesn't, I'll make his life hell."

Ollie's eyes widen but his grin is back, making him seem like any other kid. One who didn't grow up around drug abuse and violence and gangs. Then, in the blink of an eye, a mask comes down over his youthful features.

That is Oliver.

I guess we all wear masks; work exposes some and loved ones draw out others...

That's why I insisted on calling him Ollie.

I want him to know he's not just Oliver. He can be 'Ollie' too.

"School is close, right?"

He nods.

"Make sure you keep your attendance up—"

"Or you'll go to the cops." He rolls his eyes. "I get it, la—" He coughs. "Gracie."

Smirking, I watch him go, but not for long—Hudson's obviously worried about his hubcaps and he takes off when I shut the door to the back seat.

As he returns me to the stadium, I start reading through one of the essays I have to hand in to my professor tomorrow, but my mind swiftly drifts.

I don't know what I was thinking when I lied to Officer Brownhill, and I sure as hell don't know if I've made the right decision here, but at least I tried.

Not every kid is as lucky as Noah—he had a family who cared about him. Who worked hard to keep him on the straight and narrow.

That Ollie's mom didn't give enough of a damn to head to the precinct with him or that DiPascale didn't hang around to make sure Ollie went to school today tells me all I need to know.

There isn't much I won't do to preserve the remaining innocence in that boy's nature.

By the time I'm in the stands, I watch Liam and Lewis practice some plays that Bradley's set up. He probably thinks they're cutting-edge, and they might have been when Gretzky was on the ice. Still, they're a power duo, much like Lemieux and Jagr once were, one that the Stars need while they're working through the kinks from new management, kinks that remain even though we're deep into the season.

As I continue proofing my essay, I'm tempted to ignore Paddy when he pops up and sits beside me like a *clurichaun* that doesn't want to take the hint.

"How's his head?"

Such a greeting.

"From the hit the other day or in general?"

"Both?" He scratches his nose. "The other day, first, though."

"He's fine."

"They lost yesterday."

"Can't win them all." At his worried frown, I sigh. "They didn't lose because of his head. I'm sure he'll be 100% fine for tomorrow night's game."

"Perfect."

Something about his tone has me asking, "You betting on him again, Paddy?"

He scowls at me. "That's none of your business."

Because he's right, I just shrug. "Your funeral."

"It *isn't* any of your business but I haven't gambled since my older brother died." He sniffs. "Can't a man want to know how his kid is doing?"

"Depends. I met your daughter yesterday."

It isn't a figment of my imagination that he blanches. *Interesting.* "You met Jennifer?"

I nod. "She was in the lobby of Liam's building. Waiting to see me."

"To see *you*?" He frowns. "What's her game?"

"No game. She wanted me to ease the way for them both."

"Smart of her. You and I both know that Liam doesn't like change at the best of times."

The best of times haven't come around since before the kidnapping...

Funny how Liam would say that Paddy doesn't know him at all, but he knows *that.*

"You going to do it?"

"Haven't had the chance to yet, but I will, yeah."

"You never ease the path for me."

"Not my job to. You're his dad. You fucked up along the way. That's on you to heal that boo-boo." I cut him a look. "How come Liam doesn't know about her?"

"He does. You know how he's been since the kidnapping, focused on getting through each day."

"Maybe he doesn't want to know her."

"Maybe. He won't talk to me, period, not since I forced his hand to get him here, so I can't figure out where his head's at.

"Still, my girl's as much of a ballbuster as you. Maybe you can make it work." Paddy heaves a sigh. "He's got other family that'd like to meet him too.

"Cousins and nephews plus their wives—great girls the lot of 'em. Even an aunt who'd like to bring him into the fold."

"Liam likes being in the Bukowski fold."

"Don't you think, after what happened, he's isolated enough?

Don't you think he deserves to be surrounded by people who'd like to call him family?" He hitches a shoulder. "I know I'd like that for him. Don't you?"

I can't deny that I do.

Still, Paddy isn't finished. "These folk ain't just your average guys either. Conor bought this hockey team to bring Liam to the city because he wasn't doing well."

"Did he do that for Liam or for you? Because I don't think Liam wanted to come here."

"Liam was alone in Montréal," he growls, his temper bristling at my admittedly prickly tone. "That wasn't going to change any time soon. He needed to be with people who matter to him. Including you."

"You brought him here because *I'm* here?" My brows lift. "Thought you didn't know I'd left Canada..."

"I brought him to the city because *we* are all here." Sniffing, he clambers to his feet. "Anyway, I've been patient. This Sunday. Dinner."

My eyes widen at his demand. "Excuse me?"

"No excuses," he retorts, purposely misunderstanding me. "I want him to meet the people who care about him."

Annoyed but unsure why because Paddy seems as if he's trying to be a father for once, I mutter, "I don't even know where you live!"

"Same building as you. Couple of his cousins do too. Top floor is where we'll be having Sunday dinner though. The doormen know to show you to the private elevator that'll take you up there. I'll expect both of you at three."

Brows lifted as the jerk swaggers off, I find Liam on the ice. Because he has some kind of radar where his father is concerned, he's watching so I shoot him a smile, not wanting him to think that Paddy pissed me off.

I mean, he did, but Liam doesn't need the distraction during practice.

Because I *am* agitated, I figure it'd be a good time to deal with another asshole so I can scratch something off my growing to-do list.

Momentarily dismissing my essay, I get to my feet and head for the bench where Bradley's watching over the scrimmage.

"Kerrigan's baby momma's got cancer," I drop as my greeting.

His head swipes to the side as he finds me in the stands. "What?"

"You heard me. Keep it on the down low—his kid's mom's sick."

"How do you know that?"

I shrug, unwilling to give him an answer.

"That's probably why his temper's running on a shorter fuse than usual," Bradley muses.

I roll my eyes at that insight, barely refraining from countering, *You don't say.*

What I *do* say is, "You should probably bench him tomorrow."

"Bench one of my stars?"

I scoff. "He's not one of your stars. He's barely kept his shit together this season. He's -4 in the last 3 games. For a player that plays on your offensive line, it's, shall we say, unbecoming? It's no wonder Liam doesn't pass him the puck."

"We discussed how he favors Lewis over Kerrigan—"

"I heard. Which was dumb. A goal is a goal."

"Kerrigan was a top scorer for San Jose. He's barely scored this past month. If his teammates aren't passing to him, then—"

"Then he should make sure he's open for a pass. Look, these guys aren't machines. You don't need to be their drill sergeant." When his glance turns mutinous, I grouch, "I didn't come over to tell you how to do your job—"

"That'd be a first. You think I haven't heard the 'tips' from Padraig O'Donnelly? I know exactly where they're coming from. My question is, what's your angle, Bukowski?"

"No angle. But I'm on your side, Bradley. Liam's your captain and if I can make things easier for him, I will."

"You consider this 'easier?'"

"You should see me when I'm trying to be difficult," is my sweet retort. "Anyway, I didn't come over here to tell you about Kerrigan."

"No? Then why are you gracing me with your presence?"

"Liam wants to sponsor a kid for the outreach program."

"There's a process," he dismisses, his gaze knowing. "One Liam is aware of. *You* might think you're above the rules, but you're not."

"We both know that's bullshit," I counter, unoffended as I watch Liam ignore Kerrigan and target Lewis—who immediately scores. I don't comment on the fact that Greco's injured shoulder is acting up again because Bradley should have caught that. "I could just talk to

Padraig and he'd make it happen, but I thought I'd talk to you instead."

Bradley cuts me a look. "I don't like you, Bukowski."

Well, hello, open season.

"The feeling is mutual—"

"You clowns—get your asses moving!" he shouts. "What is this bullshit with you peewees on the ice?"

I narrow my eyes at him. "I think you're a dinosaur who's hanging onto his laurels of winning gold for Canada when you should have retired once you added that medal to your meager collection.

"Your plays are outdated, and how you manage your players is out of touch with their reality. Greco should have been given a reprieve from this practice. It's clear that his shoulder's bothering him and you still put him in net. Never mind that you tried to get Liam to play when he might have had a concussion.

"I get that you have to make your mark and that you want to put the Stars on the map. I mean, the mafia owns the team. I don't even want to know what they've threatened you with if you lose," I comment, tone sugary. "But sacrificing your players or letting them play when they need to rest isn't the way to go about it."

"I don't need to be lectured by some nobody cunt from the prairies."

Eyes flashing with annoyance, I turn on him. "If the nobody *cunt* from the prairies is the only one who'll tell you that you're wrong, then that's just proof that we raise them right in Winnipeg.

"Do what you want with my criticism, I don't give a shit, but when I bring a kid to the outreach program, you get him an open spot, do you hear me?"

"Or what?" he snarls.

"Or I'll speak to Liam's *family* and make it known that you're mismanaging the team. They're probably not hockey fans because if they were, they'd see you for what you are—a washed-up has-been ready for the retirement home."

Not letting him answer, I retreat through the rows and head up the stairs toward the exit.

A smile curves my lips, though.

I probably shouldn't have enjoyed that as much as I did, but fuck if

I don't hate it when people bring up my province and dismiss me as if I'm from the sticks.

I'm not.

I'm from the best fucking city in Canada, and anyone who argues with me can suck my donkey dick.

CHAPTER 32
LIAM

"WANT the good or the bad news first?"

That greeting has me groaning. "Man, that's how this is going to go, huh?"

She smiles at me and somehow, that smile makes everything so much better.

"I'm giving you a choice. That's more than I need to do."

"Good news first."

"Bradley's going to get Ollie Nolan into the program."

It's hard to be happy about that when the kid hurt Gracie, made her cry, took her bag, and destroyed her stuff, stuff that put another massive smile on her face when she bought it...

But he's a child.

And kids make mistakes.

So, all I say is, "I'm glad."

I don't know how Ollie'll respond to Gracie's *offer*, but only time will tell. She's being generous when I don't know if I would be.

For her sake, though, I hope he doesn't fuck up.

She shoots me a knowing look. "Things will work out. He's only a baby, Liam."

"A baby with street smarts. But I understand why you're doing this."

"You do?"

I shrug. "I saw him in the lineup. He was the youngest there."

"Too young for that life. We have an opportunity to right a wrong. We have to try!"

"Hmm, so what's the bad?"

"Your father's putting his foot down. He wants us to come to Sunday dinner at his place this week."

"No way."

"Yes way."

My brow puckers. "Us?"

"Huh?"

"You said, 'He wants *us.*'"

"Apparently, I'm one of the reasons he wanted you to be in New York."

My head whips to the side at that piece of news.

I haven't spoken to my dad since I came here. Gracie was the *only* reason I was willing to move to the city, but the letter from him that was included in the contract package, for my eyes only, irritated me to hell and back.

Him attempting to use evidence of my purchase of a ghost gun to force me into the trade was a low blow.

Still, her answer has me demanding, "Are you kidding me? He wanted me here because of you?"

"Nope, no joke. He told me before but he said it again—he thinks I'm good for you." She graces me with another smile but this time, it's softer. Her hand reaches for mine over the console that separates the two seats in the back of the SUV. The gesture is hesitant. Unsure. My fingers instantly entwine with hers. "Do you think I am?"

"I know you are. No 'think' about it." Her blush is so cute that I could bottle it and drink from it every damn day. Reaching out, I trail my knuckles over her cheek. "You embarrassed?"

"No," she mumbles, but she ducks her head which tells me she's lying.

Taking the heat off her, I drawl, "So, what you're saying is that my old man decided to act like a father for once in his life?"

"Well, that's what he implied. He also implied that he wants you to know your family because they care about you."

"They don't know me," I dismiss.

"Isn't that the point? They want to. *I* want us to go."

"Why?"

"Shall I answer honestly?"

"Why would I want you to lie?"

"Your aunt is Irish," she informs me with faux innocence.

"So?"

"And the offer was for Sunday dinner."

It hits me.

Groaning, I demand, "Please tell me you're not asking me to sit through some fucked-up Donnghal reunion because you're craving a family get-together?"

Her eyes are practically twinkling. "It's more than just that. Food cooked by moms is always better than anything you can make yourself."

"Lies."

"In my family, it is."

I huff. "I don't want to meet them."

"Why? Why wouldn't you want more people around you, Liam?" she asks earnestly. "He made a point about you being isolated in Montréal and that's when you bought a goddamn gun.

"I've always cared about you, Liam. I knew you weren't doing well in Montréal, but I didn't think things were that dire, and looking back, I should have. That's on me.

"So, if forcing you to attend a family dinner is what I have to do, then I will." Her gaze turns merciless. "I might even talk Kara into giving you some time off from the PR shit for good behavior."

I narrow my eyes back at her. "You'd do that?"

"I would."

"For a family dinner?"

"Yup. And while we're talking about family, your half-sister approached me as well.

"You're going to start talking to her too. You have nieces who should have a cool Uncle Liam in their lives because their mom's prissy as fuck."

"You're so bossy," I complain, but her words resonate more than I'd like.

Maybe that's why I don't argue, why I don't bitch at her. I just rub my hand over my face and think about how shitty the last couple of years have been.

I *was* alone.

So fucking alone.

It's hard to think back to that time, mostly because I haven't been alone since New York and Gracie's personality is so big that I pretty much forgot about Montréal when she agreed to work with me.

She eclipsed the misery of that time in less than a week.

Because I don't want to think back to those days, I force myself away from them. That shit is for my session with Mike.

Suddenly, a soft hand is cupping my chin and it's urging me to look at her. I don't fight the hold.

"Hey," she soothes. "I didn't mean to upset you."

"Takes more than that to upset me," I mumble, but my gaze locks on hers. "Thank you."

Her brow arches. "Huh?"

"You heard me."

"What are you thanking me for when I'm making you do shit you don't want to do?"

"For giving a fuck." I swallow. "And while we're doling out bad news, Kara's decided that controlling how our relationship is outed to the press is the way forward. We have to attend a charity function next week."

Her mouth gapes.

Despite myself, I smirk at her. "Fair's fair, Gracie."

"Don't you want to attend alone?"

I scowl. "No. Why the hell would I want to do that?"

"I won't wear a dress."

I sniff. "As if I'd make you."

The tension in her shoulders lessens, but she grumbles, "I'm going to have to wear heels because you're ridiculously tall."

"Hey! Maybe you're ridiculously short."

"We're both ridiculously incompatible height-wise."

My grin is wicked. "I disagree. We're very compatible when we're horizontal. I already know that you're the perfect size in bed."

"Shut up!"

"Hudson's not interested in our conversation," I counter. "He's wearing AirPods to avoid the emo rock." When she sucks her bottom lip in to bite it and doesn't pick up on my comment, I muse, "Every time you do that in the future, I'm going to have to kiss you."

"Shut up."

"I won't." Resting my elbow on the center console, I lean into her. "You're not a lip-biter, Gracie. You weren't made for nerves."

"What does that mean?"

"It means that if you're nervous, I need to make it better. I figure a kiss'll take your mind off of whatever's bothering you."

She blinks. "That's some logic."

"Tell me I'm wrong," I rumble, moving deeper into her space so that I can press a kiss to her lips. As a soft breath soughs from her, I whisper, "Go on, Gracie. Tell me."

She doesn't.

And that says everything.

CHAPTER 33
GRACIE

MY HEART IS POUNDING when we make it into the elevator after a car ride where we made out like teenagers.

Our whole world is on the brink of changing forever and, God, I'm so beyond ready for what's about to happen that I'm jittery—not with nerves, just excitement.

Not only have I been waiting a lifetime for him, but last night was definitely a canapé and this morning was my appetizer. I'm starving—this girl needs her entrée.

I stare at him in the mirror's reflection, knowing that he's staring back at me.

My hand drifts until my pinkie connects with his.

He scoops it up in a soft clasp, like a pinkie promise, and it settles my soul in a way I didn't anticipate.

Everything about this *is* a promise.

One I know he'll never break.

That's what I'm depending on here because a life without Liam Donnghal in it? I just can't bear to contemplate that.

We're silent as we make it into the apartment.

As we walk down the hall.

As we enter his bedroom.

That, it seems, is where all bets are off.

One moment, I'm twisting on my heel, about to reach for him. The next, I'm in his arms and he's swooping me against his chest, holding me firmly and securely as he carries me, bride-style, toward the bed.

I don't even have a chance to shriek because he swallows it with his mouth, taking mine in a searing kiss that brands my soul as his.

He doesn't drop me on the mattress. Instead, he places me at the foot of the bed with our lips still locked.

My arms slide around his neck as I cling to him, loving that his focus is on our kiss. He doesn't tear at my clothes; his fingers aren't trying to find the fly of my pants.

No, his hands stay on my hips.

They're there, like branding irons—this time, he leaves an imprint on my body, not just my soul.

I lean up on tiptoe, wanting to get closer, feeling the height difference more than I ever have before. His head lowers as his tongue thrusts against mine, not exactly gentle but not rough either.

I can feel it though—*it*. Building. Growing. Liam's never this controlled aside from on the ice and I just know that once he's let loose, that's it. I'll be ruined for any other man.

Still, I love how he's taking his time. How he's coaxing me to life like the gentleman he is. He doesn't need to bother—I'm so ready for him to fuck me, it's unreal.

Because chivalry is sweet but I need to unleash the beast, I hook my leg on his hip. Not that it gets me far, seeing as he's so goddamn tall, but still, the Lord loves a trier, doesn't he?

Liam freezes for a count of one.

Two.

Thr—

I'm in the air, both my legs around his hips as he cups my butt. Fingers dig into the soft curves as his mouth tears into mine.

Fuck!

This is what I craved.

This is the unspoken promise I've felt between us for months. No, *years*.

I sob into his mouth with the relief that the dam is broken and I cling to him, arms tight around his neck as we feast upon one another.

It's so beautiful. So... *everything*.

When he draws back, my eyes drift open.

"Gracie, are you crying?" he rumbles, his thumb coming to cup my cheek.

"I want you, Liam. I want you so badly."

"*Bébé*, I'm yours," he rasps, his mouth edging toward mine again.

Except this time, he doesn't kiss me.

He nips my bottom lip, tugs on it, then bites harder.

"Mine."

I groan then whimper the word, "Yours."

He lowers me to the floor much to my disgruntlement, but that's when his fingers find my fly. Methodically, he unfastens it, then the zipper, and helps me out of my pants while I struggle to toe off my flats. As he works, I unbutton my blouse and toss it aside, leaving my bra for him to deal with.

When he's kneeling at my feet, my heart skips as I whisper, "Liam?"

"*Oui, minou?*"

I swallow. "I need you."

"You'll have me," he growls, pressing a kiss to my knee before letting his tongue slide over the length of my thigh until he finds my panties.

When he nips at the fabric with his teeth, I shiver then gulp down oxygen as he drags them off, not stopping until they're with my pants —discarded in a pile on the floor.

He looks up at me again, his gaze locked on my slit. One hand smoothes over my thigh and his thumb edges inward once he reaches the apex. I hiss as he slides through the folds all while he's staring at me as if he's a penitent sinner and I'm his salvation.

I work my heels apart, spreading my legs so he can see more. His gaze flashes where I wanted it to go and he licks his lips before he leans into me.

I can't even be embarrassed when he takes a deep breath, one that has to be loaded with my scent because, suddenly, he's there—head rocking back as his tongue sweeps through my folds on the hunt for my clit.

When he finds it, I arch onto my tiptoes before resting on my heels, one hand sliding through his hair as I grip him in place and hold him firm. The way he devours me has me shuddering.

"That's it," I weep. "That's it. Oh, God. You… don't stop. Please, don't stop. I need you, Liam. I need you so fucking much!"

This is Liam.

LIAM.

A part of me can't wrap my head around it, but another part, the part that's me from the waist down, doesn't give a fuck.

This is Liam. He wants me. I want him. Ergo, we need to get slot A fitted into slot B. ASAP.

His hands cup my ass and, with brute strength, he lowers me to the bed.

I flow with the move, following his dominion as he continues to eat my pussy, burning me up with the hungry noises that escape him, teasing me while delivering on that promise of his with every suck of his lips and flick of his tongue.

"Oh, God, Liam, your mouth is so fucking—" I groan. "You're driving me crazy!"

When I'm inches away from coming, the precipice so close that I sob with the power of its proximity, he pulls back.

One hand flicks the clasp of my bra, bearing my breasts to his hungry gaze, but he surprises me by getting to his feet and not mauling my nipples.

I can't complain, though, not when I have a feeling that I know what's about to happen.

Leaning on my elbows, my lower body quivering with how much of a tease he is, I watch as—*yes, I was right!*—he shucks off his sweater.

Then his tee.

Then his hands find his fly.

Then he unzips it.

"Hurry the fuck up, Liam," I whine.

His smirk has another shudder wracking my spine when he shoves at the waistband of his boxer briefs and suddenly, I'm eye to eye with him, able to study more than just his size but everything else too.

In my opinion, cocks are ugly, but his genuinely isn't. It's straight, no bend to the left or the right. It's long, thick, cut, and there's the faintest ombré from the tip to the base.

Seriously, this dick deserves to be part of a still life.

In fact, fuck that.

If anyone's drawing it, it's me.

My tongue is cleaved to the roof of my mouth as I take it in in all its freakin' beauty, and then, I see the silver glint at the base of his shaft.

When he retrieves a condom from one of his pockets, I don't argue as he sheathes himself, but, sitting up and with no shame, I touch the pubis piercing. "Why do you have this?"

"You'll feel it rub your clit when I'm fucking you deep."

Hello, swoon.

I stare at him, wide-eyed, not even annoyed when he chuckles.

Biting my lip, I trail my finger over his length, watching as it bobs. "Good thing you ate me out."

He just hums.

Narrowing my eyes at him, I rock back on the bed and spread my legs.

His brows lift but he grabs his dick and slowly strokes it.

I find my clit and start to finger it, watching as his gaze locks on my slit, which is weeping with my arousal.

As I play with my pussy, he continues to jack off, then I thrust two fingers inside me, scissor them, and whisper, "Takes a lot more than two fingers to replicate how thick you are."

"You don't need a replica," he rumbles. "You got the real thing, *minou.*"

That was obviously the catalyst.

He snags a hold of my legs and drags me to the edge of the mattress, moving me around like I'm a doll. I didn't know I needed that, but it's so hot to feel this petite in comparison to him.

He levers my thighs wider apart as he settles at the foot of the bed on his knees. That's when he rests his cock on my folds.

A heavy breath escapes me when, leaning on my elbows, I see the size difference.

"God, I've never wanted to be broken so much in my life," I croak.

His gaze collides with mine as he places his fingers on the tip and presses down.

My pussy is clearly magical because it welcomes him.

Inch.

By inch.

By inch.

Each one has me shuddering because Liam is packing, but fuck if I didn't realize how empty I've always felt before.

As I take him, slowly, surely, excruciatingly, I know that tomorrow, I'm not going to be able to walk without feeling it.

But there has to be some perks to having a hockey player for a lover —he can carry me everywhere, no?

Before I know it, he's inside me. Liam. Taking up every inch. *Liam.* Not leaving any part of me empty.

LIAM.

When he's *all* the way inside, that pubis piercing, so innocuous in appearance, peeps out and gives my clit a little hello.

Which is when my already wide eyes flare wider because *fuck.*

HELLO.

I practically shriek it, Adele-style.

My head rolls on my neck as I groan at the slippery pressure which is both oddly cool and deliciously warm.

He gives me a moment to acclimate to his size before he starts to thrust.

Carefully.

I know it must be killing him to take it slow, but I also know that he wants to get back in my pussy at some point in the future so destroying it isn't the way forward.

Fuck, those slow thrusts are torturous though.

I can feel prickles of sweat beading through my pores with every move he makes, so I can't even imagine what's going on with him.

Just when I think he intends to drive us both crazy, his thumb finds my clit.

In soft circles, softer than I usually like, he rubs it.

"You like that, *ma belle?*"

Suddenly, with that tumble into French, my lungs are burning and my heart is pounding and I'm there.

I'm fucking *there.*

"Oh, God, Liam. No one has ever made me—" I groan. "Fuck. You feel so good. You hit me so deep. Jesus Christ, I need you. Faster, please. Don't stop. More. More! MORE—"

I scream out my pleasure. Its suddenness has me jerking upright, flinging myself against him, unable to bear the feet that separate us.

"That's it, Gracie. You take my cock like a good girl. You fucking earned this pleasure. It's yours," he growls in my ear. "My dick is yours. You earned it."

As my arms clutch at him, his move around my waist and he hauls me tighter which thrusts him deeper into me, filling me so fucking full that I scream, "Liam, you're so fucking big. How the fuck am I—" I start sobbing before I can finish the sentence.

I cling even harder to him, bucking back so we're almost dancing together as he pumps into me, impaling me on his length.

"You're taking me so well," he grinds out. "This beautiful pussy was made for me. You're driving me crazy, baby girl. So fucking good. So fucking—"

"I can't... I just can't... Please. No more. No. I mean. *More.* Don't stop. Give me all of you. Don't ever stop," I shriek, which is when I get my second miracle.

I come again.

And this time, it's darker and deeper, plunging me to Stygian depths that are warm and comforting: a place I never want to leave.

Only, I have to.

And as I do, I hear him grunt as he comes inside me. The throbbing pulses of his cock cosset my pussy like a warm hug, making me wish there were no condom there to spoil things.

When he pushes me into the mattress, blanketing me, the only thing I can think to say is, "Knew you wouldn't break your promise."

But he's already breathing heavily in my ear, sleep having robbed him from me.

I clutch at him, settling beneath his heavy weight and, feeling like I could start purring, snuggle into him and find my own rest.

Not before I make a mental note to tell him when he wakes up that I'm on the shot.

CHAPTER 34
GRACIE

IT'S cute that he's nervous.

As we head to the penthouse, he tugs on the neckline of his sweater for the millionth time in the thirty seconds it takes to get up there.

I don't say anything because these are the kind of nerves that I can't help with.

This'll go however it goes.

Paddy, for all that I'm annoyed at his edict, was in the right to give this a shot, and, with that in mind, I get to work on making this easier for him.

"Okay, so Conor O'Donnelly is behind purchasing the Stars. He has five brothers. Conor's engaged, but the rest are married. He's also got a stepdaughter; her name's Katina.

"Declan and Aela have two kids, Shay and Cameron," I drawl as I fluff up my hair in the elevator mirror with one hand, the other clutching onto a ridiculously expensive bottle of wine. "Finn and Aoife have a preschooler named Jake.

"As for Brennan, his wife is Camille, Eoghan's is Inessa—those wives of theirs are sisters. Aidan Jr. is married to Savannah Daniels."

"From TVGM? The news anchor?"

"Yup."

"Okay. Got it."

When he tugs on his neckline *again*, I turn to him and press my hand to his chest. "It'll be fine."

"Will it?"

"Yeah, it will, and if nothing else, Mom food. That's gotta put a smile on your face."

When he graces me with a mocking grin, I roll my eyes and turn back to the reflection to fix my blouse. He bought me this darling little corsage pin holder that's barely the size of my pinkie finger. Earlier, he popped a tiny frond of lavender in there and the sweet scent's still prevalent enough to perfume the small space we're standing in.

"You like that, don't you?" he asks after catching me toying with it.

"The pin?" I can't resist returning my hand to his chest. "I do. It was very thoughtful of you."

Such an old-fashioned gift but I'm coming to learn that, in some ways, Liam *is* old-fashioned.

His finger taps the underside of my chin. "Whenever you smell whatever I put there, you can think of me."

My lips widen into a smile but before I can answer, the elevator doors open and spit us out onto the penthouse floor, only I'm not sure what I expected but *this* isn't it.

Even Liam jolts in surprise and the hand that was hovering beneath my chin shifts so he can grab me by the arm, tugging me behind him as he retreats into the elevator when a girl, back flipping down the hallway, lands a bare inch away from us.

"KATINA! How many goddamn times have I told you not to do that?"

I peer around Liam's arm to find a woman standing a mere foot away from us, clearly in lecture mode.

Personal space obviously isn't a thing in this family because there are four of us in the elevator now. As large as it is, it's not large enough for us to witness a lecture.

Katina is utterly unapologetic. "I didn't mean to land in the elevator. The doors just opened out of the blue!"

"Leave the kid alone, Star." A soft rumble comes from somewhere. "She's only playing."

"Playing? Do you know what happens when elevators crash, Conor?" Star growls.

Immediately, I push Liam and say, "Let's get out of it before it takes flight, huh?"

Star blinks as we both alight and finally stand on relatively *terra firma*. "Sorry. Not much of an introduction."

"I don't know. It's pretty fitting for this madhouse," the guy, who I recognize as being Conor from seeing him around the stadium, greets.

"This is Conor," Star introduces. "I'm Star, and this is our brat, Katina."

My lips curve. "Those were some mad back-flipping skills even if you surprised both of us." I elbow Liam in the side. "This is Liam. I'm Gracie."

"We know," Katina grouches. "We've been waiting all morning for you."

"You have, huh?" I tease.

"Yup. Grandma Lena is nervous. She almost burned the beef!"

Because she sounds scandalized, I immediately know that we're in for a treat.

"You know, for a kid who used to be vegan," Conor muses, "you sure like Ma's food."

Katina shrugs. "I'm Irish now."

Star snorts. *"We're* Irish."

Conor's smile is smug.

"Why was your grandma nervous?" Liam asks Katina.

Clearly, he's with me in appreciating the massive icebreaker that Katina is.

"Because you're Uncle Paddy's son, of course." Katina scoffs. "Everyone's scared that you're going to run, but I've seen you on the ice. I bet you suck at running without skates."

His brows lift. "Is that a challenge?"

She smirks. "No challenge. It's aerodynamics. You're big. Big doesn't run fast. It can't."

"You should see him on the treadmill," I answer with a chuckle. "He's faster than me."

"You have little legs. Conor's a good runner. He's the right ratio—"

"Sorry about her," Star apologizes. "I don't know what her school is teaching her but it's weird."

"Not weird! It's physics!" Katina sputters, more scandalized than ever. "And human biology. Certain bodies are better adapted for certain sports." She peers at Liam's legs. "I saw on TikTok that hockey players find it hard to buy pants. Do you?"

Liam's eyes bug. "Excuse me?"

"Jesus, Kat!" Star grumbles.

Laughing, Conor retorts, "Yeah, cuz. Do you find it hard to buy pants?"

I grin. "I can confirm that he needs to have his pants tailored."

Star rubs her forehead. "I'm going to have to start restricting your access to TikTok."

Katina shoots her a winsome smile then, out of nowhere, twists into another backflip and goes up the hallway the same way she came.

Whistling under my breath, I ask, "That takes some skill."

"She's got a lot of energy today," Conor excuses. "Because my brother has zero idea about kids, he gave her some of his coffee when she asked."

"Fucking moron. Who doesn't know that it's a dumb idea to give an already precocious teen caffeine?"

"In Brennan's defense," Conor reasons, "Katina is pretty persuasive."

"Yeah, and now we have an already hyper kid who's more hyper than usual!" She throws her arms up in the air. "Anyway, Conor was right. That's pretty much all the introduction you need. This family is crazy. Welcome to the madness."

I know it's unusual, but that 'welcome' couldn't have been better. Even Liam's nerves have abated some.

"Thank you for having us over," he says politely, without needing me to prompt him.

"It's our pleasure," Conor answers as I pass Conor the wine I bought for this occasion. "Uncle Paddy said we had to wait before we brought you into the circle. Said we're overwhelming, but I don't know what he means."

Star snorts again.

Hooking his arm over her shoulder, Conor hauls her into his side and smacks a kiss to her lips. "You love it."

The flush on her cheeks is all the answer I need.

Again, that sense of welcome overwhelms me and they're not even my family.

Conor remarks, "Come on, let me introduce you to everyone."

"There are a lot of faces," Star says. "Don't worry if you don't remember their names. They answer to anything."

"Curse of coming from a big family," Conor agrees. "We should have made everyone wear name tags."

Star beams a grin at him. "I'd pay to see Eoghan with a name tag on."

Chuckling, Conor offers, "I think I might have some stickers in our office. Pink ones that Katina left in there last week after that book project."

Star ducks out from his hold. "Bear with me and I'll make this happen."

"You don't need to," Liam argues, eyes wide. "Gracie's family is big. We're used to it."

Star wafts a hand. "Putting a sticker on Savannah's Gucci dress will be priceless too."

"And Inessa's," Conor chimes in.

Star's cackle of agreement echoes down the hall as she retreats to their office.

Conor, on his own now, studies us both. "Paddy says you're together?"

And *how* did Paddy know that?!

Still, I'm not sure why, but his words trigger a welter of nerves inside me. I don't even know that I've done it until Liam is there, swooping in and pressing a kiss to my lips.

"What was that for?"

"You bit your lip," he rumbles.

Conor clears his throat, but he's smiling at us.

Somehow, I think I have his approval and I never realized that I needed it.

Especially when, a couple minutes later, he and Star, stickers and pen in hand, introduce us to the O'Donnelly clan…

CHAPTER 35
LIAM

I CAN'T SAY that I had any expectations of how this would go.

I figured it might be stilted for us, but knowing how big families work and how big family dinners go, I thought we'd just blend into the background if things were awkward.

Instead, each of the O'Donnellys is wearing a hot pink sticker on their chests, most of them good-naturedly, as they talk over one another, drawing us into several conversations at once while the matriarch of the family, Lena, coordinates the meal as if it's an orchestra and she's an experienced conductor—which reminds me of Hanna.

Mostly, what fascinates me is how comfortable Gracie immediately is.

You'd think this was her family, not mine. I'm almost jealous of her ease with the bunch of strangers and how she dives into an argument with Declan and Conor over how Acuig is managing their soccer team.

"They're overwhelming *en masse*, aren't they?"

My gaze doesn't have to drift to the sticker to know this is Aoife, mostly because I already associate her with the brownies she offered me and that I had to turn down.

Did I mention that I'm so sick and tired of not eating what I want to goddamn eat?

"I'm used to big families," is my answer, but because she's so sweet, I continue, "I think I'm just jealous of Gracie."

"Why?"

"Look at her. She's in her element."

"Probably because there are no expectations on her. It's different for you. I remember when I experienced my first family dinner—it was nerve-wracking." She tilts her head to the side. "She makes you happy, doesn't she?"

My brows lift. "What makes you say that?"

"You only smile when you've got your eyes on her." Her own smile is gentle. "I know what happened to you, Liam. I understand more than you can know what it's like to overcome that kind of trauma. We find our joy where we can."

Her words have me releasing a sharp breath, one I feel like I've been holding in since Conor started harassing his brothers (mobsters) and sisters-in-law (literal mob wives) to wear name tags. "My therapist tells me I'm supposed to find joy in myself."

"Therapists are all theory. Sure, we need to find it in ourselves to a certain degree, but there's joy in being with the people we love and who love us in return." She flicks a look at her family. *Our* family. "There was a time when I wouldn't have been here, wouldn't have seated myself at the same table as Lena... I'm glad I overcame that because to see Finn here, to see Jake here, is worth it."

"Why didn't you want to be at the same table as Lena?" I ask, my curiosity getting away from me.

Her gaze is calm as she rests it on me. "You know what Acuig is?"

"I know my cousins are Irish mobsters."

"Well, when you ask questions like that, you need to know the path you're diving down." Her smile brightens. "It doesn't matter anyway. That's in the past. It has to be."

"The past affects the present."

"It does, yes, but only as much as you allow it."

"Tell that to my nightmares. You think I 'allow' them?"

She rests a hand on my arm. "I didn't mean to upset you, Liam."

Recognizing that I'm overreacting, I sigh. "I'm sorry, Aoife. I didn't mean to bite your head off."

"You're fine. If there's anything I can do, please let me know?"

Some people make that offer and don't mean it.

Aoife isn't one of those people.

I clear my throat. "I appreciate that."

"But you won't take me up on it, hmm?" She grins. "That's okay too. You'll come to learn that we're all here for you, Liam. That's why Paddy wanted to bring you here and why Lena was nervous—" Something Katina had declared at the table, much to my aunt's mortification. "—she wanted you to enjoy being with us so you'll come again."

"I don't see why it matters."

"Because you're family. Nothing matters more to the O'Donnellys than family; it's a failing of theirs."

"A failing? Not a strength?"

"Depends on who you ask," is her flat retort before she perks up again. "Are you going to resist brownies for dessert? I'm famous for them, you know?"

"Please, don't tempt me," I groan. "I'd kill for one."

"Everything in moderation?"

"Not when you're a pro athlete."

She snorts. "I leave the sports and working out to Finn. Inessa and Star are trying to get me into Pilates. That's torture enough."

A thought occurs to me—I owe Quentin, the doorman, big time for helping Gracie. A city-famous brownie would hit the spot. "Can I take one with me?"

"Sure. How's the move to New York been?"

As she draws me into a conversation about that, suddenly Aidan and Finn are trying to tell me about the best steak place in Midtown while Declan and Brennan argue that the Brazilian steakhouse on Fifth Avenue is a thousand times better.

Gracie's still arguing soccer with Conor, who does *not* know the game, while Lena and Paddy, both seated at the respective heads of the table, watch on, seemingly content to sit in peace.

I get the feeling they're both on their best behavior and that's for my benefit.

Out of nowhere, Aidan's wife, Savannah, declares, "Oh, my God, I just had the best idea."

Inessa groans. "I don't want to know."

Eoghan's smile flashes into being—he's the most severe of the brothers. "If it's anything like her last 'best idea...'"

Aidan sighs. "Little one, do we—"

"Player cards."

I blink. "Player cards?"

She nods at me. "Player cards. But for mobsters." As one, the brothers start groaning and a flurry of napkins are tossed at her but she beams a grin. "I'm going to make this happen."

Star cackles. "I'm with you, Savvie. Aela, you'll have to take the pictures."

"Why me?"

"Because you're artistic and we're not," Savvie retorts.

"I think we should all do it for each of our men," Aoife chimes in calmly. "But they have to be naked."

Finn hisses, "Traitor."

She shoots him a grin. "You'll love it."

"I'll need mine framed," Savannah purrs.

Gracie and I share a look then quickly glance away from one another with a smirk as the conversation derails into Conor trying to make this marketable for the Stars.

"Naked calendars!"

A couple hours later, with the promise of a basketball game on the big screen and no more talk of mobster trading cards and naked calendars, Finn and Brennan draw me and Gracie into Conor's man cave.

The rest of the brothers join us at some point, and I can tell they're mostly happy to let me settle into the fold, a feat that's only possible because of Gracie.

Is it strange that she's the bridge between us?

As she argues about why the Knicks are playing like shit this season with Finn, I can feel myself relax more and more until I actually start talking stats with Declan's son, Shay.

When Paddy takes a seat beside me, sandwiching me between him and Gracie, I don't tense up like I usually would. I have a childhood of his absences to back up my distrust of him. A childhood of him cheating on *maman*. A childhood of *maman's* sacrifices while Paddy's only donation to his offspring was the sperm that made me.

With that in mind, I just turn to look at him as he says, "You seem to be getting comfortable."

"That a problem?"

"The opposite of a problem," he dismisses. "And I won't let you rile this into an argument, son. I wanted *this* for you. They're your family. You should be here.

"Trouble is I know you and I know that you're difficult when it's me-related. Don't let my being here act as a deterrent. These are your cousins. They'll welcome you home whenever you want to be a part of it and you should want that. You need it, son.

"Whether you like me or not—and we can both agree that I've been a shitty father—I *can* give them to you. That's the best thing I'll have done because these kids are a gift.

"They'll fight for you, they'll go to war for you, but mostly, they'll let you come and sit at their table and eat roast beef with their children in attendance which is the greatest gift of all."

It's not like my father to be poetic, and that's how I know he means every word.

And I can see that he's right.

Not that I tell him that.

His smile lets me know he's aware I'm not going to cut him any slack, but it also says he's okay with that. "Gracie likes them. That's a good sign."

"Looks as if she's getting along with them better than I am." I huff out a laugh. "Be funny if she got *really* close, wouldn't it? We'd both prefer each other's families."

Paddy shrugs. "Only if you close yourself off from them. You have a lot in common with the boys."

"They're all pro athletes in their spare time, are they?" I scoff.

"No, but is that your measure for friendship? If it is, it's no wonder you were isolated in Montréal because most pro athletes are assholes. Including you when you're in this mood." He lifts a hand before I can interrupt. "Not going to get into an argument with you. I have no intention of upsetting Lena. She's tried very hard to get everything right today for you.

"She wanted you to know you're welcome here and you haven't even thanked her for the meal—"

"Fuck you, Paddy," I snap. "I thanked her at the table."

"And that's all. You didn't think to bring her any flowers?"

"Whatever. Your gift is me being here when I didn't want to come," I argue. Though, knowing point blank I'd have brought flowers for Hanna, I add, "I'll know to be a better guest next time."

A hint of surprise appears in his eyes. "I guess you will."

When Shay drags him into an argument about Coney Island of all places, Gracie places her hand on my knee. "Everything okay?"

Entwining my fingers with hers, a gesture that's startling in its newness and all the better for it, I glance around the room and find that the entire family has ended up in here.

"Yeah," I tell her eventually. "I think it might be."

CHAPTER 36
GRACIE

BY THE TIME we head downstairs, it's midnight.

"What's with the brownie?" I ask, eying the box in his hand.

"It's for Quentin." At my confused expression, he explains, "He helped you the other night. I owe him."

If my heart goes thunk, then that's between my chest cavity and my lungs.

Still, I tighten my hand around his and because I can't deal with that level of *sweet*, I state, "You had fun," the moment the front door closes behind us.

Maybe I sounded smugger than I thought because the next thing I know, a cake box is being dropped onto the hall console and I'm being pinned against a door with a whole lot of Liam Donnghal pressed into me.

When his mouth collides with mine, it comes as some surprise because hell, it was unexpected, but the boner burrowing into my stomach is a clue as to where this is heading.

Never let it be said that I'm not smart.

Seeing as I'm also not crazy, my lips part to welcome him in.

Fuck, he tastes good.

Like after-dinner mints and a hint of a forty-thousand-dollar bottle of whiskey that Aidan, who's apparently a connoisseur, strong-armed him into sampling.

Man, I can taste the dollar signs in his kiss as his tongue thrusts into my mouth and his hips pump back and forth, rocking his dick onto my stomach.

The ache in my core is 'steal the breath from my lungs' strong, hitting me like a sucker punch because it's surged from out of nowhere.

My arms slide around his waist, hands digging into his ass to draw him closer. He's so big, all muscles and strength and height, and while my neck is going to have a permanent crick in it, I'll suffer for the cause because I don't want this to end.

Ever.

As he tastes me, sampling me like I'm better than that whiskey he just drank, I groan into his mouth. There's no nicer way of saying it— he fucks me there. The way he thrusts into me, mimicking what his dick could be doing to me right now, is nothing short of criminal.

Because I need more friction and it acted as 'open sesame' the other night, I hitch my leg on his hip.

Unfortunately for me, I'm a short ass so I barely reach him mid-thigh, but there's the beauty of dating a hockey player who has massive thighs and huge biceps—he lifts me and pins me to the door. My legs immediately cup his hips and the friction, dear Lord, the fucking friction!

Because it's more than I anticipated, I pull back to cry out as he grinds into me.

For the first time in my life, I regret that I hate skirts and dresses because if I didn't, he could be doing more than dry-humping me.

When his mouth attacks my throat, my eyes flare wide and my heels dig into the small of his back while I wriggle and writhe as the sensitive area has my core zooming ever nearer toward a critical meltdown.

"This is so hot," I moan.

He stills before he starts back up again.

"Your dick feels so good," I whisper, tilting my head so I can bite on his earlobe. When he shudders, all his muscles seeming to lock up in response, I figure that was a smart move to make. "I love how big you are, Liam. Did you know that? You make me feel tiny. Every woman needs to feel tiny."

He grunts out a laugh before he sucks down on the join between neck and shoulder.

"Are you going to mark me again? I loved that. Loved everyone seeing that you'd claimed me—"

"Jesus, fuck, Gracie!" he exclaims. "If you keep it up, I'm going to come in my pants."

"That would be a waste," I tease, moving into him so that I can kiss him.

This time, it's slower. Softer.

Our heads tilt and angle just so, each part of the ongoing caress like it's choreographed—that's how perfect it is. No noses colliding, no accidental clashing of our teeth. One time, I even managed to damage a guy's glasses. There's none of that here.

It's seamless.

Perfection.

Nails digging into his sweater, I start to draw it up his back, wanting it gone, craving the sensation of his bare skin, those thick muscles against my palms.

I know how hard hockey players have to work to stay at the peak of their form, but seeing Liam grit his teeth when he had to say no to Aoife's brownies made me appreciate it even more.

He lets me drag his sweater off him, ripping it over his head and tossing it onto the floor.

As I take in those massive shoulders and the pecs that are totally biteable as well as the abs that go on forever, I don't even care that he's doing the same to me—messing around with the hem of my blouse too.

I'm no skinny miss, but I like my curves. If I'm bothered about inches, it's height-wise because being so short is a severe pain in the ass. So when he starts to drag it over my head, I don't even bother sucking in my stomach.

This is Liam.

I just don't feel the need to.

And he rewards me for my faith in him—when his eyes lock on my tits and they drift over my upper body, his Adam's apple bobs.

"Fuck, Gracie. How am I supposed to forget you look like this?"

I blink at that. "Why would you want to forget?"

"I have to work. I have to focus on my game," he complains, his voice thick as he discards my blouse.

The sound of tinkling hits me. "You threw my pin onto the floor!"

"It's silver. It won't get damaged," he promises—though he'd probably tell me blue was black to shut me up—before he messes with the front clasp of my bra.

That's when the groan turns guttural as my tits spill free.

His hands are immediately there, cupping them, pinching the tips, squeezing them together in a way that'd probably annoy me if it were another guy but which I rather enjoy because it's him.

When he bows his head and grazes his teeth over one of my nipples, a hiss breaks free from me and all thoughts of lavender and his gift to me fade. I arch my back, wanting to give him better access, and he rewards me by sucking down, alternating between gently biting and flicking it with his tongue.

I'd never have said that I had much of a response to a guy playing with my boobs, but hell if I don't feel the connection between my core and my nipples right the fuck now.

Unable to stop myself, I unfasten my jeans and because he's busy, I slide my hand into my open fly, behind my panties, and I find my clit.

I'm wetter than wet and it makes it easy to jill off, especially with the show in front of me.

My clit's so goddamn sensitive that with barely a couple strokes and him teasing me, I'm whimpering and rocking into him, scant seconds from getting off.

That's when he figures out what I'm doing.

Damn.

He stops his tormenting, killing my mojo, to rasp, "I need to see you playing with your pussy again, Gracie. You gonna show me how you like to be touched?"

I go to bite my lip but the second I do, he's there. On me. Kissing me.

A man of his word.

Like I didn't already know that, yet here he is, backing up my belief in him anyway.

Though his tongue thrusts against mine, before I can retaliate in this battle, he's gone. Those heavy-lidded eyes of his are staring at me as he whispers, "Well, Gracie? You going to show me how you like that sweet little cunt of yours to be played with?"

He did *not* say that word!

And yet, why did the pulse in my C U Next Tuesday throb as if he were sliding into me?

Panting, I promise, "I'll teach you but I expect you to take notes and not to forget what I like."

His grin is cocky. "I won't forget, baby girl. Don't you worry about that."

Hands drifting beneath my ass, he shifts away from the door, making me shriek. When he walks us down the hall, he doesn't continue to his bedroom—he stops at the kitchen.

Placing me on the breakfast bar, he orders, "Lift your butt. I'm going to take these off."

I obey, watching as he strips my jeans down my legs.

"You looked hot as fuck in these tonight, Gracie. But then, you always do. You're so goddamn beautiful it drives me crazy."

A shaky breath escapes me. "Really?"

"When I saw you come out of your room tonight, my cock was so hard for you. I wanted to pin you to the wall and fuck you then."

I think back to how hot *he* looked when I first saw him. "I almost wish you had."

"Next time," he vows.

With my jeans hooked around my ankles, he tugs off my ballet pumps and then whips the denim so that it flies across the room.

When I'm sitting there, practically naked, there's not an ounce of shyness in me because there's no time to feel it. His eyes are fastened to my panties like they're shielding the promised land and I tease him further by sliding my hand behind them.

He watches my knuckles protruding through the fabric, then he rumbles, "You're wet, Gracie. That for me?"

"Y-Yeah," I mewl. "It's all for you."

"You going to give me another taste? Already addicted to it, Gracie. Need more."

I cry out as I slide a finger down to my slit and soak it with my arousal. Carefully maneuvering away from my panties, I circle the drenched tip around his lips.

When he licks around the edges, I whimper, the sound shattering when he growls, grabs my hand and sucks on my finger like a popsicle.

It's supposed to be the girl who does that to the guy, but Jesus, that's hot. So hot.

I'm panting by the time he lets go, and my core clutches at nothing when he says, "Get your clit nice and wet with my spit, Gracie, and let me see." He snags his finger behind the crotch and pulls it away, using his hold to draw my panties over my thighs and knees.

Once I'm free from their constraints, I spread my legs and bare every inch of me to him.

Unashamedly.

Unreservedly.

Because this is Liam.

Because. This. Is. Liam.

My Liam.

When his gaze locks on my pussy, he orders, "Show me how wet you are for me."

With the finger that glistens from his saliva, I part my folds and show him what he did to me.

As his nostrils flare, he murmurs, "You going to take every inch of me, *minou?*"

Not the French. Dear Lord!

Thickly, I rasp, "Always, but it's your turn for show and tell first."

Though he smirks, he's quick to comply. His hands drop to his fly and before you know it, his briefs and jeans are being shucked off.

My eyes flick over the piercing that hits the top of his pubis, but that's before I take in his massive dick—it still comes as a surprise that the gossip was true about him and his third leg.

Honestly, you could rest your drink on it.

"You keep looking at my cock like that, Gracie, and you know what'll happen, don't you?"

"You don't have any pants left to come in," I retort, gingerly rubbing his piercing while I watch his hand slide over his length.

Slowly.

It takes a while because he's so long...

Thick...

Heavy…

Damn.

My pussy does a little shimmy because it knows how wonderful it's going to feel having that fill it up nice and full.

"What are you thinking?"

"Huh?"

"Something just crossed your mind. What was it? It made you release a shaky breath."

"I was thinking how good you're going to feel sliding into me again."

He steps forward at that. "You know that's true, *ma belle*." His shaft lands on my slit as he steps into me.

The second I feel his heat against me, I release the deepest of moans because, God, that feels good too.

"When you get inside my pussy, I'm going to die," I whimper.

"No dying," he snarls.

My lips twitch of their own volition and I mock, "You're the French speaker. Aren't you going to give me *la petite mort*?"

He releases a soft laugh even as he's thrusting his hips back and forth, making his length collide with my clit.

Every.

Fucking.

Time.

"We don't call it that."

That's when he breaks me. He goddamn ruins me.

He starts talking.

In French.

It's a blur of words that I don't understand, but I don't need to because it's in his tone, in his cadence. Every sentence is like a song and the key is tuned to my body.

"I want you, Liam," I whine, breaking into his lyrical torture.

Hands curling around his biceps as I draw him into me, I dig my nails in deep so he experiences the same kind of pain as I am.

"Where do you want me?" he rasps. "You have to tell me what you want, *bébé*."

I reach between us, grab his shaft at the base, and circle my slit with the head. "There. I want your dick in my pussy, Liam. Fill me. Please. I need you—"

His groan is more music to my ears, but my appreciation of it fades as—miracle of miracles—he listens.

The tip starts to penetrate me. It's thick and fat and, Lord, I need it.

Deep.

I bear down, trying to relax so he knows I want him inside me, then as he hisses because the tip pops in, I clamp around him in a nonverbal welcome.

"You're a fucking cocktease, *minou*," he growls, his hands coming to my hips before one slides high and cups my tit.

"I'm not a tease," I deny, rhythmically pulsing my pussy around the head of his dick. Not just to torture him but because it feels awesome for me too. "Teases don't fulfill their promises, but I always will."

His nostrils flare as he pinches my nipple. Hard. In time to the way I'm squeezing and releasing his cock. I yelp as the pain ripples through me, sending sensation bursting around my system. In that split second of inattention, he thrusts into me.

All.

The.

Way.

Then, when I'm still groaning at how he fills me, my ass is in his hands again and he's drawing me off the counter and into his hold. I yelp, certain he'll drop me, but he hugs me to his chest, embracing me with his strength.

I half expect him to carry me to the bedroom but he doesn't. He just starts walking. It's weird but good. Each step acts like I'm riding him, yet there's none of the effort which is nice. Plus, he feels thicker.

Thicker than I already thought he was.

And that piercing...

Wow.

Slightly warm with him, oddly slippery from my wetness, the rub of it over my folds has me shuddering against him.

"You like me in you, *ma belle*?" he asks, nuzzling his nose into my jaw.

When his lips mimic my earlier path and he nibbles on my earlobe, I release a breathy sigh. "You feel so good."

Humming, his hands cup my butt, the thumbs tipping inward toward the pucker. As he moves us around the room, my mind is focused on those thumbs.

Of all the things, that's what I can't let go of.

Every step he takes is torture because it impales me deeper onto him, but those thumbs!

"Your pussy is so tight," he rumbles. "Silk. Hot, so hot. *Tabarnak*. I used to think you'd feel like heaven, Gracie, but instead, you feel like hell, and fuck, I don't care if you burn me to ashes."

That low growl has me staring blindly at him as I whisper, "We can burn together."

He mutters something in French that I don't hear properly. It sounds like *for too jures* but I know that's wrong and right now, I don't care. One of those thumbs shifts. And it starts to rub around my asshole.

It should feel dry and chalky—in fact, screw that—it should feel uncomfortable.

It doesn't.

My wetness has spilled down, gravity letting it flow south, so when he teases the rosette, it's *delicious*.

In surprise, I tighten on him as I release a shocked gasp. When he thrusts deeper, the thumb hitting higher, I slide my arms around his neck and bury my face in his throat.

When that thumb burrows inward, pressing against the tight confines of my pussy, I release a soft cry. Eyes closing, I focus on that. On the heat and the thickness and the fullness and the way I bounce on him with each step and how good it feels and how right this is and how—

I come.

I don't even know that's what's happening until the keening wail that escapes me hits my ears.

The darkness behind my eyes would ordinarily concern me, but I'm past caring.

All I can feel is him.

He's at the center of my universe.

His heat pulls me in.

His *heart* draws me deeper.

The depth of my need for him is something that ricochets from the crown of my head to the tips of my toes and in between, an agonizing pleasure whips around my nervous system.

That's when his pointer finger torments me further.

I have no idea how he's doing it, but the tip starts playing with the already-stretched entrance to my pussy.

Grinding into him, feeling so unbearably, delightfully, wonderfully full, I just know I'm going to shatter into a million pieces because of it.

The scream I release will make 'tomorrow me' glad Liam has no neighbors. 'Tonight me' doesn't give a fuck. Especially when he groans in my ear, each one deep and guttural and loaded with his need.

For me.

Fuck.

Fuck.

We cling to one another as if we're the only stable points in each other's universe, and maybe that's how it's supposed to be.

Maybe that's how *we're* supposed to be.

One another's epicenter.

As I fall back down to earth, I'm relieved we talked about me being on the shot because he came inside me. It's warm and wet and it feels too fucking good. My pussy definitely approves.

Everything about this was perfect and the only question that's on my mind is:

When can we do this again?

CHAPTER 37
LIAM

I WISH Gracie were a miracle cure for my sleep, but as embarrassing as it is to wake her up in the middle of the night, there's nothing better than having her wrapped up in my arms when the dreams strike.

In the darkness, with the faint stars from the sky visible thanks to how high my floor is, it's easier to take a deep breath, to slow down the beating of my heart by dissociating from the nightmare when she's here.

When she doesn't push me or pressure me to talk.

She's just there.

Awake, aware, her hand cupping my forearm, her body curled up beside mine.

"Kow still hasn't called."

She tenses at that. "Why are you thinking about my brother at a time like this?"

"Because you're not my dirty little secret."

Immediately, she relaxes. "I didn't think I was."

"Really?" If I sound disbelieving, well, that's because I am.

"I'm not the kind of thing you can keep secret. Sooner or later, you'd have called him to complain about something annoying I'd done."

The mouth that was trembling a couple seconds ago in the aftermath of a dream that took me back to the worst moments of my life curves into a grin. "You have a point."

She sniffs.

"Are you going to tell your mom?"

"And have her lecture me? No. Kow can tell her." She yawns. "Or Page 6."

Grimacing, I think back to this evening and rasp, "You got along fine with the O'Donnellys tonight."

"You're an O'Donnelly too. They're *family*, Liam. Say it."

"You got along fine with my family tonight," I grumble.

"I did. I liked them. Aela, in particular. Did you know she's an artist?"

"I didn't, actually."

"She's wicked smart."

"It's the wicked part you like best, isn't it?"

I can feel her smile against the arm that's tucking her close to my side. "Maybe."

"I wish things were easier for you with your family."

The smile fades. "They love me. That's all anyone can ask for."

I know what she means, but because we're talking about her, I want more for her.

"I wish your mom knew how shitty she makes you feel."

"Did you ever watch that show about Queen Charlotte?"

I blink. "Does it have ice hockey in it?"

A laugh barks from her. "Nope. Definitely not."

"Then, it's unlikely," I tease, happy she's laughing.

"Her mother-in-law's like this grade-A bitch, even to her kid, the king, and it seems unnecessarily harsh until you see Charlotte being the same pain in the ass to her own kids. Making demands that she bristled about when they were being made of her."

"Right. And your point is?"

"I think it's a rite of passage. Or an Eastern-European thing."

"Which one?"

"I don't know. I just know that I'm happier with a border between us and it's unlikely that'll change soon." She huffs out another meaner laugh. "Of course, that *could* change when they realize I'm dating you.

They'll either come visit and be happy that you're settling down or they'll question your sanity."

"Gracie," I chide.

"What? You know I'm right."

I pull a face at nothing because I can't argue. My Bukowski world-view has been shaken at its core and I'm still reeling. "I hope you're wrong."

"Safe answer." Quiet settles between us for a moment, then she muses, "You never did tell me *why* you let Kow know about the mugging."

My expression morphs into another grimace. "He texted me to ask why you weren't answering his calls."

Gracie twists in my embrace to stare at me. "What did he want?"

"To talk to you, I guess."

"No. What did he *want*? He always wants something."

I sigh. "Gracie—"

"Liam, it's okay," she soothes, which makes me feel shittier because she shouldn't be the one trying to make me feel better here. "I know my role in my family—part peacemaker, part disappointment, part fixer. What did he want?"

I don't want to lie to her, but I don't want to hurt her either.

"He was calling about your mom's upcoming birthday." There, that doesn't sound too bad, does it?

Her chuckle is low. "Ohhh, of course. He needs me to buy her a gift for him, doesn't he?"

"Did he message you?"

Surprisingly, Ollie hadn't stolen her phone, just wrecked it, but the SIM card worked fine. So I know Kow *could* have gotten in touch.

"About what? The gift?"

My brows lift. "About the mugging."

"No."

"Did any of your brothers?"

"No."

Anger licks at my heels. "Those assholes!"

"Yup."

"What about your dad?"

"He lectured in the background while Mom was on the phone with me, but you know his ways. An hour later, he emailed me a link to a self-defense class that he paid for. We don't always show love by saying the words. I know he cares. Heck, that he went online and figured out how to pay without calling me for help is a declaration in and of itself."

I drag her into me for a tight hug. "You deserve better from your brothers and Hanna."

She nuzzles her face into my throat. "Maybe I found better."

Pressing a kiss to her temple, I mumble, "No 'maybe' about it."

"You can talk to me, you know?"

I swallow. "I know."

"You don't have to... but... the nightmares... I'm here."

My arms clench around her but she doesn't complain. I can feel my heart start to pound, can hear it in my ears. Nausea punches me in the gut from out of nowhere, making sweat bead on my face and the small hairs at my nape stand on end.

That's when I hear her soft hum and feel her hand starting to smooth along my back as she tries to calm me.

I probably wouldn't have answered if she didn't whisper, "You know how I always have the news on?"

"Yeah?"

"It's a coping mechanism," she confesses. "I got into the habit when you were... taken. It was the only way I could get any sleep."

"I'm sorry," I choke out.

"You don't have to be sorry," she counters. "I didn't tell you for that. I told you because it helps me sleep. I wanted to... I *needed* to know what happened to you. I figured that would be how we found out first seeing as we weren't your next-of-kin and Paddy might not have prioritized contacting us.

"You were gone so long that we couldn't stay together as a family. We had to carry on like you—" She shudders, and that shudder tells me exactly how rough it was for her when I was gone. "You're not alone, Liam, in still dealing with the aftermath of that time."

My mind skips back to those days when she was all I saw, when she was what got me through. I wish I could tell *that* Liam I was on her mind. That she was as aware of me as I was of her. But I can't. That's in the past.

This is the present.

"I die without getting to see you again."

God, hearing it out loud makes me sound like such a child but without her confession, I'd never have said dick.

A shocked breath escapes her, though, and her hand stills for a split second before she starts up again. "But you didn't die. And you *did* get to see me."

"I know." My eyes close as I repeat, "I know."

"I'm here, Liam. I'm not going anywhere."

"What if I'm targeted again? And what if, this time, you're in danger because of *me*? Fuck, Gracie, I can't—"

"Stop," she chides, her tone firm but kind. "I'm going nowhere. Can you imagine the amount of buyer's remorse a kidnapper would get if he tried to take me?"

"That isn't funny!"

"I'm being deadly serious," she retorts. "You don't have to worry, Liam. I'm here. We're here." Gracie presses a kiss to my arm before she reassures me, "I'm not going anywhere."

I don't argue.

I can't.

I'm too busy fucking praying she's right.

"Do you need the news on now?" I ask a few moments later.

She swallows. "Do you mind?"

My answer is to switch on the TV and find her favorite news channel before I put the volume on low.

As I tuck her closer, I hear her relieved sigh before she snuggles into me.

Reassurance or not, prayers or not, in the morning, I'm going to increase our security detail.

Just in case.

CHAPTER 38
LIAM
TWO DAYS LATER

Stacy's Mom - Fountains of Wayne

"YOU BILLETED WITH COLE KORHONEN, didn't you?" Deschamps, one of our left defensemen, asks.

As I settle my shin guard into place and pull up my sock over it, I hitch a shoulder.

"You must know his weaknesses."

I grin at Boucher, who's a right wing on our second line. "Brunettes and hot wings."

Boucher harrumphs. "That's every fucker in the league."

"Lewis likes blondes," I reason as I start to strap tape over my shin guard. If my tongue sticks out as I work, that's something I stopped giving a damn about when I was eighteen.

"I don't discriminate," Lewis argues, throwing a towel at me.

"What? You'll fuck anything in a skirt?"

"I will now."

"What happened with you and Lizzy anyway?" McIsaac, a left winger, asks. "I knew her. She was nice."

Lewis's expression immediately shuts down.

"When you woke up today, did you think about the stupid questions you could ask to fuck with people's heads?" I snap.

Boucher snorts. "Good point. McIsaac, since when do we talk about exes in the locker room anyway?"

Ha. "When *don't* we? But in this instance, we shut our traps *before* a game. Understood?"

"Gagné talks about his wife all the time," McIsaac mutters, practically fucking pouting.

I hoot. "Jude? Did you hear that?"

"Hear McIsaac malign my woman? Yup." As he draws his jersey on, Gagné bares his teeth. "He's lucky he's on our fucking side."

"So, what you're saying is, I could bring this up *after* the game?"

I roll my eyes. "If you can't read a room, you're not allowed to talk. Period." With McIsaac still pouting, most of the limelight's off Lewis by this point, but I ask, "You gonna be okay?"

He shrugs. "I'll be fine."

My gaze is watchful as he strides off. The damage is already done—McIsaac fucked with his routine.

We've all got our idiosyncrasies when it comes to pregame shit, and I can tell Lewis's is broken. He should be on track to doing a hundred star jumps, *not* heading off to the showers.

"If we lose because you're a dumbass," I drawl, scratching my jaw which I shaved smooth ten minutes ago. "I'll make the 'green dye affair' look like small potatoes, McIsaac."

With a snort, Gagné inserts, "I'll help."

"Why the fuck not? We can call it a team-building exercise—I'm in," Boucher chirps. "Worth the fine."

"What fine?" Gagné demands.

"Raimond pulled some stunt on Greco. He got fined. If more 'pranks' happen, there's a fine now."

"And you didn't tell me?"

"Since when do we gossip?" I preach.

"Ha. You said it—since when *don't* we?" Gagné frowns as he casts a glance at Greco and Raimond, who have switched cubbies with other teammates since the last game. Clearly, he just noticed. "What went down between them?"

"Rumor has it," Boucher muses, stepping close enough to us that I can smell the stench of his aftershave. Jesus Christ, skunks stink better than he does. "Raimond was 'tormenting' Greco."

"What? You heard about this?" Gagné asks me.

"No. I talked with Bradley, even stated that I should know what was going on as captain, but he wouldn't say a word." Finally, I get started on my skate.

The laces have to be precise, otherwise it'll drive me insane the whole game.

I was anal before but now, I could get a ruler and measure the distances between each eyelet—that's how precise I like things to be. These fuckers have no idea they're messing with my math.

"Fuck," Boucher rumbles. "I was hoping you'd know."

"Nah. Just that he's being 'tormented,' which I find hard to believe seeing as they've been thick as thieves from the get-go."

"No smoke without fire," Gagné points out.

I hum my agreement even as I check the time and see I need to hurry the hell up.

When Lewis comes out of nowhere with a massive tub of pasta and what looks like ranch dressing, my nose crinkles as he shifts into grand pliés. "Seriously, dude?"

"Isn't it a little late to load up on carbs?" Boucher agrees.

"That's not what I meant—he's got ranch dressing. On pasta." I gag. "Gross."

"It's the Quebecker in you," Lewis mocks, grinning wide so that I can see the pasta in his teeth.

"Or the leftie," Gagné jeers. "You know they're hellspawn."

"Well, it's nice to know we've settled in the twenty-first century," I mock. "Speaking of, Gagné, you're a redhead so that means you're also hellspawned."

"Never said we wouldn't burn together, *mon frère*," Gagné jokes, his words making me think of that vow Gracie pledged to me... My lips quirk into a dopey grin as my teammate continues, "And we will be roasted if we don't beat Jersey. I hate those motherfuckers."

"Why?"

"Every time I take a ride to the Garden State, some jerk-off crashes into my car."

"That's a coincidence," Boucher argues.

"Hell no, it isn't. My insurance stopped paying out," he grumbles. "We gotta show those motherfuckers, so Liam, you'd better tell us what weaknesses Korhonen has or I'll wreck *your* car."

I grin. "As your captain—"

Lewis starts playing his bowl of pasta like it's a violin.

"—I can only tell you that he's got a weak knee."

"We all fucking know that," Boucher complains. "He had surgery last year."

My grin turns smug. "Exactly. What happens in the billet, stays in the billet."

Lewis snickers. "Not everyone ended up with the Bukowskis. Some of us got the Condons. I'd spill shit on that asswipe so fast, you wouldn't see me coming."

I blink. "Fuck, I forgot you were billeted with them!"

"Yeah, Dean Condon and I never got along. I doubly appreciated you snapping his ACL," Lewis cheers.

"Jessica Condon was hot in her day though," Boucher rumbles, whistling beneath his breath as he jacks his dick.

Lewis groans. "Fuck off."

For some reason, Campbell, who plays on McIsaac's line, starts singing, "Stacy's Mom" but switches it out with Dean's.

I have no idea why these clowns bust a gut laughing, but I ignore them and try to reason with myself that my laces *are* straight.

Even if, from this angle, they look off-center.

Wonky laces or not, we beat Jersey.

3-1.

CHAPTER 39
LIAM

35

"IT'S ABOUT GODDAMN TIME," I grind out when my phone rings and I see the asshole's name on the caller ID.

"Hey! You told me to call when I had the chance. This is the first chance I've had!"

Kow's bullshit might work on everyone else in his life, but not on me. "Fuck off. I said it was important."

"I don't remember that part," Kow reasons. "Better late than never. By the way, did Gracie mention anything about a gift for Mom?"

"Why would she?"

"Because I brought it up with you so I figured you'd pass on the message."

"I didn't realize that's what that was," I mock, even though I did tell her. "Since when am I your voicemail service?"

"Touchy!" Kow mumbles. "Who shoved a puck up your ass and never told me about it?"

My eyes narrow at the treadmill console. "You. Are you aware of how much you take advantage of your sister?"

"Huh? What does that have to do with anything?" I hear the sound of the refrigerator door opening. "Is she whining to you already? Man, it was such a bad idea her coming to work for you."

"That's where you're wrong. It was the best idea I've ever had."

Because I recognize the noises from my own routine, I know that he's making a protein shake. When the blender starts blitzing a couple moments later, I'm prepared for it, but the noise still has me wincing and pulling the phone away from my ear.

Shoving it into the slot on the treadmill, I switch to speaker then decrease my speed.

As I start my cooldown five minutes early, I wait for my dipshit friend to hurry the hell up.

"Now, have you chilled out some?"

Jesus H. Christ. *"No."*

"Ah, shit. How about I call back another time? I'm not in the mood for a lecture—"

"I'm not lecturing you about dick. I'm telling you the facts. You take advantage of Gracie. End of statement. Now, I have to share something with you."

When he slurps in the background, I want to punch him in the face —he knows I hate those sounds. "What?"

"Your sister and I are dating."

For a second, there's silence. That's all the response I get. Until he starts cackling. "Good one, bro."

"I'm not joking."

"Sure you are. Who the fuck would want to date my sister? She'll be celibate until the day she dies. Might as well go into a convent now."

Offended on Gracie's behalf, I retort, "It's not a joke."

"Stop messing around, Liam. I get it. I take advantage of her. Yadda, yadda, yadda. Now, what's the news?"

"I don't know what to tell you, Kow. Gracie and I are an item. We're heading to a charity function tomorrow for the Stars. If you don't believe me now, maybe you will once we hit *Page 6*."

A snort gurgles in the background. "Wow, way to roll with a joke, Liam. Your dedication to pranks is coming back to its legendary level."

I cringe at the reminder of the dick I used to be.

I totally deserved how uncommunicative Gracie was with me before I got kidnapped.

"Kow," I growl. "This isn't a joke. For the last time, I'm dating your sister."

"If you *are* dating my sister," Kow says easily. "Then you have to know what you're getting yourself in for."

"A black eye? I'd appreciate one. At least then I'd think you actually give a fuck about her."

Silence is my only answer until—

"Jesus Christ, you *are* dating her, aren't you? That's where this 'You're a shit brother' BS is coming from!"

"No. That's because you're a shit brother," I snap. "You all are. Not one of you asked her how she was after she was mugged."

"Well, she's Gracie. I mean, the mugger was probably petrified after she was finished with him."

I shake my head. "She isn't invincible."

"She is," Kow argues. "She's my fucking sister."

When the belt on the treadmill comes to a halt now that my cooldown is over, I'm left staring at the city ahead from my gym window.

It's clear to me that Kow genuinely believes what he's saying.

Which is strange.

I know how he is with Gracie, know how they all are.

Could a lack of interest be something else?

"What the fuck are you thinking dating her?" he grinds out, finally sounding as if he's mad. Which he should be.

I shouldn't be this relieved that he gives a shit.

"I'm thinking like a man who's looking at a beautiful woman, who enjoys being with her, who respects her and appreciates her and never takes her for granted, Kow. How about that?"

"Just you wait until Trent and Noah hear about this."

Okay, now we're on track.

Good.

"I'm shaking in my skates. You should bring it. If you think I'm frightened of the Three Stooges, you're mistaken. Gracie's worth a fight, and I can promise you this, you'll be the ones being force-fed the knuckle-fucking-sandwiches."

Hanging up, I smile at nothing.

That went better than expected.

Now, I just have to warn Gracie that her brothers are going to be flying into New York at some point to beat the shit out of me.

That'll almost be as fun as the four of us finally getting to hang out again for the first time in months.

LATER THAT NIGHT

Les Boys - Eric Lapointe

Cole: So, it's true.

Gray: Called it.

Gray: Still, I need to remind you that if you hurt her, I will bust your balls.

Matt: Same here.

Cole: For sure.

Trent: I still can't believe it.

Gray: I think I can. They've always been close. Apart from when @Kow fucks shit up for them.

Kow: Fuck off.

Gray: Can't fuck off farther than where I am, dumbass.

Kow: This is all kinds of wrong.

Gray: What is?

Noah: It's weird you have to ask.

Kow: Them dating. I can't even with this conversation.

Matt: Good. Go away.

Liam: He's got a problem with this. Figured you would too, tbh.

Gray: Nah. I got a problem with you maybe hurting her...

Gray: You'd better not be dicking her around, Liam.

Liam: I'm not.

Gray: Good thing.

Matt: I wouldn't just bust your balls, I'd sever them and toss them on the ice for shooting practice.

Liam: Noiiiiiice.

Gray: Bet they make great pucks.

Liam: They're big enough.

Matt: He shoots, he SCORRRRRRES!

Cole: Wonder why @Kow hasn't told Hanna yet.

Gray: Maybe he has.

Matt: Nah. It'd be all over the family chat.

Liam: How did you find out?

Matt: @Kow told @Noah who told me lol. And I told everyone else. You're welcome.

Liam: Huh. Maybe they're in denial?

Gray: Either that or they want to keep it on the down-low so they can beat the shit out of you first without her giving them crap for it.

Cole: Bahahahaha! That's so the reason why.

Liam: They can bring it.

Matt: *snorts* Three against one? Don't like your odds.

Cole: He's got someone to kiss his... boo-boos now though.

Gray: True. War wounds = sexy.

Gray: Ugh, I don't need to think about Gracie this way.

Cole: Me either tbh lol.

Matt: :/

Liam: Haha, you freaked yourselves out. Thank you for doing the heavy lifting on my behalf.

Cole: You can thank me by telling Gracie that I'm coming over this weekend and I expect pierogi.

Liam: You can tell her what YOU expect. You think I'm frightened for my balls with you dipshits? HA. I got the queen of ballbusters in my bed.

Liam: So, YOU tell HER that you want pierogi.

Gray: Record her reaction for us if he goes through with it, Liam.

Liam: Oh, I will.

CHAPTER 40
LIAM

"YOU LOOK INCREDIBLE," I rasp when I see her head out of the elevator and walk toward me in the living room where I've been waiting for her.

But the power suit I expected her to wear is nowhere to be found.

Her smile is so effervescent, she makes me feel drunk as she mumbles, "Wasn't going to let you down, not when I knew you'd be wearing the Brioni." A whistle escapes her. "You look incredible too."

Her hands settle on my chest and the pressure of her fingertips soothes something inside me. Something that's restless whenever she leaves to go back to her apartment.

We've been dating for, like, two minutes, so it's way too soon for her to come and live with me permanently, but fuck if I didn't wish she would.

Cupping her cheek, I murmur, "You could never let me down."

She turns pink. "Should have shown up in my cutoffs and hoodie, hmm?"

I grin. "No way anyone is seeing your ass in those cutoffs but me." Still… "Thought you weren't going to wear a dress."

"It's not a dress," she says smugly.

That smug smile—kill me now.

"Sure it is. It has a skirt."

"There's more to a dress than that," she retorts with a sniff then retreats. "See?" When she pulls at the skirt, it parts!

"They're *pants?!*"

"Yeah. Flowy ones." She spins in a circle. "Neat compromise, huh?"

"You could have shown up in a tux, Gracie, and I'd have thought you were beautiful," I counter, watching how the floaty silk skims over her legs in a way that reveals her curves.

When she stops messing with them, the fabric settles in place. I look back at her and realize she's studying me with a somber gaze.

"What?"

"You really mean that?"

"The tux? Of course, I do," I scoff. "Hell, you rock pantsuits, Gracie. Your ass..." I kiss my fingers. "Perfect in them."

Her grin is swift to blossom. "I do like a man with good taste."

I snag her hand. "Then it's official—you *like like* me."

"Shut up. What are we? In ninth grade?"

"More like tenth. That was when you started dating *Chad*." I gag at the memory. I'd only been with the Bukowskis six months before she started hanging out with that assface. "I hated him."

"Oh, my God. *Chad!* I forgot about him. How the hell do you remember his name?"

Because I remember all the assholes she's dated.

"I wonder what he's doing."

"He's probably got a beer gut and a receding hairline."

"He wasn't *that* bad."

"He was. Don't you remember how he hurt you?"

"Not really." Her gaze drifts. "Didn't he sleep with Marie-Beth Letterman?"

"And half the cheerleading squad."

"I was punching above my weight," she excuses, which, more than the fact I thought she was wearing a goddamn skirt, has me gaping at her.

"You sure as hell *weren't*. Fuck my life, Gracie. Look at you! You're gorgeous. And you were back then, too."

Her gaze is suspicious. "Even with the spiky hair?"

"Even with the spiky hair and the fact you used more of my hair gel than I did."

A laugh bursts from her. "Mom wouldn't let me buy any. Man, you've got a better memory than me."

Only for memories that revolve around her.

I was such a moron back then.

Watching her, knowing who she was dating, teasing her mercilessly... wanting to kill every last bastard who got to touch her when I couldn't.

All the signs of a teenage asshole in love.

I wasted so much goddamn time not opening my eyes to my real feelings for her. I figure that's why it's important to me now that I don't waste anymore.

I could play it cool, probably should with Gracie. She's the kind of woman who likes to be kept on her toes. But fuck it.

If she seriously thinks she was punching above her weight with Chad of the Neanderthals, she needs the confidence boost.

"My memories revolving around you survived the many hits to the head over the last decade or so."

"Shut up," she argues with a snort.

I grab her hand. "I mean it, Gracie."

That color I enjoy seeing in her cheeks makes another reappearance.

"Are you sure you don't want to tell Hanna first?"

Her nose pops up. "And ruin our night? Nope."

The words might be confident, but her uncertainty comes through as she signs her death warrant—her bottom lip pops in and is sucked between her teeth.

Needing to lessen her nerves and uncaring about the pink lipstick she's wearing, I duck and press my mouth to hers.

A soft breath escapes her, but her arms immediately swoop up, curving around my neck as she leans into me.

When her lips part, I keep it gentle, wanting her to know that she matters. Needing her to know that she always has.

Her body collides with mine, her softness hitting my muscles, her tits rubbing up over my chest in a way that makes me want to explore the neckline of her soft silk camisole so I can release them and get another taste of her.

With a groan, I pull back, but only so that I can unfasten the button that keeps her jacket together. As I do, the golden silk beneath the navy pops even brighter.

I run my finger along the deep V of the neckline and murmur, "How do you make smart casual look glamorous?"

Her smile is shaky. "I'm just glad you like it."

"I like everything about you, Gracie Bukowski," I rumble, pressing a kiss to the tip of her nose.

One of my hands cups her breast, and she arches her back, pushing into me, moaning. "We have to leave soon. We should have left twenty minutes ago."

My gaze darts to the clock on the back wall and I find she's right.

Ordinarily, I'd say fuck it.

Screw anyone or anything that'll get between her and me.

But this is so much more than a charity function. Sure, the program matters to me, but that's nothing to what it represents—our first time in public.

That's more important than bending her over the counter and sliding into the sweetest cunt I've ever known.

I'll do that later.

Twice.

Once the whole world knows that Gracie Bukowski is *mine*.

CHAPTER 41
GRACIE

I'M WET.

Really wet.

And I'm pouting.

Really pouting.

The craving for him sticks with me as we ride toward the event because every time his knee brushes against mine in the backseat of the SUV, my dumb body reacts like I'm jilling off.

It's a crazy phenomenon, one I'll call the 'Donnghal Effect.'

Still, it's better than just being nervous.

Which I am.

Very.

This is the first time we'll be out in public and, to be honest, I almost wish we'd stayed back at the apartment. That kitchen counter and I have very fond memories and I'd have appreciated being bent over it and fucked into oblivion.

Instead, I'm here, wearing a suit that'll probably get shredded in the gossip rags for being inappropriate attire at an event like this, but it doesn't make me feel as if I'm selling out.

I hate dresses and skirts. Hate girly shit. It's just not me. This was the outfit I was supposed to wear to the Christmas formal event at my college last year but I didn't get the chance—I've never been so happy to get the flu in my life.

With my nerves at an all-time high, that I feel authentic in my skin as well as horny is a good sign, I think.

It's a reminder of why I'm even going through with any of this.

The 'Donnghal Effect.'

And man, it packs a punch.

When we get out of the car, I know I'm not the only one in the throes of experiencing it.

How the reporters swoon as we hover for photos and they beckon him nearer for interviews says it all. *But,* that's when he proves he can still surprise me.

One of the reporters from the sports networks calls out, "Liam, can we get a photo alone?"

I immediately start to move aside, letting go of my hold on his waist to slip away.

Liam, however, shakes his head and casts an easy smile at the blonde chick behind the microphone.

His hand digs into my hip, where it's been clamped since we alighted from the car, and he whispers in my ear, "We're in this together, Gracie."

I knew Liam had the ability to steal my breath, but *this?* This goes so much deeper.

All the cameras, the intensity of the flashes, the general body heat from so many people being in such confines—it's a lot. More than I'm used to. More, in fact, than I've ever given my brothers credit for handling.

Having never been in the spotlight before, this is my first time and it's overwhelming.

But his words sink into me.

He means them, and that means I can believe in them.

So, I settle into his side but I look up at him and gift him with a smile. Not a nervous one. Not one that's loaded with anxiety. A private one.

He presses a kiss to my lips.

I can feel the flashes from a hundred cameras, but I don't mind that this kiss will be in the papers tomorrow or that my mom will be calling to yell at me about it.

I just revel in this moment.

Because it's Liam and he makes me feel crazy and he kisses me like there's nothing more important to him in the world than us reaffirming our connection to one another.

"How will you respond to fans who say you lost against Tampa Bay and broke the Stars' winning streak because of your new relationship, Liam?"

That has me tensing up, but Liam acts as if he didn't hear the reporter at all.

When he pushes his forehead to mine, he murmurs, "You doing okay, *bébé*?"

Heat immediately flashes through me, erasing the bitter chill that came from the reporter's bitchy question.

"No fair," I mumble.

His grin is wicked. "What isn't fair?"

"Bringing out the French." I narrow my eyes at him. "Payback's a bitch."

That wicked grin widens, turning devious and so much hotter, as he agrees, "It is when you dole it out."

"So long as you're aware you're walking on thin ice."

"I'm a pro ice walker, Gracie. Literally a part of my job description."

His cockiness should be annoying but, actually, it's pretty adorable. Though I'd never admit that to him. Not under pain of death.

Still, our short conversation gives me the buzz I didn't know I needed to get through the pre-party bullshit. Once we're inside, it's all ass-licking and cheek kisses. *Mwah-mwah* nonsense isn't my thing.

Liam's ease in this situation doesn't come as much of a surprise seeing as this has been his life for years, but later, when we're in the car and he slumps back in his seat, I know how much this evening has drained him.

For months, Kara, his publicist, has been complaining about how few parties he attends, trying to encourage me to push him, but I never have because hockey is the priority, not parties. Still, now, I'm glad I haven't.

This is why he's been a hermit when he wasn't before.

The charade is too much for him.

For whatever reason, that makes me like him a little bit more than I already do.

It also means that Kara's job got that much harder because to get him to attend, she'll have to go through me.

And that's a feat not even Kow can manage.

THE FOLLOWING MORNING

Unknown: Saw you in the papers.

Gracie: Who is this?

Unknown: Aela O'Donnelly. Paddy gave me your number.

Gracie: Oh! Hey! You saw me in the papers at the function?

Aela: Yup. Where did you get that outfit from? I loved it.

Gracie: Really? I didn't fit in, lol. All the other women had short dresses on, but I felt comfortable. Like I stayed true to myself, you know?

Aela: Man, I get it. It's so hard to remain authentic when you have to go to these galas and charity functions. Bleugh.

Aela: I was politely told once that women with blue hair aren't allowed to attend such events and it's only because Declan is who he is that I was allowed inside.

Gracie: Fuck off!

Gracie: No way someone told you that!

Aela: They did. I swear! Hahaha. It was hilarious, tbh. We weren't even there because of him. It was this art thing for charity. It was all about me.

Gracie: Man, that sucks. I'm so glad you didn't listen. I love your hair!

Aela: Me too. After I told Declan what that bitch said, he told me that he'll get mad if I change my hair color now.

Gracie: LOL. Gotta love a supportive man.

Aela: Ya do. Of course, I'm thinking of going purple... but I don't think he'll mind. Do you? :P

Gracie: Nah. I bet he won't.

Aela: You were cute together. I saw that at the family dinner, but last night, you looked smitten.

Aela: I know, I know, that's an old-fashioned word, but I mean it. It sums the pair of you up.

Gracie: Smitten? Haha. I don't think so.

Aela: Why not? You seen the pictures?

Gracie: Not yet. Just woke up tbh.

Aela: You should check them out.

Gracie: I'm fine with not seeing myself in the papers lol.

Aela: If you say so. :P

Gracie: Liam was exhausted last night. It took a lot out of him.

Aela: It's a pressurized situation.

Gracie: For sure. I don't know how they do it, but they do. Part of the job, I guess.

Aela: I'm glad you could be there for him.

Gracie: Yeah, me too actually. I was surprised when he invited me. I figured he'd attend alone.

Aela: Why would you think that when you're dating lol?

Gracie: I dunno. I just did. Anyway, I'm glad you got my number from Paddy.

Gracie: Hey, hit me up when you're going to go purple, yeah? I'm feeling like a cut myself.

Aela: It'll be sooner rather than later.

Gracie: Looking forward to it!

LATER THAT MORNING

Dad: My Gracie girlie look beautiful last night

Gracie: Ah, Dad, thank you <3 You okay?

Dad: Mom on warpath but I fine

Dad: You happy, golden girlie?

Gracie: Very

Dad: That all matter. Tell Liam I make suffer if hurt you.

Gracie: I'm sure he knows already.

Dad: Good

Dad: Love you, my Gracie girlie. X

Gracie: I love you too, Daddy xoxoxo

CHAPTER 42
GRACIE

SOME THINGS in life are worth regretting—not telling my mother that I was dating Liam before we went public isn't one of them.

Sometimes, you have to take the bull by the balls (not the horns) and do what *you* want.

I did that when I moved to New York.

I'm doing that now by dating Liam.

I don't need anyone's permission.

I'm almost thirty years old—my mom doesn't have to approve of my dating decisions so I don't get grounded.

That's why, as she berates me, I'm not stressed or tense. If anything, I'm eating ice cream for breakfast because it's the weekend and I'm an adult who can do whatever the fuck I want.

"Mom?" I state, breaking into her tirade. "I don't feel like spending the rest of my Saturday morning listening to you tell me that Liam and I shouldn't be dating. We're not related. It isn't incestuous and you implying otherwise is just weird."

"Gracie," she snaps. "It's all kinds of wrong. You grew up together!"

"From sixteen years old! Auntie Virginia knew Uncle Jak from when they were in kindergarten. You don't think that's creepy. Or do you?" I inquire, sticking the spoon back into the carton as I kick my legs up on my favorite part of this kitchen—the counter.

No, I didn't get bent over it yesterday because Liam was exhausted after the party, but today is a brand-new day filled with exciting opportunities.

"Jakub and Ginnie have nothing to do with this. Why are you bringing them up?"

"Because you're implying that my relationship with Liam is strange. I'm trying to understand what the problem is."

"The problem is that he's part of the family."

"Isn't that all for the better?" I insert smoothly. "What are you saying? That he's not good enough for me or that I'm not good enough for him?"

"You lead completely different lives."

That that's her answer kind of kills my buzz because by not responding directly to the question, she's saying that *I'm* the one who falls short here.

Typical.

I laugh to myself as I stick the spoon back in the ice cream. "Mom, I don't have time for this conversation. If you want to moan and gripe about it to anyone, call Liam. He'll tell you that we're the only ones who matter in this relationship. Not you. Not Dad. Who, by the way, texted me earlier to tell me I looked pretty last night." *So there.* "Regardless, I'm over what anyone thinks because no matter what I do, it never compares to what Kow, Noah, and Trent—"

"That isn't true!"

"Sure it is. Maybe if I'd stuck around the printing shop, you wouldn't have such a massive problem with me, but I don't think that's the case. I think you'd always have a problem with me because I'm a girl and, for whatever reason, you think that means you can give me crap when you don't give any to my brothers.

"Kow's a manwhore. Literally sticks his dick in any honey pot that buzzes around him. Noah's got that little problem that the family doesn't talk about, ya know, *rage*. And Trent, well, we both know why you don't give him shit because he'd walk out of the door as soon as you tried to tell him how to live his life.

"They might earn millions for hitting a puck around, but you know what? I could earn the same at some point. Once I've got my MBA, the sky's the limit, and my career won't have an expiration date like the boys' have.

"But what do you gripe about? That I should be working in one of the printing shops! Why don't you care that that isn't what I want to do with my life?"

When she stops spluttering, I muse, "Maybe we shouldn't talk for a while, Mom."

"Gracie!"

After everything I've said, that that's all she can blurt out makes me narrow my eyes in annoyance. "What?"

"You can't talk to your mother like that."

"Too late. I already did. I'm tired of being the family punching bag. Tired of taking shit for the team when the team doesn't want to take shit for me.

"One of your precious sons wants me to buy you a birthday gift because he can't be bothered trawling the stores for you, and I'm the moron who'll do it for him—but *I'm* the problem child.

"I'm the one who shouldn't be in the city because it's a dangerous place though a little boy is alive because of me. Yet, I'm also too dumb to keep from being mugged and it's my fault someone targeted me. None of you, by the way, have even asked me how I'm doing after that.

"As for last night—"

That's when Liam walks in, his cowlick scooped upward as he scrubs his hand over his face. "Your mom?"

"Who else?" I mouth back.

"You should have told me privately. You shouldn't have let me find out from the newspapers," Mom inserts now that I've given her a chance to reply.

"Why?" I demur. "So I could get this lecture a day early? I don't think so. Your birthday card will be in the mail, Mom. I think I'll be radio silent until you come to terms with the fact that I'm not only an adult, but that I deserve to be treated like one too."

When I hang up the phone, Liam starts applauding.

Returning the tub of ice cream to the freezer, I have to grin. "Shut up."

He rounds the counter with a smirk. "That was a long time coming."

"It was. Trust me." Wriggling my shoulders, I mumble, "That was a massive load off."

His hand rubs the back of my neck. "To be honest, I'm surprised you took as much as you did from her."

"Says the man who didn't even realize my relationship with her was strained."

"Hey!" he complains. "I might be slow out of the tunnel but once I pick up speed, I've got your back."

Lips twisting, I nod. "You're right."

"What was her problem? I thought she'd be happy. She always says I'm like family."

"You are. But you're not the problem, Liam. I am."

His frown turns immediately black. "What does that mean?"

"It means I'm the one who's flying too close to the sun by being with you."

His mouth gapes and I'm faced with the wonderful sight of *the* Liam Donnghal being stunned into silence.

I gently tap under his chin to encourage him to close his mouth. "I'm not overly shocked that that's her opinion. So you shouldn't be either."

"She actually said that?" he growls, moving nearer to me. So close, in fact, that I can smell his aftershave from last night.

We'd come in, he'd drawn me into the bedroom, then, after dragging off his clothes and setting my news channel on mute, we had fallen back onto the mattress and he'd almost immediately tumbled into sleep.

I hadn't minded. Sure, he was a pussy tease, but I'd seen how the evening had drained him and I'd been quietly content to just lie there, relax, and read after the relatively stressful night.

"Gracie?!"

I blink up at him. "What?"

His hand rubs my neck again, his fingers taking the weight of my head as he urges me to answer, "Did she say that to you?"

That's when I make the glorious mistake of biting my lip.

Immediately, he swoops in and kisses me.

It's the most wonderful way to reset. Just that single peck, the sharing of personal space, breathing each other's oxygen, grounds me. Brings me back to this moment.

It lets me say with a nonchalance I wasn't feeling at the time, "About my not being good enough for you? Not in so many words, but I asked if that was her problem because she wasn't making any sense and her nonanswer was my confirmation."

I shrug as he tips me forward, pressing me into a hug that I didn't need, because I *am* fine, but I'll accept because he's warm from sleep and smells good and feels even better.

"I'm so sorry," he rasps. "I knew we should have told her privately."

"Like I said to her—and get the lecture a day early?" I harrumph. "Nah. I'll send her a birthday card and after that, I don't want to hear from her for a while." My hand settles on his arm as a thought occurs to me. "I don't want this to affect your relationship with her, Liam."

"How can it not? Jesus, Gracie, she can't talk to you like that, one. Two, I won't let you think I'll back up that kind of behavior."

"She's practically your second mom and family matters to you," I reason; hell, I'm not trying to 'season' his life with more people who care for him only to take Mom out of the picture. Talk about a step backward. "But my relationship with her is not yours. You get me?"

When he just scowls at me, I continue, "Look, Liam, she's always got a problem with me. No matter what I do.

"This time, I'm just past the point of giving a damn because life is too short and if I want to spend my days with you pestering me, then that's my prerogative and not hers."

A chuckle escapes him, one that I feel as it rumbles through his chest. "Tell me you don't enjoy me pestering you."

With a smirk, I murmur, "Oh, I enjoy it. Very, very much."

If that sounded more like a purr than anything else, that's my voice box being a tease. Not me.

When he tips backward, urging me away from that little divot between his pecs that smells of *him*, I almost pout, but before I can, his lips are on mine and that's even better than a hug.

I melt into him.

Literally, I just fall right into him because I know he'll catch me.

Always.

As my arms slide around his waist, I hug him tighter, needing to be as close as I physically can be. Needing that more than he can know because this right here?

It's acceptance.

It's happiness.

It's him knowing who I am and liking me anyway.

So when my lips part and I welcome his tongue inside me, my hand slides toward his hip. My fingers mess with the waistband of his shorts and, barely a second later, I slip them beneath the fabric and find his shaft.

He jolts, but he doesn't stop me. If anything, how he groans against my mouth is sheer perfection.

As I shape his length, I take him into my palm and squeeze as I start to show him how much I appreciate him.

How much I want him.

Crave him.

When he pulls back, his forehead falls onto mine so he can rumble, "Fuck, Gracie. Fuck, *bébé*, you drive me goddamn crazy," I just smile and drag his boxer briefs down the rest of the way.

Holding the base of his shaft, I tug free of his clasp on my neck and, bending at the waist, lower my head. When my lips find the tip of his dick, the guttural moan that he lets loose is music to my ears.

I made him make that noise.

Me.

I open up, sucking down before smoothing my tongue over the mushroom-shaped head.

Little beads of pre-cum have gathered there and I use that to lubricate the tip, smoothing it over the silky flesh.

Nibbling on the edge just so he will jolt in surprise, I switch tracks and suck. Hard. Making him buck into my mouth and hiss: "Gracie! What the fuck are you doing to me?"

I grin and hum around him, sucking on the tip in short pulses so that he can feel it on the most sensitive part of his cock.

When his hands find their way into my hair, I don't argue. If anything, I enjoy the tug and pull at the roots as he steers me but mostly, I ignore his silent orders and do as I want.

This is my rodeo, not his.

I gather spit in my mouth and let it trickle down his shaft. "Cat got your tongue, Liam?" I ask, aware he's been relatively silent since I started.

His chuckle sounds pained as I trace the veins at the back of his dick. "No, Gracie's got it."

"Right answer," I croon, tilting my head so that I can press tiny bites to his length that I soothe with long licks that take me from root to tip.

"Stop teasing me."

Maintaining eye contact, I flick my tongue over the slit. "But it's so much fun."

I shudder when his fingers tighten around the grip he has in my hair and he grinds out, "Shut the fuck up, Gracie, and take my cock like a good girl."

Those words go straight to my clit.

Deliciously incentivized, I find the head again and start to take him into my mouth, bobbing low, rocking back and forth while I suck in my cheeks to give him the pressure I know he needs.

Hands finding his balls, that's when I'm the one who comes across a surprise—right in the softness there, in that taut flesh, there's a piercing.

Eyes widening as I explore it, I let my finger gather the slick spit that's caught at the base of his dick, bubbling away with how fast I'm moving, then I let it drip onto his perineum, playing with the piercing as I go.

When I find the pucker of his ass, he doesn't yell in distress or moan about men not liking that shit. If anything, he broadens his stance so that I can play.

At that moment, I have a problem of my own.

I'm wet and aching and *in need*.

Deciding that the good Lord gave me two hands for a reason, I find the waistband of my pajama bottoms and, parting my legs much as he had, I find my clit and, thoroughly busy, I start to rub it while I thrust a finger into his butt.

While he groans, he clenches around me and releases the deepest grunt I've ever heard him make.

For whatever reason, that's broken him because he starts to growl, "That's it, Gracie. You take my dick in your mouth. How wet are you, baby girl? That's all for me, isn't it? Because you love what you're doing to me. You love teasing me, *ma belle*, don't you? Don't lie."

There's no chance of lying, not when my mouth is full of his dick, but he changes the parameters of the game and I've never been so grateful that I didn't drop to my knees—his hands move from my hair and he presses against my pussy through my pajamas from behind.

As he rubs me there, it feels better than my own fingers. Suddenly desperate, I retreat and lower the waistband onto my hips. A hissed laugh escapes him as I swallow around him, each gulp letting me take him deeper until my nose is burrowed in his pubis and the silver piercing cocooned there rubs the tip in a soft greeting.

That's when he takes over—his hand finds my clit, one sliding into my pussy, the other just pleasuring me like no one ever has. The parameters of our position mean that I'm pretty much deep-throating him, but choking on a dick has never been more fun.

What a way to go.

"You're so wet. I knew it. My filthy *bébé*. So fucking filthy for me. I wouldn't have you any other way, Gracie." The words are snarled but it's when his fingers find my G-spot that I start shuddering. Then, he reels me in for the kill. "You're perfect to me, do you know that? This sweet cunt—there's no better out there. It's made for my dick. And your mouth? *Tabarnak*. I couldn't have known that it'd be perfect. But it is. So perfect. You take every fucking inch. *Mon Dieu!*"

His words take me higher than I ever thought possible.

As ecstasy whistles through my system, I wiggle my fingers, wanting to overwhelm him with pleasure in return.

He has his own special spot that I hunt with my homeland security skills, and I don't stop until I make him jerk in my mouth. Until his seed explodes down my throat. Until it pours inside me as he releases the darkest, deepest of moans while I milk his prostate and I almost choke on just how much cum he releases.

But he doesn't stop teasing me either.

His fingers carry on, continuing their torture, and because we're in sync in a way I didn't anticipate, as I swallow his release, I find my own and it's *incandescent*.

Overwhelming.

So loaded with him that it might as well be Liam-shaped. Just like that part of my heart that's starting to exist solely for him...

CHAPTER 43
GRACIE

"GRACIE."

My brows lift when I see who just shuffled into the box beside me.

"Cole," I squeal, sliding my arms around his neck as I drag him into a hug. "I didn't expect to see you so soon. Not after we hung out yesterday."

He grins—women around the continental US have creamed their panties to that grin because last year, he appeared, nationwide, on buses advertising a pair of boxer briefs.

Doesn't matter that he dresses like a clown the rest of the year, Cole's got a crew of ladies who lurve him now.

Even *I* was surprised by what he was packing, but that grin does nothing for me. My ovaries are one and done thanks to the 'Donnghal Effect.'

"What are you doing here anyway?" I demand, looping my arm through his then shooting an apologetic smile at Lacey, who's been my neighbor in the family box ever since our first heart-to-heart, for almost elbowing her in the process.

"I got blown off by Kara Kingsley so I figured I'd—"

My eyes flare. "KARA? As in, Liam's publicist?"

He shrugs. "You seen her ass?"

"I have no interest in her ass."

"You're missing out. It's banging."

"I'll take your word for it," I drawl with a chuckle as I take in what he considers date-night attire—a lime-green turtleneck with black jeans and purple leather loafers. It's a good thing he's hot is all I'm saying. "You break her heart and I'll break yours. I need her working at full speed for Liam."

"Why?"

"Because he's difficult."

"The kidnapping?" he asks, his gaze locked on the ice when the puck drops and Liam immediately snatches possession.

"What else? He doesn't like going out anymore."

"Makes PR awkward."

"You think? Understatement. Still, if you did date Kara, maybe she'd teach you how to dress."

"My wardrobe is offended but I'll rise above your mean girl comment." At my snort, he grins but it fades as he asks, "So, things are still bad with Liam? He seemed brighter yesterday."

"Aside from never leaving his place without a security detail, he goes home, to the stadium, and then to a private ice rink in Jersey."

"In West Orange?"

"Yup."

"Told him about that one." He whistles again. "They have some figure skaters that practice there—"

"Lemme guess—they've got banging asses?"

"You know it."

"I don't actually but I know your type. Butts as big as the Michelin Man's."

"Don't yuck my yum," he grumbles, making me roll my eyes. "Liam either cancels or says he can't make it whenever I invite him out." He arches a brow at me. "Either we've got a problem and he isn't sharing it with the class, which I doubt because we banter like fuck on our group chat and he's yet to kick me out of his apartment whenever I visit, or... he's agoraphobic."

"Like I said. Unless it's work-related, he rarely leaves his building. He *can*, but he prefers to be at home."

"That's..."

"Worrying? I know. But he's seeing someone about it. What else can I do apart from have his back?"

Cole nuzzles the crown of my head with his chin. "That's exactly what he needs.

"Anyway, look at you wearing his number. Soooo cute," he jokes as he retreats solely so he can tug on my pendant.

My nose crinkles and I whack his hand. "Shut up."

"I'm surprised he didn't put you in his jersey," he says pleasantly.

Color blossoms on my cheeks.

I shove him in the side with enough force to wind him. When he starts coughing, I know I distracted him so I slide in with, "If I'd known you were coming, I'd have brought you pierogi."

His eyes immediately light up.

Any thoughts of Liam and my necklace are forgotten as he whines, "Shit. I haven't had any in ages."

I tut. "I can rectify that."

"You're willing to be my pierogi dealer?"

"You bet."

"I'll hold you to that," he warns.

I snort. "You can. Anyway, how come you're here? Recon?"

"And I didn't even get my ass kicked," he mutters.

"Huh?"

"Never mind. Anyway, not here for recon. This was a spur-of-the-moment thing. Kara gave me her tickets."

"Thought you'd have brought someone else. Ya know... with a phat ass."

"I've got *some* class."

"Just not a lot of it," I mock.

"Ouch."

"My sting is still sharp."

"Hell, these Sting Rays wish they were as sharp as your tongue."

Because Trent plays for them, I have to smirk. "He's lagging behind tonight," I muse as I watch the lackluster effort from the away team.

"The joys of getting old."

I snort. "I'm not the only one with a sting."

"I learned it from the best."

"You sure did."

"Too many men on the ice," I state, just waiting for the ref to call it.

"Man, Järvinen was slow to react."

"They're *all* slow."

Cole taps his nose. "It was Järvinen's thirtieth last night."

"And they went out and partied? In fact, you don't need to answer that. I can tell. Considering the Stars are hot shit this season, they were dumb not to bring their A-game."

He hums his agreement.

Resting my head on his arm because his shoulder is way too high up for my short ass, I admit, "Liam's more alone than you think. Even before we became a thing, Kow never came and saw him, barely called him either. The big jerk."

At least Cole keeps on trying and *does* visit—Kow, the so-called 'best friend,' hasn't done either!

When the forward high-sticks Raimond and manages to get away with it, I screech, "YOU BLIND OR SOMETHING, REF? GET SOME NEW GLASSES."

Because Cole has to be a good boy and can't show any support for the Stars, he stays silent but I just know he's biting his tongue.

His voice is crazy calm when he asks, "You and Kow still grind each other's gears, huh?"

"Haven't even seen Kow in person for years and he always manages to infuriate the hell out of me. I think it's one of his gifts."

"You haven't forgiven him yet?" he asks, watching as Liam intercepts a snap shot from Gagné and he slaloms down the ice before passing it to Kerrigan.

"For being an asshole?"

"Nah. I'm talking about what preempted the 'green dye affair.'"

"That was about Charlotte."

"Huh. That cock hungry chick who you hung out with?"

I gape at him. "She came onto you too?!"

He shrugs. "Can you blame her?"

I shove him in the side. "That bitch." Then, huffing, I murmur, "Kow's pissed me off since then, trust me." Though I *haven't* forgiven him.

Never let it be said that I can't hold on to my grudges.

"I didn't realize that whole mess was about her. Kow didn't know her name and Liam wouldn't say."

"He wouldn't?" I frown as I think back to that game where I turned them both green. "I wonder why." When the San Jose left defenseman shoves Lewis into the boards, I shriek, "REF! I hate this fucking guy. How the hell he got into the NHL is beyond me."

Gaze locked on the puck, he grunts. "Liam was furious with Kow, you know? After you transmogrified them into four-leaf clovers, I mean. Didn't speak to him for months."

"I knew I was right to like him," I drawl, but I appreciate him telling me that.

Liam had my back long before I even knew it.

I hiss when Greco barely manages to deflect the puck via a wrist shot from Trent.

Cole chuckles. "Ms. Hard Ass."

I shoot him a cocky smile.

A smile that gets even cockier when Liam scores the first goal against my brother's team.

Until, that is, the defenseman shadowing Liam takes him out with his knee, hard enough that Lewis has to help him up.

That asswipe skates over to the sin bin but his smug face needs a meeting with my fist.

"Kosinski's got an attitude bigger than Texas," Cole grates out as we both watch Liam settle heavily on the bench before, a few minutes later, he's led down the tunnel.

A sight that has my heart sinking.

It's always tough watching him get hurt. You think I'd get used to it with all the games I've watched, but I never have.

Ten minutes later, he's back, but Bradley keeps him there.

Knowing the coach is an idiot, it doesn't fill me with much relief.

After the Sting Rays manage to level the playing field, I see some Stars' fans start to get up and leave their seats now that Liam's not on the ice and the other team has scored.

I know that shit affects players' morale, but it's not like I can do anything other than grumble, "Fucking traitors."

Cole, seeing what I'm seeing, shrugs. "Always the way with a new team. You haven't got the tried-and-true fans yet. And the Liberties were so godawful that not even the governor supported them."

Though I snicker at that, I still glower until we reach overtime.

Which is when Bradley lets Liam back on the ice.

I can see his energy is high, but I'm still concerned as every collision hits differently, especially when—

"He'll burn out fast if he keeps this up."

"Yeah, he's pushing too hard." I bite my lip. "Come on, come on."

That's when the magic starts to happen.

San Jose knows Liam's dangerous so they buzz around him like
flies on a rotting corpse. Kosinski and Trent don't give him any rest,
skating so close that they might as well be in his pants.

"About time," I yell with the rest of the fans as the ref calls on Trent
when he shoves his stick in front of Liam, practically feeding it to his
skates so Liam trips and falls.

"Man, was he behind on that call," Cole mumbles, but he starts
clapping along with the rest of the stadium when Liam's left alone on
center ice.

"Come on, Liam!" I yell, tacking on, "Serves those fuckers right for
leaving early," because I know exactly what'll happen now that all eyes
are on him.

With a couple of bounces, Liam takes it lazily slow, coming in super
close to the net then whipping it to the back, slinking under the
goalie's glove hand, scoring his second goal and giving the Stars a 2-1
lead, which ends up being the winning goal and another W for NY.

I pump the air with my fist and, ignoring Cole's scowl, I forcibly
embrace him as if I'm the one who did the heavy lifting in the game.

"What about Trent?" he demands with a smirk.

"I'll deal with him later," I growl.

CHAPTER 44
LIAM

THE SECOND we're in the elevator is the second I pick her up and stack her legs around my hips.

Adrenaline is coursing through my veins and there's no other way that I want to celebrate than *inside* her.

Trent riding my ass like a bronco in tonight's game was worth it because it's proof that at least one of her brothers gives a damn.

It makes our kiss even sweeter when I know I convinced her that my injuries aren't too severe because she's totally on board—her mouth opens to my invasive kiss as I thrust home, tasting her, teasing her, feasting and ravaging her all while we travel to my floor.

When the doors open, I stride forward. The key gives me some trouble, but only enough that it ratchets up our desperation for one another.

As I finally get inside my apartment, I waste no time—I head for her bedroom.

It's the nearest to the entrance and I just need to be inside her.

Stat.

She clings to me as I drop us onto her bed, grinding my dick into her softness while her fingers stroke feverishly through my hair.

When her nails make an appearance, I groan into her mouth and arch my hips so that I can kneel on the mattress and work on getting her naked.

"Fuck, you need to start wearing skirts, Gracie," I complain as I struggle to get the stretchy yoga pants down her thighs.

Her eyes burn with need as she studies me, then she grins. "This isn't the first time you've been in that position. It suits you."

With a frown, I look at how I'm kneeling and roll my eyes. "Want me to stretch my groin on top of you?"

She snorts. "Maybe that'll sound sexy if you say it in French."

Obeying, I rasp the words, watching the flames lick higher as she studies me.

That's when she snaps.

She wriggles beneath me, drawing her tee over her head as she flings it to the floor.

When her bra comes next, my eyes lock onto her tits. "Fuck this," I growl, and my hands find the crotch of her pants and I tear at the seams.

She yelps as I rip the fabric off and make a space for myself.

"Oh, God, Liam," she moans as I twist her over and around so that she's on her stomach.

Making quick work of my fly, I pull out my cock, hissing with relief now that the zipper isn't welding an imprint into my shaft.

"Fuck," she groans when my fingers slide between her thighs.

"You're always so wet for me," I growl, slicking up my digits and spreading her juices over the tip of my dick.

That's when she does the unthinkable—she writhes against the mattress.

And it makes her ass jiggle.

Unable to stop myself, I grab a firm hold of the soft curve between my teeth and bite.

Hard.

Her shriek morphs into a high-pitched wail when I lathe my tongue over the bite mark I left behind.

More pussy juices have slipped down, coating her inner thighs, so I use them to further lubricate my shaft before I rest my dick between her ass cheeks and place one of my hands beside her shoulder. "Are you ready, *minou*?"

"God, so ready."

I tilt my hips forward. "You want this inside you, *bébé*? Can you feel how hard I am? Just for you—"

"Stop making me wait, Liam," she snarls, head snapping to the side so she can glower at me.

A wicked grin lights up my face as I readjust her, snagging a pillow and thrusting it under her hips so it's easier on us both.

When the tip of my dick finds her slit, her eyelashes flutter as she whispers, "You're too big, Liam."

I tease, "Want me to stop, Gracie?"

"You stop and I'll kil—" The threat fades as she starts moaning, keening wails that let me know exactly what I'm doing to her. "Ohmy-God. OhmyGod. OhmyGod. OhmyGod," she chants as I start to forge a path inside her. "You're so fucking big. Too big. *Good* big. No, too... fuck. Liam. Don't stop."

"You need me inside you, don't you, *bébé*? You need me to fill you up until you don't know where I end and you fucking begin. This is how it should always be—you taking every inch of my cock like the good fucking girl you are."

Her hands tear at the sheets as I continue to thrust into her.

Sweat beads on my forehead from how tight she is and how fiercely she's clutching at me.

Gritting my teeth, I continue tormenting us both until my hips encounter the softness of her butt.

She shudders, sharp jolts of her muscles letting me know that she's in overload, so I give her my weight, blanket her with me, then I find her hands and bridge ours together.

Nuzzling my face into her throat as she squeezes my fingers to death, I ask, "You with me, *ma belle*?"

Gracie shivers but mewls, "You feel so good, Liam. I'm too full. You're—" Her gulp is audible. "I'm going to die if you move."

"You're not. You're going to live," I rumble, not wanting that word to spill from her lips. "You're going to explode, sure, but you're going to fucking love it. Are you ready?"

She jerks beneath me with a full-body nod.

My fingers tighten around hers as, slowly, I make my retreat.

Her sharp cry whittles into my nervous system.

I don't pull out fully, just over halfway before I rock back into her.

"OhmyGod. OhmyGod. OhmyGod," she mumbles again, the words more delirious than ever.

I pick up the pace, aware that this isn't the quickie I intended, that it's deeper and slower and all the more meaningful for it.

I can feel her—every inch.

I can scent her—honeysuckle today.

I'm breathing her air and my skin is sticking to hers.

It's intimacy at its finest and it is glorious.

Nipping at her shoulder, I start to suck on the tender spot, giving her some attention there because finding her clit is—

"Did you leave a vibrator in here?" I demand when the thought occurs to me.

She jerks. "W-What?"

Knowing she'll be no help if I don't stop, I pause, ignoring her whine of complaint. "I know you, Gracie."

She stills. "Maybe."

Called it.

"Where is it?"

"Nightstand." She groans. "Top drawer."

Reaching over, I find the vibrator she left there.

I rub the toy on the sheet, knowing that's not the same as soap, but fuck if she doesn't need this to stoke the fires ever higher.

Burrowing beneath her, I'm careful with the setting as I click it on once before I let it come into contact with her pubis.

"Lower," she shrieks. "Oh, my fucking—"

Taking that as a positive, I do as she asks then settle it where I know she needs it before I leave the toy there to do its thing as I start to fuck her again.

When she locks up around me a scant thirty seconds later, I can feel her orgasm as if it's my own.

Her muscles shudder and judder and she freezes then melts then freezes again, and through it all, I'm impaling her on my dick, trying to find my own release as I struggle to thrust into her.

That's when her cunt turns into a jail cell—one I never want to leave.

She clamps around me tighter than a vise and literally drags the cum from my balls.

As I explode inside her while she's still detonating, I know, point blank, that was the best orgasm I've ever had in my life.

TEXT CHAT

LATER THAT NIGHT

Gracie: What the fuck was that about?

Trent: He broke the code

Gracie: So, you nearly breaking his head makes it okay?

Gracie: You asshole

Trent: The code fucking matters

Gracie: So this BS was about YOU...

Gracie: Why am I not surprised?

Trent: What are you talking about?

Trent: He can't just start dating you without speaking to us first.

Gracie: I didn't realize we were in the 1800s.

Gracie: The next time you face off, if you hurt him again, I'll hurt YOU.

Gracie: You know I can back up my word.

Trent: You wouldn't dare.

Gracie: Try me.

Matt: Ommmggggggg, you and Gracie look soooo cute together.

Cole: LOLZ. Yeah, just SOOOOO cute. So perfect.

Gray: A match made in heaven.

Liam: What have you done to my brothers?

Liam: Alien abduction?

Liam: You guys been probed too hard?

Gray: No, we're just overwhelmed by how cute y'all are.

Gray: Your pictures are all over the tabloids. Haven't you seen?

Liam: No.

Liam: Shit.

Cole: Can't believe I'm having to give you this advice, bro, but only kiss her once you get into your ride. Not before.

Gray: Rookie move.

Matt: He's losing his touch.

Cole: Nah. He's just whipped. I've seen Gracie wearing his number, guys.

Cole: Diamond-encrusted.

Matt: Already, Liam? ALREADY?! Why don't you piss on her?

Gray: Do not do that to our sister!

Cole: What if she's into it?

Matt: EW. We do not talk about what Gracie is into.

Cole: Well, consent is key. Liam, if Gracie consents to you pissing on her, then that's another thing entirely.

Gray: Yeah. It is. But I was talking metaphorically, dumbasses.

Gray: Still, yes, if Gracie consents, then... ummm, go ahead?

Liam: It's great I've got the green flag from you guys to urinate on her?! Tabarnak. Why can't I have normal brothers?

Liam: I've got Noah, Kow, and Trent giving me the silent treatment but you three are talking about golden showers and consent?

Liam: Why can't you all just hogtie me and force me to Tiffany's with a shotgun up my ass to get me to buy her an engagement ring?

Matt: HA! As if we'd be a party to that gross crime.

Cole: Agreed, criminal negligence.

Gray: Do we look stupid?

Liam: From where I am, sure. But you're right. If I pick her engagement ring, I'm a dead man.

Gray: Damn straight.

Matt: You really thinking that far ahead?

Gray: It's been, what, a day?

Liam: A day or a decade, this'll end the same whichever it is. You heard it here first.

Matt: *Calls Page 6*

Liam: Fuck you lol.

Gray: Better than us fucking you up though,
no? ;)

CHAPTER 45
GRACIE

MY NEXT CLASS after my face hits the papers for the second time in a week is my least favorite—principles of management.

Liam thinks that's hilarious seeing as I manage everything and everyone around me, but the course goes deeper than that.

It also helps that I loathe my professor.

McMahon never liked me, but now that my dating Liam has been made official, it's clear that dislike has turned to hate.

Maybe she's an ex and unsuccessful puck bunny?

When I receive a text from Kara about the tabloid photos of Liam and me kissing as well as the character assassination that's being attempted on my person as the press drags up a timeline of how long we've known one another—my hair looked like shit when I was seventeen. What was I thinking?—I barely let it pierce my concentration, knowing how McMahon rolls.

Unfortunately for me, she notices my screen light up.

"Ms. Bukowski, are the fourteen principles of management no longer of interest to you now that you've hooked yourself a hockey player?"

I refuse to blush, even though her question triggers a welter of laughter from the other students.

Unfortunately for her, I've already had to deal with Hanna Bukowski and, no matter who she is and what she can do for my educational career here at NYU, I retort, "I'm not sure that my personal life holds any weight in this class, professor."

McMahon narrows her eyes at me. "Cellphones should be switched off during a lecture."

"That wasn't a requirement before. Putting them on 'silent' was the only stipulation.

"I *was* taking notes on my laptop, professor. If you'd like to see them after class so you know that you have my full attention then I'll be more than willing to share them with you," I counter, saccharin-sweet.

Professors at undergrad level leave you to write or die when it comes to notes—the responsibility is yours. At MBA level, it's amplified. That she's deciding to call me out speaks of her distaste for me.

McMahon sniffs and continues with the lecture, but I can feel the eyes of my fellow students on me at varying points during the class. Those who didn't know about Liam and me have probably run a Google search by now.

When the lecture's over, I slip from the hall without her dragging me to the lectern, but a woman I've never spoken to before is waiting outside the doors.

"Gracie?"

I frown at her. "Yes?"

She smiles. "Nina, remember?"

"Not really." I check the time on my phone. "Sorry, Nina. I have to run."

But Nina doesn't care that I'm not interested in whatever she has to say. She storms ahead with: "I didn't realize you were one of *those* Bukowskis."

I release a heavy sigh—and so it begins. "What type of Bukowski are you talking about, Nina? The pain-in-the-ass variety of Bukowski?"

She flutters her lashes as she titters with laughter. "No, of course not! You know, the one related to Kow."

I frown at her. "Why is it always Kow? Trent is *so* much hotter than Kow. Plus, Kow's been around the block so many times, he's got the keys to every city he's ever played in, which is a *lot*." I sniff. "But if you're hoping that I'm desperate for a friend when you've barely talked to me throughout the entirety of this two-year program, Nina, unfortunately for you, I'm not.

"And I sure as hell won't introduce you to Kow, Trent, or Noah. They can make their own hook-up arrangements—"

"They're on Hooked-Up?" she bursts out.

My eyes boggle at her audacity. "I don't know which dating app they use, Nina. Jesus—" I hold up a hand. "I don't have time for this."

As I stalk off, the last glimpse of her face imprints on me—her mouth round as she blows bubbles like a goldfish.

Okay, I was rude. But seriously, I'm so sick and tired of having to deal with this bullshit and it's barely even begun.

Before the event, I knew it'd happen, though. That I was working on borrowed time before people would eventually link me to my brothers. It happened when I was a teenager but faded after I left the circuit and stopped following Kow and Liam to their games.

Simply being the sister of a Bukowski is to invite BS from guys hoping to score tickets or to meet my brothers or chicks wanting me to set them up...

Actually dating a hockey player, though?

I'm literally begging to be scorned and ridiculed and gossiped about in the press.

I'm going to be vilified and judged and every wrong move he makes on the ice will somehow be pinned on me.

My brow furrows at the thought.

But my scowl eases when he texts:

> Liam: Did the freesia arrive before class?

A smile curves my lips as I look down at my corsage pin-holder where the soft fronds of the flowers he gifted me this morning are sitting against my suit jacket.

> Me: They did. I was going to thank you in person...

> Liam: Did I ever tell you that I love how you're a woman of action?

Outright grinning, my thumb smoothes over the screen.

He's worth it.

The judgments, the hate, the ridicule.

I accept them.

Embrace them.

Because nothing in this life comes for free, not even my feelings for him.

CHAPTER 46
LIAM
A WEEK LATER

THE NOISE from the crowd heats up as I face off with Gray.

Playing against any of my billet family always amps up the competition but tonight, I'm leaving Arizona with a win.

My mind is firing at a hundred miles a minute and it's fucking exhilarating. My game usually goes to shit when I'm happy, but if this is me playing like shit, fuck the critics.

Swerving around Gray, who's riding my ass like I'm a bull at the Calgary Stampede, I manage to race toward the goal, just in time for Lewis to take his shot.

The puck bounces off the goalie's glove, forcing me to chase after it behind the net. Their defenseman closes the angle, almost ramming me in the boards, but I make it around the net and fire off a shot.

I miss.

Kerrigan catches the ricochet but their offense swiftly seizes the opportunity of him sucking ass and takes back control of the puck.

Ignoring the screams of the crowd, I channel my *joie de* fucking *vivre* as I go after Gray in the corner and dig out the puck.

Skating to the front of the net, I try to put it in the top corner on his glove side but their goaltender is on it again. Still, he loses his stick in the process.

Lewis jumps on the rebound and passes it to me.

I try to one-time it home, but the guy is on fire tonight and he hurls his body in front of the puck.

I'm nothing if not stubborn—to the boos from the crowd, I race to the back of the net, pick the disk, wrap it around, and finally put that sucker away.

At long fucking last.

I play like shit when I'm happy, mon cul.

In the momentum, heart racing, lungs burning, Lewis and I hug in celebration.

While I skate back toward the center, Gray shouts, "You still eating four-leaf clovers for breakfast, you asshole?"

Sweat pouring down my face, I beam a grin that not even my mouthguard can hide.

On the days when *that* is the first goal of a hat trick, I feel like I really do have the luck of the Irish with me.

Or, maybe it's my Polish girlfriend who's bringing me all the good *juju*?

YOUR DAILY DOSE OF SPORTS NEWS

NEW YORK STARS PROVE THAT DONNGHAL IS UNTOUCHABLE

BY MACK FINNEGAN

Liam Donnghal leads the Stars' offense with 10 goals as the New York Stars racked up 9 out of 9 points this week.

Toronto, Calgary, and Seattle seemed mesmerized by the power demonstrated by New York, while Greco held strong in nets.

Despite the impressive performances, whispers of Donnghal's new relationship causing a strain between him and the Bukowskis have come out of the Stars' camp. Can the Leprechaun hold strong when his love life is such a major distraction?

Gracie: This sucks.

Liam: What does?

Gracie: If I tell you, you'll laugh.

Liam: Bébé, it's 2am.

Gracie: I thought you'd be asleep.

Liam: Can't.

Gracie: Why not?

Liam: Hate hotels.

Gracie: I don't have that excuse. Did you get my mugs?

Liam: As if I'd forget. They're here. Waiting for you to get lip gloss all over them.

Gracie: HA. HA. HAHAHAHAHAHA. Not.

Liam: ;-)

Liam: Are you in your apartment?

Gracie: No.

Liam: Fuck...

Liam: Are you in my bed?

Liam: Please, tell me you're naked.

Gracie: If I tell you that then you'll never get to sleep.

Gracie: And I don't want to be accused of ruining the Stars' winning streak. Especially not against Vancouver. Bleugh.

Liam: Now I'll never sleep.

Liam: That was tantamount to CONFIRMATION.

Gracie: I'm naked beneath pajamas.

Gracie: How about that for an answer?

Liam: I'll accept text sex.

Gracie: Lol. No. Sex only if you win.

Gracie: If I have to incentivize victories, I will.

Liam: I'm sorry. That article today was out of line.

Gracie: Kara sent it to you? :/

Liam: Yeah.

Gracie: If their critique is this forceful now, with you winning, you really can never lose.

Liam: Bébé, Lewis is out. Sprained his shoulder. You know I hate Kerrigan. A win... might not be possible. Even if it is against Wankouver.

Gracie: Then you'd better work extra hard lol.

Liam: I'll give it all I got.

Gracie: Oooh, okay, so your willingness to apply yourself earned you a blowjob.

Liam: Let's not talk about blowjobs.

Gracie: You can send me pics if you deal with your boner on your own...

Liam: Deal.

Liam: But before I go, what sucks?

Gracie: Doesn't matter.

Liam: Gracie.

Two minutes later
Liam: Gracie!

Liam: Your silence had better be because you're touching your pussy and not because you've gone shy on me.

Gracie: This bed is too freakin' big without you in it. Do you know how cold your side of the mattress is? It should be illegal.

Liam: So, what you're saying... is that you miss me?

Gracie: Did I actually say that? Look at the words I used, Liam. I didn't say that.

Liam: I'm good at reading between your lines.

Liam: I'm the Gracie-whisperer.

Gracie: *pouts*

Gracie: Okay, so I do.

Gracie: But it's been a week!! First Toronto, then Calgary, then Seattle, and, tonight, Vancouver. You don't even land until 6am.

Gracie: They totally wouldn't pull this bullshit schedule if the Stars weren't new.

Liam: I like that you miss me.

Gracie: Sadist.

Liam: No.

Liam: Because I miss you too.

Gracie: What are you wearing?

CHAPTER 47
GRACIE

Last Resort - Papa Roach

"THIS IS HARD."

As I skate backward on the ice, I watch Ollie, who's clinging to the boards. "Nothing good in life is ever easy."

The same goes for me. However, not unlike Ollie, I've been tutored by the best skater around—Liam.

With Bradley threatening to toss Ollie out of the program because he's making no progress with his skating, Liam agreed to work with him after school twice a week on top of their other sessions.

I'm here for morale.

And the promise of sex in the Zamboni shed.

"You just need to find your balance," the NHL god himself insists, but his tone is far more patient than mine.

Not that that comes as a surprise.

It's way too early to think that he'll be a great dad, isn't it?

Yup, practically preemie.

Leaning beside Ollie, his arms across his jersey-covered chest, I watch Liam and try not to think about the things he's been sharing with me in the dark of night.

Of both the good and the bad varieties.

Dads *should* be emotionally available, right?

Mine wasn't, but he's Polish so that means he cries at weddings and isn't afraid of hugs. Eastern Europeans might look stoic, but get a vodka in them and sheesh, oversharing FTW.

Liam is a perfect blend of…

I'm getting ahead of myself.

Again.

"My balance is in the stands," Ollie grumbles as he wobbles on his blades. "On the ground. I've been practicing for weeks and I still can't do it—"

"Kid, you're getting skating lessons from Liam Donnghal," I snipe, annoyed at his whining. "Do you know how many fans would die to be in your skates?"

"Kill me now and they can take my place," he mumbles, sounding far too old for his years.

Words like that are triggers for Liam.

His frown is immediate. "There are other sports, Ollie. We said we'd figure something out if this one isn't for you."

Ollie's feet windmill beneath him though he didn't even move an inch. With a yelp, he clings harder to the boards.

"I wanted to try this out," he screeches. "But it's impossible!"

When he screams the last word, I roll my eyes and skate toward him, letting flurries of snow shower his jeans. "You think everyone gets on the ice and just flies across it?"

"No," is his sullen answer.

"So, why should you be any different?" Though I arch a brow at him, I ask Liam, "What happened the first time you were on the ice?"

"I fell over so many times that my mom thought I'd been beaten at school," he says cheerfully.

Ollie frowns. "Why?"

"I had bruises on top of my bruises."

His eyes flare before he ducks his chin. Which, of course, is when I get it.

Man, I'm losing my touch.

In my defense, I haven't hung around my dipshit brothers for a while.

He's *embarrassed* about falling on his ass in front of Liam.

"You fell the first time you got on the ice?" Ollie demands. "Really? You're not just saying that to make me feel better?"

"I fell the second, third, and fourth times too," Liam drawls with a snicker, but with a practiced ease, he leans back against the boards, elbows resting on the low wall like he doesn't have a care in the world.

Considering he got off twice yesterday and once this morning, I guess he doesn't.

Me either, for that matter.

I might be walking like I've been riding a horse for two days straight, but that's a small sacrifice for the upper that is a Liam orgasm.

"I fell over too," I concur. "All the time. When I haven't been on the ice for a while, I still will. It's not like riding a bike. Liam had to coach me too."

"You haven't fallen over yet," Ollie accuses.

"Want me to fall on command?" I retort, hiding a smile when I think about how that was Liam's tactic to get me to skate with him.

"No," he mumbles because he's kinder than I am. "But, just, I've been doing this for weeks and my ass has more bruises than when I've gotten a beating from Ma so, just, I dunno, don't lie to me."

"Why would I lie?" I insert, though my heart is pounding at that admission. How many beatings? How often? "I have no need to. Whether or not you make something of this practice is up to you, Ollie. I'm trying to give you options that take you off the path you were on— one that has you landing straight in juvie.

"What you choose to do is your own decision."

Ollie blinks at that but, for whatever reason that probably only makes sense to teenage boys, he relinquishes the fierce grasp he has on the boards.

With a soft exhalation, he straightens up.

Almost immediately, gravity takes him under until Liam swoops down and catches him.

Man, he really does suck.

After we share a look, Liam commandeers control of the lesson, and after he saves Ollie, though the kid turns pinker than a beet in mortification, he seems to take direction better over the next forty or so minutes.

By the end of the session, he's spent most of the time with his ass on the ice but he's smiling, which I consider a win.

"You're a total liar," Liam tells me when Ollie, with his shoulders hunched, slouches on his way out of the stadium after gracing us with a quick wave goodbye.

We offered to have Hudson drive him home, but he prefers the bus.

I'm not going to push things too soon...

Not for a week.

At least.

"What am I lying about?" I ask absently, wondering how I can get Ollie to accept a ride home sooner rather than later.

He's barely thirteen.

My mom thinks I'm too young to ride the damn bus in Manhattan and I'm sixteen years older than him, for God's sake.

"Not caring what he does. That the whole thing is on him."

"It is," I argue, grumbling when he snatches my hand and tugs me along with him as he skates backward.

I'm no figure skater, but I flow with him as he draws me around the rink in circular patterns that mimic a dance.

"Is not," he says. "If he decided he wasn't interested, you'd be in his face, working to convince him otherwise. Especially after what he admitted."

"Think she beats him often?"

He winces. "I hope not. From what he's said, she seems more neglectful than..."

"Neglect is a form of abuse."

"Yeah." He rubs his nape. "I'll keep an eye on him."

"Thank you." I let him spin me around a few times before I admit, "Never heard of reverse psychology? It's how we keep him in line. That's the only thing that works on boys his age. You were the same. Don't pretend that you weren't."

He grins at me. "I never said I wasn't but I'm keying into your wiles, Gracie Bukowski."

"What wiles?" I demur, fluttering my eyelashes at him.

"That this crinkles when you tell a lie." He taps the bridge of my nose. "I don't know how I missed it before, but I did. No more."

"You're just going to go around studying my nose for lies, are you?"

"Would you prefer me to study other parts of your anatomy?"

"How about my ass?"

"It's one of your finer features," he agrees with a twinkle in his eye as he finesses me into a twirl worthy of a waltz. That's when his eyebrows start waggling. "Anyway, just to get you back on the ice again, the lesson was totally worth it. You need to come to West Orange again. It'll make private ice time even more interesting."

When I collide with him, hands settling on his chest, a sigh of pleasure escapes me as he spins us around with a freedom that's only possible on this medium.

For all that I'd grown to dislike his sport, there's no denying the simple joy of skating. Especially with him.

But that's my trouble.

With the ice *and* with Liam—it's easy to fall.

Hard.

Even he's surprised when my skates fly out from under me. Just when I think I'm done for, he scoops me up and plasters me to his chest.

Nothing in this life is a certainty, definitely not with a pro hockey player, but it's too easy to start believing that Liam will always be there to catch me if I fall.

Especially if it's for him.

YOUR DAILY DOSE OF SPORTS NEWS

STARS' WINNING STREAK CONTINUES DESPITE INJURY-PLAGUED TEAM

BY MACK FINNEGAN

As fans rave about the luck of the Leprechaun, the Stars are facing a daunting few games with both Kerrigan *and* Lewis still out on injury.

Can Liam Donnghal lead the team to another victory against Tampa Bay?

Gracie: Sorry <3

Liam: We were fucked without Kerrigan and Lewis.

Gracie: You were at the top of your game and TB sucked.

Liam: Apparently not.

Liam: Gotta focus. Bradley's being a bigger dick than usual. Practice is gonna be hell tomorrow.

Gracie: Ugh.

Liam: Speak later xo

Hanna,

I hope you like the flowers—Happy birthday!

My absence from the Bukowski dinner table will hopefully be understandable.

Gracie and I are together. She makes me happy, probably far happier than I make her, and I won't have anyone, not you or the press, try to tell her that she isn't good enough for me.

If anything, it's the other way around.

I love you but I don't accept you treating Gracie badly.

Liam

YOUR DAILY DOSE OF SPORTS NEWS

THE IMPENDING FACE-OFF BETWEEN KOW AND THE LEPRECHAUN

BY MACK FINNEGAN

For the first time since the news broke that Liam Donnghal is dating Kow Bukowski's sister, the two players, known to be best friends, are set to face off.

Rumors abound of a divide between Donnghal and the Bukowskis after Trent failed to settle the score in New York. Tonight, we'll see how the new family dynamic will pan out on the ice…

Gracie: How's home?

Liam: You should have come with me.

Gracie: I'm needed here, plus the deadline for that essay on strategic management is looming.

Liam: You could have worked on it across the border lol.

Gracie: Uh-huh.

Liam: It's good to be back in Winnipeg.

Gracie: I'll bet. Tell you what... Next time you're in Montréal, I'll come with you but only if we can go to a Sugar Shack together.

Liam: FUCK. Now I'm going to crave ragoût and oreilles de Christ from la Cabane à Sucre all day!

Gracie: Oops, lol.

Liam: How about we fly out to Pierrefonds tonight?

Gracie: I'm in New York. And it's Mom's birthday. I figured you'd be heading over to the house to eat with the fam.

Liam: No.

Liam: I think we should go to Québec!

Gracie: You have practice tomorrow.

Liam: I'll take the fine.

Liam: Tell my EA to make it happen. She's a boss-ass bitch.

Gracie: LIAM! I have to study.

Liam: Not for one night you don't.

Liam: Anyway, you owe me.

Gracie: Why?

Liam: You said Bradley would get rid of that fuckface Greco and dipshit Raimond before the trade deadline.

Gracie: I never said that.

Liam: You did!

Gracie: But I'm never wrong. Like, ever. This can't be.

Liam: Yeah, yeah, mon p'tit cabbage. You were wrong this time. So you owe me. BIG.

Liam: We'll hit the Sugar Shack, I'll ruin my diet and get bitched at by Coach, and you can be home by tomorrow night.

Liam: Don't tell me you don't miss Canada because I'll call you a liar.

Gracie: I can't tell you I don't.

Liam: Is that a convoluted way of saying yes? Lol.

Gracie: Well, if my boss insists...

Liam: Cibole, is that how I get to have my way?!

Gracie: Don't get your hopes up.

Liam: Actually, OTHER things were up...

Gracie: Tonight?

Liam: Fuck, yeah. Tonight.

Liam: A win, my girl, and ragoût—what more can a man ask for?

Gracie: Do you need me to send Mom flowers on your behalf? She means too much to you not to recognize her birthday, Liam.

Liam: I organized it myself. You shouldn't have to do that. <3

Gracie: <3

CHAPTER 48
LIAM

THE FOLLOWING EVENING

"THIS ISN'T how I intended for our day to go," I mutter as Gracie's arm slides around my waist.

Only, it's not because she wants to be close.

It's for support.

Literal fucking support.

"I'll turn him navy blue this time," she seethes.

The notion amuses me enough that I regret laughing. I've had so many bruised ribs in my time that I should be able to adapt and move on, but God, the way they wind you is something you *can't* adapt to.

I'll take it though.

My ribs are literal proof that Kow gives a damn about her.

"Sorry," she mumbles, patting my abs in double apology. "I'll stop making you laugh, but I wasn't trying to be funny."

"That's why it was hilarious," I choke as we make our way across the parking lot toward the *Cabane à Sucre*.

When she huffs, I'm not sure if it's thanks to annoyance or exertion —it's not like I'm a snowflake on the scale, but neither am I bearing down on her that much. Having my arm raised hurts, but having it curved around her is pain relief in itself.

Then, there's the fact that being back in Montréal is like a breath of fresh air.

I know she feels it too, even if she's from Winnipeg, not Québec.

When I pull us to a halt, she peers up at me. "What is it?"

"Just look around, Gracie."

The ground is still covered with snow. The walkways and parking lot have been plowed and shoveled, but you can't shovel a forest. The trees are snow-capped, dusted here and there with mounds big and small, and that scent, the undeniable smell of maple syrup being cooked just ten yards away, seems to perfume the wintery night air.

Above me, I can see the Milky Way.

I haven't seen that since I moved to New York, where the light pollution puts a stop to me experiencing that natural phenomenon.

It's chilly and crisp and *Gracie* has her arm around my waist.

Gracie flew here when she hasn't been back to Canada in too long, just to be with me.

Gracie is propping me up.

Gracie is going to share my hotel bed tonight.

Sure, it's a day late because there were no seats available on any flights last night and I had to spend most of the morning and afternoon alone but that's better than her refusing to come home.

My grin is dopey and it has nothing to do with the pain meds I took back at the hotel before I got a taxi to the airport to pick her up.

It's just because of *her*.

Because she's here, with me, and we're together.

No hiding. No secrets.

I don't care that my so-called best friend is why I'm using my girl as a crutch. Nope. Nothing can shake my good mood.

"I missed this place almost as much as I miss skateboarding, but not as much as I missed you."

She grins at me. "That's the drugs talking."

"Naaaah."

"I forgot you liked skateboarding."

"Haven't done it in years."

"Not since you sprained your wrist when you were seventeen?"

I click my tongue. "Yup. Couldn't damage the moneymakers. The Mounties put it in my contract that I couldn't skate. S'how it goes."

"Sucks."

"Yup. What doesn't suck though is..." I lean down, ignoring the stabbing pain in my chest, and press a kiss to that beautiful mouth of hers.

Because I can.

She jumps in surprise but her lips part and immediately beckon me in.

What a welcome.

"What was that for?" She hiccups breathily when I make a retreat.

I *could* take this further if I wanted to, but I have a game in two goddamn days and as much as I want nothing more than to take her right here in the forest, I can't.

And not just because she'd kill me if she got frostbite.

Fucking responsibilities.

"Just a hello."

Her smile is sheepish. "You said hello to me at the airport."

"Not how I wanted to," I grumble, lifting a hand and pressing it to her cheek then curling a strand of hair around her ear.

"The second I saw that hit, I knew your plans were scuppered."

Amused that she's still as furious today as she was last night when she called me to check I was okay, I huff. "Kow can't put a stop to my plans."

She ignores me to rant, "You're supposed to be best friends so no wonder it's going viral. That asshole. What the hell was he thinking just hitting you out of nowhere like that? Five minutes in the box wasn't enough."

I have to agree.

The collision wasn't one for the record books, but the impact of Kow connecting with me, *then* momentum knocking me into the boards means I'm lucky that bruised ribs are all I'm dealing with.

I still managed to score twice.

As if I'd let Winnipeg win after that stunt.

"And if Kow wasn't bad enough, that Rydel asshole should have been thrown out of the game. Period."

"Rydel's never liked me," I state, pressing a kiss to the tip of her nose, loving her defense of me.

"Why not?"

"I was top of the draft our year and he wasn't." I shrug and immediately regret it. "You know how these stupid grudges are born."

"Like yours with Greco?" she says not-so-sweetly.

"Greco's an asshole."

Admittedly, he's gotten better over the season.

He's morphed from bragging about parties and the women he's fucked to focusing on the game.

Maybe that shit with Raimond changed him or maybe almost getting snitched by Gracie to Bradley about taking RED made him see the error of his ways.

Like she knows what I'm thinking, she merely grunts and encourages me to start up again.

"Told *Maman* about you today."

She stills. "You visited her grave?"

"I did. Always do when I'm in the city and I had time on my hands until you got in." I whistle. "She'd have approved. She always liked you."

Gracie swallows. "I always liked her."

Humming, I press a kiss on her temple. "Why do you always smell good?"

"It's a curse," she teases, but she settles deeper into me as she asks, "You sure those meds aren't messing with you?"

"Naaaaaah."

She snorts.

Even though it hurts, I hug her tighter to me. "I mean it. This is just you and me, *minou*. No meds, just maple syrup. My preemptive sugar high. You know it's gonna hit like heroin."

Her chuckle, however, is better than maple syrup-crack.

Together, we walk toward the cabin in the woods that gleams with soft, welcoming lights.

"I thought they might be closed."

"They were. I paid them to stay put."

Her disapproval smells like gardenias. "In tickets? Or cash?"

"Tickets are king, not cash, in my world, *bébé*." My mouth waters. "You ready for meatball ragoût?"

"No, I want the glazed ham and beans. Been thinking about them since you forced me onto that plane."

"Forced, *right*. Because I was there, dragging you into first class..."

She sniffs, but I can see her smile. Even better, she darts forward and places a swift kiss on my cheek.

My brand of charm offensive might come with a no-refined-sugar diet, but I know she's falling for it and me.

TEXT CHAT

LATER THAT NIGHT

Gracie: I will never forgive you for tonight.

Kow: Fuck off, Gracie.

Kow: He broke the code.

Gracie: Ah. This mythical code again. Trent already told me about it.

Gracie: Since when do you give a fuck about me, Kow?

Gracie: You fuck my friends, but I can't fuck yours?

Kow: Is that what this is about? PAYBACK?

Gracie: NO.

Gracie: I know diving into a random puck bunny's pussy is your goal in life but dicks aren't the center of my existence.

Kow: Did this all start as bullshit? This PA crap was just a front?

Gracie: Of course it wasn't.

Kow: He should have ASKED.

Gracie: As far as I know, King Charles III is our king not King Charles I. He doesn't have to ask you dick.

Gracie: Do I ask you about your relationships?

Kow: This is different and if you can't see that then there's nothing to say.

Gracie: I told Trent, and now I'm telling you. Hurt him again, I'll make the 'green dye affair' look like small potatoes by comparison.

Liam,

Thank you for the flowers, son.

I'm sorry about Kow. Fryd has had a word with him and the other boys. While I don't approve, I won't have them injuring you on the ice over your relationship with Gracie.

I hope you're okay. The news said you were but if you could let me know, I'd appreciate it.

I love you.

Hanna

Hanna,

I'm fine. You don't have to worry. I can take care of myself.

Have you sent a note to Gracie too?

Liam

YOUR DAILY DOSE OF SPORTS NEWS

STARS LOSE IN MIAMI—LEPRECHAUN'S NEW GIRLFRIEND TO BLAME FOR HIS GOAL DROUGHT?

BY MACK FINNEGAN

The New York Stars' streak lasted nine games, but fans are blaming the center's girlfriend for the team's recent loss in Miami, which is the second game with no goals for top-scorer Liam Donnghal.

Sister of hockey legends, Kow, Trent, and Noah, Gracie Bukowski was recently pictured with Donnghal at the Stars' fundraiser for its new outreach program that hopes to cultivate homegrown talent in low-income neighborhoods.

Ever since the event, many have been saying that the Leprechaun's game is not as focused as it once was, especially after the showdown in Winnipeg that saw a fight between Kow

Bukowski and Liam Donnghal go viral. It seems not even the family approves of this relationship...

Mary Quinn, 58, from Queens, points out, "Donnghal's definitely slowed down since they got together. That's what happens when a man falls in love. It'd be romantic if we weren't so close to the playoffs. It's wrong of that Gracie Bukowski to get between a man and his friend though. I blame her."

Suzanne Hapsburg, 27, from Westchester, remarks, "I don't think their relationship will last long. Not when she's making his game suffer."

Whether or not Ms. Bukowski *is* to blame, talking heads have more faith in the Leprechaun—they're backing the Stars in tonight's game against Philadelphia with odds of a 4-2 win.

———————————————————————————————

CHAPTER 49
GRACIE

KEEPING AN EYE ON HUDSON, whose AirPods are in his ears as usual, I lower myself into the shadows, fully aware that Liam's pouting over not scoring again in tonight's game.

A win is a win even if it was in a shoot out where he failed to follow through, but there's no way I'm dealing with his grouchy ass all night long. Some cheering up is definitely required.

Carefully, I grab his zipper, aware that his head whipped away from the window at my first touch.

When I tug it down, he snaps out a breath and then grunts as I pull his dick from within the folds of his dress pants. Not that he tries to stop me, but he rumbles, "Gracie—"

I don't let him finish.

I just suck the tip into my mouth and flutter my tongue around it. His hips jerk back in surprise and I can feel the muscles in his abs flex as his whole body responds to that one move.

If that isn't great for my confidence, I don't know what is.

Staring up at him as I flood his shaft with spit, I start to rock my head, letting him sink deeper into my mouth. One hand rakes through my hair as he holds me to him. As for the other, he settles his elbow on the armrest and leans his head on it to watch me in the play of lights from oncoming traffic.

His posture is so lazily indulgent that sparks of pleasure whisper through me as if I were touching myself.

His hand on the back of my head starts to tighten and release in my hair, encouraging me to take the pace he's setting.

Because this is for him, and because I can't take this much further with Hudson so close, I follow his wishes.

He pushes me past my comfort zone, but he does it in a way that would give me time to stop him if I needed.

I want to please him though.

I want that so much, it shocks even me.

We're both getting shit from the press so reconnecting in this simple way nourishes something in me that's been on edge since the Stars' winning streak ended.

I know what it means—he's happy.

When he's miserable, he plays like a god.

How can I be on edge about making him happy?

Welcome to the bittersweet world of being a PAL for a pro athlete.

Head bobbing in his lap, I swallow around him. As I suck him and tease him, the hold on my hair is interspersed with soft strokes of his fingertips at my mouth.

It's a tender caress. Dare I say… a loving one?

Tongue fluttering along that thick vein on the underside of his shaft, I draw him ever closer to the edge.

It's weird having to be silent, especially when I realize how noisy we are together, but there's no denying it makes this even hotter.

When his hips rock forward, the motion sharp and unexpected, I cough around his dick then quickly force myself to relax because he's exploding in my mouth—cum jettisoning down my throat as he hisses with pleasure.

My eyes are watering, but hell if I don't feel proud as I swallow everything he can give me.

When he's finished, when I lick him clean, making sure I get every last drop, when I pat his closed fly once I tuck him behind it, I press my lips to his.

He groans as his tongue swipes out to taste himself, but I pull back to murmur, "Told you I was a good girl."

OVERTIME

TWO WEEKS LATER

Gracie: OMG, you did it! You're in the playoffs!!

Liam: Bébé, this isn't my first rodeo lol.

Gracie: It is with the Stars. AND the Liberties weren't in the playoffs for over a decade, Liam. Jeeeez.

Liam: I don't play for the Liberties. ;-)

Gracie: Okay, okay, Mr. Cocky.

Gracie: We're not celebrating the not-so-massive win, then?

Liam: I didn't say that.

Gracie: Pretty sure you did.

Gracie: Thought it wasn't that special?

Liam: You're right. It's very special. Epic, even. Fuck, what an achievement.

Liam: I can't believe we did it. We're miracle workers. Stars by name AND by deed.

Gracie: That's right. You are.

Gracie: When does MY star think he'll get home?

Liam: Flight's due in two hours.

Liam: You going to wait up for me?

Gracie: I'll let you be my alarm clock, hmm? How about that?

Liam: It can be arranged.

CHAPTER 50
LIAM

Delicate - Damien Rice

LIKE I TOLD HER, this isn't my first rodeo, but it's still a good feeling to know that we haven't sucked ass this season despite the growing pains the team has had and the injuries we've been plagued with recently.

Everyone's in a good mood on the ride to the plane because not even Lewis and Raimond start bickering, a miracle that continues for the entirety of the flight.

By the time we're back in New York, fatigue has set in for a lot of us.

It's been an intense month and the pressure was high. Thanks to a couple of fuckups at the start, where we mostly lost, we had a lot of ground to make up for.

The worst part was that Gracie was getting blamed in the press. I'm actually a douche for downplaying what tonight's win means for the team. Her relief must be intense.

No one realizes how hard it is dating a pro athlete.

Earlier this week, the papers were saying I'd gained weight and that was because Gracie hadn't been cooking the right food for her boyfriend...

How chauvinistic is that?

Like we don't have nutritionists anal-retentively managing our macros and micros, for fuck's sake.

Vowing to make my assholery up to her, I trudge off the plane and head toward the car.

Hudson greets me with an open door and I slip inside and sink into the cushions with a yawn.

"Great game, sir."

"Liam, Hudson. Liam," I correct for the millionth time. "How have things been?"

"Fine, sir. Gracie was accosted by the press outside the apartment building yesterday afternoon and she managed not to punch the reporter. I think we both know how much of a win that was."

I grin into the darkness. "Yeah, a massive win."

More massive than what just happened in Calgary.

"What did they want?"

Hudson has picked up on the fact that Gracie won't tell me everything that happens when I'm away or when I'm not with her, so we've got a bro code situation going down.

Honestly, if the Stars stopped paying Hudson to drive me around, I'd pay him instead. The guy's smart, sees more than he should, and picks up on more intimate details about Gracie than her security does.

Not that she realizes I have more security on her.

Hudson does though.

That falls under the bro code limitation too.

"They wanted to know why you failed to make that penalty shot in Minnesota."

Grimacing, I dig my fingers into my eyes. "Like that was her fault."

"They do seem to be targeting her. I'm not certain why. She's a Bukowski. It's not as if she doesn't understand the hockey mentality."

My grimace darkens.

The 'hockey mentality.'

I'm pretty sure that Gracie's happy with me, but it's shit like this that could wreck things for us.

Her being vilified by everyone under the sun because the team lost a couple games... How long is she going to be willing to put up with that bullshit?

I'm the top scorer but I'm only one fucking man. It takes a team to win but you wouldn't know that from what they print in the press or say on PSN.

By the time Hudson drops me off at home and I'm making it up to my floor, I'm wearier than ever.

If the media ruins this for Gracie and me, I'm not sure what I'll do.

Retire to Manitoba, maybe?

Become a legit hermit?

Go full wild man of the wilderness just to punish the hockey fans who have supported *me* but have turned their backs on the one woman I want because God forbid I'm allowed to be happy?

Dumping my suitcase by the door to sort in the morning, I slip out of my shoes so that I don't squeak as I walk down the hall, which is when I see the bedroom door is open.

Just as she said she'd be, she's sleeping. I can tell because she switched off that wax melt thing she burns and there's a glow from the TV screen that she leaves on all night.

Except, it's always on mute and...

There's a buzzing sound.

I know exactly what it is.

"Ah, fuck, Gracie," I groan, tearing at my shirt buttons and dragging it off as I make it to the door.

My pants come next as she whimpers and my mouth immediately waters as my cock leaps to attention.

The sight of her with her legs spread and a vibrator pumping in and out of that delicious cunt is honestly spank bank material, but it's the fact that she's moaning, "Liam, fuck, Liam, please, come and give me your dick. This doesn't even fill me," that's got my blood pressure soaring.

As I clamber onto the bed, the scent of her arousal perfumes the air.

I could glut on it. Glut on *her*.

Jesus fuck.

Bowing my head to get a better view, I snag the vibrator away from her. As I rub it over her clit, I watch as she lowers her hand and thrusts two fingers into her slit.

"Oh, God. I can't. You're too... Fuck. I need to come. Now! Liam, please. Please. Fuck!"

Groaning, I lick those digits, joining in the fray, loving how she wails and the tendons in her inner thighs pull taut and strain as she burrows her heels into the bed and rides the waves of release.

Retreating, I drag the vibrator away from her clit, ignoring her hissed breath of complaint. Instead, I move it through her folds, collecting her juices and getting the device wet.

In a coordinated attack, I press an open-mouthed kiss to her clit while I place pressure on her ass. As the vibrator sinks home, I nip and suck and lick the nub until her screams impact me louder than a crowd of twenty thousand at the Stars' stadium.

This is my oxygen now.

She is what breathes goddamn life into me.

As she comes and comes and comes, I don't stop feeding her pleasure, wanting to give her this when, sometimes, I feel like I give her nothing but misery.

When she spreads her fingers, as if she isn't full enough, I'm tempted to work my way into her. But instead, I surge up the bed and rest my dick against her slit as I kiss her, letting her taste herself, moaning with the delight of it when she moans in return.

As I rock my hips, as I kiss her and distract her, my hand digs into the nightstand. It's not like I don't make a racket but keeping her busy, I find the lube I put there weeks ago in preparation for this.

"You want me to fill you, Gracie?"

She cries out, "Please. Fuck, please. God, Liam, I need you inside me. Now." Her knees dig into my hips and she jerks hers up as if that alone will get my dick to go where she wants me.

"You feel like something different?"

Immediately, she tenses.

And I know we're on the same page.

"You're going to break me," she whimpers, her arms clutching at me in a way that speaks louder than words.

Her claws are out and I've never wanted to be mauled more.

"You telling me you don't want to be broken," I rasp, nipping her bottom lip, tugging on it before letting it fly back.

"Only by you," she mewls.

Fucking A.

Grabbing my pillow, I change her position, altering how her ass rests on the bed. Levering her upright, I try not to blow my wad at the sight of her pussy clutching around her slim fingers.

Unable to stop myself, I quickly press a wet kiss to her clit before I get to business.

"God, Liam, what you do to me. You drive me crazy. Please, baby, I need you! Fuck me. Hard. Please."

We haven't been using condoms, but I still snag two from my stash, ones that have been hanging around for this very moment.

Pushing away from her, I swiftly enrobe the vibe in one, and then my dick. Coating my cock in the lube, I cover my fingers in it too then slide them over and around the pucker.

"Touch your clit, *bébé*," I rumble, watching as she obeys with surprising-for-Gracie alacrity.

As she fingers herself, I slide one of my own into her ass, getting her used to the thicker invasion, then I start to thrust a second and a third in.

"I'm so wet for you," she cries. "Do you see?"

God, I see.

When I think she can take me, I press the tip of my cock to her rosette and slowly start to slide home. While she's touching her clit, I get the vibe and switch it on as I thrust that into her cunt.

"LIAM!"

With the triple attack, she immediately goes off like a light show.

How she clenches around me is brutal.

"You are so fucking tight," I bite out as she writhes against the bed.

"Nothing feels as good as your dick. God, I love it. I need you to fuck me, Liam. Fuck me, please. Don't stop. Don't ever stop."

The pleasure's too much, though, because she rears up, her arms coming around my waist, nails digging into my shoulders as she draws me into her.

With our mouths colliding, she fucks me there while I'm careful not to hurt her.

As her hips start to buck back, I know she's ready for more, so I quicken my pace, sliding in as deep as I can.

"God, you take me like such a good girl, baby, but I need you to relax a little. Let me…" She obeys immediately, and we both groan as I slide in deeper. "Fuck. Fuck." My head rears back as the sheer exquisiteness of this moment rams me in the solar plexus.

This is Gracie.

Not only is she letting me inside her, but this is her ass. She's trusting me with this. With her. She's in my bed. In my apartment.

We're in this *together*.

That, combined with her sheer, exquisite tightness, is what gets me off.

I'm so close to saying the words, letting them spill from my lips, but I don't want to ruin this for her if she isn't ready.

The trust she's showing me here has to be enough.

It has to be.

To stop myself, I thrust my tongue into her mouth, riding the burst of ecstasy that only she can give me, soaring even higher when she comes again, screaming into the kiss, her entire body tensing up as her orgasm annihilates her.

When she slumps into the bedding, I follow her. One hand falls beside her head, and the other drags the vibrator from her slit. Switching it off, I toss it on the floor, ignoring the clank as I give her my weight and feed her a softer kiss that she melts into.

"I need to thank Hudson," I mumble against her lips.

She freezes. "What?!"

When her nails dig into my shoulders again, a warning and a threat imparted, I chuckle. "There's no way that that wasn't a coordinated effort."

Immediately, the danger from her claws fades. "Damn, you figured that out?"

"As much as I'd love to think of you in my bed touching this beautiful pussy all day and all night, *bébé*, I can't see it. You're too practical for that."

She snickers. "Damn. Hoist by my own petard."

Grinning as I kiss her again, I murmur, "It's like if we ever *do* get to have phone sex, I know for a fact you'll be lying if I ask you if you're naked."

"Shut up! You're ruining my aura of mystery," she wails, but she's laughing and I feel it even more because my dick, though softening, is still partly in her.

"Wow, that feels even better than just seeing you laugh," I muse, resting my forehead against hers.

Her butt clenches down, making me hiss. "What about now?"

My chuckle is goofy. "Perfection. I like making you laugh." Her amusement morphs into a hiccup as she nuzzles into me. "Like your dirty mouth even better. Fuck, Gracie, wherever you come up with that stuff, keep hitting me with it. *Please*."

"Remember you asked me if I worked for a sex line?"

I pause. "No way."

"Yes way," she coos, her voice extra breathy.

"Fuuuck," I rumble. "God, talk about an apprenticeship and I'm reaping the rewards."

She hums. "I'm glad you enjoy it. My exes never did."

"They're fucking idiots then." I knew that anyway because they let her go.

Thank God they did.

"I missed you."

The relief that sinks into my veins is better than a pure shot of heroin. "And I missed you, Gracie. So fucking much."

She clings to me, her arms sliding around my shoulders again as she draws me close. The condom needs to be dealt with, and we should probably shower, and I need to shave again, but for the moment, we just lie there, together.

In this, *together*.

Here, together.

And somehow, I know I won't have to deal with any nightmares tonight.

YOUR DAILY DOSE OF SPORTS NEWS

NEW YORK STARS REACH THE PLAYOFFS

BY MACK FINNEGAN

In their first season as the Stars, the newly renamed New York team cinches a spot in the playoffs.

Can the Leprechaun bring home the silver cup for NYC?

CHAPTER 51
LIAM

Numb - Linkin Park

THE NIGHTMARE-LESS NIGHT was a blessing sent from above.

Getting eight hours of rest is a luxury I won't take for granted, but it's followed up with three nights of solid hell.

The dreams have shifted. *Twisted.* She's been with me every night since I got back, but the terrors have morphed into her not just being kidnapped, her not just enduring what I went through.

Of her being tortured.

Of her being killed.

The third night, I don't just wake up screaming. I wake up crying.

And I know why—Hudson downplayed the press situation while I was away.

Gracie got roughed up and she only didn't land a punch because one of them knocked her into Ludvig who dealt with the assholes. Ever since, I've been imagining worst-case scenarios.

That she was in danger, because of me, is literally driving me insane.

"Oh, sweetheart," she rasps as she takes me in her arms and holds me like I'm goddamn fragile when I'm supposed to be the one who's strong for *her*. "What's wrong? How can I make this better?"

Shaking my head as I hold her tighter, enough that I know I must be hurting her but unable to stop myself, I don't answer.

I can't.

There are no words that can convey the horror of what I just endured. Of the movie that my subconscious crafted as my own personal hell.

As she holds me, I start to relax, and she takes that as a sign to as well. Though she switches channels from one of her anime shows that she fell asleep watching and over to the 24/7 news channel, eventually, she falls back into a deep slumber.

As she does, I concoct a plan.

That alone takes some of the strain off, so when I finally get some rest and wake up without a nightmare, it makes me wonder if everything happens for a reason.

She eyes me with concern but takes my cue and says nothing. We both know I'll talk if I want to, and I don't.

Not to her, not about this, at any rate.

When she leaves for a class with her least favorite professor, I do the unthinkable—I call my father.

"Liam?" he greets, his tone loaded with surprise.

"I need help."

As I stare out onto the city, I hear him release a breath. "Whatever I can do, I will."

Swallowing, I mutter, "Thank you."

"Never been a good father, Liam, but that doesn't mean I don't want to be a better one now." He doesn't let me answer, just continues, "So, tell me, what do you need from me?"

"It's Gracie."

"What about her?"

"I need extra protection for her."

"Conor foots the bill for three-quarters of your security personally, Liam—" That was news to me. "—so I know that you already put four bodyguards on her."

"That's not enough," I rasp.

A soft sigh sounds in my ear. "Oh, son. She won't be targeted. Not like you were."

"How do you know that?" I demand. "If I was kidnapped, who's to stop someone trying to grab her? I'd empty my bank account to get her back, Dad, but that doesn't erase whatever they'd put her through. They cut my ear off, but what would they do to *her*?"

There's silence on the other end of the line until he muses, "Been a while since you called me that."

"I need your help," I repeat, not wanting to get into this. Not now. Maybe not ever.

If he can help me protect the most precious person in my world, that'll go a hell of a long way to righting a childhood of him skipping out.

"What are you asking for, Liam? Guards from his ranks?"

"Please."

"I'll talk to Conor."

"Thank you." I release a shaky breath. "*Dad.*"

"You're welcome." He clears his throat. "Son."

Liam: What are you wearing?

Gracie: We already had this conversation.

Liam: Lie to me.

Liam: After the day I've had, I'll take that over jacking off by myself. Fucking Coach. I'm sick of losing because of his dumb plays.

Gracie: What kind of lie do you want? The full works or...

Liam: The full works being?

Gracie: Nudity or lingerie lol.

Liam: If I get a choice, nudity.

Gracie: Men. You're such simple creatures.

Liam: Simpler than you think.

Liam: Are you at my place?

Gracie: Yeah.

Liam: Good. I like it when you're there.

Liam: Check in your nightstand.

Gracie: Checking...

Gracie: Ooooh.

Gracie: Give me five so I can clean it.

Liam: You can have two.

Liam: My cock is aching, Gracie. I wish you were here to suck me off.

Gracie sends voice note

I'll be waiting in the entrance for you on my knees when you're back, Liam, if you want…

You did so well today. It's not your fault you're having to carry McIsaac and Fortin because Kerrigan and Lewis are injured. Nor is it your fault that Bradley is an asshole.

> Liam: Ah, Christ. Thank you, ma chérie.

> Liam: xo

> Liam: But I don't want to talk about that BS.

Liam sends voice note

Nothing's better for improving my mood than your mouth, ma belle.

Gracie: Not even my pussy?

Gracie: Even five-hundred miles away, your voice when you call me 'ma belle' gets me wet.

Gracie: Want to FaceTime?

> Liam: No. Lewis crashed in my hotel room. I'm in my bathroom.

Gracie: I don't want to know, do I?

> Liam: Problems with his ex.

> Liam: And no. You don't.

> Liam: But fuck, tell me how wet you are.

Gracie: I don't need lube for the toy…

> Liam: Slide it over your clit.

> Liam: It's got a jackhammer setting lol.

Gracie: Mwah. I love that you know I like me some pressure.

Liam: Figured that out whenever I pound you into the bed and you almost, ALMOST squirt.

Liam: Fuck, I can't wait for that day. When you burst all around me and I get to see what I do to you.

Gracie: Jesus, Liam. This is really strong.

Gracie: God

Gracie: I wish your cock were inside me while I was using this vibe.

Liam: I do too, minou. You're so beautiful when you come. I love it when you're overstimulated. That pretty mouth of yours that's always racing a mile a minute with so much sass goes silent.

Liam: That's how I know I've done my job right.

Liam: Slide a finger into that delicious cunt, Gracie. Send me a picture.

Gracie sends picture

Liam: Ah, Jesus. Think of me, baby girl. Think of me with my hand around my dick, jacking off and wishing that you were here. That your fingers were in my hair, that your pussy had my cock in a chokehold.

Gracie sends voice note

Oh, God!

Liam: It's only been a few days and I miss those sounds. You're close, bébé. I can tell. You're glorious when you come. Do you know that?

Liam: You light up like a fireworks display.

Liam: I will never get tired of seeing you explode.

Gracie sends voice note

Fuck, Liam. Fuck. Why can't you be here? I'm so empty. My fingers don't fill me like you do.

Liam: If I were there, I'd make you beg for it. Just so I'd know how desperate you are for me, for something only I can give to you.

Gracie: Liam, I'm going to come.

Liam: Do it. Give it to me, bébé. I want to know you're getting off even though I'm away from home.

Gracie sends voice note

Liam! Liam. Oh, fuck. Please. Yeah. Jesus, yes—

Liam: Beautiful, so beautiful. I love hearing you get yourself off.

Liam: Ah, shit, Gracie. I'm not going to last. I'm going to think of my cum falling onto that pretty tongue of yours.

Gracie: I'll suck it clean and swallow it down whole, Liam. Get you nice and hard. I'll make sure I don't miss a single drop. Just like the good girl I only am around you...

Gracie: Then, I'd lube up my finger with my spit and I'd get everything out of you by thrusting it into your ass and playing with your prostate as I suck on that piercing you have on your perineum.

Gracie: You like it when I do that, don't you?

Liam sends voice note

I love it when YOU do that. Tabarnak, *GRACIE. What you fucking do to me.*

Gracie: When you whisper and your voice goes deep, it drives me wild.

Liam: Ostie

Three minutes later
Liam: I needed that.

Gracie: Do you feel better?

Liam: Yeah.

Liam: I do.

Liam: Thank you, bébé.

Gracie: I should be thanking you. That vibe is phenomenal.

Liam: You're welcome. :-*

Liam: Wish you were here.

Gracie: Me too, tbh. Not long now. <3

Liam: No. Not long.

Gracie: Everything okay with Lewis?

Liam: He wanted to go out for a drink, but I don't really do that.

Gracie: No. I know. You can though. You used to enjoy hanging out with your team.

Liam: Not the same when you're afraid to sit with your back to the room or are checking out the place for exits.

Liam: That's where I was taken from. Did you know that?

Liam: I was heading out of a club in Montréal?

Gracie: FUCK. How did you never tell me that? I thought you were snatched off the street.

Liam: I didn't tell anyone. The cops thought it was outside... but it wasn't.

Liam: It's why I don't like going out, though.

Gracie: They drugged you?

Liam: Yeah.

Gracie: I'd kill them if I could.

Liam: I know. :-* But that's over with. For the most part.

Liam: ANYWAY, that's why I invited Lewis to my room.

Liam: I like the kid but he can't handle his beer lol.

Gracie: Bet I can drink you under the table...

Liam: All four feet nothing of you?

Liam: We should have a drinking competition once the season's over.

Gracie: Last man under the table wins...?

Liam: It worked last time.

Gracie: What?

Liam: Never mind.

Liam: A day at Coney Island on the other's dime. How about that?

Gracie: No fair! You already owe me that.

Liam: Two days, then. I'll get us a hotel room there. :-P

Gracie: That sounds like a date...

Liam: Because it is.

Liam: Do you hate that we don't get to do normal stuff?

Gracie: Normal stuff like you not being able to leave the building without needing to sign your autograph a million times?

Gracie: Normal like you watching me eat toast as if I'm starring in a porn movie but not because you want ME, just the carbs?

Gracie: Shit like that? :P

Liam: Yeah, lol. And you're wrong about the toast. Watching you eat is a religious experience.

Gracie: Fuck off, LMAO.

Liam: I can't fuck off any farther than Montana!

Gracie: Sure you can. Outer Mongolia's farther away.

Liam: Mostly, I just meant, you know… never being able to hit up a restaurant together. Never being able to go dancing. You used to love dancing.

Gracie: At indie concerts lol.

Liam: You owe me a date when Simple Plan plays in NYC.

Gracie: OMG. We totally need to go to that! Songs of our misspent youth. :P

Liam: You can hold me to that promise.

Gracie: No. It's no fun if you're not happy too. We'll go if you can handle it. Agreed?

Liam: Agreed. <3

Gracie: Don't even THINK of saying that you're sorry. You have nothing to be sorry for.

Gracie: I still can't believe you got me a Cameo from them.

Gracie: Where's this month's BTW?

Liam: Incoming. :-P

Liam: Thank you, Gracie.

Gracie: For what?

Liam: Just being you.

Liam: Now, I'm going to go crash.

Liam: Sleep well.

Gracie: You do, too.

Gracie: And you never have to thank me for being me. Not when I'm a better Gracie around you. Sleep tight. <3

CHAPTER 52
GRACIE

Paris - The Chainsmokers

IN A STRATEGY that stinks of Bradley's interference, Liam favors Kerrigan over Lewis throughout the game. Kerrigan causes three turnovers and the fans aren't happy.

The Stars, with their new lineup, have been drawing a lot of interest and have gained some notoriety, meaning the crowd is beyond vocal as they chant their displeasure at Kerrigan's failure to follow through.

Liam's furious.

I can see it from here.

It wouldn't take a mind reader to figure that out anyway, but it's in how he stews on the bench, whacking his stick on the boards, throwing a water bottle when he never has hissy fits. And in the way his skating is aggressive rather than graceful like usual as OT hits.

We win but the score doesn't reflect the Stars' performance.

As always, Liam's the first to get off the ice and down the hallway that'll lead to the dressing room.

After all these years of knowing him, there are some stunts of his that still come as a surprise. Like, until recently, I didn't know that he wears a St. Anthony medallion.

Before every game, he kisses it. After every game, be it a loss or a win, he polishes it.

I'm not sure what St. Anthony can do on the ice—find lost goals?

If so, that didn't work today.

Watching him go, I don't bother moving from the VIP box where friends and family sit as the rest of the stands start to clear.

I won't be leaving until he does, so there's no need to get involved in the crowd rush.

Instead, after I wave farewell to a wan Lacey, I check my notes and get some studying in after I peep at the family chat and see very few messages on there—since Kow and Liam faced off in Winnipeg, things have been all quiet.

It's weird.

Like the calm before the storm.

When the stands are dead, with the maintenance crew working on the ice and the clean-up crew picking up the trash that people are too lazy to throw out themselves or to recycle, I drag off my PALs jacket and shove it in my purse as I head for the bowels of the stadium.

The Stars have over twelve thousand square feet of locker room— it's massive and a way of getting my steps in as I traverse from one end to the other on the hunt for my pissed-off hockey player of a boyfriend.

On the journey, I see Greco punching the wall in fury over letting those two goals in.

If he and Liam didn't have beef, I'd probably tell him to cut himself some slack. The goalies have it the hardest in my opinion. How they're treated by the rest of the team, it's almost like it's all on them if a game goes south when that's just not true.

Still, Liam *does* hate him so I decide to be loyal and leave Greco to his busted knuckles.

Because the locker room is crazy busy with the press, I sneak past them and find Liam in the rehab whirlpools which are totally off limits but... fuck it.

There are a lot of naked asses in here, but I've seen worse in my time so, ignoring them, I head over to the side, evading the stares from the physiotherapists who watch my progress but don't reprimand me for being here.

When I move in behind Liam, I know he hasn't seen me. So, resting my elbows on the edge of the water, not caring if my sweater gets wet, I call out over the whirlpool, "You did everything you could."

He twists around in surprise, sending a wave of water over me.

Standing there, drenched, I look at myself then let out a laugh.

When I glance up, I can see that all the players are watching me, waiting for my reaction.

What do they think I'm going to do?

Curse him out?

Turn him blue this time?

Brows lifting, I dump my purse beside the tub then clamber into the water next to him.

Fully dressed.

A cheer goes up around the room that has both Liam and me chuckling and gracing them with one-fingered salutes before the surge of interest fades and Liam's left staring at me as if he can't decide whether to be amused or annoyed.

"You look like you're constipated."

That has him snickering. "Shut up."

"I won't," I tease, resting my arms along the edge, mimicking his earlier position. "You really do. Maybe the tub isn't where you need to be right now."

He scoffs. "Gracie!"

I just smirk.

Scraping a wet hand over his head, he ducks below the water so that only his face is bobbing on the surface. "Sorry I got you wet."

"Did you do it on purpose?"

"No."

"You don't have to apologize, then."

He sighs. "Now I know I fucked up bad if you're being so under-standing."

"Hey! I can be nice."

"Since when?"

"Since forever." I roll my eyes at him. "*Honestly.*"

"You don't have a rep for nothing, Gracie."

"That was years ago."

"Years ago and yet, most of these guys know to stay away from you."

My lips curve of their own volition as I study my nails. "You're exaggerating."

"Do you remember that time when you were following Kow and me and you put water in the vodka because you said we were drinking too much to score goals?"

I snicker. "And you still thought you were drunk?"

His grin is sheepish. "Kow flashed that photographer."

"There are probably photos of that night buried away on someone's hard drive," I agree with a laugh. "You deserved that anyway. Plus, the Mounties owe me big time. You pulled your head out of your ass."

"Kow didn't."

"Kow cherry-picks the advice he listens to. He probably wouldn't if my water-vodka had given him cirrhosis of the liver or my green dye had made his dick fall off."

A bubble of laughter escapes Liam. "I wish I could say otherwise."

"But you can't because my brother's a moron. A very lucky moron."

"Some of it's skill."

"Most of it isn't. Don't get me wrong. I know he's good at what he does, but if he truly applied himself, he'd be a thousand times better. That's why you've got the clout to be a franchise player and he doesn't."

"Better than the Stanley Cup winner he already is?"

I hum. "You know it too. Twenty-three men win the cup. Only some of them become legends."

He pulls a face, aware that I'm including him under that banner —*legend.* "Maybe."

He bobs in the water again before coming to the decision to not be annoyed about what went down on the ice, though I know Bradley will have shifted most of the blame onto him.

When he moves over to my side, letting his hand slip around my waist, he murmurs, "I'd drag you onto my lap, but I think the physios would call Coach in and he'd shit a brick."

"Sounds painful."

"Yeah, probably is. They'll be leaving soon. Bradley wanted us all in here so we can get some relief before early practice tomorrow."

"That wasn't on the schedule."

"No, he amended it after our 'horrendous' performance. We need to work on playing together 'more cohesively.'"

I can't disagree. "He'll never get that level of cohesion he's after when there are so many grudges between the lot of you."

"You're not wrong."

"Rarely am."

His lips twitch. "You okay?"

"I'm okay if you are. You did great out there. He told you to bypass Lewis, didn't he?"

"Yeah." His hand scrapes through his hair. "I listened. Shouldn't have. Kerrigan's more of a nightmare than usual."

"I know you're cutting him some slack but Lacey just told me her prognosis is... She doesn't even have six months, Liam. That's a lot of pressure."

He heaves a sigh. "Don't make me be kind to him."

"I won't make you do anything," I drawl, but I slide my hand over his head and rub the back of his neck.

"Less than six months?"

Sorrow fills me when I think about Lacey—she was coughing like crazy earlier. "Yeah."

"Fuck." He shoves a hand over his hair. "I'll try to get Lewis on board."

My fingers don't stop massaging the back of his neck. "I think that'd be a good idea. Just FYI, Greco's knuckles are going to be busted tomorrow."

He frowns. "How do you know that? I didn't see him get injured on the ice."

"He was just punching the wall when I was coming to find you."

"Punching the wall?" he repeats, tone dubious. "Why would he do that?"

"Maybe he's a masochist." I hitch a shoulder, then, seeing the physios finally leave, I wade my way onto his lap.

Maybe the green-dye incident remains as notorious as ever in hockey circles because no one catcalls or says dick when I take the best seat in the house. Nor do they when he curls his arm around me.

"You guys need to not hate each other so much. You're stuck together until the end of the season, at least."

Especially now that the trade deadline has gone the way of the dodo.

"Greco's a jerk."

"Sure he is. Lots of hockey players are." My brothers included. "It's a common trait among you Neanderthals."

"I think I should be offended."

"You probably should be. You used to be a jerk too." I tap the tip of his nose with my finger. "You're not anymore though. Good job on being a better person."

A burst of laughter escapes him. "You'll always keep my feet on the ground, won't you, Gracie?"

I wink at him. "I'll do my best."

"How was class today? I didn't know if you'd make it to the game."

"Finals are coming up so shit's getting more intense." I yawn. "I'm tired, to be honest."

"We'll head back home soon."

I like how that sounds, but I rest my head on his shoulder and mutter, "I should go to my apartment. School is nearer to my place and I have an early class tomorrow."

When my next yawn makes my jaw creak, he asks, "Am I working you too hard?"

A laugh combines with a yawn. "Nope. You're a pushover boss, Liam."

"Glad to hear it," he teases, but I know he means it.

"It's just things are heating up in class, you know?" I yawn again. "Lots to prepare for, ton of shit to reread."

Do I tell him that it's less fun than it used to be?

"Everything okay?"

"It's weird how well you can read me."

He smiles. "You study for your MBA, and I study you."

I huff. "Smooth."

"That's me. Smoother than peanut butter."

"You're only saying that because you know I hate the crunchy variety."

"Which makes no sense considering you eat nothing but nuts all day."

"You just want me to eat nothing but *your* nut all day."

His eyes flare wide before the most massive laugh booms from him. Honestly, it's a wonder it didn't pop a blood vessel.

Smug from making him laugh like that, I look around to see if anyone witnessed the earthquake-like laughter only to find that we're alone.

All alone.

Huh.

"You doing all right there, Liam?" I jeer, amused that *he* is so amused.

He rubs his watering eyes. "Yeah, I'm fine. But you're right. About the nut."

"Of course I am."

"But you didn't distract me from what we were talking about earlier. You can tell me what's going on, Gracie, you know."

"It's nothing."

"Not if it's important to you." He sits up. "Why are you always okay with talking about *me* but never yourself?"

"I'm not interesting."

"Since when?"

Since forever.

"Liam—"

"No, Gracie. Seriously. I don't think you're interesting—" Ouch. "I think you're *fascinating*." Oh. "Now, tell me what's going on in that head of yours."

Watching him for what feels like endless moments, endless in that he doesn't break the silence, doesn't relent, and all the while the bubbles from the whirlpool churn around me, lulling me into relaxing, I heave a sigh.

"What I'm studying…"

"It's too hard?"

I sniff. "No."

"Then?"

"I'm getting there," I grumble, tracing my fingers through the water. "It's boring."

"Boring," he repeats.

"Yeah."

"Why? Because there's a lot of work? We can figure something out so you have more time—"

"No. That isn't what I mean." I peep up at him. "If I tell you this, you can't let anyone know. Ever."

His eyes widen. "Your secret's safe with me, Gracie."

I know it is.

That's why I shift on his lap, straddling him, then, moving closer, I whisper in his ear, "I think I only picked it up to piss off my mom. Which means I'm almost in my thirties and am rebelling against her like I'm a teenager."

He snorts. "Makes sense."

I pull back. "It does?"

"Sure. I never realized how contentious your relationship was. Now that you've made a stand, I guess it makes sense for you to reevaluate your life and where you're at."

Something flickers in his eyes, something that makes me cup his chin. "I'm not reevaluating you, Liam."

"No? I wouldn't blame you, not when tomorrow's papers will say it's your fault we played like shit because you're my girlfriend and you should have put me to bed at 7pm to make sure I got enough rest for the game. Never mind the other bullshit with that reporter roughing you up."

His gruff tone has me murmuring, "Takes more than that to frighten me off."

"Yeah?"

I don't bother confirming or denying, not verbally anyway.

Letting my arms crisscross on his shoulders, I surge high on his lap so we're closer, then I press my lips to his.

He sighs into my soft kiss, settling deeper in the water so both of us are just two heads lolling on the surface.

His mouth opens, letting me in. As I slip inside, he angles his head, inviting me deeper, an invitation I'm more than happy to accept.

There's something special about kissing Liam.

It's as if we have all the time in the world when we don't, but it's like the clock is irrelevant.

I figure that it's part of the 'Donnghal Effect.'

His hands go to the hem of my sweater. One slides beneath it, skimming over my waist, before he starts to shove it higher.

Both of us know that anyone could walk in right now, be it Bradley or one of his teammates. Though I've never really been into exhibitionism, the thrill is electrifying.

He nips the tip of my tongue, startling me into jerking back. His eyes are like pools I could swim in but his smile is anything but apologetic, something that makes complete sense when he jerks my sweater off and over my head. It makes a plopping sound when it falls onto the floor.

Both hands settle on my ass as he rumbles, "You going to stay in that wet bra, Gracie? Or are you going to show me those beautiful tits of yours?"

"Think I'm afraid to show them to you?" I taunt, tucking my arms behind my back and unfastening the clasp.

When the tension in the straps eases, I snag the now-heavy fabric and let it join my sweater on the tiles.

"I know you love them, Liam. I think you should leave a love bite right here, next to my nipple. Just so that—"

When I lift my breast and motion to where I'd like a hickey, one of his hands settles between my shoulder blades and he hauls me closer so that they're smushing up against his pecs.

"I'll leave a reminder you won't forget," he confirms with a growl, but then his nose trails along my jawline. "You're so soft, Gracie. I love that."

"More curves than you can handle?" I try to joke, but it comes out like a croak.

"I think I can handle you just fine. Reach down, Gracie. Feel what's hard just for you."

Fuck.

Swallowing, I do as he says and let my fingers curl around his hardness. "I love how thick you are."

"You like how I spread that perfect pussy of yours apart, hmm?"

"Y-Yes," I whisper, well aware that he's the only man I've ever known who's made me stutter. "And you go so d-deep inside me. It's like I don't know where you end."

His fingers dig into my ass, the curves giving way to his tenacious grip. "Is that beautiful little cunt hungry for my dick?"

"You know it is, Liam."

He shakes his head. "How can I? You're still wearing too many clothes. I think you should rectify that, don't you?"

Nodding meekly when I'm never meek, I slip off his lap and stand in the water. When his gaze lands on my bare tits, I watch his nostrils flare before they're hidden again as I duck down and start to strip out of my wet yoga pants.

When they and my panties plop onto the floor, the intensity of his gaze pins me in place.

I stand there, breathing heavily, knowing that someone could walk in, but it'd be worth it.

To be looked at like *that* is worth any price.

He grits his jaw, the muscles clenching in a way that makes his handsome face less *pretty* and more alive, more vibrant, more everything.

Before I know it, he's in front of me. But instead of keeping us chest to chest, he spins me around. I have no clue what his game is, and I find I don't care.

Trusting in him to pleasure us both, I let him maneuver us until he's satisfied with our positions, and, boy, is it worth it.

I find myself kneeling on the bench seat, but where he's positioned me, holy fuck, the bubbles come straight out and hit me at my core. When he lines up behind me, he blankets me as one arm comes around my hips, his hand finding my slit.

As he touches my clit, he rasps, "How do those bubbles feel, *ma belle?*"

My only answer is a groan.

He spreads my lips apart and shuffles me forward. I nearly choke on the water when it bucks in a wave as I jolt in surprise. My yelp is both pleasure-filled and desperate.

God!

"Liam," I mewl, my arm sliding back to grab him behind the neck.

This new position gives him access to one of my tits and as he cups it, nipping and pinching the tip, I can feel his dick settle between my butt cheeks. It's hot and heavy and it's lying there like a threat and a promise all wrapped into one.

When the bubbles continue tormenting me, I press my arm to my mouth and bite into the tender skin when he slots the tip of his shaft to my entrance. It spreads me wider, but the torture is worth it because he growls, "FUCK!"

That rumble vibrates in my ear, making me shiver.

Knowing the whirlpool is teasing him as much as it is me, I tilt my head to the side and mutter against his jaw, "I want you to fill me, Liam. I need you inside me. Please, give me your cock. Please."

"When you ask so goddamn nicely," he snarls, "how can I say no?"

In contrast to his aggressive words, he slides into me so slowly that I'm whimpering by the time he's all the way inside.

I tense up with every inch he claims because with the bubbles and the teasing of my clit and how he's pinching my nipple, it's too much.

I cling to him, the only stability in this insane world, and let him take me where I need to go, giving myself over to him when I trust no one with *me*.

And he doesn't let me down.

I don't think he ever will, either.

Still moving too slowly, he thrusts in and out, making sure I feel every part of his dick. My pussy clamps around him whenever he retreats and returns, silently begging him to stay inside me, to fill me. Forever.

Without a word, he seems to understand because instead of pulling out, he stays deep. Rocking his hips, grinding into me, pushing me toward the flow of the bubbles so that my clit and pussy are bombarded on all sides.

When my orgasm finds me, it hits me with the force of two freight trains colliding.

The water makes me feel everything with more intensity because I'm not tethered to gravity as I usually am. I'm lighter, more buoyant, and so is my release.

Crying out his name, I beg, "Fuck me, fuck me, fuck me, Liam. Please, please—"

That's when his hand comes up to my mouth and he muzzles me.

I have no idea why but that makes this ten times hotter.

With his hand right there, I have no alternative other than to grip him with my teeth and to bite down. He groans in my ear, thrusting harder, faster—

"What in the hell is going on in here?!"

The words should be like a bucket of cold water being hurled at my face.

But they're not.

I know it's Bradley.

I *know* it is.

But my pussy clamps around him as pleasure shuttles its way through my veins with the force of one of Liam's penalty shots to the back of the net.

When I release a deep, keening cry, Bradley screams, "Ms. Bukowski, get out—"

I should be leaping from the water, shoving a towel over myself to cover up, but Liam's doing a great job of that. His bulk comes in handy because there's no way that fucker can see me.

Maybe it's because I have no respect for the coach, maybe it's because Liam'll be the one who suffers at practice as a punishment tomorrow, and *maybe* it's because this room will definitely be off-limits to me in the future, but I open my eyes and purposely seek out the coach who is looking at me.

There's hatred in his expression, disrespect as well as disgust—a whole cocktail of it.

Unaffected, I smile at him like the cat who got the cream while Liam jumps, making water surge over the sides of the whirlpool.

Face practically puce with rage, Bradley's nostrils flare as he shouts, "What the fuck do you think you're doing, Donnghal? You're the goddamn captain!"

"Can you imagine the scandal if the PR manager hadn't gotten the press out of here early tonight? Get your ass on the tiles now."

It's cute that even with Bradley breathing down his neck, Liam rearranges me so that my modesty is intact with his hands on my tits until he dunks me below the surface, simultaneously flashing his still-hard dick.

"It's a little late for that!" Bradley growls.

I hide a smile even as Liam mumbles, "Tomorrow's gonna suck." He climbs out of the water then shoots me a wink and, while Bradley's cussing up a storm and he's snatching a towel, whispers, "You're worth the reaming I'll get at practice."

"I'll take care of your blue balls later," I croon.

His ass is the last thing I see and the *only* thing I'm interested in before I flop back into the water.

Gray: When we said look after Gracie, we didn't realize we had to include 'don't dick her down in the dressing room for your coach to see.'

Liam: How the fuck do you know about that?

Cole: How else?! Gagné told me.

Cole: It's spreading over the Eastern Seaboard better than Kow did when he finally got his green card.

Matt: Don't you mean chlamydia spread?

Cole: Well, let's face it. Chlamydia definitely became more of a problem with him this side of the border. LOL.

Liam: @Cole, you're an asshole for telling everyone!

Cole: You did that yourself.

Cole: What the fuck were you thinking?

Liam: I wasn't!

Matt: Little Liam was, huh?

Liam: Less of the little.

Gray: RUMOR

Liam: What? No pics or it's a lie? Do you really need to see my dick AGAIN, Gray, because I'm not afraid to share with the class. It's only gotten bigger since the last time you saw it, hahahaha.

Matt: Apparently, this exhibitionism kink of yours is extending to incest. I'm scared. I'm going to tell Hanna.

Gray: LMAO. In the family chat?! PLEASE.

Liam: I'm not talking to her.

Matt: Ohhh, yeah. I forgot about that.

Gray: Even though it's your birthday tomorrow?

Gray: And you know she'll send cake.

Cole: I'll eat the cake if you don't want it.

Liam: Greedy asshole.

Cole: Hey, I'm not afraid of refined sugar like you are, OLD MAN.

Liam: Fuck off.

Gray: Seriously, though. You're not going to take her call? She always phones on birthdays.

Liam: Gotta back my shit up, guys. Hanna treats Gracie like crap.

Cole: :/

Cole: But I'd still eat the cake if she overnighted it.

Cole: Hint: I take donations.

Liam: I'll be too busy to answer a call. We're heading to Coney Island.

Liam: Gracie and I are spending the day there.

Cole: Dude, I can't get you to the golf course for eighteen holes and you're heading to Coney fucking Island?!

Liam: I'm going to TRY to go there.

Matt: Still struggling, huh?

Gray: I guess we were hoping Gracie had a magic pussy that'd make everything better.

Liam: Firstly, if you mention Gracie and the word pussy in the same sentence again, I'll wing my way down to Tucson to beat the crap out of you.

Liam: Secondly, as magical as it might be, it's not that magical lol.

Gray: Boo.

Liam: Yeah. But one day at a time, right?

Cole: Can we build up to you playing a round of golf with me?

Liam: Never gonna happen.

Cole: Aim high!

Liam: Golf = aiming low.

Matt: You're the only hockey player alive who doesn't like golf, you freak.

Gray: So, the plan is for you to head to Coney Island AFTER Bradley puts you through the punishment of your life?

Liam: Pray for me.

LATER THAT DAY

Liam: Heard about your argument with the wall. Everything okay?

Greco: Everything's fine.

Liam: I'm a better listener than the wall.

Liam: Here if you need to talk.

YOUR DAILY DOSE OF SPORTS NEWS

LACKLUSTER WIN FOR DONNGHAL'S TEAM

BY MACK FINNEGAN

In a game full of setbacks, the New York Stars' offense failed to take it all the way. Lewis and Donnghal are still the breakout power duo this season, but Kerrigan caused three turnovers, spoiling the lead the Stars had fought to rack up.

More and more, the team is depending on shoot-outs to win, showing the limits of Coach Allan Bradley's offensive strategies.

Despite the setback, the Stars remain the favorite to win this series.

CHAPTER 53
LIAM
TWO DAYS LATER

Heaven Is A Halfpipe - OPM

"WE NEED to cut Kerrigan some slack."

Lewis pins me with a look. "He sucks."

"I know he does," I mutter, scraping a hand over my head as I toss my helmet onto the bench, unable to deny the indefatigable truth that Kerrigan is blowing harder than a chinook this season.

"Then why do we need to cut Kerrigan any slack?" Lewis demands, practically pouting at the notion.

"He's got a lot of shit going on at home. We need to help him out."

"He wouldn't help *us* out."

Knowing he's right, I pull a face. "Maybe he wouldn't, but we don't always do shit for something in return. Isn't that the whole point of being on a team?"

Lewis huffs. "Don't expect me to play nice with Raimoron is all I'm saying. I'll suck this one up, but he can go fuck himself."

"What is it with you two? It's getting so long and drawn out that I'm actually interested in knowing."

"The NDA I signed says I can't tell you," he grumbles, then he asks, "Get anything nice for your birthday?"

Grabbing my cell, I show him what Gracie got me.

He eyes the skateboard. "Old school."

"Very. Vintage."

"Why?"

"Why what?"

"Why did she get you a skateboard? It's not like you can use it during the season. It's in our contracts. 'No fun allowed.'"

Though I snicker, I share, "She knows I had one as a kid."

"You don't go out much, do you?"

"You're a genius for working that out," I mock.

He chuckles under his breath. "No offense, man, but how are you going to use *that* if you don't go out?"

"I won't use it. It's to hang on my wall." Behind a glass case.

"Do you…" He pauses. "Do you think you have agoraphobia?"

"No. Just don't enjoy being outside."

"Sounds like agoraphobia to me." He eyes my uniform. "You're not getting changed?"

"No point. Got some extra coaching time with Ollie."

"He's the outreach kid, right?"

"Yeah. *Ollie*. Remember his name and don't call him the outreach kid or I'll have to slap you upside the head."

"You're grouchy today," Lewis remarks, but he's grinning as he swipes a towel off the side with one hand and snags two bananas in the other.

"I'm not."

"You are."

I huff. "Early morning."

"Uh-huh."

I'm not about to tell him that I hate it when Gracie stays at her apartment and not with me.

I feel better now that Conor's on the case but still, it blows when she's not around. Though it *was* my birthday yesterday, she had another early class so it made sense for her to return to her place.

Still sucked.

"You want some help with the kid?"

"With *Ollie*?"

"Yeah. Him."

"Nah. Thanks, though. He's shit on the ice but we're getting there."
Sort of.

He's managing to stay upright without falling over for a solid ten minutes—that's a massive improvement to how much time he was spending flat on his back during those early sessions.

He's more tenacious than I expected though.

"Why are you giving him private lessons?"

"Gracie."

He tosses a banana at me. "They're related?"

"No. She doesn't want him to end up in juvie."

Lewis scratches his forehead. "And the likelihood of that is high?"

Having recently seen Ollie's home after dropping him off there, I nod.

Once the banana is peeled, I take a big bite before I decide I'll head to the equipment room and start working on the curve of my blades.

Leaving Lewis to get changed, I spend some time at one of the workbenches until the alarm on my watch blares. I switch it off then return my stick to the stick locker.

Storing it there, collecting the skates I bought Ollie a month ago, and dragging the strap with my cell hanging from it over my head, on my way out, I see Greco's taping up his knuckles which look fucked.

I make no comment because he hasn't messaged me back so I have to assume he doesn't want to talk about his recent foray into self-harm.

Instead, I just head onto the ice, unsurprised to find Ollie in the stands waiting for me with a hotdog in one gloved hand and a can of soda in the other, a tuque on his head, and a scarf around his neck like it's midwinter.

When he sees me, as he's taken to doing, he waggles the hotdog at me. "Thanks, Liam."

"You're welcome."

Didn't take me long to figure out that the kid doesn't have enough money to eat.

I think of the banana I just devoured and sigh.

I'd kill for a hotdog.

Skating over to him because he's behind the visitors' bench, I lean against the boards and ask, "How'd school go? You get that history assignment finished?"

Shoulders hunched, he grimaces. "I hate history."

"We learn from history that we learn nothing from history."

Ollie studies his hotdog. "I've heard that before. Do you think it's true?"

"I do."

"Why don't we learn?"

"Because we choose not to." I angle my head to the side. "What's your choice, Ollie?"

He takes a big bite of his hotdog and, for a second, I think that's all the answer he'll give me. Then, his gaze locked on his beat-up sneakers, he mumbles, "I stopped hanging around with Arnie's crew."

"You have?!"

He scowls at me. "You think I'm lying?"

"No. I just didn't expect that." A nasty thought hits home. "They didn't hurt you, did they? For coming here?"

"I didn't tell them." He stuffs the rest of the bun into his mouth. "They never ask, so I don't say dick."

It's not hard to read between the lines.

"You doing okay?" I ask carefully—it's never nice to feel unwanted.

"Been better." He starts unfastening the laces of his sneakers then leaves them next to his trash—we've already had a conversation about throwing our garbage away—before he steps over to me barefoot.

I pass him his skates, watching as he sits on the bench nearer to the gate and ties them up how I showed him with an ease born of practice.

Him eating just before he gets on the ice isn't ideal, but the way he scarfs his food, I'm not about to stop him, not when he needs the energy.

Plus, right now, loading down with carbs isn't an issue. Case in point, how he moves around at a snail's pace while circling the rink with me.

"Liam?"

With my mind drifting between thoughts on my portfolio and Gracie's exam schedule, which starts tomorrow, alongside this week's training schedule, absently, I answer, "Yup."

"You know knives?"

Well, that ripped me away from thoughts of the NASDAQ. "For cooking, eating, or stabbing?"

That has him flinching so I already know the answer.

"Stabbing," he whispers, then he pulls his jacket aside. In the inner pocket, there's a goddamn hunting knife slotted in there.

"Jesus Christ, Ollie," I snap, skidding to a halt in front of him. "Where the hell did you get that?"

Gaze darting from left to right, he swallows. "Jamie. He's taken over Arnie's place on the crew. When I stopped hanging around with them, he didn't like it. He says I have to look after this, prove I'm still loyal to them."

Speechless, I grab his shoulder. Then, I realize how massive this is that he came to me, that he didn't squirrel it away. I let go of his shoulder, wishing my misunderstanding of him and his friends growing apart was correct.

My brain whirs with the repercussions and the potential that we have here for shit to go wrong.

"How does keeping that for them prove you're loyal to the crew, Ollie?"

His bottom lip quivers before he firms it. Too late. I saw. That and the fear in his eyes.

"They think I'm hanging out with someone else. W-With a bigger gang, when I'm here. I-It's to make sure I'm tied to them."

Fuck.

FUCK.

Gracie never planned for this!

"Ollie, you can't keep that."

"I know," he whispers, his tone miserable.

The kid literally hangs his head.

For the first time in a long while, I'm not sure what to do.

Money won't solve this, neither will my position or fame.

Speechless, I stare at the handle that's peeking out from his jacket pocket, part of the blade visible…

Is that blood?

Tabarnak.

"We have to take this to the cops."

"If we do, they'll know I snitched."

"Is that so bad?"

He peers at me with eyes that are too old. "Yeah. It's bad. Real bad, Liam. I wouldn't have come to you with this if it weren't."

Fuck my life.

If I didn't have a headache before this, I do now.

"I-I don't want this no more. I want what Gracie said. I want to be better."

Jaw working, mind racing, I blow out a breath. "Okay, you're going to skate around this rink twenty times without falling. You fall, you restart the count. Do you hear me?"

"I mean, sure, but—"

"No. No buts. You're not going to complain, or whine, or tell me you're bored. You're going to focus on skating rather than this because I'm going to handle it." The relief that hits his eyes has me dragging off my jersey. "Give it to me. I'm heading over to the stands. I'm going to call a cop I'm friends with—" Before he can protest, I continue, "We'll work something out. A fake arrest. Make it look like you were caught with it."

"You can do that?"

If I sign enough of Brownhill and Adamson's memorabilia, *maybe*.

"If we can't, we'll work something else out." Then, I grunt. "We have to fix this, Ollie. Permanently."

"How? I can't change where I live. I go to school with them and everything."

When his gloved hands pass me the knife and I tuck it into my jersey, I tell him, "Are there any sports fans on the crew?"

"Jamie likes hockey." He gags. "He's a San Jose fan."

With the makings of a plan in mind, and a potential favor from Trent in the works if things go south with Brownhill, I tell him, "Okay. Get started on your laps."

Clearly, I mistook his earlier mood because the way he takes off tells me the weight that's been lifted from his shoulders is gargantuan.

Seeing as I'm bearing that burden now, I get why that'd affect his goddamn state of mind.

Wrapping the jersey into a bundle and tucking it under my arm, I skate over to the side and clamber past the gate.

Once sitting, I unlock my cell and scroll through my contacts until I find Brownhill's number.

As the ringing tone hits my ear, I focus on the kid who, for the first time since I met him, isn't bitching about skating. If anything, he looks happier.

Maybe these issues with his so-called 'crew' are why he's been a pain in the ass to deal with so far.

I know that he's been better in the outreach program, otherwise I'd never have heard the end of it from Bradley. But I figure that's because his inability to stay upright is something he and I have been working on in private.

"Only for Gracie," I mutter even if the kid isn't *all* bad.

"Excuse me?"

I grimace at Brownhill's greeting. "Sorry, officer. This is Liam Donnghal speaking."

It's only as I utter his name that I realize how weird it's going to appear to the cops that the kid they hauled in for the lineup of mugging suspects is the kid in question now.

Shit.

This is going to be harder to sell than I originally thought.

"Hi, Mr. Donnghal!" Brownhill gushes.

"Liam, please." I clear my throat. "Officer—"

"Sam," he corrects.

"Sam," I parrot.

"How can I help, Liam?"

"I've got a problem."

"You do?"

"Did you know the Stars has an outreach program for underprivileged kids?"

"I didn't know that, but it sounds like a worthy mission."

"It is. One of the kids from the lineup is a part of that program."

Silence sounds down the line.

"Okay." His tone has flatlined.

He knows.

Slowly, I justify, "He and I have been working together on his skating skills."

"Right."

The man's not an idiot, just a superfan.

I rub at my eyes. "He's come to me with an issue that he's been having with some friends of his."

"This kid wouldn't happen to be Oliver Nolan, would he?"

"Yeah, that's him."

Brownhill grunts. "His crew is a piece of work, Liam. I hope you know what you're getting involved with."

"I don't know the crew, just the kid, and he's decent. The whole point of the program is to take someone from a shitty area and to give them an opportunity to better themselves."

"In my experience, that's not always possible."

I grit my teeth. "Well, the team has to try. We have to give back to our community."

"If you say so, Liam. What 'issue' is Oliver having?"

"He's been tasked with proving that he's loyal to his friends."

"What kind of task?"

"Holding a weapon on their behalf."

Brownhill hisses, "Jesus Christ. A gun?"

"No. A knife. With blood on it."

"Do you understand what you're asking of me here?"

"I'm just asking for help with a kid who wants to better his life but his past is clinging to him."

"You're trying to make it out like this boy is a good egg. I have no idea why Ms. Bukowski lied about him being her mugger, and I've no idea what game you're playing with him being a part of this outreach program, but—"

"Any help you can offer me, Sam, I'd be grateful." My voice is gruff with how badly I dislike having to manipulate this situation.

He knows what I'm saying, too, because he clears his throat. "Playoff tickets?"

"Club seats," I immediately offer. "For as long as we're in the playoffs."

Brownhill scoffs. "All the way to the end, then. No way you guys will lose with how you're playing this season."

"Maybe. That's something I can't guarantee. Tickets, however, I can. For you and how many?"

I hear the tapping of a pen in the background. "Five. That's how many friends I'll need to help me clear up this mess."

"I understand." I release a sigh. "It can't look as if Oliver gave you the knife."

"No. I understand that. His crew… When I tell you they're not good eggs, I mean it. Arnie was the original leader but James is worse. Arnie was too hopped up on drugs to accomplish much.

"The rest are as young as Oliver but eager to prove their worth to the new 'leader.' One of my friends works their patch and they've been bombarded with dozens of petty crimes this week alone; that's why I know so much about them. You're getting involved in something you don't understand."

"I'm sure that once this situation is under control, things will get easier," I try to appease.

His grunt tells me he doesn't agree. "I'm going to treat this as a tip-off. We'll bring the boy in for questioning and go from there."

"He won't be arrested?"

"No." A gust sounds in my ear. "But I make no promises about any of his crew whose prints may be on the weapon."

Praying to fuck that Ollie didn't touch the knife, I state, "Understood."

"This won't be the last you hear of his crew, Liam. I'm warning you —once you're in, they don't let you out."

I know he meant that as a warning, but if anything, it makes me all the more determined to liberate Ollie from those ties.

Staying noncommittal, I tell him, "I'll get the tickets to you as soon as they're available."

"I appreciate that. I'll keep you updated."

"Thank you for this, Sam."

"You're welcome. Tell the boy that we'll take the knife from him at the precinct."

"Got it."

When Brownhill puts the phone down, I release a soft breath as I stare at the bundle I dumped on the seat beside me.

Watching Ollie as he completes his task, I don't disturb him, just wait for him to finish.

As he skates over to me, I can see the expectant look on his face.

He saw me on the phone and knows my plan, for what it's worth, is underway.

"Everything okay, Liam?" he asks, his tone hopeful.

"Did you touch the knife?"

"No. I'm dumb, but I ain't that dumb."

"I'm glad you said it first," I snap then bite my tongue because he doesn't need me to add to the pressure he's under. "Okay," I murmur eventually. "The cop I know, we've made arrangements. He's treating my call like a tip-off.

"Tomorrow, he's going to show up at your school and bring you in for questioning. The knife will be taken from you at the precinct."

"I-I won't be arrested?"

"No. He said you won't. But if there are prints on the knife, then someone will be. You understand me?"

He scratches his cheek. "If Jamie goes to jail, someone will probably take his place. No one is as old as him."

"How many are on this goddamn crew?"

"Six now."

Tabarnak. "How do we get you away from them?"

"I don't know," he mutters, shoulders hunching again.

We never talk about anything outside of what's going on with him at school or what he's learned in the program, so I ask, "Your mom…"

"What about her?"

"You never talk about her."

"Not much to say. She's always strung out."

That has me cringing. "Aren't you tired of dealing with that?"

"Maybe." He shrugs, and the move is bizarrely adult for a boy so young. "I used to like it. Meant that I could do whatever I wanted, whenever I wanted. Things are different now, though." His brow puckers. "I-I like this hockey shit, Liam. I might not be good at it, but I like it."

"You've only been playing a few months," I counter. "You need to give yourself a chance to adapt. Have you tried it in nets?"

"Nah. You know that they just give us sticks and try to keep us from falling on our asses in the other classes."

"I'm going to assume that Gracie's wasn't the first purse you stole?"

"No." He shoves his gloved hands into his pockets. "I'm real good at snatching 'em."

"Not anymore," I retort, though I can't help but think that could be a useful skill for a goalie to have.

"No. Not no more," he quickly agrees.

"You enjoy it? Outside of Gracie's rules?" I ask. Now is as good a time as any to ram that home.

"I wish I didn't suck at it, but yeah. You think I'd be good in the crease?" he asks hopefully.

"I think the same instincts that have you targeting a particular mark, that help you snatch a purse, might make catching a puck easier. It's something to think about."

He peers at me. "Why were you asking about my mom?"

"If you want away from your crew, maybe it's time to speak with ACS."

"Ha. Like they give a fuck. Anyway, I'm not going in no home."

"Wouldn't it be better than what you're dealing with now? It isn't like you'd be on your own in the system."

"Isn't it? You and Gracie are only interested in me at the moment. My crew was... *is* my family."

"So why did you tell me about the knife? You said it yourself, Ollie —you want to go a different way. I think that Gracie and I have shown you an out and you want to take it—like you said, you're not that dumb. *And* we're not going anywhere.

"Gracie, for good or bad, has taken an interest in you. She's not the kind of person who gives up on someone. I'd know because she's with me."

"And you're a lost cause? You're *Liam Donnghal!*"

"So? Do you think that's easy? You think it's all fun being with me?" I shake my head. "Do you know what being 'Liam Donnghal' got me, Ollie?"

"What do you mean?"

"I mean that it got me kidnapped. I mean that Gracie gets shit in the papers for wearing pants at an event where she 'should' have worn a dress simply because she was on my arm. I mean that money in the bank doesn't always lead to you sleeping without nightmares and it sure as hell doesn't grow your ear back. I mean that living in a big house doesn't take away from the fact that you don't feel safe because being Liam Donnghal got you abducted once—what's to stop it from happening again? And what's to stop those same people targeting the woman you love?"

Ollie clambers over the boards and takes a heavy seat at my side. "You have nightmares?"

I stare at him. "I do."

He points to my prosthetic ear. "That happened while you were kidnapped?"

"It did."

"I thought it was a skating accident. One of the instructors in the program has a massive scar from a skate."

"I wish that were what happened to me but it isn't." Leaning forward, I rest my elbows on my knees. "I'm helping with this, Ollie, so maybe I can help with social services too."

He blinks at me. "I'll be alone."

"You won't be," I counter. "You'll have Gracie and me."

"You won't be in the home they put me in."

"No, but you'll sleep under a roof without a mom that's high. There'll be food in the refrigerator that you don't have to steal—" His blush tells me I hit the nail on the head there. "You won't have to be afraid of a drug dealer coming around, demanding payment for her addiction."

For a while, he doesn't say anything, just stares out at the ice. Then, he rasps, "I'll still see them at school."

"Not if we make sure you're moved to a different district."

"You can't promise that."

"Maybe I can't *promise* it, but I'll do everything in my power to make sure it happens."

He swallows. "Really?"

"Really."

His small shoulders hunch again, and just when I think that's a sign he's going to turn me down, with a trembling bottom lip as he shifts focus from the rink and back onto me, he mumbles, "Okay."

Our gazes locked, I nod. "Let's make it happen then."

CHAPTER 54
GRACIE

Let Me Blow Your Mind - Eve, Gwen Stefani

THE DOOR'S unlocked when I get back to my apartment. The only reason I don't freak out is because Ludvig is behind me. Then, the knob twists and the door pulls in to reveal *Kow*.

I was supposed to stay at my place again tonight, but when I shove past him and find Trent and Noah sitting on my couch as well, I forget about charging my dying phone or the fact I'm supposed to text Liam once I arrive home—I'm just tempted to turn around and leave.

I don't even have to ask how they got in.

My bodyguards.

Makes sense now that I think about it—Ludvig didn't exactly panic when the door opened, did he?

Making it a top priority to fire anyone who's a hockey fan on mine and Liam's security detail, I slam the door in the asshole's face.

"Why do you have bodyguards?" Noah asks.

"Why do you care?" His eyes widen but, ignoring him as I drop my bags to the side, I snap, "How did you even know who to bribe?"

It's not like we advertise who our security is.

"Bribe?" Kow rolls his eyes. "That's coming on a little strong—"

I hiss out a breath. "Andrews." Liam's agent, as well as Kow's and Trent's. "*He* told you."

"Calm down, Gracie. It's not a big deal." Maybe not to my baby brother. "Seriously, though, why do you have bodyguards?"

"Why don't you ask Andrews? Seeing as he has all the answers," I snap at Noah before demanding, "Have you seen Liam?"

"No, why would we have seen him? We're not talking," Kow mutters as he leans forward, elbows on his knees, casting a serious expression my way. "Because of you."

"You sure he wants to talk to *you* after that stunt you pulled in Winnipeg?" At his dismissive sniff, I try again, "Liam doesn't hang out here."

"We didn't come to New York for him," Noah grouses. "We're here to see you."

"Breaking into my apartment kind of gave that away but before I got my hopes up, I wanted to check," I retort as I retreat into my kitchen.

Only to find a pig sty.

"You assholes," I snarl. "Look at the mess you left behind!"

Trent calls out, "You had nothing in the refrigerator."

"Haven't you heard of trash cans? And if you ordered in, did you bother to get me anything?"

"We're not animals," Noah complains. "There are some leftovers in the fridge."

"There better be," I warn.

When I find a cold Vietnamese noodle salad, I stop huffing and snag a fork and dig in as I riffle through the bags of takeout in there.

Shit must be bad if they're eating out, though.

Kow's shadow darkens the archway that acts as a divider between the kitchen and my poky living room. "Mom called."

So that's why they're here.

"I have one of my first exams tomorrow and you pick tonight to come and bitch at me about a conversation that happened with our mother a while ago, Kow?" I demand, hefting my ass onto the counter because that way, we're at the same level.

There's nothing worse than always looking up at someone during an argument—the curse of being short.

"This was the first time we could all make it into the city," Noah excuses, shouldering past Kow who's still leaning against the aperture.

Trent also pushes his way in and takes a seat at the kitchen table.

The apartment's never been spacious, but now, these hockey hulks are taking up far too much of my oxygen.

"So, this is on *your* schedule not mine. Got it." *More like they all got tossed out of the playoffs.* "My exams are important. If you think I'm going to waste time getting stressed about your reason for being here, you can walk out the door and come back when my finals are over."

Kow frowns. "You told Mom that you were cutting the lines of communication with her."

"You actually spoke with her long enough to find that out, hmm?" I inquire, entwining noodles around my fork before I shove it in my mouth. "Shame it's old news. Like pre-playoffs old. Back when each of you were still in with a shot of winning the cup..."

His top lip curls into a sneer. "It's all she's been able to talk about since it happened. You hurt her, Gracie."

"I didn't know I was capable of doing that, to be honest," I muse, hunting for a peanut and chomping on it. "Go me."

"Gracie!" Trent chides, his voice deep and low.

"What?"

"That's needlessly mean."

More like she was.

"I don't think it is. I thought my response was an intuitive reaction to the tenor of our conversation—"

"Stop talking like a lawyer!"

"Sorry to disappoint, Kow, but Cornell says you can suck my donkey dick because they awarded me with a juris doctorate," I retort. "And if that's too confusing for you, it's Latin for 'fuck you.'"

"Look, you hurt Mom's feelings," Noah rebukes. "We're here to get you to apologize so that she'll stop bitching about it to us."

"Then you might as well leave now. I'm not saying sorry for something that she's to blame for." I stab my fork at him. "In her opinion, I'm not good enough for Liam."

Kow shrugs. "Let's face it. You're not, are you?"

Each word winds me, acting like a slap to the face that amplifies every single insecurity I possess.

Because, deep down, I want to cry, instead, I blink at him. "Here was me thinking that maybe you guys meant it when you said you were defending my honor on the ice…"

"You're you, Gracie. You're difficult and outspoken. Liam needs someone who'll put his career first."

"If you weren't standing over there, I would stab you with this fork."

But my other brothers are nodding at me like they're in total accord with Kow, the dumbest of our siblings.

"Liam doesn't feel the same way. Or do you think I tied him to the bed until he agreed to date me?"

They don't know me well enough anymore to recognize that the gruffness in my voice stems from the tears I refuse to shed.

First time I've seen them in years outside of on the ice and this is their welcome back to the fold…

The fuckers.

Somehow, it's even worse because this feels like a double blind.

Did I actually *like* that they were hurting Liam? Did the sister in me feel as if that was proof her brothers cared?

God, that is so messed up.

Hockey—every. Fucking. Time—it turns me into a pick-me cunt.

Unaware of my thoughts, Noah pulls a face. "Talking about tying him to the bed is just plain wrong. You're like brother and sister."

"No, we're not. At all. Not just because I enjoy doing a lot of filthy things with him when I can barely stand being in this kitchen with the three of you," I snarl.

"Liam needs someone soft and caring," Noah argues. "Gracie, I love you but that is not you."

"After the kidnapping, he needs someone who'll be there for him," Trent concurs.

And I'm not?

"Funny how I'm hearing this from you three who, at the start of the season, barely called him and who canceled on him whenever he tried to make plans for you to catch up at his place. Do you even realize how small Liam's circle is?"

"We fly in for the game; we fly out afterward. You know how it goes," Kow states unapologetically.

"He's a recluse but you couldn't make time for him? Hell, you don't even call and there's no flight required for that. I think when Liam wanted to talk with you about our relationship, Kow, it took you nearly two weeks to get back to him."

"We're busy men, Gracie. We're not girls," Noah counters as he riffles through the leftovers. "We don't need to talk every night to know that we're buds."

Because this is getting us nowhere, I settle a stony look on him. "If you need to convince someone that I'm no good for Liam, it's the man himself and, like I said, he isn't here."

"This can't go anywhere," Trent tries to placate. "You're just wasting your time with him, Gracie. We're doing you a favor by telling you this now. You're not wife material for a hockey player."

My brow furrows. "Who said I wanted to marry Liam?"

"Don't you? Isn't that what all women want?"

Angrily, I toss the container into the trash. "Not all of us. Look, I get it—you agree with Mom. I, on the other hand, don't."

"He skipped her birthday meal because of you," Noah grinds out. "You know how close they are. Do you think that's fair? On either of them?"

"After everything that happened, you have to know that's bad for him," Trent concurs.

"I told him that he shouldn't let my issues with Mom affect his relationship with her." Pursing my lips, I jump down from the counter. "I repeat—you're having this conversation with the wrong person. You can convince him that I'm bad for him because I'm not listening to this bullshit anymore."

As I storm through the kitchen, Trent tries to grab my arm to stop me, but I avoid him.

Unfortunately, Kow's blocking the exit.

"Move," I snarl. "Or do you want to lose your balls?"

"Not until you listen to reason," he bites out. "You need to break things off with Liam. He's clearly not adapting to New York well and you're taking advantage of him—"

"Fuck. You," I spit, wishing I were taller so that I could get in his face instead of earning myself a crick in my neck as I glare up at him.

"Don't you dare tell me I'm taking advantage of a man I've loved for longer than I can put a number to.

"I've dealt with your shit for decades. You've ruined my life in so many ways that you can't even know and if you did, you wouldn't care. Here I was, thinking that you finally did give a damn, and more fool me because it's always about *YOU*. But I'm the dumb one because you told me. You said it was because he broke the bro code and I didn't fucking listen.

"The crazy thing is you've not only stolen friendships from me, but I have no identity because of you and now you're trying to take Liam from me as well.

"You've robbed me of *every* single win I've ever had because it's nothing in comparison to your achievements, to the point where I had to leave my home, *my country*, to get away from YOU. To make a space for myself. To be somewhere I'm not continually compared to you when I'm three times the friend, confidante, and partner any of you will *ever* be—"

"God, stop with the whining, Gracie," Kow growls. "So, what? I fucked a few of your friends! What does it matter? It's only sex!"

It's a miracle steam isn't coming out of my ears.

A few?!

Meaning more than Charlotte?

Ignoring him like he didn't speak, I continue, "You come into *my* home, invade *my* space to tell me that I'm not good enough for a man who I make happy, who I bring peace to, who I make smile. Well, you can do your own dirty work because I'm not dumping him."

"You've got some nerve, Gracie," Trent rumbles. "He's been off his game—"

"So off his game that he's led the Stars to the playoffs for the first time in years. Unlike three Bukowskis I know...," I mock. "You're the ones who are out of line. You think you're here to defend your bud, but you're not.

"We're an item—I won't break things off with him, so he'll have to dump me. And I won't say sorry to Mother either." I stab my finger at Kow. "You've just added yourself to the incommunicado list because if I don't hear any of your fucking names for a decade, it'll be too soon."

With that, I put every ounce of force into it as I shove Kow out of the way.

Because he didn't expect me to be strong enough, he staggers back. I head for the door, leaving them to deal with securing my apartment seeing as Ludvig will have gone home now.

At this point, I'm so mad that I don't care if they abandon it unlocked.

Of the many offensive things they said, I'm mostly furious about the fact that the first time I verbalized my feelings for Liam, I didn't tell him those words. I wasted them on the three men who didn't deserve to hear them.

I race out of the building, unsure if they'll come after me, and only when I'm on the street do I let the tears flow as I run down the block and away from them. Hell, away from everyone.

Turning into an alleyway, stopping at the mouth for safety because I'm upset, not an idiot, I sniffle into the lily I tucked in my pin this morning. The bunch was waiting in the passenger seat when Harvey, my other bodyguard, came to pick me up for school.

My thoughts are racing and the urge to sob is growing stronger as that scent permeates every inhalation I take.

All I want to do is call Liam but...

I can't.

If I do, he'll react to the sound of my grief and that will make everything devolve.

I can't deal with that.

Not when a lifetime's insecurities of never being enough are starting to worm their way inside of me.

"Liam's different." I practically snarl the words to myself as I swipe at my cheeks. "They're wrong. I know they are. H-He won't... They can't convince him to leave me."

But, like always, the three nightmares the stork brought to darken my door have already worked their insidious magic.

The fear is there and it's real.

Sucking down air to calm my agitation, I snag my cell from my pocket and groan when I see there's only 1% of my battery remaining.

Realizing I ran out of my place without any of my stuff, including the power bank *or* Liam's business phone, I know my options are limited.

Thankfully, I have some juice to message someone who has enough distance from the situation to not judge either side.

Someone who, might possibly, be a friend one day.

If I can let her in long enough to trust her…

> Me: Aela?

Then, because Liam will think I've been freakin' kidnapped if I don't loop him in, I message:

> Me: Everything's fine. I just have some shit I need to talk through with a girlfriend.

Relief hits me when Aela replies:

> Aela: Hey!

> Me: Do you mind if I come around for a coffee?

> Me: I wouldn't ask but I really need to go somewhere neutral.

> Me: My brothers basically just told me I'm ruining Liam's life, game, and everything in between. I can't be where they are, and they're probably on their way to Liam's apartment.

> Aela: Assholes. They need to keep their noses out of other people's business.

> Aela: This is my address.

I'm lucky I've got a good memory because as I step outside of the alley, my focus is more on her address than the sidewalk so when someone bumps into me, my phone goes flying.

Already battered and repaired from Ollie stomping on it, it gives up the ghost.

Fuck.

CHAPTER 55
LIAM

Where's My Love - SYML

I HAVEN'T DATED anyone for as long as I have Gracie.

Ever.

Mostly because I was a hockey fuckboi before the kidnapping and after, well, I made a monk look promiscuous.

It's weird how you get used to the small things—the bitching about a professor or a teammate over a protein shake in the morning, the kissing her after she drinks maple ambrosia so I get to savor the taste of two of my most favorite things together, the sharing of a vanity mirror while I shave and she plucks her eyebrows, the apartment never *feeling* empty when she's around.

I like those small things.

They're not so small to me.

After the day I've had and the strings I've had to pull, I'd have appreciated seeing Gracie's welcoming smile when I got in.

Instead, the apartment is dark and there are no smells in here aside from cleaning products and marinara sauce for the endless bowls of pasta I eat because the housekeeper came today.

When Gracie's in the building, she's got one of those wax melts burning, the smell of which always makes me crave the butter pecan ice cream she thinks she's hiding from me at the back of the freezer.

She isn't.

I know where it is and what it's next to—fucking lean proteins.

Dumping my shit by the door, I head into the kitchen and take a seat at the counter once I've pulled out a bottle of kombucha.

The quiet is already too much so I switch on the TV and leave her news channel playing.

Checking my cell for any calls or texts, be it from her or Officer Brownhill, instead, I find a bunch of emails from Kara with invitations to events I have no desire to attend, a circular the team has sent about the upcoming travel to L.A. for our next game, and a missed call from Kow of all people. But not even an 'I'm home' from Gracie.

Which is unusual.

Another small thing is us keeping each other in the loop about where we're at. I started it when she became my PA; now, it's a habit we both indulge in. Her because it's expedient, me because it stops me from worrying about her.

Refusing to be concerned because it's still only six, I call Kow, set the phone on speaker, and take a sip of my drink.

"Yo," he greets like we're back in the 90s.

A message pops up on my screen:

> Gracie: Everything's fine. I just have some shit I need to talk through with a girlfriend.

Girlfriend? What girlfriend?

Confused, I text back:

> Me: Okay. Lemme know when you get home?

"Liam?"

Blinking, I focus on my conversation with Kow. "We talking now and I didn't get the memo?"

He grunts.

"You ever miss beer?" I ask wistfully, staring at the raw fermented drink I'm sipping.

I'll miss it even more if he's calling to give me shit about dating Gracie. Especially now that he's out of the playoffs and suddenly has the time to care about his sister...

My knuckles ache with how hard I clench down on the bottle in my hand.

"Nah. I don't punish myself like you do."

"You're the same age as me and I know you're not ready to retire."

"Not for a couple years, but a few beers never killed anyone." He clears his throat. "You at home?"

"Why?"

"Answer the damn question."

"I'm here."

"You heard from Gracie?"

My brows lift. "No? Fuck, have you two fought on the phone or something?" Is that why he broke radio silence?

Kow grunts in my ear. "Trent, Noah, and I are in the city."

"Which city?"

"New York," he mumbles.

"Why the hell am I only just hearing about this? Where are you staying? Are you coming here?" I'm not in the mood for a fight but at least they'll liven this place up.

"We're about ten minutes from your apartment."

"Should I prepare myself to duke it out with you?" I half-joke.

He doesn't laugh just mutters, "Nah."

Huh. "I'll let the doorman know to send you up."

Leaving the bottle of kombucha on the counter, I contact the front desk then use the guest bath before they arrive.

When I open the front door, I get a read on their expressions, brows high, I ask, "Who died?"

Considering the day I've had, that's too apt, but it doesn't trigger a reaction from these asswipes.

Noah shoots me a look as he leaves the elevator, his outstretched arm as he draws me in for a hug coming as a shock. Kow dips his chin, telling me he's still pissed—that comes as less of a surprise. Trent just whacks me on the back and, because he's the largest brother, tipping me by three centimeters, I actually get shoved forward with the momentum.

It was a toss-up between him sticking to ice hockey or switching over to basketball as a teen, but I think he should have been a plow horse.

"What's going on?" I demand, studying their solemn countenances after I lead them through the front door, along the hall, and into the kitchen.

Since Gracie burst into my life, that's become the heart of my home so it's second nature to bring them in here rather than the living room.

"Anyone want a kombucha?"

Kow pulls a face. "Nothing stronger?"

"No booze in the house. Temptation." I've been practically teetotal since the night of Amelia's wedding.

Noah shrugs. "I like it. Got that ginger-lemon stuff?"

"Yup. Trent?"

"Same."

Kow huffs. "I'll just have water."

After sliding the three glass bottles over the marble counter, I lower my elbows onto it and study them.

"What's going on? Is one of the folks ill or something?"

"Nothing like that. You genuinely haven't seen Gracie?"

I arch a brow at Noah. "No."

"She isn't here?"

"For fuck's sake, *no*. Why would I lie?"

Kow starts messing with his bottle cap. "We wondered where she went."

"*Where she went,*" I repeat blankly. "Meaning that you know where she was before she 'went' wherever she went?"

"Yeah. We met her at her place."

"She never mentioned that you were coming to the city for a visit."

"She didn't know either. It was a… surprise."

A surprise.

Noah's tone tells me it wasn't a good one.

Suddenly, Gracie's message takes on extra connotations.

"I figured I'd be your first port of call. You know, that you'd give me the whole, 'She's my sister. Don't you mess with her or I'll mess with you,' spiel. I was looking forward to it, in fact."

There are so many crickets in here, it's turning into an infestation.

"Okay, fuckers, what's going on? You're acting really goddamn weird," I say as I snag my phone and check my messages again—no reply from Gracie.

Noah scrapes his nail over the paper sticker on the front of the bottle. "She didn't like what we had to say and she took off. We informed her bodyguard. What's with that anyway? Why does she have security on her?"

I'm not sure which part of that triggers the most concern: that they know her bodyguard or that she ran out. But knowing security is with her eases some of my worry.

She's safe... but *hurting?*

She said everything was fine though.

I figure that I'm slow to process the undertones here after the day I've had, so it takes me longer than it should to reason, "You came about your mom, didn't you?"

The way the three of them hunch their shoulders clues me into how right I am.

Nostrils flaring, I send out a text:

> Me: Ludvig? Do you have eyes on Gracie?

He should be making his way home, but if these assholes contacted him, as per his new schedule, if she goes out, he does too.

Still, Kow doubles down on his assholery by grumbling, "Gracie can't just cut Mom out because she cares about you."

"That isn't what happened. Hanna basically said that Gracie wasn't good enough for me, which is bullshit.

"If anyone has a lot to put up with here, it's Gracie. Since the start, she's been blamed in the papers whenever we lose a game—either she's fattening me up or draining my concentration.

"God forbid, it has anything to do with me having a life outside of the game." I grit my teeth when I see Ludvig still hasn't replied. "Besides, I've wasted too many years not telling her how I feel about her.

"After everything that happened, she was the only thing that got me through—she was my lifeline. The last thing I need is Hanna convincing Gracie that she shouldn't be with me—"

"Gracie? *Our* Gracie? That's who we're talking about right now, right?"

"Do you have to sound so surprised?" I snap at Kow. "*Yes*, Gracie. Your sister. *GRACIE.*

"I remember sitting in that hellhole, dried blood on my face, my ear gone, my entire head feeling like it was about to fall off as infection set in, thinking that I was going to die, and she was my biggest regret."

Eyes wide, Trent leans back on his stool. "You not dating Gracie was your biggest regret?"

"Not dating her. Not being able to see her again... The idea of *never* seeing her again, of the last time we met up being the end," I explain in a rush as the words take me back to the darkest of days I've ever known.

Grieving what I went through has been an arduous process, one that Mike has spent a long time trying to encourage. But through it all, Gracie has been a cornerstone of my recuperation—not that she or any of her family know that.

But that's not the problem here.

"Did I play well after I was freed?"

Kow frowns. "Yeah, but that's how you roll. You always play your best when you're stressed AF. That's how you won the Stanley Cup that year."

I figure I have to spell this out for them: "How would you say I've been playing lately?"

"You never play like shit, but this entire season, it was clear that your mind was elsewhere."

I stare at him.

Really fucking stare.

Grace each of them with that stare.

Trying to see if they'll pick up on what I'm saying.

They just look back at me, confused.

"Fuck you. You're just like the press, blaming her if the wind turns when we all know that I've been playing the best hockey of my career. And do you wanna know why? *Gracie.* Because I've finally found a fucking balance. I'm actually living my life and enjoying it. And you asswipes call yourselves my friends and are questioning all that?"

"I don't understand," Noah eventually says.

"What's to understand? I used to play my best hockey when I was miserable. Now, I do it when I'm happy. Because. I. Am. Because I have other things on my mind—good things. Things I want to think about like..." I suck in a breath. "...how much I love your sister."

Trent blinks at me. "You love... Gracie?"

"What's with the hesitation? She's awesome. The best thing that's ever happened to me. How couldn't I love her?"

Noah crinkles his nose. "But she's difficult."

"No, she's not difficult. She just has opinions, and those opinions mean she isn't constantly kissing my ass or thinking I'm a god because I chase a puck around a patch of ice."

"Her career doesn't align with yours," Trent points out.

"Who says it has to?" I frown as realization strikes. "You're not just here to fix things for Hanna—you're here because you agree with her."

Her message reads differently now.

What the fuck did they say to her?

"Of course," Kow grumbles.

"No 'of course' about it. Hanna's harder on Gracie than any of you." My temper snaps at the limits of my control. "I pity the Bukowski family because not a single one of you knows what you're missing out on by taking Gracie for granted.

"Look, I figure that you're here for my sake and I appreciate that to a certain extent. But I wish *en ostie* that you were here to kick my ass and to tell me to watch myself because you'll be there to break some bones if I hurt her. I actually appreciated when Kow and Trent beat my asses because I figured you gave a fuck, but you're all so busy being mommy's boys that you can't see the forest for the trees." Kow rears backward at that but I snarl, "Why would you think I needed you to protect me... and from Gracie of all people?"

"You've been different since the kidnapping. We have your back, bro," Kow states.

"Since when?" I demand, checking my phone again.

Nothing.

Is she working up to breaking up with me over something these assholes said to her?

"I don't need you to have my back," I growl, fury leaching into the words. "I can guard my own. Gracie needs her family, man. The people who are supposed to love her unconditionally are the ones who should have *her* back. Instead, she's out in the cold.

"It wasn't until she started working with me that I realized how much of a disconnect there is between you all. It's sad as hell, but you're the ones missing out because Gracie is a beautiful human being.

"Now, I'm going to have to ask you to leave because I've got to fix whatever mess you made with her. If you've ruined this for me, if she breaks up with me, that's us—done. Do you understand?"

Kow jerks back like I slapped him. "Fuck off, Liam. You'd never do that—"

I don't let him finish. "No *brothers* of mine would purposely wreck the best thing that's ever happened to me without consulting me to see whether I'm happy or not.

"We haven't even talked in months, not really, even before this stupid falling out, yet you've taken it upon yourselves to think that I must be crazy to be with her.

"I tell you what—she's the one who's out of her mind for dealing with me." I snag my phone and hit dial on her number when Ludvig still hasn't responded. "Just leave, would you? Before I throw you out."

"What the hell has she done to you, man?" Noah demands as I round the counter, the phone to my ear as I await her answer.

"She's done dick. Why do you intentionally see the worst in her? All she's done is be *here* for me. She's had time for me. She's the one who hooked me up with a shrink. She's the one who's there whenever I need her, who remembers that I missed skateboarding, for chrissakes. Where the fuck have you guys been? Sure, you're busy. We all are. But I will always pick her. Always—"

"Bros before hoes, man," Kow rumbles.

That's when I see red.

"Your sister is *not* a ho." My fist flies to punctuate that declaration. Kow's head tumbles back before he has the chance to shield his face, and Trent's there to stop me from lighting into him anymore. "Don't you dare put that word and Gracie in the same sentence," I snarl, letting him hold me off because I don't want to waste time on them when Gracie's somewhere that isn't *here*, their poison in her ears.

"What the fuck is wrong with you, Liam? We came here because

Gracie's ruining everything," Kow snaps. "You're letting her poison you against us—"

"Are you all so fucking unhappy with your own lives that you can't let me have some happiness for myself? Or is it that you hate Gracie so much for being different that you can't let her be with someone who loves her for who she is?" Disgusted with them, I shake my head. "Seriously, get the fuck out of our home and take your bullshit with you."

Kow sneers. "Did we not even deserve to be looped in? You're the shitty friend here. You just thought you could fuck our sister without any blowback?"

"I'd be happy with that. But you're sulking with me is one thing. Agreeing with your mom and siding with her is another matter entirely. *That* is my problem. She's the best thing to ever happen to me. Understood?"

"Kow, leave it," Noah urges, grabbing him by the shoulder and forcibly shoving him toward the door.

"Some fucking friend you are," Kow roars as he lets Noah drag him away.

"Some fucking *brother* you are," I shout back, preternaturally aware that Gracie's radio silence is probably the beginning of the end of our relationship. That's when I see Trent hasn't moved. "What do you want? I swear to God, Trent, if you call her names, I'll—"

"You love her?"

His question has me releasing a breath. "Yeah. For a long time."

He scrapes a hand over his jaw. "You said *our* home."

"It's her place as much as it's mine."

"Mom misses you."

"I miss her too," I say honestly. "But I'm not going to let anyone disrespect Gracie—even if that's the people I love the most in the world and the people who should have been looking out for her since she was born."

He flinches like I struck him. "Gracie's always been difficult. Always gone her own way."

"As if the rest of us haven't," I scoff. "Do you know she only came to the US to get away from you? To make a life for herself out of the shadow of the famous Bukowski brothers? Your mom constantly compares her to the three of you. You and I know that without even having to talk to her about it, Trent. Your dad's better but he's as hockey obsessed as we are."

His grimace says it all.

"Get out of here, Trent. I don't want to argue. It was a shitty day *before* this conversation happened. Now, I've got to find the woman I love and convince her whatever her asshole brothers said that had her running off is wrong."

Trent surprises me by nodding. "Text me when you know she's safe."

"I'll let her decide whether she wants you to know that or not," I counter.

Another flinch but he nods and finally leaves.

When the call goes to voicemail again, I check Find My and see that her device last registered at her place.

An hour ago.

When I know she's not there.

That's when I let my fear for her, not for our relationship, run riot.

I call Ludvig, who finally deigns to answer, but I can hear his feet thudding on the sidewalk. Is he running?

"We'll find her, sir," he assures me, breathing heavily from exertion. "The Bukowskis told me she ran out—"

Blood draining from my face, I cut the call.

Knowing I have no alternative and grateful for my backup plan, I call in the big guns.

The Irish Mob.

CHAPTER 56
GRACIE

Erase/Rewind - The Cardigans

WHEN THE TAXI drops me off at Aela's house after a crazy long journey thanks to an accident that got us stuck on the Hudson River Greenway, it's with relief that she guides me to the kitchen.

Not only is this my favorite room in any house, but it's also silent in here.

After making sure I'm settled with a drink, she puts Cameron to bed with the promise of her return in fifteen or so minutes.

The quiet, after the day I've had, is nice enough that I don't even miss the news.

Someone once told me that peace feels like boredom to a child raised in chaos, and truthfully, it's only since Liam came back that I realized how bored I've been.

The fear of being betrayed again made me isolate myself. And that I'm here, in the kitchen of a woman I've met once, tells me how extreme I've taken my isolation.

"Oh, hello."

I blink at the young blonde girl who takes a seat at the empty kitchen table beside me. "Hello." It takes me a couple moments to recall who she is, then I tack on, "Victoria."

"You've got a good memory." Her grin tells me that mental workout was intentional. "No one remembers my name."

I grimace. "Been there."

"You look upset. Are you okay?"

"I just had an argument with my brothers."

She tips her head to the side. "A bad one?"

"Yes. The worst kind."

"I argued with my sisters tonight too."

"Oh?"

"I told them I've decided who I'm going to marry and they're not happy about it." She waves a hand as I sputter. "Family tradition."

"To marry young?!"

She chuckles. "I'll marry when I'm older, but I still know who it'll be. Anyway, that doesn't matter. I'm just saying their opinion's their opinion. I don't give a flying fuck what they think in the long run. You should feel the same way about your brothers."

My lips curve. "You're not wrong about their opinion being theirs..." The rest? I didn't know what I was doing with my life at her age, never mind knowing who I was going to marry. Unsure if I'm impressed or terrified, I ask, "So you're finding refuge at Aela's too?"

She nods. "With Seamus. He's a good listener and even better at shutting up when I don't want to talk."

That has me snorting.

"Why are you here?"

Her curiosity tells me how weird it is that I came to Aela's, of all places, after an argument with my family, but I mumble, "I needed a breather with someone who wouldn't judge me."

"And Liam would judge you? Huh. I misread him, then."

"No, he's not like that."

She purses her lips. "I don't know much about relationships, but aren't you supposed to run to the person you're in one with when the going gets tough?"

"He was my first choice," I assure her. "But he's close to my brothers."

"You thought he'd take their side?"

"No, I—" I don't. *He won't.* Right? "—I knew he'd take mine and I didn't want it to ruin their friendship."

Her brows lift. "That's a very kind thing to do."

My nose crinkles because the words are a compliment but her tone isn't.

For a teenager, Victoria is more adept at giving shade than the media.

"What did you argue about?"

"They said I was dragging Liam down."

"Down where?"

"You know, hockey? Making him play worse."

She scoffs, "That's it?"

"That's all that matters to hockey players."

"That's dumb. They sound like shitty friends."

I can't disagree but... "Liam doesn't have many people in his life. I don't want to make that worse."

She hitches a shoulder. "Sounds like he has three more than you if your brothers take his side."

Well, ouch.

I rub my forehead. "Liam took my side with a couple family arguments and they say that's my fault too."

"Is it?"

"It's not that cut and dry. He took my side because if it's not hockey-related, it's unimportant. He was just sticking up for me."

"He looks like the type of guy who'd always have your back. I'm glad I didn't read him wrong.

"If it's any consolation, you two looked very happy together when you were at Conor and Star's apartment." She smiles as she gets to her feet. "I think your brothers sound like idiots."

"You're a very smart young woman," I drawl.

Victoria chuckles. "Do you need another drink? I'm just about to get one for Shay and me."

"No, I'm fine. Thanks."

I watch as she gathers some soft drinks from the refrigerator and waves a brisk farewell at me on her way to the door.

Just as I think she's going to leave, she says, "Only you can decide your worth, not your family. And it certainly has nothing to do with how well someone plays a sport."

Her derisive snort tells me what she thinks about *that*.

"She's very wise for someone her age."

I jump at the next intrusive voice, one who happens to be another un-Aela-shaped person. Twisting in my seat, I find Conor standing in *another* doorway. This one looks like it could head to a basement.

"Hello, Conor."

"Hi. Didn't mean to startle you."

"You're fine." I glance at the door. "And you're right. She's very wise."

He strolls over to the kitchen table, where I'm at, and sits opposite me. "Do you mind if I ask you a question?"

In this madhouse, I wouldn't be surprised if he asked me to sit for a lie detector test.

"I retain the right to not answer," I say lightly.

"Spoken like a lawyer."

"I can talk the talk."

He wafts a hand. "What do you think of Bradley?"

I frown. "The Stars' coach?"

"Yes."

Though I want to tell him that hockey and the Stars are not my priority right now, I hate Bradley enough that I'd like to share my opinion with the team owner. "He's a jackass."

Conor grins at me. "You say that like it's a bad thing. Star often tells me I'm a jackass."

I groan. "I just realized why you changed the Liberties' name!"

He winks. "It's not something everyone has picked up on, but why is he a jackass?"

"He's antiquated. Doesn't listen. Stubborn. Uses plays that undermine the talents of his players. I also don't think he gives them enough RnR time. Like, when Liam had a concussion this season. While Bradley stuck to the letter of NHL law when it came to medical advice, Liam could have used a couple more days to recuperate.

"They're men. Not robots."

Conor studies me. "Padraig told me that you had many opinions about the team."

Studying my nails, I mutter, "I have opinions about a lot of things. Especially idiots who have no right to lead one. I bet you picked him as your coach because he won Olympic gold, am I right?"

"Of course."

"They have the crème de la crème on their team. And he coached *Canada*. The motherland of hockey. Dude, he had an easy job. You should have gone with Robbie Mitchell from Vegas."

"I should have? Why?"

"He's got fresh ideas and he cares about his players." I shrug. "Coaches should. You know when Liam was released, he dropped thirty pounds. *Thirty*. His agent had him convinced that he should keep the weight off.

"The following season, Mitchell moved to the Mounties. He told Liam that he should get a new agent and worked with a nutritionist, *personally*, to make sure that he gained the weight back even though it slowed him down on the ice because he knew that there was more to Liam's magic than his physical prowess." I click my fingers. "*That* is the sign of a good coach."

"Did Liam fire his agent?"

I huff. "No." But he'd better after that BS stunt he pulled today.

"Are you passionate about this because of Liam or because Mitchell's good? Vegas didn't make the playoffs," he points out.

"Vegas sucks. They fucked up with the draft last year." I sniff. "Their GM is a pile of horseshit. So's the Stars'. Whoever thought it was a smart idea to put Liam and Greco on the same team then not trade Raimond before the deadline while Lewis is vital in offense is insane…"

He chuckles. "You know Justin Delaney?"

"Not personally but I know he sucks harder than Vegas's GM. Trust me, that's saying something. You went for what you perceived as being the best, but your inexperience with the game is clear."

He pulls a face at my criticism but only asks, "When do you graduate?"

"I might not. Finals start tomorrow."

"You'll pass though. I've seen your grades."

"Excuse me?"

He wafts a hand. "I'm a hacker."

I play with my '35' pendant. "That doesn't come as much of a surprise with your associations, I guess. Still, are you supposed to admit to that?"

"Conor's a renegade," Aela drawls, returning to the kitchen and making me jump *again*. "He doesn't care who knows what he does."

"I'm untouchable," is his smug confirmation. "And the only woman who could get to me is my fiancée so I'm all set."

Aela tosses something at my chest. "Shay bought this for me as a gag gift."

It's in the Stars' colors and I know it's a jersey, so when I see the name on the back, I chuckle. "I'm sure Declan loved you wearing Liam's name."

"Didn't get it over my head," she says with a laugh. "You should take it. Wear it when you go home."

I grin. "You're a devious woman, Aela."

"More than one way to stake a claim," she counters as she pulls a pop from the refrigerator, tosses it at her brother-in-law when he asks for one, then plucks some juice out for herself. "And if your brothers *are* there, that'll show him." To Conor, she gives him the basic rundown of what I texted her earlier. "They told her she was ruining Liam's game and his life."

"As the team owner, I take offense at that."

Aela snorts. "And as the man's cousin?"

"I also take offense. He's quite clearly besotted with you, Gracie.

"In fact, I'll incentivize you *not* breaking up with him. I never cared about the Stanley Cup winner before but this year, I'd like to win it and you breaking my star player's heart isn't the way to victory."

My grin widens. "Shut up." But damn, that's good to hear.

I know I'm not the easiest person in the world, but with how my brothers were talking, it was like I was half-demon.

Aela strolls over to the kitchen table and takes a seat at the head. When I'm surrounded by O'Donnellys, she murmurs, "What's going on, Gracie? I'm happy you messaged but why did you need someplace neutral? Why not go to Liam?"

"Why? She's family. Family finds solace together," Conor says, confusion lacing the words.

She rolls her eyes. "Ignore him. He doesn't share dick with his family."

"Lies."

"The filthy truth more like," she mumbles. "Anyway, this is a safe space, Gracie, so if we can help, tell us how. Conor's right about one thing: we're all family here."

"Or we will be when Liam proposes."

Aela barks, "Conor!"

"You don't know that," I point out.

His smile is smug.

"So," Aela prompts, rolling her eyes at her brother-in-law's non-answer. "What's going on?"

Still fiddling with my pendant, I mutter, "Do you want the long story or the short?"

Conor's smile is kind. "Whatever helps you make sense out of what's going on."

Ugh. Liam has *the* best family ever.

"When I graduated high school," I croak out, "I followed Kow and Liam around the circuit as they played in their rookie season.

"I had this friend from my last year of elementary school. When I moved to Montréal, it was the first time we were apart and I missed her, so, one time, I invited her to stay with us. I was excited when she came to visit. We hung out and caught up with everything we hadn't been able to do when I was a thousand miles away.

"On the penultimate day of her trip, we were supposed to watch Liam practice—"

"Not Kow?" Conor inquires.

"He was resting up for game day. He'd gotten whacked in the head so they were being cautious, making sure he was ready to play." My smile is weak. "Anyway, after practice, we were going to hang out with Liam, but she had food poisoning so she told me to go watch him on my own. I did because he's *Liam*. He was so raw back then, all the makings of the talent he'd develop but so powerful it was intoxicating to watch."

"I'll bet," Aela teases.

Flushing when I see their knowing looks, I mumble, "I skipped out early because I realized what a shit friend I was for leaving her to watch some boy run hockey drills. I came back and—"

Groaning, Conor interrupts, "You caught her fucking Kow?"

Aela gasps. "Shut up! That's not what happened. Is it, Gracie?"

"It is," I admit, trying not to smile at Aela's double gasp. "We argued—"

"Of course. She broke the code," is Conor's immediate response. *The infamous code.*

"In a sense," I agree. Then, I snort. "Of course, Liam's breaking it now too. And I'd have gotten over seeing them have sex *on my bed*—"

"So tacky," Aela snipes.

"—if she hadn't told me that I had no right to be upset about Kow and her being in a relationship. Not when she'd been putting up with me for years just to be close to him."

"What a bitch!" Conor grouses, leaning forward, obviously invested in my story.

Oddly comforted that a guy agrees, especially after Kow accused me of whining, I nod. "I'd have dealt with it, really I would, but Kow's Kow. He has so many notches on his bedpost, it's now a toothpick.

"When she said that shit about them being in a relationship, he already had one foot out of the door and I knew he didn't have a clue what her name was. And that just feels like the story of my life," I finish glumly. "No matter what I do, where I go, who I meet, it's never about me. It's about the hockey players in my family.

"So, tonight, for them to tell me that I'm not good enough for Liam, it stung and it made me question some stuff, and I didn't have anywhere else to go," I admit. "If I went to Liam, he'd react and things would just... Their friendship is already on thin ice because of me. I didn't want to do anything to wreck it further.

"I didn't feel like being in a bar or a restaurant either. I just wanted—"

"A safe space," Aela inserts. "You said it made you question a few things... like what?"

The ride over here might have been long, but it came with the benefit of permitting me a moment of introspection. That's why I can answer:

"I ran from Montréal even though I was very close to Liam. I barely managed to graduate high school, but after I cut out the toxic family bullshit, I managed to get my bachelor's in business. I came here and studied for my LSATs and then I got into law school. I forged my own path. Made my own way. All without the help of my family. I disconnected myself from them—emotionally, physically, *financially*. I realized that sticking around them was turning me into a 'pick-me' girl—"

"God forbid," Aela jokes, making me chuckle.

"Now, I'm dating Liam. Things feel so right, like how they should have been years ago. And nothing's how I thought it would be." I rub my brow. "I hate my MBA classes."

Aela blinks. "You do?"

"I do. I hate law. I hate... I *hate* hating hockey. How much of my life has been a ridiculous rebellion? Do I even know who I am anymore? I made myself loathe a sport that I love. How crazy is that?

"Hockey started because, when I was younger, I wanted to hang out with my dad, but all the shit I know isn't just because I have random factoids in my head—"

"You're passionate about it," Conor remarks, his tone soft.

I nod. "I kept up with the game through following Liam's career, though, admittedly, I didn't realize I was doing that, dammit. It's like I dissociated or something. It's nuts."

"Family does that to you," Aela concurs.

"It does," Conor chimes in.

"Everything's changing in such a short space of time and Liam's the catalyst," I whisper, biting my lip.

The part of me he's trained immediately expects his kiss.

My lips tingle with the loss.

"You can't blame Liam!" Conor argues.

I raise his jersey to my chest and hug it like it's him. "I'm not. I'm thanking him."

Conor's frown is loaded with his disbelief. "Then why are you here?!"

"Conor! She's processing! Leave her alone."

"No." I blink. "He's right. *Victoria* is right. Self-sacrifice, my ass, when they're shitty friends. He's my end game, just like I'm his. And if I have to knock some sense into his skull to make him see that and unteach whatever BS they tried to indoctrinate him with then I will.

Fuck them." I jerk to my feet, ignoring the scraping of the chair as I stand up. "Aela, can I really keep this?"

She chuckles. "The jersey? Of course!"

Aela's barely had the chance to finish the sentence before I'm dragging it over my head as I make my way to the foyer, racing like I've got a rabid pack of wolves at my heels, which is when there's a banging on the front door.

The noise has me braking to a halt. I *am* in the front hall of an Irish mobster's house, after all.

Checking the peephole, I find Liam waiting for me there on the stoop.

The relief I feel at seeing him tells me I was a dumbass earlier—I should have gone home because he always, *always* makes me feel better.

I open the door.

CHAPTER 57
LIAM

35

Like I Can - Sam Smith

THE MOMENT CONOR sends me Gracie's location, I call Hudson and light it out of my apartment.

I don't care that when I get to the lobby, Fryd and Hanna are arguing with Quentin, the doorman. I barely even notice until he shouts, "Mr. Donnghal, sir! Do you know these people?"

My head whips to the side in annoyance, but when I catch sight of Gracie's folks, I pause but only long enough to snap, "I have no idea why you're in New York but it had better be to reconcile with Gracie. I've already had it up to here with the Bukowskis thinking that I'm not the lucky one in this relationship tonight."

Fryd chides, "Liam! Not talk Hanna like that!"

I'm about two seconds from flipping him the bird. All I say, however, is, "Shame you didn't stop Hanna from treating your own daughter terribly."

Hanna flinches. "I came to apologize to her, Liam."

"You did?" After the conversation I just had with the boys she fed her narrative to, I eye her dubiously. "Really?"

"Yes. You not coming for my birthday... not answering my call on yours... it made me see how seriously you were taking this. I-I didn't—"

"I have to go stop Gracie from realizing she'd be better off by dumping me, Hanna. Something that's only a risk because your dumbass sons told her *she* wasn't good enough for *me* while they tried to defend *you*.

"While I'm gone, you need to stop stuttering and work out exactly what you're going to say to her to make her realize that she's a valid and important member of your family." Uncaring that Quentin is eavesdropping, I continue, "I'd invite you up but I fully intend on bringing Gracie back home and proving how much I love her and I don't think any of us are comfortable with you hanging around in my apartment when that happens."

Hanna flushes but Fryd snorts. "Son, go get girlie. What are waiting for?"

Hanna whacks him on the stomach. "Fryd!"

"What?" He shrugs. "I saw writing on wall years ago. I not know why you all surprised."

Shocked he figured out my feelings for her but glad he did, I slap him on the shoulder and tell him, "Good man, Fryd. I'll call you tomorrow, Hanna, and tell you when Gracie's ready to see you."

Fryd interrupts my thoughts with: "She make big apologies. I already spanked her—"

"Fryd!" Hanna shrieks.

"Jesus Christ, I didn't need to know that," I mutter, deciding to get out of there before I'm scarred for life even more.

Hanna already looks like she's about to melt into the ground, and I don't blame her.

Waving at them as I depart, I find Hudson waiting outside.

Each mile is torture.

If Declan lived closer, I'd have run to his place, but instead, I just white-knuckle it as we finally make our way there.

When his brownstone is in my line of sight, I jump out of the SUV and run to the door, slamming my fist on it until someone shows up.

That's when it opens.

And Gracie's standing there.

Right there.

IN *MY* FUCKING JERSEY.

I don't give her the chance to speak, don't spoil this by messing it up with anything *I* might say. She's heard too many words today—she needs action—so I haul her into me and hug her.

Tight.

So tight that I know she'll never be able to figure out where I finish and she begins because that's how we're going to be.

For-fucking-ever.

As I hold her, she sobs against my chest, nonverbally describing how devastating the day has been for her. Gracie's not a crier, but this has been a special kind of hell—I know that without her telling me what her brothers said. Just dealing with the aftermath of it was bad enough and they were trying to support me, so I can't even imagine how traumatizing that was for her.

Over her shoulder, I see Aela watching us, a soft smile on her lips. That's when I notice another girl there too—Victoria? If memory serves, Brennan and Eoghan's sister-in-law.

With both of them smiling at me, it could be creepy, but mostly, I realize it's just confirmation that I'm exactly where I'm supposed to be.

I don't know if this is the right place or the right time, but I'm done with gatekeeping the words.

Aela and Victoria are about to be Gracie's family so it's fine if they overhear.

"I love you," I whisper in Gracie's ear. "I'm the lucky one. I'm the one who doesn't deserve you—"

She jerks back at that. Slaps my shoulder. "Shut up and stop talking smack about the love of my life!"

Fuck.

Just, fuck.

What's that making my eyes prickle?

"You love me?" I croak. "I thought you were going to break up with me."

"Screw that," she growls. "That was never what this was about."

"Then why didn't you come home? Or just come to me, period? Why didn't you answer your phone?" I snap, gripping her shoulders— I swear I'm about two seconds from shaking some sense into her.

"My cell is a goner." Then, she tacks on with a grimace, "Do you understand how isolated I am, Liam? Before we went public, before you came into my life, I literally locked myself away.

"I have no friends. None. The ones I thought I had were from work and they let me down the second they knew who you were and who was related to me." She presses her hand to my cheek. "I don't want you to be like me. I want you to have people who love you in your life. My brothers do. They're idiots, but they do. I was just trying to protect you from arguing with them and making things worse."

"They did come to *our* apartment," I say. "But with or without you there, we argued. That was always going to happen. I told them to get the fuck away from me with their bullshit."

"Yay!" Victoria cheers from the background.

Aela claps. "Totally! That's how it's done!"

Gracie turns around and mutters, "You guys. You're not supposed to be listening in to this conversation."

"I kind of live here," Aela drawls with a chuckle.

Victoria shrugs unapologetically. "I wanted to see what he'd do." She waves. "But I'll leave you to it."

Aela grins. "If you'll just close the door on your way out, I'll let you kids make up on your own too."

"I'll make sure the latch is on," I tell her with a smile.

"Thank you." Aela tips her head to the side and informs Gracie, "You're not alone anymore, babe. From the look in his eye, you're going to be an O'Donnelly sooner than I thought.

"So, just FYI, I also need more friends in my life. I know how it feels to be betrayed, for different reasons than yours, but it still hurts."

"It does," Gracie croaks.

Aela shoots her a half-smile. "See you later, friend."

Gracie waves at her sheepishly. "Bye... *friend*. I'll call you sometime this week and we can get your hair dyed purple."

Aela grins. "Can't wait."

As she makes a retreat, I snort. "You two are so cute."

Gracie whips around to glower at me. "I'm not cute."

"You are," I argue, cupping her chin so I can tilt it backward for a kiss. "And you're even cuter in my jersey."

If my voice meandered into a growl at that then it can't be helped.

"You like it?"

"I do. Where the hell did you get it from?"

"Aela gave it to me."

"Then I owe Aela."

Gracie's smile shifts from nervousness to smugness. "Yeah, you do."

"It means what I think it means, right?" I ask, just making sure that we're on the same page here.

Her chin tips up even higher than it did with my help. "That you're mine? Yeah. It does."

My grin is wicked. "I like the sound of that."

"Just so you know," she admits, "I was on my way to you because... screw them."

I wink at her. "No thanks." Still, her words have me pressing a soft, grateful kiss to her lips before I whisper, "You'd better not be changing your hair color. Blue all the way, *bébé*."

Her cheeks practically glow. "I just need a trim."

"Good," I rasp, sliding my hand through the silky locks and wrapping the ponytail I make around my wrist. "I think Aela asked on my behalf but..."

"She did?"

"Yeah, but it's not the same without me doing the proposing..."

Her eyes widen. "Gracie, will you marry me?"

"You might regret asking me. I doubt I'll be a normal wife."

"That's not the threat you think it is," I counter, pushing my forehead back onto hers.

Her soft chuckle tells me I answered correctly.

I grin and raise her hand to my lips. "I'd be uber romantic and have a ring all ready, but I know better than to choose something for you."

"You really *do* know me," she wails, her arms sliding around my neck as she hugs me fiercely. "I fucking love you, Liam Francis Donnghal."

"And I fucking love you, Gracie Agnieska Bukowski." Then, in her ear, I murmur, "I've wanted you to be mine for a long goddamn time, Gracie, and now I'm never letting you go."

CHAPTER 58
GRACIE

Until I Found You - Stephen Sanchez

ENGAGEMENT SEX DOESN'T GO ACCORDING to plan.

Which had better not be indicative of the rest of our lives.

Minutes away from Liam sliding into me, his cell rings. I know he put it on silent when he set it to charge so that means only a favorited number can reach him.

Knowing that, Liam pushes his forehead against mine and I growl, "Answer it."

Panting, overheated, I scream in frustration as he rolls off me and grabs his cell.

"Ollie? Why are you calling so late at night?" he demands, setting the phone on speaker.

Immediately, my earlier sexual frustration shifts to concern even as my body is fully revved and ready for action when a soft sniffle whispers over the line.

"She's dead. S-She d-died."

"Oh, honey. I'm sorry, but who's dead?" I ask dumbly.

"My mom. She overdosed." I can hear him crying. "S-She l-left m-me."

Heart twisting in my chest, I stare at Liam when he tosses the cell on the bed and starts dragging on the jeans he threw aside earlier.

"We'll be there soon, Ollie. Send me your location?" he urges.

"I-I'm in the hospital."

"Which hospital, buddy?" he asks softly.

But Ollie can't answer, he just weeps. "She's gone, Gracie. S-She's really gone."

"I know, sweetheart. I'm so sorry. So very, very sorry." My throat clutches, making it hard to get the words out to assure him, "We'll be with you as soon as we can, okay? You stay there. We're on our way."

Ollie sniffles. "Don't go. D-Don't leave me too."

For the second time that night, I start to cry but I don't care. I don't even hide the tears in my voice. "I won't go anywhere. I just need to get changed."

Liam, already dressed, takes over for real: "We're coming, buddy. I'll handle things. I handled everything earlier, didn't I? I'll handle this too."

"She's gone, Liam. I-I know I was supposed to leave but I didn't think I'd never see her again." This time, he starts sobbing and I swear my heart doesn't just twist, it breaks. Shatters, even, into a thousand irreparable pieces.

I know the woman was scum for how she abused him, but his hurt feels like *my* hurt.

I have no idea what they're talking about with Ollie 'leaving,' but whether or not she was a junkie who died because she didn't put her son first or not, he loved her.

And she left him.

"I know, champ, I know," Liam rumbles. "I swear we'll be there soon."

"I'm ready," I rasp, swiping my hands over my cheeks before Liam snags one of them in his own.

The night of our engagement might not have ended how we figured it would, and I'm definitely curious about what Liam 'handled' earlier, but I guess there's only one thing that matters—we're together and we'll deal with it *together*.

CHAPTER 59
LIAM

LATER THAT NIGHT

CLOSING Gracie's bedroom door behind me, I sneak away so I don't disturb Ollie's sleep.

It's been a long-ass day for him, and I know the upcoming week won't be any easier—he needs all the rest he can get.

Retreating to our bedroom, I climb into bed and draw her against my chest. She's been somber since he called, naturally so.

"Your mom and dad are in the city." When she tenses, I'm quick to explain, "Your mom's here to apologize. I told her that she needs to make it a good one if you're going to forgive her."

"What's with the tornado of Bukowskis heading to Manhattan tonight of all nights?"

"Terrible timing," I mutter. "Anyway, I wanted you to know that before you go to sleep."

She turns her face into my throat. "I'm lucky to have them."

"You can't live like that. I didn't tell you they're here to guilt trip you.

"You're a wonderful person, Gracie. You deserve her apology. She did wrong by you. She's going to make it right."

"I'm not wonderful. I'm prickly."

"I like you prickly." At her snort, I continue, "Because of you, that kid has somewhere to sleep tonight that isn't in the system. That doesn't sound like something a wonderful human being would do?"

"That's on you," she mumbles. "No way would social services have let me take him."

"It's not a permanent solution, though," I say with a sigh, my chin rubbing the crown of her head. Having already explained about the knife and Brownhill, I also share, "We arranged earlier for him to leave her, to go into the system, but it doesn't sit well with me, him going into a group home."

"No," she agrees. "But we can barely look after ourselves, Liam. It's not like we're ready for a family."

I can't deny that she's right.

Maybe in a few years, we'll be ready, but that doesn't help Ollie now.

"Do you think Mom and Dad would pitch in? Oren—" The last kid the Bukowskis offered to billet. "—left last year to be one of Pittsburgh's goalies. Maybe that's why Mom's been more manic than usual. She's used to a full nest."

"There's a difference between billeting and fostering a kid," I point out. "Plus, there's the fact Ollie's American and they live in Canada."

She hitches a shoulder. "Dad should retire soon."

"What? And you think he'll move away from the greatest country on earth?"

"—the greatest country on earth?"

We both chuckle as we speak the words at the same time.

"Maybe he would," she muses. "I mean, most of his kids are based here."

"Aside from Kow."

"Kow doesn't count. The farther Dad is away from him, the less risk there is that he'll have a heart attack."

I snort out a laugh. "I told Hanna that I'd let her know when you're ready to speak with her."

"I love that you did that."

Gently grabbing her chin, I tip it up so that her focus can only be on me. "I will *always* have your back, Gracie Agnieska."

"Stop with the middle name, dude," she chides, but the words are definitely watery.

"There's power in it," I tease. "Whenever I use it, you know that I might as well be speaking a vow."

Her throat bobs. "Liam?"

"Yes, Gracie."

"I love you."

"I love you, too."

"Thank you for being here."

"You never have to thank me for that." I place a soft kiss on her lips. "There's nowhere else I'd rather be than by your side."

"Oh, Liam," she wails, her arms practically choking me as she slides them around my neck and squeezes.

I smile into her hair but arrange her so that she's half off/half on me. "Okay, we need to catch some Zs. Tomorrow's exam is coming sooner rather than later."

Though she groans, she settles into me with a sigh.

I clap my hands to switch off the lights.

"We need to fire Andrews and my bodyguards," she mumbles.

Amused, I ask, "Any particular reason why?"

"Andrews told the Three Stooges who my security details were and they let them wait in my apartment until I got back."

My mouth tightens with annoyance. "I'll deal with it."

She sighs. "No more Andrews. Yay."

I'm too annoyed to find any humor in this. Instead, I tuck her tighter into me as the light from the TV soothes her to sleep.

Except, she isn't.

Five minutes later, her face turns toward me, her lips brushing my Adam's apple. "I'll talk to her. After my exam tomorrow."

I kiss the crown of her head. "I'll call Hanna in the morning."

CHAPTER 60
GRACIE

Vindicated - Dashboard Confessional

CUTTING someone toxic out of your life is never easy, especially when it's a mom who, technically, has always been *good*.

I saw Ollie's apartment when we went to pick up his things last night—Mom would have died rather than let her kids live in that environment.

There were used tampons on the floor.

On. The. Floor.

Needles littered the table.

It stank.

And the refrigerator contained nothing but mold.

Fucking mold.

As I settle in front of Mom at the coffee shop I agreed to meet her in, it's hard to reason that I had the right to protect myself from her ways.

Sure, she favors my brothers over me to the point where I struggle with my place within the family, struggle, even, to have an identity that isn't linked to hockey, but she never starved me. Never put me in unsafe environments. Never chose to avoid seeking help for her addiction. She always fought for me, *for us.*

God, Liam's making me so emotional—because just thinking that has tears pricking my eyes.

"Gracie," she rasps when she sees me, shocking me by snagging ahold of my hand from across the table. "I've missed you, darling."

Uncertainly, I squeeze her fingers back. "I don't say this to hurt you, Mom, but I haven't missed you."

Her throat bobs. "I deserve that."

"I love you," I whisper. "But I'm tired of always being the disappointment."

Mom's face crumples. "You could never be a disappointment."

"No? It's how you've always made me feel. Like nothing I do could ever compare to what the boys do. My achievements mean nothing in the face of theirs. Do you know how hard it is to get into Cornell?"

"Do you know how it felt not to be invited to your graduation ceremony?"

My eyes flare. "What?"

"You think I didn't know they have those?" She scoffs. "Your undergraduate ceremony passed by without a single mention. Not a single one. If I hadn't looked it up on your school's calendar, I'd never have known." Her bottom lip wobbles as she reaches for her phone. Suddenly, she's shoving it at me. "I had to take these like some kind of spy, Gracie Agnieska. I had to bribe one of the security guards with tickets to one of Kow's games. Do you even care how that upset me?"

I gape at the pictures of me on the stage. The mortarboard on my head, the scroll in my hand, a smile on my face even though I never bothered to glance at the audience because there was no one there to see me, no one I'd invited because I didn't even think Liam cared, never mind my siblings or parents.

"I didn't think you'd be interested," I admit, my fingers gently brushing the screen.

"Of course, I am! But I won't force myself on you when I'm not wanted." She grabs her coffee cup and takes a deep sip. "You've always been an unusual child. We never knew what to do with you."

"Do you know how that makes me feel?"

"How do you think *I* feel hearing that you left one of the safest places in the world to go to New York City? And not only do you go around getting mugged, I have to hear about it from your brother who heard about it from Liam!

"The second Kow told me, I burst into tears. Your father went stone white at the prospect of what could have happened to you!"

"I didn't ask for that to happen to me! And I didn't tell you because I didn't want a lecture about how great Canada is. I know it's fantastic. But my life is here." I heave a tired sigh; already exhausted after my exam, this isn't helping my energy levels. "Why did you never ask me how I was doing?"

"Why did you never tell me?"

"I shouldn't have to! You should have wanted to know!"

"Gracie, whatever I do, it's never the right way with you. I try to care, and you think I'm being pushy. I give you space to tell me, and you never do! I'm not a mind reader. You're nearly thirty years old. If you want something from me, *tell me*. I love you! I never want to hurt you."

"Like *I* hurt *you*, you mean?" I spit, hearing the criticism there.

She sighs. Wearily. "I didn't say that. Why must we always be at cross purposes?

"Your problem, my darling, is that you're too intelligent for your own good—mine too. I know you're smarter than me, Gracie."

Uncomfortable, I mutter, "Don't say that, Mom!"

"I only speak the truth. I remember when you were a teenager, you went through that phase where you refused to study. You wouldn't apply yourself. How you scraped through and graduated is a testament to how smart you are because you didn't pick up a single textbook that spring.

"Then, you decided to follow your brother around the country like some puck bunny! Deciding that you were going to draw those odd comics for a living." Jeez, I forgot about wanting to get into manga. "My only consolation was that Kow promised me you weren't sleeping around with the players." She pats at her forehead as if sweat is still beading there from the memories of that time. "I tried to get you into the printing shop, but you weren't interested. There was work there. A solid career. You could have inherited everything! But you didn't give a damn.

"Everyone has their own prerogative, so I never said anything but when you finally decided to get a degree. It just felt like something else you were playing at—"

I'd like to argue with her, but I think of the time I worked at the sex line or that stint at the comic book store where I got fired for reading all the comics... never mind that short-lived desire to draw manga she remembered and I didn't.

"But in the end," she continues, unaware that she lost me for a moment, "you always made me feel like *we* were never good enough. Always refusing to attend Thanksgiving, never coming home for Christmas or for our birthdays though all the other boys make the trip... You rejected us—every year. Every holiday. Every family event—"

"You don't play in law school, Mom. Or with an MBA. I get why you thought I was being flighty at first but what did I have to do to get you to believe in me? All these years later and you still undermine my career choices.

"The boys are millionaires. I'm half a million in debt with student loans. I can't just fly home whenever you think I should, and even if I could, I wouldn't." Her wounded expression has me rasping, "I want to be me, and you never let me be that at home. I didn't want to just be a Bukowski."

"Don't you see how hurtful that is?" Mom cries. "'To just be a Bukowski.' You don't know how proud I am to be one. When I married your father, I married into a family who cared for their children. Who loved them. You know my parents died when I was barely fifteen. I was alone for so long, Gracie, that to be invited into the fold was an honor.

"But you throw that away at every corner."

It might be mean of me to get to my feet when she's imploring me to understand but I do. When I step away from the table, she gasps, "Gracie! Where are you going?"

I stare at her. "I didn't choose to be born, Mom. This isn't about you. It's about *me*. Do you want me to apologize for being difficult to raise? Do you want me to say sorry for being a teenager desperate for attention when her mother only gave it to her brothers? Is it any wonder I rebelled?" Fatigue hits me. It's an exhaustion so bone-deep, it's as old as I am. "Thank you for coming to see me, for trying to reconcile things, but if this is how this conversation is going to go then I'll leave.

"I'd prefer to hang out with Liam than have every aspect of my childhood torn apart and skewed where I'm the guilty party because I'm too difficult, too awkward, *too goddamn hard to love* by the one person who'll forgive Kow for being a walking STI, who'll excuse Noah's terrifying temper, who never says a bad word against Trent even though he's certainly not perfect—"

"No! I'm sorry. I want to make this right. I don't want to leave here without my daughter back," she pleads.

My throat bobs as I plunk my ass down. "I just want to be me. I'm not sure that 'your daughter' *is* me. I know how much you wish I were like Cousin Amelia."

"You shouldn't say such things. I-I do like you for who you are."

A lifetime's experience makes me take her words with a grain of salt. "Do you know how often I get tossed aside so that people can reach one of the boys? Everything I do ends up being tied to them. None of my achievements are my own.

"It's been like that my whole life. No matter what I do, I can't escape them.

"It isn't my family I want to liberate myself from. It's the fame and the..." I pull away so that I can press my hands to my face as I repeat, "I just want to be me. I'm so accustomed to being used by friends who dump on me to get to them, I've stopped even trying.

"I am so alone, Mom, and I did it to myself because I know I'll get hurt. You think I have an attitude and I know people think I'm mean, but it's..."

"A self-defense mechanism. I know, darling." She doesn't just lean over this time. She shuffles out of the booth and plunks herself at my side. At first, I think she's trying to trap me in the banquette, but before I know what's happening, I'm in her arms and she's squeezing me tightly. "You are *never* alone. You're a Bukowski. Your brothers might drive you crazy, and their fame might have impacted your life, but you are one of us. We are always a phone call away."

"You say that and then they hit Liam up to tell him that he should dump me because he can do better! You feel the same way!" I glare at her, aware that I'm bawling like a baby in public and not giving a fuck.

"I didn't think that. I just know you, that's all. Liam hasn't been the same since the kidnapping. I didn't want you to tire of him. You get bored so easily, sweetie—"

"You thought *I'd* get bored of *Liam*?" I splutter.

"I did. It's not as if the men you date last long. I didn't want that for Liam. I was protecting him. But I understand that I hurt you in the process, and I'm very sorry about that."

For a second, I can only gawk at her.

It doesn't help I never tell her who I've been dating and that if I do, it's by accident.

The different names I've unintentionally dropped to her over the years make me cringe.

"As for the boys, I've told them off."

"You've told them off?" I repeat.

"Yes. And your father's with them now, teaching them that brothers aren't supposed to stand with the boyfriend when it comes to who their sister is dating." She purses her lips. "I couldn't believe it when I heard what Liam said. Dad will teach them the error of their ways, don't you worry, darling."

I swallow. "I love him."

She squeezes my fingers. "Truly?"

"Truly. I won't hurt him. I won't." I can see that's where her worry stemmed from, even if it still stings. "That's the last thing I want to do."

"And he loves you? Or do I need to slap him upside the head?"

A soft gurgle of snotty laughter leaves me. "No. He does. He proposed."

"He did?" She snags at my hand. "No ring?"

"He says that he knew better than to pick one for me."

"There are few who aren't related to you that know you better," she concurs with a soft, tinkling laugh.

The gentle sound of amusement, without a hint of malice, has me blinking at her. "I never thought of him as a brother and he never thought of me as a sister."

Her cheeks turn pink. "Did you… When you were younger—"

"No. We didn't mess around back then," I murmur. "I wish we had. We wasted a lot of years."

She squeezes my hand. "Life is long if you're blessed, Gracie. You have a lot to make up for but plenty of time left too."

"Mom?"

"Yes, Gracie."

She probably doesn't understand how hard it is for me to say. "I don't want to be alone anymore."

"You never were, but now that we understand each other better, we can make sure you stop feeling that way entirely. There's nothing I can do about other people. I, myself, am targeted by stupid women at the country club. It's wearisome—I know that. But now, we can complain to one another."

"I just thought you were showing off how jealous people were about the boys being your sons," I admit, thinking back to her conversations about women trying to set their daughters up with one of my brothers.

"Good lord, no! I'm proud of them, Gracie, but I'm not totally blind to their faults even if I willfully hide from some of them."

"I'm sorry I was mean."

She sighs. "Back anyone into a corner and they'll come out swinging. Never mind a Bukowski. But if anyone understands what you're dealing with, it's me." She squeezes my hand. "Now then, tell me about you and Liam. I want to hear how he proposed."

For the first time in decades, there's no resentment in me at her demand.

For once, I just spew it all out, gradually gaining more and more steam as I go because she's right—if there's anyone who can understand, it *is* her.

CHAPTER 61
LIAM

THE FAMILY DINNER comes as a surprise.

After a day filled with practice, handing over a dangerous weapon to Brownhill, and a conversation with my lawyer to break my contract with my treacherous agent, it's a nice surprise though.

When I make it back to my apartment, I find it filled with Bukowskis.

Though Hanna and Noah are the only ones making pierogi, everyone's in here. Gracie's sitting at the counter, talking to her, not bickering, while Hanna clips Noah's ear every time he grumbles about the tedium that is making individual dumplings one by one and by hand.

As that goes down, Ollie's brow is furrowed with his tongue sticking out the side of his mouth as he concentrates on his task, uncannily reminding me of when I'm fixing my laces. The chore is one that Hanna is obviously instructing him on.

Fryd and Kow are complaining about something, and Fryd's still-thick Polish accent booms across the room like cannon fire, helping me pick out that the Bukowski patriarch isn't happy with his son's man-whoring ways. Trent, ignoring everyone, is on his phone, scowling at the screen. Even Cole's here, bitching with Gracie and Hanna about something.

For a moment, I just lean against the door, taking it in with a soft smile.

This is my family.

It doesn't take much to figure out that Hanna and Gracie resolved some of their issues this morning and I'm glad. It hurt something in me to know that there was such dissent between them even as I understood it and applauded Gracie for standing up for herself.

Maybe it's seeing how Ollie's been included, maybe it's knowing that they're all in the same room without trying to kill each other, but it makes me take a step forward—not just literally but figuratively.

Heading straight for Gracie, I don't stop until I'm by her side.

A wave of greetings pop up at my arrival, and though I was close to beating the shit out of them last night, I just grin at the guys before I press a kiss to Gracie's head. The greetings morph into boos which I ignore by placing a kiss on her lips instead.

Tasting her smile is the best thing I've sampled all day.

"You doing okay?" I ask, checking in. "The exam went well?"

"I'm fine and it did." She turns her face into my throat, a move that's becoming more and more common for her. "Thank you for asking. We cleared the air."

"Good. With the boys too?"

She points to three bunches of gardenias on the kitchen table. "Their version of an apology. You know they're my favorites." She gives me the side-eye. "Did you tell them?"

I raise my hands. "Nope. We haven't spoken since last night. Still, I'll kick their asses if they give you any crap in the future."

"We'll kick them together. I have more than just green dye in my box of magic tricks."

Grinning, I give her a quick squeeze, then I shift and find Hanna watching us with a soft smile. "Hanna?"

She lights up at my warm tone. "Yes, son?"

"Would you mind if I invite some people over for dinner?"

"Of course not, the more the merrier and it's a wonderful excuse to enlist Kow, Cole, and Trent into the pierogi production line," she chirps to a chorus of groans. "Who did you want to invite?"

I swallow. "My dad. And my half-sister."

Hanna's eyes widen. "You have a half-sister?"

"I do." To Gracie, I ask, "You have her number, don't you?"

"I do." She shoots me a proud smile. "A real family dinner sounds good to me."

CHAPTER 62
LIAM

35

"STOP BEING NERVOUS," she chides as she fusses with my sweater. "She wouldn't have given me her address if she didn't think we'd be coming over."

"Are you micromanaging my feelings right now?"

Her grin is sheepish. "Only a little."

Shaking my head at her, I mock, "Reassuring. If you're micromanaging, you're nervous too—"

Before I can finish that sentence and she can choose a rebuttal, the elevator doors to my sister's apartment open.

I can tell she's as surprised as I am because, not only does she startle enough to jostle the baby in her arms, she stops fussing with her daughter's cowlick and stares at me with wide eyes.

For a moment, both of us just study one another.

It's weird because there's nothing masculine about her at all and yet, I can see myself in her—it's as if I put one of those social media filters over my face that predicts what I'd look like as a chick.

Aside from that, I can see why Gracie once called her prissy. She's immaculate. Her makeup, her hair—it's like she just came off a movie set.

Someone clears their throat.

My gaze skitters toward the source and I find a man standing there. I already know from Gracie's pep talk on the way over here that this is

Jennifer's husband and the father of her two daughters—Luciu Valentini.

"Welcome to our home," he says simply once he realizes my attention is on him.

"Thank you," Gracie replies in my stead, tugging on my sleeve to drag me out of the elevator.

The kid in Jennifer's arms starts playing with her hair but that doesn't jerk her attention away from me. If anything, it makes it all the more apparent that I'm right at the center of her focus.

"Hi."

She swallows. "Hello."

Luciu mutters something that sounds like, "... you well, *bedda mia?*"

Her gaze darts off him and onto me before she takes a hesitant step closer. "I wish I'd known that I had a baby brother. It might have made things easier when I was growing up."

"You had it tough?" I ask gruffly.

Her nod is slow.

"I'm sorry. I wish I'd been there to kick the ass of whoever needed it."

"It made me a survivor, and now I have Luciu for that." She licks her lips. "I still need a baby brother, though."

I never expected her to say that.

It makes me scuff a hand over my jaw as I mumble, "I need an older sister too." This might be premature but I'm going with my gut. "You know, to be my best man?"

A grin peeps through her shock. Man, that's Paddy's smile through and through. This shit is fucking weird.

"You're getting married?" she demands.

"I am."

"And you'd want me to be your best man?"

Kow's the only other person I'd have asked and though he'll be offended, I figure he's yet to apologize to me for being a douche, *and* if he takes over those duties, one of us will end up in the hospital. Not just because his idea of a bachelor party will probably put us in jail...

Gracie will definitely kill me if that happens.

"Yeah. I like to do things the nontraditional way."

"Don't listen to him," Gracie chimes in. "He's as traditional as they come."

Jennifer shoots a look at her husband. "Can't be worse than Luciu." As he snorts, she murmurs, "I'd love to be your best man."

"Saverina could be a flower girl if you want?" Gracie tacks on before she nudges me with her elbow again. "Introduce yourself, Liam."

"They're babies," I mutter. "How do you introduce yourself to babies?"

Jennifer's smile is rueful as she shifts the one in her arms onto her hip. "Saverina, this is Uncle Liam."

Her eyes turn big and wide as they settle on me. Then, louder than the commentators at a game, she screeches, "Unka Lee-Lee."

Gracie bursts out laughing while I let loose a wry chuckle.

Luciu snickers. "You're in luck—Bella doesn't talk yet."

"Be thankful for small mercies, eh?" I drawl sheepishly, even as I stroll closer to my nieces and stroke Saverina's cheek with one hand and allow Bella to gnaw on the other.

Those baby teeth, man, they fucking sting.

This close to Jennifer, it's weird to see even more of my father in her features. I find myself tracking them—the slant to her nose, the shape of her eyes. How her mouth quirks into a grin as Saverina practically throws herself at a startled Gracie, somehow knowing she'd be open to catching her.

"So, we came over to invite you to a family meal we're holding today," Gracie says primly even as Saverina, who's fascinated with the blue tips in her hair, starts yanking on them like the color will slide off with enough force.

As Jennifer and Luciu share another look before they both nod, that's probably when it hits me—Gracie and me... we're not alone anymore.

We never will be again.

CHAPTER 63
GRACIE

"YOU OWE ME."

Jennifer jumps with one foot out of the bathroom door and one foot inside it. "Jesus, Gracie! Warn a girl, would you?"

"You pee a lot."

"I'm pregnant. Sue me."

I cock a brow at her. "You're crazier than my mom. She had three kids under the age of seven. Yours are under the age of four."

Jennifer shrugs. "We want a big family."

"Apparently. Anyway, if I didn't catch you here, how else was I supposed to talk to you tonight without Liam overhearing?" I don't let her argue, just grab her arm and tug her toward the gym.

Her nose crinkles. "You don't have somewhere else we could sit?"

Admittedly, the room stinks of *boys*.

"The spare is being used by Ollie."

She winces. "Such a sad story. I wish…"

"You wish?"

"I had a similar childhood. My mom was—" She blows out a breath. Sucks one in. "—a terrible parent. Though Padraig was absent, he did a better job than her. Let's put it that way."

"Paddy sucks on the providing front."

"He says he's trying to make up for it. I only met him a few years ago."

"Can you make up for something like that?" I ask her softly.

"He's trying. It's better than nothing. It's not always easy, but I'd prefer to have him in my life than not. It helps that he's terrified of me."

I snort. "I noticed that."

"He's very cautious about upsetting me." She hesitates. "Liam struggles with him, doesn't he?"

"He does. I was surprised when he invited him over today. They've never been close and he grates on Liam." My brows lift as I lean against a stationary bike. "We agreed that if I made this happen, you'd give me some clues about his kidnapping."

She grimaces. "I can't tell you everything."

"Why not?"

"Like I said before—because a lot of illegal things happened to get Liam home." She clears her throat. "I can tell you that the people who took him were killed when he was retrieved.

"I can tell you that he was targeted by a kidnapping group. I can tell you that my husband was pivotal in making his release possible, and I can also tell you that the cops didn't bring him home—the O'Donnellys did."

My brow furrows. "The mafia helped more than the cops did?"

"Yes." She blinks at me. I get the feeling she's trying to impart some knowledge with that blink but I'm pulling a blank—

"Your husband's... mob-adjacent?" I ask carefully.

Thinking about Luciu Valentini, who looks exactly like Jennifer—as if they stepped off a magazine shoot together ten minutes ago despite the fact they've been here for hours—I could see that.

He doesn't scream Don Corleone but there's definitely something... dangerous about him.

"He is."

Curious, I ask, "How come you didn't know Paddy when you were growing up?"

"Because he'd faked his death and was hiding up in Canada. That's when he met Liam's mom."

Eyes wide, I blurt out, "You're shitting me?"

"I wish I were," she drawls, clearly amused at my reaction as I stagger over to Liam's multigym and sit down heavily on the padded bench. "He came back to New York to beg his brother for help with paying Liam's ransom demand."

Mouth gaping, I sputter, "This is like something from a book."

She tosses her hair over her shoulder. "If it were, it was written by someone with a whacko sense of humor and a fucked-up imagination."

Definitely. Stunned, I ask, "Instead of paying the ransom, they got him back by force?"

"The Irish Mob weren't going to hand over tens of millions of dollars when they could deal with it in-house... What do you know of the O'Donnellys?"

"Nothing."

"Well, Liam's uncle was the head of the mob. Now, his cousin is." She shrugs. "The kidnapping group had no idea what they'd gotten themselves involved in."

"I'm glad," I spit bitterly, thinking about last night's nightmare and the thousands prior to it.

"Me too. I hope they suffered," she says pleasantly. "I can assume that they did. Anyway, do you consider that enough info to leave me alone about this?"

Though I'm still taken aback, I have to chuckle. "Yeah. I know more than I did before so that's something. I just want to help him."

"I don't think you can. Some trauma is unfixable. But you can be there for him. You can stand by his side and prop him up when he's too weak to hold himself tall. That's all anyone can ask from their partner." Her smile shifts, softens. "I'm going to go hang out with my brother, husband, and father." She shakes her head. "Never thought I'd say those three words in the same sentence, but here we are."

I let her go but stay in the gym while I gather my thoughts.

My family has gone back to their respective hotels, and Ollie's sleeping in the spare bedroom, so it's only Liam's family in the living room.

Laughter drifts from that way and a smile curves my lips at the sound.

Liam's earned this. He deserves happiness.

Jennifer's right—that's not solely a burden a partner can bear, but moral support is where I can come in handy.

Mind still buzzing from what I've learned today, I return to my fiancé's side and slump onto the couch next to him.

Absently, and all the more powerful for it, he grabs a hold of my hand, gently tilts my wrist, then presses a kiss to where my pulse beats merrily away.

Jennifer, cuddled into Luciu's side, smiles at the sight and rests her head on her husband's shoulder.

"Always knew you two were meant to be."

Padraig's out-of-the-blue words don't rile Liam up for once. Instead, he says, "Wish you'd told me sooner. I might not have spent nearly twelve years without her."

Paddy shoots me a wink. "Damned if I do and damned if I don't."

CHAPTER 64
LIAM

"I'M surprised you forgave them as easily as you did."

Her brow puckers. "Liam, I can be cordial and forever hold a grudge."

My grin makes an appearance. "So, we're in agreement?"

"About?"

"Forgiving your brothers on the surface but then making their lives hell at one point or another?" I drawl, because Kow might have said sorry to me earlier but that doesn't make up for the heartache he caused Gracie IMO.

She snorts. "Of course."

That's one aspect of their family that has forever amazed me—their capacity to move on so swiftly.

It was why, when I came home, I knew all was technically right with the Bukowski world again.

They're innocent.

No highly traumatic pasts, no major problems—they're just a family. Two folks, four kids, an ice hockey addiction, and a five-hundred-dollar-a-week grocery bill when they're all together.

Feeling a touch nervous, I approach the bed once I've dragged off my clothes. "I have something for you."

Yawning, she flops onto her back and studies my dick with mild interest. "If you think I'm going to fall for that after how long today has been—"

"Not that." I chuckle. "You don't have to read it. You don't have to even look at it, but I'm going to leave it on your nightstand." She won't have a clue how tough it is to do this, but I texted Mike today and he said if I was ready, I should go ahead.

But that I could also never show her what are my most intimate thoughts and feelings and memories...

That it was my choice.

This is Gracie, though.

My Gracie.

She blinks at me as I place the blue leather journal beside the lamp on the nightstand. "Why so cryptic?"

"Not cryptic," I counter. "Just something I'd like you to have if you want to read it."

She leans up on her elbow and stares at the small leather-bound book. "What is it?"

"When I first started with Mike, he told me to write a journal because I was struggling to open up to him. I couldn't do it, but Mike and I figured how to—I pretended I was writing to you."

When her eyes widen, I try not to feel embarrassed.

This is Gracie.

She loves me.

Clearing my throat, I continue, "There are entries from back at the beginning. You can read them or not, but I didn't want to hide it from you anymore. It would have felt deceitful."

Reaching over, she touches the leather. It's tentative. Cautious. "I'm glad I could help you even without knowing because I'd never want you to think you couldn't come to me or share something with me. Whether it's in person or in word. And as much as I'd like to read this, I won't—"

"But—"

"—let me finish." She holds up a hand. "Unless you share it with me."

That's a solution, only...

I huff out a laugh. "I figured there'd be distance between us when you read it."

"Physical distance?"

"Yeah. Like if I'm at practice. I didn't think I'd be in the room or that I'd be actually seeing your reactions live, you know?"

"Does it matter? I don't mean to make you uncomfortable. I just thought, this way, you control what you share with me."

Though I'm willingly sharing all of it with her, I appreciate what she's saying.

Deep down, I like her suggestion even if, on the surface, some of the shit I said will be cringe.

"Yeah, okay," I mumble.

Those beautiful eyes of hers stare at me warmly as she asks, "One now?"

I grimace. "Really?"

"Really."

Though I heave a sigh, I pick up the book and flick through the pages. Scanning where it falls, I nod to myself then read aloud:

"*'Dear Gracie,*

Today, I watched you eat ice cream and I thought I was going to come in my pants—'"

She howls with laughter and slaps my arm. "Shut up! You did not write that!"

I grin at her. "I did. If you don't believe me…" I shove the journal at her before pushing her over to what's usually my side.

Snorting, she leans on her elbow again and, with an expectant look, says, "Go on then. Tell me the rest."

"*'Honestly, watching you eat ice cream is a holy experience. You eat it like you do everything else in life—with your heart and soul. I both admire that about you and am jealous of that personality trait. But then, how can I be jealous of something that I love about you?*

"*And being at the center of that, knowing that you're there and with me, not just a member of my team but my partner, it's a beautiful thing to be a part of.*

"*I'm a lucky bastard. I think you should know that.*

"*Yours,*

"*Liam.'*"

She doesn't say anything, just sniffles then burrows her head against my shoulder. "Read me another one?"

"'Dear Gracie,

"I'm so embarrassed about my nightmares—'"

"You have nothing to be embarrassed about!" she spits, head snapping up to glower at me so quickly that she almost bumps her forehead into my chin.

Ignoring her, I continue, "'I know you're down the hall and that you can hear me cry out like a baby in the middle of the night but the truth is, I'd prefer to be embarrassed and have you close than be alone and wake up to an empty apartment.

"You don't know what you bring to my life by simply being here.

"Thank you.

"Liam.'"

Her throat is croaky as she whispers, "Read me another one."

And that's how we spend the next hour.

Me reading snippets of my life since the inception of this journal and her listening, arguing with me, laughing over some shit I wrote, weeping a little over some of the entries about my nightmares that revolve around *her* getting hurt, or growling at me over what she perceives as my ridiculousness.

I fucking love it.

Love her.

Love what she brings to my days and how much warmth she imparts simply by breathing.

I really am a lucky bastard—now, I just have forever to prove to her that she was right to have faith in me.

CHAPTER 65
GRACIE

"'DEAR GRACIE,

I don't think I'll read this entry to you.

I think I'll wait until your patience runs out and you read the journal from front to back or until we're old and gray and have kids like Kow running around our heels and driving us crazy.

The deal with Amelia's wedding...

We'd just sung "Fuck Her Gently" and your mom was upset because Amelia had run off crying and I sneaked outside with a bottle of tequila. I never thought you'd follow me, certainly not with lime slices and salt in hand.

The tequila is why you don't remember what happened. If my life hadn't changed, it'd probably be a blur for me too.

Man, you were under the table after three shots that night.

Anyway, we got drunk and you splashed into the lake. One thing led to another and we're making love on the shore. It was like all my wet dreams coming together in one fantasy, except it was reality.

You passed out after you came (yeah, two orgasms. TWO. Never let it be said I have tequila dick.) Anyway, I carried you back to the lodge and that was when Kow, as usual, had to go and wreck shit.

He was drunker than a skunk and I cuffed him to the bathtub in his room so he couldn't get into any mischief while I was gone. I returned but you burst into tears minutes after I got into bed—'"

I break off from reading to scoff at that. "I didn't cry."

"You have barely any recollection of that night," Liam retorts easily, staring at me from the bed while I pace in front of it, reading his journal. This time because Liam said he'd never read it out loud. "So who's going to paint a more accurate picture, huh?"

I sniff.

"Just read it, would you?" he mumbles. "Your ass needs to be sitting on my dick. If I'd known it would interfere with us fucking, I'd never have given you the—"

"Because you're being a jerk, I won't sit on your dick. I'll sit on your face instead."

"*Bébé,* if you think that's a punishment, you're wrong."

My lips curve but my smile fades. "Oh, my God. We fucked on the lakeshore, didn't we?"

"Yeah. Why?"

"Do you know how many times I got off to that 'fantasy?' And all along, it was a memory that tequila erased?" I shriek. "Fucking tequila!"

"Trust me, I was just as mad that you forgot what happened. It's why I don't drink that much anymore. Still, you touched yourself and thought about that?"

I blow out a strained breath. "More times than I can count. Now, don't distract me." Before he can follow through with the promise in his eyes, I continue with my reading:

"'*So, I'm lying there, listening to you talking about how you'll never get married, trying to figure out why that would make you cry, and I remember asking, "Why won't you get married, Gracie?"*

I thought you'd say because you hate the dresses or something, hate men, hate the bourgeois device that is marriage, but you didn't.

You broke my fucking heart.

"Because no one wants to marry me. I'm too much of a bitch to be a wife. I bet I'll die alone. You left me alone."

You practically slurred those words, but I knew what you were saying and it blew my mind even as I turned you into my arms and held you close.

How sharp your tongue is, is one of my favorite things about you—'"

"To this day," he preaches, "it is."

"Even when I'm sucking your cock?"

He chortles. "Especially then."

I snort.

"'You never let me get too big for my britches.

You're always the one speaking with calm and rational common sense.

The truth hurts, but with you, it's always founded in love.

You speak love.

When you started crying, I swear to fuck, I didn't know what was going on. I'd never seen you like that before. Not even when Roman died. You just locked up. Refused to talk about him. You've always been a hard nut to crack, Gracie. You loved that dog. You loved him like crazy. But you'd never tell from how you were after he died.

Anyway, it got me thinking.

And reacting.

I knew I was taking advantage of the situation, and hell, it wasn't like a legally binding contract! I wouldn't have forced you to marry me before we hit thirty-five.

But I definitely played on the situation. I figure that's because I was as drunk as you.

In vino veritas, though, because I've wanted you for so long.

That's why I said, "Gracie, you don't have to worry about dying alone. If you're not married by the time we're both thirty-five, we'll get hitched."

You squinted at me, but I figured you approved when you threw yourself into my arms and hugged me, slurring, "I, Gracie Agnieska Bukowski, do promise that if Liam Francis Donnghal and I aren't married before we reach thirty-five, we'll take each other off the market.

After I repeated the vow, you mumbled, "Let's do it, Liam. Let's be each other's end game."

That's when you passed out.

Then, the next day, you nearly broke my fool heart because you remembered nothing. Nothing.

I'll never know what made you agree seeing as you don't even know why you did it, but afterward, I was determined to let you lead your life, to find your path... until you hit thirty-five.

That was when all bets were off because I was going to hold you to that promise. After that night, I had all the confirmation I needed that we were perfect together.

But of course, nothing can ever go as planned where we're concerned.

We've saved five years of playing around one another, Gracie.

I'm glad we got our heads out of our asses because life is too short and I want to spend every minute of it with you.

35, the number I play and always will—'"

I gape at him. "Oh. My. God! YOU SNEAKY ASSHOLE!"

He's too busy grinning at me, proud as a peacock at the level of *sneak* it took to maneuver this behind the scenes, to realize that I'm about to jump on him.

When I do, he tackles me beneath him, but I shove at his shoulder. "I wondered what the hell you were doing with all those 35s. I thought you were going crazy!"

He winks. "Just for you."

I huff then press the journal into his chest and, snootily, inform him, "I haven't finished."

"God, can't you just—"

"Nope." Loudly, I continue:

"'35 flowers to make you smile.

35 Cameos (more incoming) to make you happy.

35 manga comics to make you laugh.

35 Liam mugs to make you think of me when you drink coffee.

35 songs on a mixtape I'll give you the night we get married. (Songs that I'm bribing Hudson to play in the car on repeat. You've been slow to notice that one.)

35, the number we'll lead our lives by, by getting together sooner rather than later.

But don't worry, I don't expect 35 kids. :-P'"

That has me cackling. "Bet your damn ass we won't be having 35 kids," I mutter, but I'm grinning. And it's the kind of grin that you don't know when it'll ever end.

It feels like it could last forever.

Which is fitting.

Because when I read the last three words, even I know what they mean.

"'Pour toujours,

Liam'"

I sigh. "Forever?"

His gaze is softer now. "Forever."

I toss the journal onto the bed so I can slide my arms around his neck. "I love the sound of that. You've been dating me all these years and I didn't even know it…"

"What matters is you know now."

Voice sultry, I coo, "You need to be on your back, hmm?"

"Take a seat, *mon p'tit* cabbage."

Gray: Okay, so confession time.

Liam: Huh?

Gracie: What have you done now?

Gray: Your lack of faith wounds me when I had both your backs, Furball!

Liam: What?

Gracie: Hey!

Gray: Both of you came to me, separately, and told me that you were into each other.

Gray: And I KEPT YOUR SECRET BECAUSE I'M FUCKING AWESOME

Gray: Do you know how goddamn hard it was not to tell the others?!

Gray: Now, I'm free from this limbo and it's such a fucking relief I tell you.

Gracie: Holy shit, you told Gray you had feelings for me, Liam?

Liam: Wait, Gracie, when did you tell Gray that you were into me?

Gray: She told me back at the start of the season. Liam told me after he beat the shit outta Condon. Something about Lewis coming onto you if I remember right.

Gracie: :O

Liam: Gray, why the fuck didn't you tell us sooner?!

Liam: DO YOU KNOW HOW BLUE MY BALLS WERE?

Gracie: Liam!

Liam: Gracie, I've waited for you for years and this dipshit could have told me sooner and I wouldn't have had to wait an extra four months?!

Gray: You're not blaming me for keeping your secrets, are you, motherfucker?

Liam: Two words, Gray. Blue. Balls.

Gracie: They'll be blue again if you don't shut the fuck up, Liam Donnghal.

Gracie: I can't believe you kept that secret for so long, Gray. Thank you. <3

Gray: *sniffs*

Gray: That's what I'm talking about.

Gray: @Liam Hey, asshole. I'll be sure to share with the class whenever you drop a secret on me in the future.

Liam: Blue balls.

Gracie: Stop saying that!

Liam: You had blue balls too. I've seen all your vibrators and you told me yourself you'd burned out three.

Gray: I do not need to know this.

Gray: DO NOT CONTINUE WITH THAT LINE OF THOUGHT, LIAM.

Gracie: I mean, yeah, I was really horny but you're going to give Gray the wrong impression.

Gray: I'm not getting any impression.

Gray: No impression whatsoever.

Gray: Gracie is, in fact, a born-again virgin and Liam's balls are about to drop off still.

Gray: No sex has ever been had.

Gray: I just wanted you guys to know that I never told anyone, including the pair of you, so, when it comes to Christmas, you owe me.

Liam: Ha!

Gracie: I'll make sure it's a nice gift, Gray.

Gray: You'd better.

CHAPTER 66
GRACIE

ON THE DAY of my last exam, we get some unexpected news.

Mostly, I'm just grateful the cops contacted us *after* I finished because I'd have felt like I was going crazy if I'd gotten it beforehand—the knife that Ollie had given to Liam had been used in a stabbing.

The fingerprints of the leader of the gang, Jamie, were all over the weapon and, as a result, he'd been arrested.

After we'd expressed concern that he might blame Ollie for his arrest, Officer Brownhill assured us that the gang knew Ollie's things had been searched while he was being taken in by social services.

In the upcoming days, we have to believe that there's no grudge held because none of us are targeted and we'd know seeing as Liam's got enough bodyguards on us to compete with POTUS.

Just in case.

Some of whom are definitely shifty-looking.

I don't want to think Liam has sicced mob guards on us but if it helps him sleep at night, I can turn a blind eye.

According to Ollie, the rest of the kids are his age. Without Jamie or Arnie around, they're leaderless. He seems to think that won't stop one of them from trying to become the top dog, but that's out of our control.

If there are repercussions, I know Liam and I will handle it.

No way will Ollie be dragged back into that life, even if it means making him a Canadian citizen and taking him across the border.

Extra stress isn't what we need and I won't borrow trouble.

Ollie won't eat anything unless it's Mom's pierogi, and he won't even talk to anyone that isn't her. Which means Dad's had to go back to Winnipeg on his own to manage the printing shops and Mom's practically living with us.

Then, there's the fact that the Stars keep flying through the playoffs. Win after win after win until, eventually, it's the quarterfinals.

Out of nowhere, I'm sitting in the stands, confirmation that I've gained my MBA buzzing in my head competing with the noise from the fans who are here to watch the grudge match between the Stars and the Pittsburgh Steelmen.

As I sink back into my seat to watch Liam face off against Oren's team, Saverina starts shrieking 'Unka Lee-Lee' at the top of her lungs when Liam's image flashes on the Jumbotron so I'm too distracted to notice someone take a seat beside me.

Liam didn't know if Jennifer would want to attend because she's prissy as shit, but I invited her to sit with me once Lacey, who I'm growing quite close to, had to bow out thanks to a chemo session knocking her on her ass.

"I still can't believe you left your apartment looking like that."

I scratch my nose with my middle finger. "It's a PALs thing."

"Sounds like a brand of dog food."

"You're a bitch." My lips twitch as I rub my shoulder where I'm aching—I started that self-defense course Dad bought for me and I'm paying for my 'no-exercise' rule. "I like it."

"You only just figured that out, hmm?" she teases, ignoring the starfish grabby hands that try to pull at her bob.

"Liam didn't think you'd want to come."

"Unka Lee-Lee!" Saverina shrieks.

"Yeah, kid. Unka Lee-Lee," I tease, amused at her massive Cheshire cat grin.

I have to figure that Liam's nieces are only here because it's a family thing. Something both siblings are taking to heart—we've been invited to their place for dinner this weekend and Jennifer came over with the babies for coffee the other day too.

"It's not my sport but he's my brother," she says staunchly. "It helps that I knew Luciu would get a kick out of it too."

Her husband is definitely getting *something* out of it. My soon-to-be brother-in-law, dressed in more Armani than sense, has missed the hotdog reaching his mouth twice as his eyes dart around the ice, following the game. Tucked in a sling on his chest, Bella is sleeping peacefully.

"Of course, if I'd known you were going to do your hair like that, Gracie," she muses, a coy smile curving her lips as she takes in my ultra-teased hairstyle that was *not* my idea, "I might have taken a seat with Star."

"Ahn-tee Gwac-ee!" Saverina decides that's the moment to call me her aunt—for the first time.

Even as I'm grinning at that title, one Jennifer had to have specifically taught her, my nose crinkles.

"It was a group decision."

"A bad one," she agrees. Her eyes twinkle though. "What we'll do for the men we love, hmm?"

"Yeah, *what*," I say with a huff as I snag Saverina's hand in mine and press a kiss to her tiny fingers.

While she's busy trying to catch the blue tips of my hair, someone drawls, "I heard you completed your degree."

Gaze darting to the side, my brows lift when I realize Conor has slipped into the space on the other side of me. "Yeah. I got the news today."

"That's a shame."

"It is?" I question, surprised.

"Yeah. You have to share the day with a potential win."

"You want to know what's a 'shame?' If the Stars move forward, the day of my graduation will likely be in the middle of that series."

"Whether it is or not, we'll find a way to get him to the ceremony."

"I don't want him to feel torn between—"

"What? The woman he loves or his job?" Conor scoffs. "I might own the team and I might want them to win, but I have my priorities straight. I think Liam does too."

I think about all those journal entries and my lips twitch into a smile. "Maybe you're right."

"No 'maybe' about it." He crosses his legs, resting his ankle on the opposite knee without man-spreading to a ridiculous degree. "Nice outfit, by the way. And..." He wafts a hand at my head.

I grimace as I peek at the monstrosity I'm wearing while nervously toying with an ultra-teased lock of hair. "You have to take one for the team sometimes."

"Is this a ritual I don't know about? All the women have hair like yours." His confusion is real. "And you're all wearing the same jackets too."

I hum. "It's a thing."

"A thing?"

"A thing," I confirm. "Don't have to like it, just have to do it."

As it's the first time I've ever been included by the PALs, I wasn't about to sit this out even if I do look like hell. It was okay before we hit the quarterfinals—we just had to wear the damn jacket, but now, Lacey is insisting we all tease our hair. I know why too—she's got a wig she's ready to rock.

Fuck cancer.

Especially as she's the one who suggested this monstrous hairstyle and isn't even here to see it.

"Teamwork makes the dream work," Conor says with a soft smile, but before I can answer, he continues, "Now that it's official, I wanted to come to you with a proposition."

"What kind of proposition?" I ask dubiously, wincing when Liam gets high-sticked by a Pittsburgh defenseman as the asshole tries to intercept a pass between him and Lewis. "You have to be kidding ME," I scream as the crowd boos after the referee misses that. "Fucking asshole," I snap at no one. "Sorry, Conor, you were saying."

He chuckles. "Your passion's there. No denying that."

"Passion? For referees to use their fucking eyes?" I grumble, my hands flaring wide when Kerrigan, bare seconds later, passes to Lewis, who takes a shot and misses. "Shit."

I have a feeling it's going to be one of those goddamn games—stuck in a gridlock with relief only coming in OT.

Already preparing myself for the irritation, I frown when he says, "I was thinking about what you said at Aela's."

With everyone else on this side of the stadium, I scream, "THAT WAS OFFSIDE!"

Jennifer mumbles, "Jesus Christ, Gracie. You have a set of pipes on you."

Ignoring her, I answer him, "I overshared at Aela's, Conor, so you're going to have to narrow it down."

Conor, unoffended by my outburst, merely states, "Specifically, what you were saying about Bradley."

"What about him? That he's a nuisance?"

His lips twitch. "He got us this far."

"Liam and Lewis did that." I huff and concede, "Greco too. He's sorted himself out over the course of the season."

"That could be Bradley's influence."

"Maybe." If I sounded dubious earlier, that's nothing to now. "Anyway, I'm trying to focus, Conor. What's your point?" I growl at the sight of a defenseman closing his hand around the puck without the referee batting an eye. "Did Pittsburgh bribe this asswipe or something?"

Conor, ignoring me, asks, "If he coaches us to the Stanley Cup, what would you do?"

Head whipping from side to side as the Stars chase the puck out from under Pittsburgh's possession, I frown. "Keep him on for another season, but I'd have your general manager watch him like a hawk, especially the trades he requests. He either has no people skills or doesn't care that there has to be some camaraderie in a team. You can't have that with people who loathe each other."

"By your own admission, Greco was a key player this season. Yet, according to Paddy, Liam detests him."

"It's all about balance. Liam hates the ground he walks on, but if Bradley were better at managing people, it'd be easier to handle.

"If he loses, I'd toss him out. Reaching this stage is good, particularly in the face of what the Liberties consistently failed to bring to the table, but with the resources you've thrown at the team, his achievement is middling."

Slapping his thigh, Conor chuckles. "You're brutal. I love it."

"It's in my nature not to pull any punches."

"I'm learning that." He watches Kerrigan and Lewis duke it out with one of the defensemen over the puck. "Did you know I only bought the team for Liam?"

"Paddy mentioned it."

"He wanted him to be close to family so I made it happen." He tilts his head to the side as Liam manages to intercept a Pittsburgh pass. "There's little I won't do for my family."

Half-expecting him to threaten me over Liam's honor like my brothers did, I tug on my '35' pendant.

"Paddy says Aela was right."

"About?"

"That you'll be one of us soon enough."

Huh. That didn't go where I thought it would.

"We haven't set a date or anything. Hell, we haven't even picked a ring."

Conor shrugs. "Doesn't matter. You're his. You're an O'Donnelly now. That comes with perks."

"Like?"

"Nepotism."

I frown. "I don't want—"

He hushes me. "You have the qualifications to back up my decision and to tell any naysayers to piss into the wind. I'll only take nepotism so far... but I like how you think, Gracie. The Stars would benefit from having you on board."

"On board?" I mutter, tone dazed. "What do you—"

"I'd like you to be our next GM."

Mouth gaping at him, I sputter, "W-Wh—"

I'm so busy being bedazzled by him that I fail to see Liam ram a Pittsburgh's defenseman into the boards.

Conor goes on to tell me how much money I could earn, what the benefits would be, how far my responsibilities would stretch, details that both sink in while going over my head at the same time.

When he's done with his spiel, as if he knows he's blown my mind, he pats my arm. "I'll let you think about it. You enjoy the rest of the game, hmm?"

He doesn't hang around for long—if anything, as I'm still stumbling over an answer, he's already moved over to the other side of the box where, I realize, his partner, Star, and their daughter are sitting.

It's amid the chaos that the crowd suddenly goes wild. Even Jennifer screeches in glee—Liam's scored.

We're up 1-0.

And like he's got something to prove, whether it's to himself or me or the world, maybe all three considering how the press has been vilifying me whenever he loses, over the next period, he scores a second time.

When we make it into the third, Lewis and Kerrigan act like their sticks are magnetically attached to the puck as they manage to breach Pittsburgh's defense. Nothing Oren does seems to keep his net clear from my man's offense.

By the time the game's over, my mind isn't on Conor's job offer, the shitty PALs jacket I'm wearing, or the fact that Jennifer and Luciu are jumping up and down with two tired kids in their arms.

I'm too busy screaming with the rest of the crowd as we celebrate a 6-1 win that forces a game seven in the conference quarterfinals.

CHAPTER 67
GRACIE
LATER THAT NIGHT

Smooth - Santana, Rob Thomas

"I FUCKING LOVE YOU IN THIS," he growls as he presses an open-mouthed kiss to my lips. "You're like a pocket rocket Dolly Parton. But I need you out of it."

Grateful Liam moved Mom and Ollie into the apartment next door, I bite his bottom lip as he plucks at the jacket that's branded with his name on it. "Sure you don't want to fuck me in this?"

The rumble that escapes him is so animalistic, I know my core is going into overdrive.

This whole claiming shit shouldn't appeal to the feminist in me, but it does. It really does.

And that rumble is so good for my confidence, which has taken a beating tonight seeing as he's right—I do look like a Canadian Dolly Parton. With my teased hair and the dumb sports coat that's tailored to my waist and has tassels, bright-red, *glittery* tassels on the back in a deep V that brings attention to my man's name and number.

"*Ouais*, I wanna fuck you so bad in this, *ma belle*," he snarls, shoving me to the wall beside the kitchen entryway.

His mouth drops to my throat which he nips and sucks—right over my pulse point. I can feel it throbbing against his tongue, reacting to how turned on he is.

Adrenaline + a win + me wearing his name = a very turned-on Liam Donnghal.

And I volunteer for tribute.

My hands scrabble at his slacks as I try to get the ball rolling here. The last thing I want is for him to tease me when I'm literally aching.

What a game that was!

Sweet Jesus, he was good.

The way he flew across the ice and how he and Lewis and Kerrigan finally worked together to slam hit after hit after hit—so hot.

Unable to bear it any longer, I hitch my leg on his hip and climb him like a tree because that always gets me results.

When his dick pushes into my crotch, I cry out, "Liam, I need your cock. In me. Now. Like, right now."

He shudders. "Say that again."

"I need your dick, Liam." Back arching, I whimper, "I need you to fill me. I need you to slide home—"

As hot as the other statements got him, it's the last one that lights his fire.

With a final suck on my pulse point, one that has me writhing against him, I pluck at my fly until he takes over. I'm not sure what the hell is happening but my linen shorts are suddenly being ripped at the crotch. The sound of fabric tearing is obscenely loud and delicious.

"How the fuck did you do that?" I moan, not caring but still impressed because his hands are back to being busy. One circles my neck, pinning me to him with the best kind of jewelry around—a hand necklace—the other finds my slit, a finger testing me before thrusting home.

Instantly, he starts to press against the front wall of my pussy.

That meltdown I thought was happening?

Nah, that was a prequel to the main event.

As he thrusts into me, making sure to hit that spot over and over again while the butt of his wrist rubs my clit and his mouth tears into mine, I can feel the orgasm build.

It's there—already hovering within reach.

Mewling into his lips, my fingers tear at his jacket, plucking and biting into the expensive silk as I fight the bewildering urge to pee, knowing what it is, well aware of what's coming.

I tear myself away from his kiss to warn, "Liam, I'm going to come."

"Give it to me, *bébé*. Fucking give it to me. I want you to come all over me. Come all over my goddamn name."

A frantic laugh escapes me—what does he think I am? *A geyser?!*

Panicked and desperate, I rock into him, thrusting back, feeling like I'm dying and being reborn and that's when I scream, "LIAM!"

My head swings from side to side, but I ride through the wave of pleasure and experience that high-pressure burst which happens so rarely and feels like an implosion and an explosion at the same time.

My whimpers chase me, following the way he continues finger-fucking me, priming me for more until I'm sobbing, chanting his name, needing him to stop but craving his continued attention.

When it happens again and I squirt, this time, I grab at his shoulders and push my forehead against his, connecting with him even as he takes me higher and higher.

While I cry and keen and whimper, he whispers, "You're so beautiful, Gracie. And you're mine. All mine. No one else's. No one will ever see this, no one but me. Not anymore. You're mine. Liam fucking Donnghal's."

I don't even care that he's talking about himself in the third person!

I just have to screech, "Stop teasing me!"

It draws him from his caveman-like speech and he stills before he lets loose the lowest, deepest, darkest chuckle.

That's when, out of nowhere, he's no longer holding me up.

Suddenly, I'm standing, my face is turned to the wall, and I'm being bent over a console table that's a bare foot away. My hands clutch at the edge as he drags off the tattered remnants of my pants, which is when I hear his zipper.

For endless seconds, I don't even breathe.

I'm just waiting.

Waiting.

Forever waiting.

Then, his dick is there.

Right there.

And he thrusts into me, hard, fast, deep. All in one go. Taking me from barren emptiness to overwhelming fullness.

But he doesn't fuck me.

He goes slow.

"You bastard," I scream into the console table, nails scraping over the surface as I buck against him, craving everything he has to give.

He laughs but doesn't reply.

"Give me your dick," I demand, beg, plead. "I need it. Need you. Please, Liam. Please. Fuck me. Take me! I'm yours."

"That's right, Gracie. You're mine. *My* good girl. Say it. Tell me what you are."

"Your good girl. Only for you," I sob. "Please, please. I can't take it. I can't. Oh, fuck, please."

He plows into me.

His fingers bite into my hips, dragging me into him so that I feel it with every thrust. It should hurt, but I'm so sensitive that it just makes the wail that escapes me go on forever as that high plateau he discovered inside me soars toward the heavens.

When he pulls out, I freeze.

Then, he slaps my clit before rubbing it with all four fingers. Another slap. Then, those four fingers are inside me. Thrusting, spreading. I can feel it—

"LIAM!" I cry, dancing onto my tiptoes at that burst of pressure.

I can feel it drench my thighs, know it's sprayed onto him.

His cock is back in my pussy before I can take a shaky breath and suddenly, black dots flicker at the corners of my vision.

Then, those wicked fingers are dancing with the devil once again.

Both sets.

One goes to my clit.

Fast flicks in circular motions.

The other goes to my slit.

The fingertips slide around his thickness, edging into my pussy, spreading me wider.

"Li—" My voice fails me.

Those black spots don't just dance at the edge of my vision. They hover there, do a little wave, then start to surge forward, overtaking everything else.

When I come this time, it's like a detonation.

My whole being contracts then explodes, giving way to his claiming.

Because I am his.

Forever.

Always.

Endlessly.

And when he comes, his roar of completion melting into my name, I know, one hundred percent, that he is mine.

Tirelessly.

Ceaselessly.

Completely.

And I'd have it no other way.

Liam: Putting a ring on it.

Mike: 'Bout damn time.

Mike: You okay?

Liam: Never been better.

Mike: Let me know when to schedule time off for your capitalistic celebration of a bourgeois institution.

Liam: My wedding?

Mike: What else?

Liam: You're married. You sank to the depths of the bourgeoisie as well.

Mike: The decision to couple is essentially meaningless.

Liam: You told your wife that?

Mike: For sure. Before I proposed.

Liam: You romantic, you.

Mike: She loved it. Said that my buying her a ring was MORE romantic for her because I'm a nihilist. Apparently, I'm better at romance than you are.

Liam: Yeah, you beat Hallmark.

Liam: Anyway, you want to attend MY wedding?

Mike: Of course. I'll suffer through the hyperbolic displays of wealth for you.

Liam: And cake?

Mike: Ha. No. The cake will suck. You don't even know what good cake is.

Liam: Gracie does. She's already assured me that it's going to be red velvet.

Liam: It's been so long since I've had sugar that I'm not sure what that even is...

Mike: I pity you but I will come and I will eat.

Liam: I'm honored.

Mike: You should be.

CHAPTER 68
LIAM

I'll Show You - Justin Bieber

SCRAPING a hand over my hair as I check the status of my flight, I mutter out loud, "I'm fucked."

Delayed.

Across the board.

I don't know why the universe is screwing with me on today of all days when I need the airports to be working and every plane around the world to be on time so mine won't be delayed, but that's not happening.

Nervously, I study the screens, knee bouncing as I gnaw on my cheek, just waiting for an update.

I'm in South Carolina of all places. I have to be in New York in two-and-a-half hours and Charleston is a six-hour drive away.

Like I said, I'm fucked.

I have literally ninety minutes to be with her in the city for the graduation ceremony before I'm supposed to catch a return flight.

Not even that's looking like it's going to happen.

Mind racing as I consider my options, I vow, "I will *not* fail her."

I'm Liam Donnghal. I have connections. Someone will rent me an emergency helicopter—

"I'm Liam fucking Donnghal," I mutter to myself, not even thinking about the connections I have because I'm a hockey player...

I'm related to the mafia.

Not just via my father but by my sister!

If they can't make this happen, no one can.

I contact Jennifer first because I know she and Luciu own a private jet. Whatever bullshit's going on with the airport, though, is affecting small plane traffic too.

"Do not panic," I mumble when I hang up the phone, uncaring that I look like a crazy person as I talk to myself in the business lounge. I bypass my father and head straight to Conor. When he answers, I blurt out, "Conor, do you have a helicopter I can borrow?"

"I do," he says smoothly.

"I swear I'll be back in time for the game."

"Of course you will."

Thinking that he's being sarcastic, I state, "This is important. More important than the semifinals."

"I chased Star around the world, Liam. A two-hour flight's nothing."

He sends me a link.

Another one pops up on my phone.

I blink.

Wait... so, he wasn't criticizing?

"There's a car waiting outside to take you to the nearest helipad. The second link is a car that'll take you to the graduation ceremony."

I don't even care that his level of preparation is downright nuts, that he even knows what today means for Gracie—slowly, I'm acclimating to his ways and I'm just goddamn grateful that he can make this happen.

I get into the waiting limo. A quick ride later and I climb into the helicopter and, boom, we're on our way.

When I land, I almost have a heart attack when I see Kow in the car waiting to collect me.

"What the fuck?!" I demand when I sink my ass in the passenger seat. "Conor got me the most dangerous man in North America to drive me to Gracie's graduation?"

Pulling into traffic and almost getting us T-boned in the process, he wafts a hand. "I know people."

"Yeah, bad people apparently." I mean, I like Conor, but he's still Irish Mob.

"I just wanted to do something nice," he retorts. "I know I've been kind of a—"

"Jerk? Douche? Asshole? Dick? Fucker—"

"Yeah, yeah, yeah. I get it. Earned it too." He sniffs. "I'm proud of her though. One of my girlfriends was telling me it's a real big deal, this MBA shit."

I roll my eyes. "In between blowjobs?"

He smirks at me. "You know it."

My eyes roll double-quick this time.

Of course, nothing is going to go right today and the universe hates me because we're gridlocked eight blocks away from the ceremony.

"Chill out, bro. You think I'm gonna let you miss Gracie's big day?"

I scowl at him. "No. But knowing you, we'll get into a thirty-car pileup first."

His nose crinkles. "You have one near-death experience—"

"One?" I sputter.

He waves a hand at me in dismissal, but I stare at the traffic, study our location on the map and that's when, in my goddamn dress shoes, I jump out and take off through the streets.

I don't even care that my security is back in South Carolina—I can *not* let her down.

Every couple minutes, I check my watch.

Time is ticking down.

Fifteen minutes.

Ten.

Five.

The doors to the building are shut—of course they are—and I can't burst in otherwise people will know I'm there.

I grew a beard especially for her, and I didn't go through that torture so that my identity will be doxxed within the first two seconds of me showing up. Not after she's spent the past seven days threatening to shave me herself since I told her how hard it is for me to have facial hair now.

The building has a clock tower and it starts to chime just as I approach the signposts that lead me to the entryway.

I'm already late—I was supposed to be there before she went on stage.

I know she hasn't replied to my last message of:

> Me: I promise I'll be there

Because my cell didn't buzz in my jacket.

Tabarnak, she already thinks I let her down.

Panic increasing, I grab the hat and shades I shoved into my pockets earlier and put them on and try to sneak into the auditorium as silently as I can.

Thank fuck, attention is on the stage.

Thank *fuck*, no one sees me slip in once I hand over my invitation.

From the back of the stands, barely catching my breath after running faster than what feels like I could skate here, I watch as student after student collects their degree.

'B' last names come up quickly.

And then, she's there.

Right there.

A smile is on her face as she accepts her degree, looking hot as hell in her cap and gown—I will definitely be fucking her in both. I just have to wait until tomorrow. But what makes it even better?

She turns to the crowd and seeks out the people sitting here, finding Aela and baby Cameron as well as Conor, Star and Victoria in the audience first.

As for Noah, Kow, Trent, Matt, Gray, and Cole, they agreed not to attend for her sake, but Hanna, who's live-streaming the event for the boys, Fryd, and Ollie *are* here.

When Gracie finds her family in the crowd, her hand lifts and she waves to them.

Then, her gaze drifts.

I know she's looking for me…

She had faith I'd be here.

Which is the moment she finds me.

Her smile morphs into a secretive grin but she doesn't wave at me. That grin is message enough—she knew I'd make it.

Just like I knew, come hell or high water, I'd do anything to see that smile.

As she heads off the stage, I send her the link to her final Cameo.

This time from me.

Somehow, I think I'll be a disappointment in comparison to Papa Roach and Blink-182, but my ego can handle that.

Because she and I are end game.

And nothing, be it delayed flights, and no one, despite our mutual crazy families, will ever change that.

CHAPTER 69
COLE

TWO WEEKS LATER

IT SUCKS that the Blue Demons didn't even make it into the playoffs and, despite the bad juju, I have to grin when I watch Liam slide yet another puck into the back of the net.

There's an advantage to my figure-skating coach being late—I got to read some Omegaverse RH until the puck dropped, then I started watching my bro in action.

Speaking of, I cheer to the empty rink when he scores.

My celebration is between me, the ice, and my Kindle, which I bring everywhere with me.

When a notification slides into my DMs, informing me my coach has shown up at long last and has just parked outside the rink, I switch from watching the game stream to my message app. Sending her a thumbs-up, I move over to Hooked-Up when I see a chick swiped right on me.

My nose crinkles when I study her profile.

I've got nothing against hot blondes, but I definitely prefer brunettes.

Checking out the next profile, I see a hottie from Midtown. One of her pictures shows her working—her uniform has *Chuck's* embroidered on her tit, another has her hugging a cat. That's good. I don't hate cats.

As I swipe right, a second later, a notification dings around the rink, echoing and making me jump in surprise.

That's when I realize I'm not alone anymore.

I look up, on the hunt for my figure-skating coach who's the only person allowed access during this private session, and my eyes widen as recognition hits.

The chick I just swiped right on is the one skating toward me...

My grin makes an appearance as I straighten up and head onto the ice.

This whole session was born of watching Lewis, one of the first-string right wingers who plays for the Stars, spin pirouettes on the ice. While other morons were giving him shit, well, until Liam called them out for it, I was watching his landing and takeoff.

Poetry. In. Motion.

Ballet isn't my thing, but figure skating *could* be.

And now that I've seen my coach, hell, I'm more invested in my classes than ever because not only is she hotter than she looked on her profile, that *ass* of hers?

Fuck. My. Life.

She's even a brunette.

Of course, I'm too busy checking her out to see the writing on the wall because Mia Charles, of Hooked-Up fame as well as a talented figure skating coach who's supposed to be helping me with my edge work, skitters to a halt right in the center of the ice and bursts into tears before I even get the chance to ask, "How you doin'?"

BONUS SCENE & AUTHOR NOTE

FIRSTLY, I'd like to take this moment to thank you for reading END GAME. I hope you loved Gracie and Liam's story and fell hard for them.

That scene with Aela and Gracie calling each other 'friend' was totally inspired by a scene from a British TV show - The Inbetweeners. If you know, you know. :P Or, you can see it for yourself (NSFW) here:

https://www.youtube.com/watch?v=j9-hRivcIY8

NEW TO ME READERS...

If you're looking for a binge read to end all binge reads then take note! :D

CURIOUS ABOUT JENNIFER'S STORY?

Start with THE DON! It's book one of her duet and is free to read in KU!

www.books2read.com/ValentiniOne

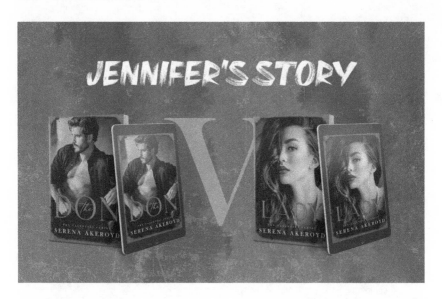

LIAM'S OTHER FAMILY?

You can read their stories too!

You can start with FILTHY! The whole series is complete and free to read on KU!

www.books2read.com/FilthySerenaAkeroyd

MAFIA MAYHEM!

While none of the books are required to enjoy Liam and Gracie's story, here's the madcap universe I created where we originally meet Liam.

It's a combination of Sicilian mafia, Irish Mob, Russian Bratva, and MC!

They're all free to read on KU too!

You can find the links in the correct reading order on my website here:

https://www.serenaakeroyd.com/my-books/the-five-points-mob-collection-universe/

YOU CAN ALSO READ a bonus scene for Gracie and Liam here:
https://dl.bookfunnel.com/mxuv5v9hsg

Once END GAME hits 500 reviews head to my reader group for another bonus scene! www.facebook.com/groups/SerenaAkeroydsDivas

Much love to you all and I hope you're excited for the next book!

Gem

xo

CONNECT WITH G. A. MAZURKE

For the latest updates, be sure to check out my website!
But if you'd like to hang out with me and get to know me better, then
I'd love to see you in my Diva reader's group where you can find out
all the gossip on new releases as and when they happen. You can join
here: www.facebook.com/groups/SerenaAkeroydsDivas. Or you can
always PM or email me. I love to hear from you guys: gamazurke@
gmail.com.